DARK CIRCLES

AN INTRIGUING THRILLER WITH AN
INCREDIBLE PLOT TWIST

DEREK FEE

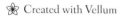 Created with Vellum

For Aine, Bobbie and Sean

CHAPTER ONE

Big George Carroll drummed his fingers on the steering wheel of the black taxi. He cast a glance at the rearview mirror and hoped that his passengers didn't notice. Two pairs of cold lifeless eyes stared back at him. Neither man had spoken a word since he'd collected them at the arrivals gate of Belfast International Airport. He wished that Sammy had given this job to someone else. However, Sammy trusted him and that made George happy. Big George shivered. His mother would have said someone had just walked over his grave. The two men in the back seat were an ill-matched pair. They reminded Big George of the Mutt and Jeff cartoon characters that he loved. The one that reminded him of 'Mutt' was tall and thin with the pale face and demeanour of a professional mourner. The second man was considerably smaller standing no more than five feet four inches. His face was as bland and pallid as his colleague's. George doubted that either man spent much time in the sun. Mutt and Jeff incited something in Big George that was unusual – fear. It wasn't a feeling he was used to. George was six feet seven and weighed in at one hundred and forty kilos, most of which was muscle. Big George didn't do fear. The people he dealt with did. Except for the two in the back of the cab. There was something about them that sent the shivers up his spine. The instructions from Sammy were clear enough. Pick up two guys at the airport and drive them to an address in the University area of Belfast. A parking place would be blocked off with traffic cones; he was to remove the cones and park. He was not to converse with his passengers and when instructed he was to move on to a second address. It was a simple, no-brainer driving job. But Sammy had said nothing that could have made George feel the way he did. The three men sat in the car in silence and waited.

BRIAN MALONE STOOD up to leave his office at the Northern Ireland Infrastructure Agency at exactly five thirty. Although he contemplated having a drink before heading home, he decided that he'd wait and have a stiff one at the flat instead. He looked around and saw that barely sixty per cent of his colleagues were heading for the exit. It was not a good strategy to quit on time if you wanted to make it in the NIIA. Members of the hierarchy would be striding along the corridors checking out who was still at their desks. Meanwhile, the pile suckers would be spending their time playing Solitaire on their computers or checking their Facebook pages. It was so damn pathetic. Malone didn't like to think about climbing the greasy pole. He didn't like to think about spending the next thirty years doing it either. There had to be more to life than shuffling papers about. He dreamt about skipping out on cold and miserable Belfast and heading to Cyprus. He was a diving fanatic and had a long-term plan to open a diving school on the island. He'd chosen Cyprus because it was English-speaking and had a regular throughput of English tourists. The question was how long term was his plan. He'd tapped his parents for a loan, but they were not receptive. Anyway, they needed the money for themselves. He'd looked at the costs, and he needed fifty grand. Said in one breath it didn't seem like a lot but for a junior civil servant, it would require more than ten years of concentrated saving. By then he might be married with a child on the way and the fifty grand would always be a mirage that he could see in the distance, but was fated never to reach. It was a fine evening so he decided to walk to his apartment. Belfast was almost bearable on an evening like this. Awnings had been installed on bars and restaurants so that when the light rain that was a constant visitor to the city made its appearance, the customers could still enjoy the continental lifestyle without getting drenched to the skin. As he walked along, he smiled at the after-work groups enjoying their drinks. Life didn't seem so bad and maybe even the fifty grand wouldn't turn out to be a mirage. You never really knew what was around the corner.

Jeff sat in the rear of Big George's cab with a photograph on his lap. The face in the photograph was etched in his brain, but he was a professional and it was better to be sure. There was not going to be a fuck-up. He was in the zone. He knew what had to be done. Two men were to be murdered, and nobody would be the wiser. Both would be made to look like natural or accidental deaths. 'We're on,' Jeff said softly as Malone turned a corner and walked slowly in the direction of their cab.

Malone took no notice of the black cab parked on the street where he lived. He was whistling and looking straight ahead as he approached the door of the house containing his apartment. He didn't notice the two rear doors of the taxi opening or the shapes of the two men exiting. He slipped the key into the front door and turned the lock. As he pushed the door open, he was shoved from the rear and stumbled into the small hallway, just ahead of the two men dressed similarly in black polo neck

jumpers and dark trousers. He turned to remonstrate, and as
he did so was struck on the side of the temple. The blow didn't
appear to be hard. It was more of a sting than a blow, but it was
sufficient to turn his lights out.

MUTT CAUGHT him before he hit the carpet. Jeff removed the
keys from his hand, and together the two men carried him to
the door at the end of the hall where a plastic '2' hung upside
down. Jeff inserted a key and turned the Yale lock. They
carried the prone body inside.

'First things first,' Jeff said in a soft Glaswegian accent. He
removed a small box from his side pocket and opened it as his
colleague sat Malone into the only easy chair in the room. He
removed a large hypodermic syringe from the box and slowly
pulled the plunger down, filling the glass body of the syringe
with liquid from a vial. He opened the young man's mouth and
lifted his tongue. He plunged the syringe into the underside of
the tongue and pushed the plunger. 'Instant heart attack,' he
said to his colleague.

Mutt turned and looked at the figure slumped n the chair.

Malone moaned and looked like he was about to come
awake when he shuddered, fell off the chair and lay on the
floor. His eyes opened, and he saw the two men looking at him.
He remembered that he was hit on the head, but that wasn't
where the pain was. His chest was aching, and he was having
difficulty breathing. He tried to get up but found that he
couldn't move. The pain in his chest was excruciating. He
tried to speak, but no words came from his mouth. He lay
back.

Jeff dismantled the syringe and put it back into the box.
He slipped the box into his pocket and then felt the neck of the
man lying on the ground. The pulse was still there. He went
around the small flat opening drawers and examining the
contents, making sure to replace them in their original posi-

tions. He looked over at his colleague who held up a plastic bag containing a laptop computer. From the corner of his eye, he noticed the man on the ground convulse. He abandoned his search and stood directly in front of the dying man. He had seen many men die. Some he had sent to their Maker, whilst for others he had simply been an observer of their last moments. He watched the man convulse again. He was not a religious man, but he carried out an experiment every time he saw someone die. He tried to identify that moment when the soul left the body. He put his fingers on the young man's neck. There was still a pulse, but it was weak. The potassium chloride was doing its job. Without immediate medical attention, death was just around the corner. He would have preferred some other method of murder but the instructions were that it had to look natural. There was nothing more natural than a heart attack. He went back to his observations. Although he was convinced that the soul did not exist, he was ready to change his mind if on even one occasion the dying person did not go from a living breathing entity to a waxwork figure in an instant. The man on the ground convulsed one last time and expired. Jeff placed two fingers on the side of his neck and felt no pulse. Brian Malone had left the building.

The two men glanced at each other and took one last look around the flat. Jeff dropped the keys on the dining table, and they let themselves out.

CHAPTER TWO

'David, for Christ's sake put your hand up for the vote.'

David Grant suddenly came out of his reverie due to the sharp pain in his side. He looked to his right and saw that his colleague had jammed an elbow into his ribs. 'What? Vote?' Grant said absentmindedly.

'Put your bloody hand up.' His colleague grabbed his right jacket sleeve.

Grant raised his hand and looked into the chamber of Belfast City Council. All the members of his party had their hands raised, as had been agreed with their leader. The Chairman made a piece of theatre out of counting the hands before declaring that the vote had been passed. Grant had no idea what he had just voted for, but he would have followed his colleagues anyway.

'What the hell's up with you?' Grant's colleague asked.

'I was away with the fairies,' he answered.

'You've been away with the bloody fairies for the past two weeks.'

Grant dropped his hand down to the edge of the bench and felt the briefcase sitting beside his right leg. It was a croc-odile skin case that had been a gift from his brother who worked for a development agency in Madagascar. He'd seen similar cases in a shop in Royal Avenue and there was no way he would have been able to afford one. The contents of the case were the reason why Grant had been so distracted over the past several weeks. He had no idea why the local Deep Throat picked on him. He assumed it was because he was the only Jewish member of the City Council. Whatever the reason, the documents were of such an import that they were certain to change his life. The question was whether it would be for the better or the worse. One of the City Councillors had launched into a speech about flag days or marching or some such other issue that was of no consequence to Grant. He wasn't very religious and hadn't been in a synagogue in years but being Jewish in Northern Ireland had its advantages. As a young solicitor, he was expected to join the Masons, but he was spared the more or less obligatory membership of the Orange Order.

'You look shot.' His colleague was staring into his face. 'You're either burning the candle at both ends, or you're coming down with something very nasty.'

Grant was well aware that he looked dreadful. His normal pallor accentuated the dark circles under his eyes. He had spent the past two weeks examining documents that would have an explosive effect on the very fabric of Northern Ireland, and on his career. He remembered the part of the Bible where Jesus had knelt in the Garden of Gethsemane and wished that the chalice would pass. As he had struggled to make sense of the papers that had been entrusted to him, he wished he had never accepted them. He was also sorry that he had involved one of his friends in the exercise of understanding what were extremely complicated documents.

'Maybe you should see a doctor,' his colleague suggested.

'Just overworked,' Grant said because he realised that his colleague was waiting for a reply.

'Take a rest,' the colleague said. 'The Council takes a break in the next few weeks. Most of the issues on the table are facile anyway, so you don't even have to turn up here for this bullshit.'

The Chairman was attempting to bring a speaker to a conclusion but was encountering a high level of resistance.

'Any more votes this evening?' Grant asked.

His colleague looked at the order paper. 'Nothing. As soon as the extremists have had their say the Chair will wrap us up.'

Grant cleared the space in front of him and dumped the documents into his briefcase. It was time to go home.

CHAPTER THREE

Mutt and Jeff sat in David Grant's small house. The lock on the front door had presented no problem to them and there was no alarm. They waited patiently and silently in the dark. The house had been searched from top to bottom. Although both men knew it was getting late, neither had looked at his watch. They would wait until they had finished their job.

Grant pushed in the door of his house. He had opted to renovate a modest two-up two-down dwelling in the Ashley Avenue rather than go for an upmarket new-build apartment. He had tried to maintain the character of the property and felt that he had succeeded. As he entered, he dropped his briefcase on the floor and made his way to the kitchen at the rear. He plugged in the electric kettle and opened the door of the American-style fridge. The remnants of a lamb rogan josh and some sticky white rice stared back at him from the middle shelf. He didn't feel like facing a reheat, so he took a packet of cheese slices and a tomato from the upper shelf. He pushed the door of the fridge closed and saw a small man standing on the other side.

'What the ...,' Grant dropped the cheese and tomato on the floor. He saw the small man's hand move, but it appeared to flash very quickly to a point on his head. He felt dizzy for a second and then hit the kitchen floor.

Mutt appeared at the door and without speaking moved to the prone man. 'We'll need help,' he said simply.

Jeff nodded. 'The Hulk in the cab?'

'Has to be.'

'Shit.'

'I'll get him.'

Jeff nodded. He never thought about his lack of stature. He had a set of skills that did not depend on physical prowess. However, the man lying on the kitchen floor weighed in at perhaps one hundred kilos and there was no way he and his colleague could manhandle deadweight of that size.

Big George and Mutt appeared at the door of the kitchen.

Jeff handed George a pair of surgical gloves. 'Put those on and help me get him into the hallway,' he said.

George looked at the prone man. Sammy had told him to stay out of the way, but he didn't want to get into an argument. He took the gloves and put them on before picking up Grant's feet. Mutt had chosen his shoulders, and together they lifted him. They walked through the kitchen door and into the hallway.

Jeff had already placed a small case on the ground and was removing an item of female clothing. 'Undress him.'

George was wondering what was going on. He knew the two boys were heavy metal, and that they had come to Belfast to do some kind of special job. The guy on the floor was out for the count and the man who had helped him carry him into the living room was taking the guy's jacket off. George removed the man's shoes, noting the level of wear, and then removed his socks. His partner was removing the shirt so George loosened the belt on the man's trousers and pulled them down. The guy was wearing a pair of white Y-fronts which had turned grey from washing. George hesitated. 'Everything?' he asked.

Jeff looked at him.

George pulled down the guy's Y-fronts. The man was lying naked on the floor. George examined his tackle and saw that he was both circumcised and fairly well endowed. He looked away and saw that Jeff had already laid out a pair of ladies' fancy knickers, a brassiere, a garter belt and a pair of ladies' stockings. He didn't like what the two men were doing. It wasn't nice to dress a man in women's clothes.

'Out of the way.' Jeff pushed George aside and picked up the garter belt. With a quiet efficiency, he dressed the man on the floor in the female items. Mutt lifted the guy up so that the brassiere could be affixed to his torso. Jeff slipped a camisole over the stunned man's head and put a pair of red high heels on his feet before standing back to admire his work. He smiled and turned to George. 'Get him up.'

They lifted Grant up into a vertical position. An open wooden staircase ran to the upper floor with a short return on the landing. Jeff climbed the stairs and tied a rope to the post at the top of the stairs. He dropped the noose-end of the rope down to his colleague who put it around the semi-conscious man's neck.

'Keep him up,' Mutt said to George. He went into the kitchen, returned with a chair and placed it directly under the stair post.

Together they hauled the prone figure up onto the chair.

Grant moaned as he was manhandled into a vertical position. His eyes began to open. Jeff, at the top of the stairs, immediately put strain on the rope, and Grant was in a semi-hanging position with his feet just about able to reach the seat of the chair. He suddenly opened his eyes and began to choke.

Mutt kicked the chair away making sure it fell in a natural position.

Grant swung in the air and started to kick his legs. He hit Big George in the face with the heel of one of his shoes and opened a cut in his cheek.

'Hold the bastard's legs,' Jeff called from above.

Big George lunged at the flailing legs and grabbed them. He held them tight. He could hear the noise of the man choking above him, but held on to the legs for dear life.

'Pull down, you big fucking oaf,' Mutt shouted.

George did as he was told and the force in the legs gradually reduced until there was one final kick, and they went quiet. He released his grip and looked up into two bulging eyes. He stood back. He hadn't bought into this. He was only the driver. He put his hand up and felt the blood running down his cheek.

Jeff descended the stairs and joined the two men below. They stared up at the body. Jeff rearranged the chair. Grant had kicked off one of the red high heels, and they left it where it lay. Jeff pulled down the top of the panties Grant was wearing and took his penis out. He moved Grant's hand over and rubbed it on the penis.

Big George looked away. He didn't mind the heavy stuff, but this was bloody sick. He didn't know what had happened with the poor bugger at the flat, and he didn't want to know. 'You need me?' he asked.

Jeff shook his head.

George made for the door.

Mutt and Jeff made a final appraisal of the hung man. They nodded at each other and made for the front door. Jeff noticed the briefcase in the entrance hall and nodded at it. Mutt picked it up and took it with him.

George was already behind the wheel of the black cab. He started the engine as the two men exited the house.

Jeff pulled the door of the house closed behind him. The

two men retook their places in the cab and it pulled away from the curb.

'Where to?' George asked.

'Belfast International.' Jeff said.

'It's night,' George said. 'There are no flights.'

'Belfast International.'

CHAPTER FOUR

Stephanie Reid looked at the ceiling above her head. She ignored the young man who was doing his pneumatic best on top of her. She had picked him up in a bar earlier that evening, and she was already sorry to have consented to what would be a one-nightstand. Her lothario took a break from pumping and looked at her. The smile froze on his face as he realised that her facial expression wasn't one of ecstasy but boredom. She felt his penis wilt inside her and she smiled. She wondered whether she had destroyed his confidence permanently. She hoped so. She had listened to several hours of bullshit, which was intended to get her in the mood to have this dope drive her to nirvana, and she realised it was giving her intense pleasure to stick a pin in the lothario's balloon.

He rolled off her and stared at the ceiling. 'This never happens to me,' he said.

'That's what they all say. Why don't you put on your clothes and get out of here?'

'Can't we wait a while?' he asked, the pleading clear in his voice. 'I'm not sure what happened there. I was really into it but then it just went off the boil. Give me a chance and I'll get it going again.'

She got out of bed. He was 'into it'; this from an arsehole who had learned his sex technique from watching someone poke a fire. 'I'm going to the toilet, and I'd be grateful if you weren't here when I get back. Close the door on your way out.'

'Can I have your phone number?' he asked.

'No,' she said just before she closed the door to the toilet. She sat on the toilet bowl and wondered what the hell she'd been doing bringing that creep back to her apartment. Every time she met a new man she supposed he might just measure up to Ian Wilson, but so far no luck. Careful, girl, she thought. You're becoming obsessive. The message was clear enough. Wilson didn't want her. That's what his mouth said, but it wasn't what his eyes were saying. Belfast had been quiet over the past three months, so they hadn't had an opportunity to work together. That didn't stop her from following his progress. What was she doing sitting here? She didn't want to pee. She realised that she was waiting for her stud to vacate her home. She flushed the toilet and opened the toilet door. Thankfully, he had received the message, and the bedroom was empty. She stared at the rumpled bed and knew that she didn't want to sleep there right now. She put on her dressing gown and went into her small kitchen. She plugged in the electric kettle and made herself a cup of tea. She carried the cup into the living room and switched on the television. *Funeral in Berlin*, one of her favourite films, was just about to start, and she settled down on the sofa.

She woke to the noise of the telephone ringing. The cup of camomile tea she'd prepared was sitting on the coffee table untouched and for a moment she was confused. Then she remembered her pneumatic friend and the Michael Caine film on TV. The phone continued to ring, and she prised herself away from the couch and to the nearest handset. 'Reid,' she said glancing at the clock. One thirty in the morning. She listened attentively. 'I'll be there in twenty minutes to half an hour.'

. . .

THERE WAS NOT much activity when Reid arrived at the house in Lawrence Street in the University area. The coroner's ambulance had already arrived and was parked at an angle in front of the house. A police car was parked in order to block access and two police officers, one male and one female, were standing on either side of the house.

'What's the story?' Reid asked as she approached the police officers.

'Suicide, I suppose,' the male officer said. He had a half smile on his face as he spoke.

Reid took an instant dislike to the man. 'Is there something funny about suicide?'

'Look inside.' He pushed the door open. The stupid grin was still on his face.

Reid ignored him and moved through the open door. She found herself in a narrow hallway with a staircase on the left. At the end of the hallway a man dressed in female clothing was hanging from the stair post. The man's head was lying on the top of his chest and from a distance the figure looked like a broken Pierrot doll. The smell of defecation hung in the air. 'Who sent for me?'

The male officer shrugged his shoulders.

'Do you know who I am?' Reid said sharply.

'A doc,' the male officer replied.

Reid looked at him. She knew the type. He looked over fifty years old, meaning he'd been in the RUC before the creation of the Police Service of Northern Ireland. He was obviously not au fait with the ethos of the new softer policing in the Province. Or, maybe he'd just skipped the course on how a police officer should behave. 'I'm not just a doc as you put it,' she said staring into his face. 'I'm the pathologist, and I'm only supposed to be called out when there's some doubt as to the cause of death. If the man hanging inside is a suicide, he could have been pronounced dead by a general practitioner, maybe even his own doctor.'

'No need to get your knickers in a twist,' the officer said. 'We called it in and someone at the station must have given you the call. Now do you want us to try and find the guy's doctor?'

Reid sighed. 'Since I'm here, and I suppose everyone wants to get on with their lives as quickly as possible.' She picked up her black bag and re-entered the hallway. Not a nice way to go, she thought as she walked around the body. The man's face had already turned puce, and his eyes bulged in his head. The face was engorged, and the tongue protruded from his mouth. She noted the drop from the chair and concluded that the deceased didn't die from hanging but from strangulation. The difference was not solely semantic. Death by strangulation was agonizing whereas death from hanging could be mercifully short. The deceased had died a death that had been protracted, grisly and painful. She tried to ignore the flaccid penis hanging over a pair of lady's briefs. The only feature of note was that the deceased was circumcised. She looked up and stared into a face that was definitely cyanotic. Petechiae, little marks on the face and in the eyes from burst blood capillaries, a classic sign of strangulation, were clearly visible. She gazed at the floor and saw a stain indicating that the deceased had ejaculated either shortly before or after death. A line of dried faeces ran down his bare leg.

'Ma'am.' The male policeman entered the hallway.

Reid turned. 'You may call me Professor or Doctor but I am certainly not a Ma'am. What's your problem?'

'The meat wagon is outside,' he said sheepishly.

'Tell them to wait. I'll let them know when I'm finished.'

She continued her examination of the face and noted that a bruise had risen on the temple. The welt showed that the injury had been pre-mortem. She had never seen the body of someone who had died from a failed attempt at erotic asphyxiation. She was well aware that the technique was dangerous and could lead to accidental death. She walked up the stairs and examined the knot that had been made around the post at the top. She slid the knot down a fraction and saw that there was no indentation in the wood. It looked like it was the first time that the rope had been tied around the post. The deceased was unlucky on two counts. First, he had given himself a very nasty death, and second, it looked like he was a first-timer. She went slowly down the stairs. Something didn't seem right. It should have been clear-cut. The deceased accidentally died trying to reach erotic bliss. He wasn't the first man to die like this, and he wouldn't be the last. She looked at the body again and wondered why she wasn't buying it. She took out her mobile phone from her pocket and opened the camera. She started taking photos of the hanging man, his face, his torso, the position of the rope, and the stain at his feet. After taking more than twenty photos, she put away the phone and went to the front door.

Two men dressed in high-visibility jackets, and trousers with high-visibility strips along the legs, were leaning back against the outer wall. One was sucking hungrily on a cigarette while the other simply looked into space. For them it was just another boring night shift.

'I'm done,' she said as she exited the house.

'Thanks be to God,' the ambulance man who had been smoking flicked the butt of his cigarette into the air where it lit an arc like a damp squib firework.

'I want him at the Royal Victoria,' Reid said sharply. 'He'll need to be autopsied.' She turned and walked towards her car. The sound of guffawing came from the open door of the house. Reid thought about returning and giving the ambulance men a piece of her mind but the idea of a return to the sanity of her apartment kept her heading in the direction of her car. Men suck, she concluded for the second time that evening.

CHAPTER FIVE

Detective Superintendent Ian Wilson sat in the living room of the apartment that he and his partner shared in Belfast. He was directly facing a large picture window with a stunning view across the early-morning city. He loved that view, and he had been staring at it since he'd risen at seven o'clock. As soon as he had woken, he had stretched his hand out in the bed and felt the empty space beside him. He wasn't surprised. Kate was waking up earlier and earlier, and the effects of the lack of sleep were beginning to show on her face and in her shortness of temper. He had expected to find her at her desk poring over some legal papers, but she had already left for the office. He remembered sitting at her bedside in the Royal and promising that things would not change. He knew then that he was a liar, but he hadn't realised how big the lie was. Losing their child had been a tragedy for him but for Kate, it had been a catastrophe. She had been told a million and one times that it wasn't her fault. A miscarriage is nature's way of dealing with some deeper problem with the foetus. However, the patina of grief hung over Kate like a veil of darkness. It began with the guilt that led to the sleeplessness that in turn led to the tiredness. Kate was beginning to run the full gamut of the symptoms of loss. It wasn't a question of nothing changing. It was beginning to feel like everything was changing.

'Sunrise over Belfast is a bit special.' The voice came from behind Wilson.

He turned and smiled at Helen McCann. Kate's mother had returned to Belfast from her home in Antibes as soon as she had talked to Kate on Skype. They say that girls generally grow up to resemble their mother. If that was the case, Kate had nothing to worry about. Her mother was well north of sixty but was still strikingly attractive. Her all-year-round tan was subdued, more sun kissed than sun blessed. She was wearing a silk kimono that probably cost more than Wilson earned in a month, and although she had just left her bed there wasn't a stray wisp of hair on her perfectly coiffed head. 'Aye, I love this view.'

'It's rare to have the city bathed in gold,' she said.

'That's why you live in Antibes.'

She put her right hand on her heart. 'Ulster is in here. And as the ad says "for everything else there's Antibes".' She smiled. 'Kate gone?'

Wilson nodded.

'I'm worried about her,' Helen said. 'She's taken the miscarriage much worse than I thought. She was always such a strong girl but behind that strength was a vulnerability that once breached ...' Her voice trailed off.

'It'll pass,' Wilson said. 'It's bereavement, and it has to go through the various stages that a death entails. Eventually, she'll accept that it wasn't her fault, and that she's young enough to have a lot more children.'

'You're right about the process,' Helen said. 'But you may be wrong about the timing.' She looked at the man sitting in front of her. He was rumoured to be one of the best detectives in the PSNI but to her, he was just one more man who had a very incomplete knowledge of women and how they work. She knew her daughter a lot better than this Johnny-come-lately. Kate was in pain, and she was a long way from healing. A superintendent in the PSNI was by nature inured to people's pain. That wouldn't serve him well when dealing with her daughter. 'Would you like a coffee? I'm nothing in the morning until I've had my first coffee.'

'I'd love one.' Wilson wondered why he didn't believe that it wouldn't take a cup of coffee to switch Helen McCann on. He didn't know much about her, but he noticed people's reaction when her name was mentioned. 'We're both grateful that you took time out to help Kate.'

'I love my daughter,' she said from the kitchen. 'And I had some business in Belfast.'

'What business is that?' Wilson asked getting up and making his way to the kitchen.

Helen McCann stood with her back to him, busying herself at the Nespresso machine. 'You like a long coffee, I assume?'

'Yes, thanks. You said that you had business in Belfast. What business is that?'

'Not really business.' She deposited two cups of coffee on the breakfast bar. 'I'm so bored these days that I consider lunches and dinners with my old friends as business. I have a few board meetings to attend, a few charitable functions. I come to Belfast when I want to be busy.'

Wilson stirred with the spoon that Helen had provided although he took neither milk nor sugar. He was the square peg in a round hole as far as Kate and her mother were concerned. They had all the advantages of money. They were educated at the best schools and colleges. They travelled the world, and not in economy class. His father had been an RUC man, and his mother was a teacher, the quintessential middle-class family. He wondered how his mother would feel at one of Helen's lunches or dinners. He knew she would be out of place. Just like him in the sphere of the McCanns.

'Kate is tired all the time,' Helen said, sipping her espresso. 'I've convinced her to hire a housekeeper.'

Wilson's eyebrows rose. He hadn't been informed about the employment of a housekeeper. But then why should he be. Until something more permanent was announced, he was simply the lodger.

'Do you see your mother often?' Helen asked.

'My mother's dead,' Wilson said.

'No she's not,' Helen sipped her coffee. 'She's living in some Godforsaken town in Nova Scotia, as you very well know.'

Wilson was stunned. 'How do you know?'

'I am one of the wealthiest women in this Province. I have one daughter to whom everything I own will pass one day. Surely you don't think that I would be so remiss as to not check into the man who currently resides with her.'

'I haven't seen my mother since she remarried and left Ulster.'

'How very peculiar. You haven't seen your mother in more than twenty years.'

'She gave up that right when she married within one year of my father's death, and when it transpired that she'd had a relationship with her new husband over a period of years when she'd been married.'

'You're too harsh.'

'This subject is closed,' Wilson said.

Helen was about to speak when Wilson's mobile rang. He picked up the phone and looked at the caller ID, it was Stephanie Reid. He thought for a moment before pressing the green button. 'It's a bit early,' he said as soon as the line opened.

'And Good Morning to you too,' Reid said. 'You're a right grump in the morning.'

Wilson wanted to kick himself for his brusqueness.

Thinking of his mother tended to leave him on edge. 'Thanks. I wasn't expecting a social call.'

'It's not totally unrelated to work. Are you busy today?'

Wilson wanted to answer 'yes' but that would have been a lie. And Professor Reid might discover that lie. 'Not really,' he said finally. 'Why?'

'I'm not sure,' Reid said hesitantly. 'I was called out by mistake last night. It appears that a Belfast City Councillor by the name of David Grant had an accident while performing erotic asphyxiation. Something seems to have gone terribly wrong, and he ended up strangling himself.'

'But,' Wilson said.

'It didn't look right.'

'Accidents rarely do. That's why they're called accidents.'

'I can't put my finger on it but I think there's more to this than an accident.'

'What might he local GP think?'

'That the chair slipped while Mr Grant was trying to get his rocks off by simulating a hanging. I should mention that he was dressed in bra, panties and black stockings at the time.'

'That must have been quite a sight. And you want me to do what about it?'

'Maybe it wasn't an accident. It looked to me like one of those tableaus they used to do on stage. It looked set up.'

'Most deaths look set up. The corpse generally looks like a mannequin that has been positioned in death. You've been down that road as many times as I have. Who was there from our side?'

'Male and female cop team, they obviously discovered the body and called it in.'

'Anyone from CID?'

'Not that I saw. By the time I was through with the preliminary examination of the body, an ambulance crew had arrived and were anxious to get the body away. It's in a morgue.'

'Was there any sign of foul play?'

'Not that I saw.'

'How about the police team?'

'They called it in as accidental death. We've all heard about erotic asphyxiation. It looked like the classic set up. Maybe that's what spooked me. It looked a bit too much like the classic set up. I took some photos if you'd like to see them.'

Wilson sighed. 'I respect your opinion but I really don't see the point. Belfast is full of people who are into bondage, domination, sadism and masochism. They hang around in clubs and beat the shit out of each other. The only surprise is that more of them don't end up in the hospital or even the morgue. Half the thrill is in the pain mixed with the pleasure.'

Reid laughed. 'I didn't know you were so well up on the Belfast sex scene. Another string to your bow?'

'I won't dignify that remark with an answer. What do you want me to do? I'm not supposed to create my own work, officially there's no case.'

'I'm going to do an autopsy this morning. Depending on what I find, I'll decide what opinion to present to the coroner at the inquest. I'd like to think that I'll do right by Mr Grant. Given that the poor man was a politician, the Press will have their claws into him before the day is out. He'll be dragged through the mud, and maybe he doesn't deserve it. Spare one hour this morning for the autopsy. Look at the photos and visit the house. If you tell me I have my head up my bum, I'll go with death by misadventure and we can consign David Grant to the dustbin of history.'

Wilson stayed silent for a few moments. If it were anyone else except Stephanie Reid, he might have considered that they were over-reacting. She was right about the newspapers. There was nothing juicier than a politician involved in some kinky sex practice. Chief Superintendent Spence would have a fit, but he could always claim that he was helping the coroner out. 'Okay,' he said. 'What time does the autopsy start?'

'Ten o'clock. You'll be there then?'

'I'll be there,' he said. 'Just for a look-see.' He pressed the red button cutting the communication.

'Who was that?' Helen McCann asked.

'The pathologist,' Wilson said simply.

'It must be important if the pathologist called you at home.'

'A Belfast City Councillor called David Grant died last night while trying to get off on erotic asphyxiation. It appears it didn't go right, and he strangled himself.' Wilson may have been mistaken, but he thought he saw some recognition in Helen's eyes when he said the name of the deceased. 'You knew him?'

'We met once, I think. Some legal do or other. He seemed like a very nice young man, and I heard that he was a hell of a lawyer. I understood that he was very committed to rooting out corruption in the Public Service. I was told it bordered on the obsessive. On a single meeting, I wouldn't have believed he was the sort who went in for unusual sexual practices.'

'It's not normally stamped on the forehead.'

'What's the pathologist's problem?' she asked.

Wilson moved off towards the kitchen. If he was going to face one of Reid's autopsies, he needed another coffee. 'Something has spooked her. She wants me to attend the autopsy and look at some of the photos she took at the scene. She wants to make sure that if she declares death by misadventure that that's what it really was.'

'How very professional.'

Wilson tried a smile. He switched on the coffee machine. 'Can I make you one?'

'No, thank you,' she smiled. 'If I drink two coffees, I'm hyper all day. How terrible that you have to attend to see people being cut up.'

Wilson picked up his cup of coffee. 'Just another day in paradise, as we say in the PSNI.'

CHAPTER SIX

I t was long past the days when Belfast was considered the murder capital of the United Kingdom. Despite that there were enough evil people out there that Wilson didn't fear for his job. That being said, he had to admit that things had been quiet since they had stopped Maggie Cummerford killing old ladies. The past few months had been taken up with preparing evidence for her trial. He enjoyed the short drive from the apartment to the Grosvenor Road entrance to the Royal Victoria Hospital. The Belfast Trust Mortuary was a two-storey modern, yellow brick building at the rear of the hospital site and was adjacent to the Northern Ireland Office State Pathology Laboratory. All bodies were transported to the hospital by contracted undertakers and were subsequently released from there. Wilson parked his car in the area reserved for staff and placed his 'Police on Duty' card on the dashboard. He flashed his warrant card at the attendant in reception and made his way through the labyrinth of corridors. He spotted Reid's assistant entering the autopsy room and caught the door before it closed.

Professor Stephanie Reid was in the act of gowning when Wilson walked into the room. She turned at the sound and unleashed her most radiant smile. 'Welcome stranger,' she said before tossing a green gown in his direction.

'Long time no see,' Wilson caught the gown and basked in her smile. The sight of Stephanie Reid had the ability to take your breath away but add that smile and you believed that you had landed in heaven. The bulky surgical gown hid her slim figure, and her blonde hair was tied back in a bow. Her high cheekbones and piercing blue eyes could probably be attributed to the visit of the Vikings to the shores of Northern Ireland many centuries before. He covered up his admiring look by busying himself putting on his gown.

'How's life treating you?' she asked. She didn't need to ask the question. She could see the lines of tiredness on his face.

She moved close to him and he could smell her perfume.

He removed his jacket to permit the gown to cover his torso. The gowns were not made for six-foot-three, one-hundred-and-twenty-kilo former international rugby players. 'As well as I expected it to.'

'How's Kate?'

Wilson was surprised. Reid had come on to him more than once. However, she had never mentioned Kate by name. 'Fine,' he said, the catch in his voice belying the truth.

'It takes time,' she said. There was a softness in her voice. 'Losing a child at twenty weeks is pretty traumatic. I hope that she's seeing someone. I know how difficult it can be to recover fully. How long has it been? Two months?' She also knew the statistics. A couple that lose a child stand a forty per cent chance of breaking up between three months and two years later. While the evidence was scant on miscarriage, what there was indicated that there was around a twenty per cent chance of a break-up.

'About that, but I'd rather not talk about it.'

'No problem.' She continued to tie up her gown. 'Before we begin, I want to set the scene for you.' She moved to the computer in the corner of the room. She held up a USB. 'I shot these photos on my mobile phone. There's no way that they're up to the standard of those taken by your forensics people but it was the best I could do under the circumstances.' She plugged in the USB and brought up the series of photos she had taken in David Grant's house.

Wilson moved in front of the screen and examined the first of the photos. It was taken from the doorway and showed the body hanging at the other end of the hallway. Wilson increased the size of the photo to the maximum. David Grant's face was contorted in the rictus of death. It was apparent that he had died in excruciating pain. Wilson noted the exposed penis hanging out of the female panties. A chair lay on the ground beneath the suspended body. Wilson flicked through the series of images, expanding each to the maximum and zooming in on David Grant's face in the final image. 'For an amateur you did a pretty good job,' he said staring at the protruding tongue in the last photo.

Reid put her face alongside his and looked at the screen. He was aware of her cheek almost touching his. She moved her body against him. He moved away and she followed him.

'This is why I send DS McElvaney on autopsy duty,' he said standing up and moving away from the computer.

'I try not to think of the Rottweiler,' Reid smiled.

'You're incorrigible.'

'Let's get professional and see how David Grant died.' She moved to a metal table where a corpse was covered with a sheet. She grabbed one end of the sheet and whipped it from the table with the theatrical flourish of a magician.

Wilson thought that he had seen most oddities, but he almost gulped as the body of David Grant still clad in women's undergarments was exposed. He saw that Reid was watching him intently.

'Ever see a "gasper" before?' she asked.

'No.' He had often heard of erotic asphyxiation, but he had never dealt with a case. 'How does it work, medically I mean?'

'The carotid arteries on either side of the neck carry oxygen-rich blood from the heart to the brain. When these are compressed, as in strangulation or hanging, the sudden loss of oxygen to the brain and the accumulation of carbon dioxide can increase feelings of giddiness, light-headedness, and pleasure, all of which will heighten masturbatory sensations.'

'Don't people realise the dangers?'

'Apparently there are quite a few who are willing to run the risk. Most of the practitioners rig some kind of escape mechanism but there was none in this case. In some fatal cases, the body of the asphyxiophilic individual is discovered naked or with genitalia in hand. Sometimes there is pornographic material or sex toys present as well as evidence of having orgasmed prior to death. Bodies found at the scene of an accidental death often show evidence of other paraphilic activities, such as fetishistic cross-dressing and masochism as in this case.'

Wilson looked at her with furrowed brow. 'Paraphilic?'

'You obviously didn't take Greek at school.'

Wilson raised his eyebrows. 'My teachers were more interested in my performances on the rugby field than in the classroom. I bet you were the class swot.'

'Not true but you're close," she smiled. 'Para meaning beside and phila meaning friendship, paraphilia. It describes the experience of intense sexual arousal to atypical objects. Most of the victims are male but there have been the odd cases of female victims. When I was an intern, I attended a special workshop given by a visiting US academic who covered the subject in detail. One of the points he made was that initial cases were considered to be the result of a murder, but as the practice became known, doctors were encouraged to look at accidental death. Maybe the pendulum has swung a little too much in favour of the accidental death theory. I'm a contrarian because I'm thinking that David Grant could possibly have been murdered.'

'But it could have been accidental?'

'It could have been. Why don't we try to find out? We've done you the favour of washing the body,' Reid said. 'As you might imagine when I examined the body initially those silk panties contained a load of faeces. However, I wanted you to see him as I did.' She nodded at her assistant who started removing the undergarments from Grant's body.

Reid pulled down the microphone to her level and waited while the assistant prepared the body. 'The body is that of a male of approximately thirty years of age,' she began. She moved around the body, recounting the engorged face turned blue through lack of oxygen. She then moved on to the little marks on the face and in the eyes from the burst blood capillaries. Then, she noted the protruding tongue. She moved along the body noting the bruising and ligature marks on the neck. Then she examined the bruise on the side of Grant's head. She reached up and switched the microphone off.

She turned and looked at Wilson. 'Up to now it's all pretty much classic strangulation. At this point, it would be impossible to say whether the death had been caused or was accidental. Except for that.' She pointed at the bruise on Grant's temple. 'That was made pre-mortem. It could have happened accidentally sometime before death, but the position is such that it would have probably concussed him. At any rate, he received a blow to the head sometime prior to death.' She picked up her scalpel. 'Now for the messy part.'

Wilson was always impressed when he saw Reid work. Her predecessor had fancied joking while he dissected a body, but Stephanie Reid was all business.

She reached up and turned the microphone on again. She worked deftly with the scalpel explaining the incisions and what she found as she went. She worked for a half hour without pause then switched off the microphone and looked at Wilson.

'What?' he said.

'Maybe I was right,' she said.

'Don't sound so surprised. Can you explain what you just found in plain English?'

'Grant was standing on a chair. It's a less than ideal long drop. If the drop is too short, or if the noose knot isn't in the correct position, it's not a hanging but a strangulation that can take several minutes and is a far more excruciating experience. These are the carotid arteries.' She pulled back the skin and revealed what looked like tubes. 'You can see that they've been compressed, when that happens, the brain swells so much it ends up plugging the top of the spinal column. The Vagal nerve is pinched, leading to something called the Vagal reflex, which stops the heart. The lack of oxygen getting to the lungs due to compression of the trachea eventually causes loss of consciousness due to suffocation. Death then follows in the same pattern as it does when the neck breaks, with the entire process ending in anywhere from five to twenty minutes. But this is the real beauty.' She pointed at a small bone in the neck. 'This little fellow is called the hyoid bone. You can see here that it's been snapped.'

Wilson saw that the small bone was indeed shattered. 'And that means?' he asked.

'That means that our friend on the table was most likely murdered.'

CHAPTER SEVEN

D eputy Chief Constable Royson Jennings sipped his tea as he sat to the right of the fireplace in the study of Coleville House just outside the town of Ballymoney in County Antrim. He looked up at the two men facing him. Sir Phillip Lattimer was the owner of Coleville House. The Lattimers were gifted the lands around Ballymoney in the aftermath of the battle of the Boyne by King William in gratitude for their support against the Jacobites. In the intervening centuries, profits from the slave trade allowed the Lattimers to increase their holdings and construct a magnificent Palladian mansion overlooking the Glens of Antrim. The current scion of the Lattimer family was a man of substance in more ways than one. He flowed over rather than sat in the button-back leather chair. His face was rotund, and florid, and a series of chins ran down his neck. Wispy grey hair covered his bowling ball-sized head. Sir Phillip collected directorships the same way some men collected stamps. There was no sector of the Province's economy where he could not connect with a 'friend'. The second man facing Jennings was in total contrast to Sir Phillip although they shared one thing in common – they were both enormously powerful. Jackie Carlisle was no longer involved in politics, but his hand could be found in every aspect of life in Ulster. Now in his seventy-first year, his pale face was thin and angular, with his nose a giant prow, accentuated by the emaciation surrounding it. In contrast to Sir Phillip, the wing-backed chair consumed him. His knees and elbows stuck out of his expensive blue suit. Carlisle liked to think that a flea couldn't fart in the Province of Ulster without his permission. Certainly, no piece of legislation moved through the Northern Ireland Assembly that he didn't cast an eye on first.

'Cheers,' Sir Phillip raised his glass of brandy and toasted the other two men. He took a deep slug.

'Your liking for the devil's buttermilk will kill you one day,' Carlisle said raising his teacup.

'You only live once,' Sir Phillip laughed.

'What time will the others arrive?' Carlisle asked.

'We start at twelve thirty and finish our meeting with lunch,' Lattimer replied. 'Most of them want to be back in Belfast in the early afternoon.'

'The agenda is fairly short,' Carlisle said. 'As Chairman I intend to keep discussion to the minimum.'

Jennings sipped nervously at his tea. Since he had received the invitation from Carlisle, he had been wondering why he had been summoned for the pre-meeting chat. Carlisle and Lattimer were the heavyweights of their group and an invitation from them was a serious affair. Roy Jennings had spent his life climbing the greasy pole in the Police Service of Northern Ireland. As a young man, he had read a copy of Machiavelli's *The Prince*, and he had lived by its rules. He had bag-carried and brown-nosed his way to the second top position in the Force, and he knew that he would never make it to the top unless he had the support of Carlisle and Lattimer and men like them. He already accepted his position as being beholden to others in furtherance of his career.

'Roy we need to know that you are completely onside with

our little clean-up operation in Belfast,' Carlisle's steely grey eyes bored into Jennings.

'So far it appears to have gone well,' Jennings said trying to hold Carlisle's gaze.

'The whole business was a total cluster fuck,' Lattimer said.

'Phillip, please,' Carlisle said. 'No profanity and none of that American crap.'

'Don't give me that Bible thumping shit,' Lattimer said. 'A cluster fuck it certainly was.'

'Our confederate, Mr Rice, is not the most intelligent or subtle of men,' Carlisle said. 'It was inevitable at some point that a trace would be left on some project involving him, and that it would have to be cleaned up. I'm assuming that Rice is at the very least competent in removing the threat.'

'Maybe we should have thrown Rice to the wolves.' Lattimer sucked the dregs from his glass.

'Rice has been an integral part of our operation for a considerable period of time.' Carlisle placed his teacup on a small table beside his chair. 'Throwing him to the wolves was never an option.' He turned and looked at Jennings. 'I assume there's no issue on the side of the PSNI.'

'Malone is not even on the radar,' Jennings said. 'David Grant is another matter. He's in the public eye and Rice's friends were very inventive in their method of killing him. It's not every day that a Belfast City Councillor hangs himself in a kinky sex act. We can assume that this one will run in the newspapers for some time. We won't be completely safe until it runs its course.'

'But you can stifle any investigation,' Lattimer said leaning forward.

'If that becomes necessary,' Jennings said.

Carlisle rubbed his bony chin. 'There is no need for an investigation. David Grant died while performing a despicable sexual act. Our friends in the Press will rightly vilify him.

There will inevitably be an inquest, but we should be able to control the result.'

'Am I the only one here who thinks that Rice has been a bit heavy handed in cleaning up?' Jennings asked.

Lattimer and Carlisle looked at each other.

'Given the level of experience of the Circle members, we could have come up with a more subtle solution,' Jennings continued.

'Did you ever meet Grant?' Carlisle asked.

'No,' Jennings replied.

'Pompous little Yid bastard,' Lattimer interjected.

'We would have needed leverage to keep Grant quiet,' Carlisle ignored Lattimer's interjection. 'And we didn't have any. The Circle has been manipulating events in Ulster for more than one hundred years. In that time the man in the street has had no inkling of its existence. It is imperative that it continues to be the case.'

'Rice is a liability,' Jennings said. 'He and his parents were useful in manipulating events during the "Troubles", but he may have outlived his usefulness. We have to recognise that we are now in bed with criminals. And criminals cannot be trusted.'

Neither can senior police officers, Carlisle thought but didn't say. 'What's done is done. Malone and Grant were potential threats to the existence of the Circle. Their demise removes that threat and for that we have to be grateful to Rice. We're counting on you, Roy, to make sure that these two dreadful accidents remain just that.'

This was the opportunity that Jennings was waiting for. Ensuring that the Malone and Grant murders never saw the light of day would provide him with leverage in the Circle to ensure that he would ascend to the top job in the PSNI. He wanted to smile but kept his face hard. 'You're asking a lot, Jackie. Although I owe a lot of allegiance to the Circle, I am, after all, a policeman.'

'And a good Ulsterman,' Carlisle said quickly. 'We're talking here about the maintenance of the status quo in Ulster. We are the glue that keeps this Province together. The Brits would have abandoned us years ago if it wasn't for the influence of the Circle.'

Jennings smiled. This was an authentic flash of the old Jackie Carlisle. 'Calm down, I already said that I would do whatever was necessary. I understand the remit of the Chief Constable runs out towards the end of next year.'

A leopard never changes his spots, Carlisle thought. Jennings was an ambitious little bugger. The job of Chief Constable at the PSNI was a heavy price to exact for keeping a few accidental deaths quiet. 'So I hear,' Carlisle said. 'I think you would make an excellent replacement for the incumbent. It's about time we had a true-blue Ulsterman in charge of the Force again.'

Lattimer glanced at his watch. 'Are we done here?' he asked.

'I think we have an understanding,' Jennings said.

CHAPTER EIGHT

Wilson was in a quandary when he left the Royal
Victoria. Officially, there was no murder. However,
he respected Reid's professional opinion. The question was
whether that was enough to bring the matter upstairs. Grant's
death was certainly more exotic than the usual Ulster death.
But Grant wasn't the first man to breathe his last breath
wearing female clothing while suspended by the neck.
Although there were no defensive wounds, in Wilson's
humble opinion there were enough discrepancies to warrant at
least a further investigation. One thing was certain, if Grant
had been murdered, someone had gone to considerable lengths
to conceal the fact. The level of inventiveness indicated the
presence of someone who was no stranger to murder.

Instead of returning directly to the office, he telephoned
Detective Sergeant Moira McElvaney and arranged to meet
her in the Crown Bar in Great Victoria Street. He was already
seated in one of the snugs in the bar with a pint of Guinness in
front of him when she entered. It was Wilson's curse to be
surrounded by attractive women. While Kate McCann and
Stephanie Reid owed their high cheekbones and blonde hair to
Scandinavian forebears, Moira McElvaney was one hundred

per cent Irish colleen. Her slightly freckled pale face was topped by a mass of flaming red hair. Her features were completely symmetrical, her nose and ears were perfectly shaped, and she possessed the most sparkling green eyes that Wilson had ever seen. She had a body to match her face, although many would consider her to be on the skinny side. Her smile widened as she entered the snug.

'Boss,' she said plonking herself into one of the button-back leather couches. 'I like the new office arrangements.'

'I wish.' Wilson returned her smile.

'You look worried,' she said. 'Secret meeting in your favourite pub so early in the day, I smell trouble.'

'I think that maybe your nose is in perfect working order,' he said simply. He waved at the barman. 'What'll you drink?'

'Policewoman on duty,' she said. 'Perhaps a cup of peppermint tea is in order.'

Wilson ordered the tea and watched the barman wince. He avoided the man's eyes by sipping his Guinness.

'What's up?' Moira asked.

'I'm just back from an autopsy at the Royal Victoria.'

'That wasn't part of your agenda for today.'

'I know but Professor Reid called me in.'

Moira raised her eyes to heaven. 'She doesn't give up easy.' She took the cup and saucer from the barman and stirred her tea before removing the tea bag. Stephanie Reid was not one of Moira's favourite people. She didn't like the way that Reid continued to throw herself at Wilson. As far as Moira was concerned, Wilson was spoken for. If not, she might have thrown herself at him, despite the fact that she had a very presentable boyfriend.

They toasted each other silently. 'It wasn't like that,' he said. 'She was called out by accident to a death by asphyxiation. The person in question was David Grant.'

Moira sipped her tea. 'It's in the late edition of the

morning papers. I don't know where these people get their information from.'

Wilson could make a very good guess. The police officers and the ambulance crew would be the perfect starting point. He took a USB from his pocket. 'Take a look at these photos when you get back to the office. Reid took them at the scene. It appears that Grant was into kinky sex. He was dressed in women's underwear and had hooked himself up to a noose tied to a stair post. It's what they call erotic asphyxiation. The lack of air is supposed to heighten the sexual experience.'

'I'll take your word for it.' She took another sip out of her cup.

'It's not something you should try at home. Anyway, Reid wasn't totally convinced that the death was accidental and she found a few discrepancies in the autopsy.'

'So what's the problem?'

'I trust Reid's intuition but if I bring this upstairs there might be a view that I'm trying to instigate a high-profile investigation on very flimsy evidence.'

'Nobody would accuse you of that.' Moira finished her tea. She'd never pictured Wilson as the paranoid type.

'I want you to get over to Grant's house and tape the place up. If there's any evidence, I don't want it screwed up. Find Grant's next of kin and contact them. His body is at the Royal and probably will stay there until the inquest. Reid intends to push for a murder conclusion with the coroner.'

'What do you think?'

'Off the top of my head, I think if it was a murder – a very elaborate one. A speeding car might have knocked him down, and that would have been an accident. But we would have looked for the speeding car and the person driving it. This way, we might think that it was either accidental or suicide. There's nobody to look for.'

'Look, Boss. I trust your instincts, but you know that the good professor doesn't overly impress me. I know bugger all about erotic asphyxiation but if someone hooks himself up to a noose that may end up killing him, either they mean to die or it's an accident. I don't want to burst your bubble, but it just might be that Reid wants to involve you in a little drama so that she can stay close.'

'I wouldn't sell Reid short if I were you. She's a lot more than a pretty face.' The door of the snug opened, and an attractive woman stuck her head inside. Wilson did a double take before confirming that the woman was not Kate. He let out a sigh of relief. He would hate to get into something in front of Moira. The snug door closed slowly.

Moira noticed his reaction and the relief that followed. The Boss hadn't been himself over the past few weeks. He wasn't open to talking about it but there was definitely something up. He wasn't a hail-fellow-well-met but she hoped that he considered her a friend as well as a colleague. If he did open up, it would be in his own good time. 'Maybe so but this is a bit flimsy,' she said.

'Put a bit of crime-scene tape around the house and get Harry working on a profile of Grant. The least we can do is look into the possibility.'

'The Prosecution Barrister in the Cummerford case wants to see you as soon as possible. It looks like we're going to be tied up with the McIver and Cummerford trials over the next few months so the question is do we really have the time to "look into" Professor Reid's possible homicide.'

'Humour me.' Wilson signalled the barman for the bill.

'What about the Chief Super?' she asked.

'Leave him to me. I'll square things as soon as I get back to the office.'

The barman arrived and Wilson rooted around in his pocket for the change.

'You OK, Boss?' Moira asked.

Wilson didn't answer because he probably would have said something like 'not too bad for someone whose life is heading down the toilet at breakneck speed'. His relationship with his partner was disintegrating by the day. The business with Ronald McIver had hit him hard. McIver had been a member of the team and was about to go on trial with one count of manslaughter and one count regarding the unlawful death of his wife. Both had happened on Wilson's watch and there were those in the Force who wouldn't forget that fact. Rumour around was that Wilson was on the slide. Maybe the rumours were true. 'Look at the photos and print them up,' he said. 'Preserve the scene and get Harry onside with the profile. If I remember right, Peter has some contacts in the sex industry. See if Grant is known around the BDSM scene. I've got a lecture at the Police College this afternoon. I'm supposed to keep the cadets amused. I'll be back in the office tomorrow so I expect you'll already have something for me to go on.'

Moira stood up. 'This could be a monumental waste of time.'

'Either that or we can get David Grant some justice.'

CHAPTER NINE

Moira sat at her computer in the squad room in the station. Detective Constables Harry Graham, Peter Davidson and Eric Taylor stood directly behind her. The photos taken by Reid, in the hallway of David Grant's house, were displayed as icons on the screen. Moira had already admonished her colleagues who had guffawed at the first sight of David Grant's suspended body.

'Put the photos up again,' Harry Graham said.

'Only if you agree to behave like Detective Constables in the PSNI and not like a crowd of titillated schoolboys,' Moira said.

'Sorry, Sergeant,' Peter Davidson said. 'It's not every day that we see a gasper. In fact, it's the first time in my twenty years on the job that I've come across one.'

Moira brought up a long shot of the hallway. The three men behind her moved closer.

'Poor bastard,' Davidson said.

'Poor unlucky bastard,' Graham echoed. 'He must have been in the middle of getting off when the chair slipped.'

'Reid thinks he was murdered,' Moira said bringing up a close-up of Grant's face. 'He wasn't hung, he was asphyxiated.'

'Same difference,' Taylor said.

Moira brought up the images one after another. They were not the kind of images she would like those who loved David Grant to see. She wondered how they were going to keep them from his family. She would leave that one to Wilson. 'Obviously not, the Boss wants us to look into it.'

'What about upstairs?' Graham asked.

'The Boss will handle that,' Moira replied. 'We need to get the scene taped up. It's more than likely that the attending officer, and the ambulance crew, and even Reid compromised the scene. But we may as well see what we can preserve.' She turned to Graham. 'Harry, the Boss wants you to run up a profile on Grant. He was a Belfast City Councillor and a leading lawyer, so there's probably a lot of Press on him. Don't approach the newspapers. Most of what you need is probably on the Internet. Peter, the Boss reserved the best job for you. You've still got contacts in the BDSM scene?'

Davidson nodded and his two male colleagues stared at him.

Moira ignored their looks and continued. 'The Boss wants you to check around and see whether Grant is known on the scene. Eric, check into Grant's movements over the few days before his death. Keep it low-key. We don't want anyone going off on a flier and reporting to the Press that we're looking into the death. One thing I want to emphasise, nobody, and I mean nobody, outside this office is to see these photos. I'm going to print off one set for the whiteboard. It'll mean someone's job if the Press get their hands on them.'

'What will you be doing while Peter is putting his life on the line in an SM club?' Graham laughed.

'I'm going to be interviewing the officers who discovered the body.' Moira pulled the USB from the computer and switched it off.

CHAPTER TEN

Wilson was a regular performer at the Police College. The fact that he was a former Irish international rugby player, and a senior officer, went down well with the young cadets. Over the years, he had got his patter, and the jokes that seemed so natural, off pat. He had expected his overall negative mood to influence his performance, but once he began he was on autopilot, and he had received the more or less obligatory standing ovation at the end of his speech. The Principal of the College invited him for a drink, but he declined citing tiredness and the need for a decent night's sleep. The Principal was a big rugby man himself and displayed mild annoyance at being denied a good chat and several rounds of drinks on the College's expenses. When Wilson arrived at the apartment, he parked the car. At first, it took him some time to turn off the ignition and when he did, he sat silently watching other occupants of the building return for the evening. It was the first time that he didn't want to enter the apartment. The arguments with Kate had been increasing and the last thing he wanted was to launch into another one. Eventually, he opened the car door and rode the lift to the penthouse. He slowly entered the key in the lock and quietly entered the apartment.

'How did the autopsy go?' Helen McCann asked as soon as he entered the living room.

Wilson was a little taken aback by the question. 'Usual autopsy,' he said moving to the bar. He poured himself a large Jameson. 'Anything for you?' he asked Helen.

'Gin and tonic and heavy on the gin.'

He poured the drink as requested and handed it to Helen. 'Sláinte,' he said touching his glass to hers.

'I don't hold with Gaelic,' she said not drinking. She touched her glass to his. 'Ulster,' she said.

Wilson didn't care much for what people said when they toasted, so he answered with the same.

They both drank, and Wilson moved to the picture window. Helen followed and stood beside him.

'You were telling me about the autopsy,' she said.

'Was I?' Wilson thought back to the conversation when he entered. It hadn't registered with him that he had been talking about Grant's autopsy.

'Yes, I read about the poor young man in the paper. It was some sort of sexual thing.'

'Erotic asphyxiation,' Wilson said.

'Which is?' she asked.

Wilson made an attempt to explain Grant's preferred method of sexual arousal to his partner's mother. The sanitised version didn't pass muster.

'I see,' she said when he'd finished. 'So, he was some kind of sexual deviant.'

'I suppose it depends on your definition of sexual deviancy. What was considered deviant yesterday is common practice today.'

'So why the urgency for the autopsy?' she asked.

So why all the questions? Wilson thought. Then he remembered the flood of questions from the cadets. It appeared that both the young and the old have the time to think up a surfeit of questions. 'There are some discrepancies in the autopsy.'

'What kind of discrepancies?' she asked.

Wilson was tiring of this conversation. At that moment, there was a noise from the hallway and they both turned to see Kate enter the open plan living room. 'Kate, darling,' Wilson moved towards her but she evaded his embrace.

'Into the whiskey already,' she said dumping her expensive leather briefcase beside her desk.

It was going to be one of those evenings, he thought.

'Kate,' Helen moved to her daughter and hugged her. 'You're looking so tired. Have you eaten today?'

Wilson could see the tears welled up in Kate's eyes as she withdrew herself from her mother's arms.

'It's been a bit hectic,' she said as she slipped away from her mother's arms and flopped onto the settee.

'I'll get started on dinner,' Wilson said. 'I've no idea what's in the fridge so it'll have to be potluck.'

'Count me out,' Kate said.

He looked at her and saw that she was on the verge of tears, again. He was now walking on eggshells. The smallest remark would be enough to set her off. 'What about you, Helen?' he asked.

'I had an absolutely huge lunch,' she replied. 'Anyway, I have to meet some friends for drinks. I'll phone for a taxi from my room.' She slipped quietly away.

For once Wilson wished she had stayed.

'What are you working on?'

'Nothing much,' Kate replied bundling and removing papers from her case before dumping them on her desk. 'The Prosecution is trying to move up the date of McIver's trial. I'm trying to delay it a bit so I can concentrate on the Cummerford defence. Oh Christ but I'm so tired.'

This was the point of return. Whatever was said next

would lead to either an argument or a reconciliation. 'You need to see someone,' Wilson said.

She turned to face him, red streaks colouring her pale face. 'I'm the one that needs to see someone.' She spat the words out. 'What about you? Maybe you should see someone who can teach you how to display a little bit of sensitivity. Don't you feel grief? Has that stupid job you love so much stripped you of the basis of humanity? Don't you feel?'

'Of course I feel.' He made to move towards her, but she recoiled.

'I don't see it,' she said. 'Show me how you feel. Show me your anger, your depression. Do you have nightmares about our dead child? Do you feel panic? I feel all those things. I'm angry with God, I'm even angry with the doctors at the hospital for not saving our child, but most of all I'm angry with you.' She marched towards him and started to beat on his chest. 'You great unfeeling brute. You don't have a sympathetic bone in your body. And you think that I should see somebody.' She slid down his body and ended up crying on the floor.

Wilson was stunned. What amazed him most was that he had no answer to her accusations. He had already accepted the fact that their child was dead. He didn't really grieve or feel anger. He had flipped through the process and had already reached the end. He simply accepted that their child had never existed. That was perhaps the dichotomy between men and women. Now the question was, how could they work their way through this period? He bent to pick her up and felt a pair of hands on his shoulders moving him out of the way. He started to resist and found Helen McCann had re-entered the room.

'Leave this to me,' she said softly. 'Kate is still raw, and you're not the one who can apply the salve.' She picked Kate up and cradled her in her arms. Then she led her to the bedroom.

Wilson fell back into the club chair. He bent his head and

held it in his hands. Through the picture window, the sun was setting over the Lagan River and the city beyond. Wilson was oblivious to the sight. He had always considered himself a problem solver. However, he had learned that one could only solve the problems that one owned. He would give anything to have Kate back the way she was. But that would have to be Kate's decision, and he was beginning to realise that he might not be part of the solution.

CHAPTER ELEVEN

S ammy Rice lifted his head and snorted hard to get all the cocaine into his nose. The white powder had an almost instantaneous effect. Deep in his brain the drug interfered with his chemical messengers, the neurotransmitters that nerves use to communicate with each other. It blocked norepinephrine, serotonin, dopamine, and other neurotransmitters from being reabsorbed. The result was a chemical build-up between nerves that caused euphoria. 'Yes,' he shouted as the high hit him. Rice had been using more and more cocaine since the death of his mother. As a major supplier of drugs in Belfast, he had always steered clear of his own product but over a period of a few months, he had gradually become his own best customer.

Big George Carroll and Rice's new number two, Owen Boyle, watched as their chief strode up and down the living room of the house he occupied in Ballygomartin Road in West Belfast. Neither man dared speak. Rice had always had a hair-trigger temper, but the cocaine had led to an increase in his irritability and paranoia. He was the godfather of a major crime 'family' in West Belfast. The core of the family had been established during the 'Troubles', and that core had segued without difficulty from terrorism to criminality. In the process, Rice and his lieutenants became wealthy men.

'What the fuck do you mean by it goes further?' he shouted at Boyle.

Owen Boyle was as hard as they come but he wasn't over-joyed at working for a man who would kill as quickly as he could praise. He cleared his throat. 'We've had some smart arse look at the stuff we took from Malone's and Grant's places. It looks like Grant went outside for some financial advice. He passed all the shit that Malone gathered on to some accountant friend of his to do a forensic audit.'

'Forensic audit my arse,' Rice shouted. 'I told you to clear this fucking mess up, and you told me that you'd done it.'

Boyle could feel his sphincter loosen. He looked at Big George and saw the spaced-out look on his face. Big George always seemed to be on another planet. Maybe that was the best place to be when Rice was on the rampage. 'We thought that we'd got to him before he'd had time to do anything about the papers but we were wrong. The bastard had digitised everything that Malone had taken from the Infrastructure Agency and Grant had already emailed them to his mate.'

'Digitised,' Rice looked confused. 'What the hell is digitised?'

'He turned it into a computer file,' Boyle explained.

'So it could be rambling about out there.' Rice stood directly over Boyle. 'Does that mean we have to kill every bollocks in Belfast before we're safe? Those papers get out, and I go to jail. Do you understand that?' He grabbed Boyle by the throat and lifted him out of his chair. 'And I'm not going to jail.'

Boyle stared into a pair of dilated black pupils. He was surprised at the strength of the hold that Rice had on his throat. He was about the same height and weight as Rice but he wasn't about to fight back. 'We know who the guy is.' His voice was a squeak.

Rice released his grip on Boyle's throat. 'If you want something done, you have to do it yourself. I can trust no one. What's the fucker's name, and where do I find him?'

'Why don't you let me handle this Sammy?' Boyle's voice was reassuring. 'We're in the clear so far. Malone and Grant are out of the way, and no one is the wiser.'

'Bloody bitch,' Rice said returning to the table where another line of cocaine was waiting to be snorted.

'What?' Boyle asked. This was the new Sammy Rice. You never knew where Sammy's brain was these days.

Rice rolled up a £50 note. 'Bloody bitch of a wife, she's down in Spain shagging some no-talent golf pro. The boys in Malaga are laughing up their arses at me. As soon as we clear up the mess here, I'm going to go down there and give them concrete boots.' He smiled then bent and snorted the remaining line of coke.

Boyle watched as the coke hit Rice's brain. His eyes followed Rice as he moved around the room. He wondered how much longer this could go on before their operation would be affected. Neither he nor many of the men in the organisation wanted to work for a drugged-up crazy.

Rice whirled around. 'What's his name and where do I find him?'

Boyle was confused. He wondered were they talking about the accountant or the golf pro. Since he had never been to Spain, he assumed it was the accountant. 'His name is Mark O'Reilly and he works for Watson Accountants in Windsor House in Bedford Street.'

'Where does he live?'

'Apartment on the fifth floor of the Tannery Building in Castle Street.'

Rice smiled. 'Perfect. I have something in mind for Mister O'Reilly. Is he a Taig?'

'I don't know,' Boyle said. 'We'll have the lads over from Glasgow again?'

'No need. I'll take care of this myself.' Rice pointed at the figure of Big George sitting stoically in the chair. 'George and I will handle it.' He walked over to the table and cut another line of coke.

POLICE CONSTABLE JIMMY CORR and his partner Rebecca Higgins were about to go out on patrol when Moira intercepted them. 'You're going to be a little late this afternoon,' she said showing her warrant card.

Corr raised his eyes to heaven. He was geared up for the evening, and he obviously didn't want whatever it was Moira was offering. He made a big deal of examining her warrant card. 'Big time detective, eh! Call my sergeant and he'll arrange an interview.'

'Detective Sergeant,' Moira said sharply as she thrust her warrant card into Corr's face. She looked at Higgins and saw a pained look on her face. Nobody liked being paired up with an arsehole.

'What?' Corr said pulling himself up to his full height of six feet two.

Better men than Corr had tried to intimidate Moira. He was the old-school RUC man, big and broad and bluff. His face was craggy and what people called 'lived in', while the purple streaks on his nose indicated the sign of a little too much whiskey having been imbibed. She could imagine him yearning for the old days when he could bash a Catholic's head in with impunity. Thankfully, those days were gone. Higgins was maybe fifteen years his junior. She was wearing a bulky stab vest, but Moira could see that beneath it she had an athletic body. She was not exactly pretty, her chin was a little too square and manly, and her blonde hair was tied back in a ponytail. 'You address me as Sergeant, and if I want to interview you now, I'll interview you now. I've arranged with your

Sergeant for the soft interview room. You can lead the way.'
She saw Higgins smile.

'What's the problem?' Corr asked when they had installed
themselves in the easy chairs of the soft room.

'David Grant.' Moira took a notebook from her pocket. 'I
asked for your report, and they gave me this.' She held up a
copy of a report sheet and dropped it onto the table.

'The sexual deviant that hung himself,' Corr laughed.
'That was some fucking sight.' He looked at the paper on the
desk. 'So, what's your problem?'

Moira smiled. 'It's what they might call "report lite".
You're not exactly Charles Dickens in the description area.'

'We followed up on a call,' Corr said. 'When we got to the
house, the occupant was dead having hung himself. The
doctor was called, and that was the end of our involvement. It
was cut and dried. What else was there to say?'

'Tell me everything and I mean everything,' Moira said.
'From the moment you picked up the radio call until you left
to resume your patrol.' She turned to face Higgins. 'Anything
he leaves out, feel free to interrupt.'

Corr removed his notebook slowly from his breast pocket and
flicked through the pages. 'We received the call from dispatch at
ten thirty. One of Grant's colleagues rang in to say that he hadn't
turned up at a meeting, and they were worried about him.'

Moira made a note to enquire with the dispatcher as to the
name of the colleague. 'Go ahead,' she said looking up from
her notebook.

'We knocked on the door and got no reply,' Corr continued. 'Then I looked through the letterbox and saw the body
hanging at the end of the hall.'

'The light was on in the hallway?' Moira asked.

'Yes,' Corr replied. 'The place was lit up like a Christmas
tree.'

'What did you do then?' Moira asked.

'I kicked the door in, so I did. Took it right off the hinges.' Corr's chest puffed out.

'Was there a deadbolt on the door?' Moira asked.

Corr looked at his partner. 'We didn't see one,' Higgins said.

Moira made a note. 'Okay, you're inside. What did you do next?'

'It was pretty obvious that the man hanging at the end of the hallway was dead,' Corr said. 'His tongue was protruding, and his face was purple. I didn't want to disturb anything in case the scene wasn't kosher.'

'Something bothered you about the scene?' Moira asked.

'I'd never seen anything like that before,' Higgins interjected. 'You couldn't put your finger on it but it looked off. Maybe it was because it was my first time. It looked a bit staged. I don't know.' She looked at her partner. 'We were both a bit shook up.'

'So you didn't check for a pulse?' Moira asked.

Corr and Higgins looked at each other and didn't answer. After a delay, Corr said, 'The guy was dead.'

Moira could understand their reluctance to check the body. 'What did you do then?' she asked.

'Constable Higgins went to the car and radioed for the doctor and the ambulance,' Corr said. 'We secured the front door and waited for the doctor.'

'Did you check the remainder of the house?' Moira asked.

Corr and Higgins exchanged a look before Corr said, 'No.'

'What happened when the doctor came?'

'She gave us a bollocking because we called her out,' Corr answered. 'Said we should have called the GP.'

'She seemed pretty professional,' Higgins added. 'Did some of the things that we should have thought of, like taking photos with her mobile phone.'

Corr shot her a look.

'What happened next?' Moira asked.

'She examined the body,' Corr said quickly. 'By then the ambulance crew had arrived and were waiting for her to finish.'

'Did she take down the body?' Moira asked.

'The ambulance crew did that,' Corr answered. 'When they took the body out, we secured the door. We put a call in to the station to have someone come out and finish the job properly. It wouldn't take long for some villain to suss the place out and remove whatever was saleable.'

Moira made another note. If Grant had been murdered, the scene had been well and truly compromised but that would be up to the chief of the forensics team to conclude, if the investigation ever got that far. 'Anything else?' she asked.

The two constables exchanged a look and shook their heads in unison.

Moira closed her notebook and replaced it in the pocket of her coat. She took two business cards from her pocket and handed one to each of the constables. 'If you remember anything, contact me.'

'So it was murder then,' Higgins said taking the card.

'We're looking into the possibility,' Moira said.

'Whether murder or not the man was engaged in a wicked act, maybe he deserved to die,' Corr said putting the business card into his breast pocket.

'Judge not and ye shall not be judged,' Moira said just loud enough to be heard as she made her way to the door of the soft interview room.

CHAPTER TWELVE

Peter Davidson watched the barman pull his pint of lager before setting it in front of him. He was sitting in the Rex Bar in the middle of the Shankill Road. One pint wasn't generally enough for him to get a buzz on, that would be three pints down the road. Davidson had spent the afternoon and early evening looking up contacts from his former life as a member of the Vice Squad. It had been two years since he had switched to the Murder Squad, but many of the denizens of the demimonde of bondage, domination, sadism and masochism were still alive and kicking, and none of them had ever run across David Grant. It was a walk down memory lane that Davidson didn't particularly enjoy. Like many who deal with the seedier side of life, he had partaken of the forbidden fruit himself, and it had cost him his marriage. His five years in Vice had led directly to him sitting alone in this bar waiting for the moment when the level of alcohol hit that critical point that banished all memories.

'DC Davidson as I live and breathe.'

Davidson turned and gave a half smile. 'I heard you were back in town.'

'Aye, they couldn't get along without me. After that

Cummerford woman stained her panties, my phone was ringing night and day with offers to replace her.'

'It's nice to be wanted.' Davidson nodded to the barman. 'What'll you have?'

'My shout,' the man said quickly. 'After all the *Belfast Chronicle* is paying.'

'Two double Jameson,' Davidson said to the barman. He didn't like the Press much but his new companion was a horse of a different colour. Jock McDevitt wasn't just a journalist; he was a drinking buddy from the old days. Davidson had been a contact who had become a friend. McDevitt's great skill was that he could get a rock to talk. He stood only five feet six in his stocking feet and weighed sixty-five kilos soaking wet, but his open face exuded empathy. When you talked to Jock, you felt that you were the only person in the world for him. His concentration on you and your problems was total. 'I see you didn't overdo the deep-fried Mars bars when you were in Glasgow,' Davidson said.

McDevitt smiled, and the glow of that smile washed over Davidson. 'I never took to the deep-fried Mars bar. Can't say that I didn't enjoy Glasgow though. Same type of villains we have here in Belfast but a lot more of them. However, the *Chronicle* found my weakness, they offered me a lot more money than I was making. It appears that Miss Cummerford did substantial damage to the reputation of the paper. Not so good to have a serial killer on the payroll. At least, I haven't killed anyone. Well, not yet anyway.' He smiled and touched his glass of whiskey to Davidson's. 'To the good old times.'

'Maybe they weren't so good.' Davidson took a sip of his whiskey. It could be a coincidence that McDevitt had strolled into the Rex, but Davidson didn't believe in coincidences. McDevitt was the best newshound he'd met, and he'd landed on Davidson for a reason. DS McElvaney's words of caution were rambling around in his brain.

'Being alive is the good times.' McDevitt smiled. 'What are you up to these days?'

'Murder Squad.' Davidson decided to keep his answers as short as possible.

'Beats Vice. You guys have been busy lately. I hear Cummerford and McIver are up for trial soon.'

'You said it.' Davidson took a slug of his whiskey and chased it with a mouthful of lager. He was beginning to feel good.

'Anything else of interest?'

'As in?'

'A little bird tells me that you've been a busy boy this afternoon,' McDevitt said nodding at the barman and indicating the empty glasses.

'What kind of little bird would that be?' Davidson asked.

'The kind that wears a studded leather bikini and likes to administer punishment to bad boys.' McDevitt took a £20 note from his pocket and dropped it on the bar.

'I didn't know you moved in those kinds of circles.' Davidson looked at the double Jameson that had arrived before him. He was entering dangerous territory. He recalled McElvaney's threat. He had no doubt that she would carry it out.

'I move in every kind of circle,' McDevitt said. 'You wanted to know whether David Grant was in the BDSM world.'

Davidson picked up his whiskey. 'If you say so.'

McDevitt sipped his whiskey. 'We're being fed the line that he died while performing a particularly dangerous sex act. Something in my gut tells me that we're being fed bullshit. I need to know whether my gut is still operating properly.'

'Although Grant was only a City Councillor, he was a personality,' Davidson said picking his words carefully. 'We're just stitching up some of the details. Like was he part of the BDSM scene, or was he simply someone who tried gasping and didn't do it properly?'

'I heard from another little bird that there are some pretty interesting photographs of the scene. The *Chronicle* would pay good money if they could get their hands on even one photo.'

Davidson downed his whiskey. 'Thanks for the drink.'

'I find out things, Pete. Just like the old days. If you share with me, I'll share with you.'

'I'll pass the word along,' Davidson said. 'This time I don't think that any of your little birds will be carrying warrant cards.'

STEPHANIE REID WAS JUST ABOUT AS TIRED as she had ever been and that was saying something. She had been on her feet since she had entered the Royal Victoria at eight in the morning, and it was now almost exactly twelve hours later. It appeared that there was an epidemic of unexplained deaths in Belfast. She had already dealt with six corpses most of whom had died suddenly, but the reasons had lurked deep within their bodies. Right now she was looking forward to a hot bath and a glass of chilled Sauvignon Blanc accompanied by the music of James Taylor. She sighed as she watched her assistant wheel in yet another body.

'The last one,' he said sheepishly.

She contemplated telling him to take the corpse back and she would autopsy it tomorrow, but who knew what tomorrow would bring. She walked to the trolley and picked up the tag attached to the corpse's toe. 'Brian Malone, age twenty-six, massive heart attack' she read. Age twenty-six and massive heart attack didn't usually go together. The assistant removed the cotton sheet from the body and displayed the corpse. It was immediately apparent to Reid that Brian Malone was not your typical heart-attack victim. In life he had been reasonably fit. The body was lithe, and he sported a six-pack that most men would have been proud of. It just showed that even the fit could harbour a small defect within their physiology that would be their undoing. 'Get him on the table,' she said heading for the sinks in the corner of the room. It was now her task to find the defect that had led to the death of an otherwise healthy man. This was the aspect of her job that she loved the most. In some ways it was similar to the job that Wilson did. He searched among the evidence to find the motive and the murderer. She dissected bodies looking for clues of frailty that had led to death. Her spirits lifted appreciably when she thought of the man she dreamt about consistently. Although she told herself many times that the pursuit was futile, she still harboured somewhere within her the hope that someday the situation would turn in her favour. The loss of Wilson's unborn child had the potential to create fissures between him and Kate McCann. The thought flashed through her head and she despised herself for it. If a man came to her, she wanted it to be because he desired her. She walked slowly to the table where Brian Malone lay and picked up a scalpel. 'Now let's find what genetic flaw caused the Grim Reaper to come looking for you.'

MOIRA MCELVANEY ENJOYED the evening at the cinema followed by dinner and a bout of lovemaking with her lover Brendan Guilfoyle. They had been together for almost nine months and Brendan's one-year sabbatical at Queen's University was coming to an end. That meant decision time was approaching, and Moira had decided that she would concentrate on enjoying the now and put off the decision that she dreaded until the last possible moment. In three short months, Brendan would be returning to his job as Professor of Forensic Psychology at Harvard University. He had already asked her to go with him, but she hadn't replied. She liked the idea that he told her continually that he loved her. That wasn't the problem. She had already loved one man and he had responded by beating and humiliating her. He had justified his action by calling it love. Love was a many-splendoured thing. It could be used to justify both care and incredible cruelty. She was certainly over Michael Regan, but that didn't mean she didn't wake up in the middle of the night running a hot sweat thinking of the beatings she received at his hands. At least she had been instrumental in putting the bastard where he belonged – behind bars. Too many women hung on hoping wife beating was a phase, only to find that it was a way of life. The current situation with Brendan was different. He was an intelligent and articulate man. He could hold his own in any company and had embraced Belfast with enthusiasm to the point where his normal Bostonian accent had taken on a distinctly Northern Irish twang. But what she liked most about Brendan was that he was fun. You could never be depressed in his company, and she could feel herself lighter when she was with him. Maybe that was love, but the spectre of her failed marriage always haunted her. Then there was her job in the PSNI and Wilson. While she might have wondered if what she felt for Brendan was love, she had no doubt about her feelings for her job. Her heart lifted every morning when she woke and realised that another day full of challenges was waiting for her. She fell into police work rather than chose it as a profession, but it had turned out to be the perfect fit. The thought of giving up her job for a life with Brendan filled her with a kind of weird dread. Almost as much dread as never seeing Brendan again. And then there was Wilson. She had been initially attracted to her boss. Who wouldn't? He might have been the perfect man if it wasn't for the fact that he was alleged to have slept with every female police officer his own age, and quite a few considerably younger. She had been disappointed when she discovered that he already had a lover, but since then their relationship had changed, and she saw him now as more of a mentor than a potential lover. He was her teacher, and she felt she had so much more to learn from him. Leaving with

Brendan would cut that learning short. She was mulling through these thoughts when she realised that Brendan was no longer in bed with her. She slipped out from beneath the duvet and making the minimum amount of noise made her way into the living room where she saw Brendan hunched over her laptop. She snuck up behind him.

'I hope you've got some clothes on,' Brendan said without looking up. 'Otherwise you're giving the guy across the way a peek.'

'What the ...' She leaned over Brendan's shoulder and saw that he was examining the photos that Reid had taken of David Grant. She tried to hit the power off button of the computer, but Brendan blocked her. 'You have no right.' She started.

'I'm expecting an email from Harvard.' Brendan cradled her head in his arm over his shoulder. 'And given the time difference I thought I'd check up now. You didn't turn off the laptop and guess what popped up when I hit the button.' He turned and saw that she was naked. 'Want to discuss this or should we head back to bed?' He smiled.

'I'll throw on a robe.' She turned and headed back to the bedroom.

'That's what I call an ass,' Brendan said admiring the view.

She gave him the middle finger as she entered the bedroom.

'Interesting,' Brendan said as they sat and flicked through the photos. 'A gasper.'

'Maybe,' Moira said. 'The pathologist doesn't like the look of it.'

'The guy I read about in the paper?'

'That's him.'

'What does the ME think is wrong?' he asked.

'We don't call them MEs here. You're supposed to be the bloody expert. What do you think is wrong?'

He blew the photos up to the full magnitude and went

through them one by one. 'I've seen a few of these in the States. Hell of a way to die. Did you look at the scene yet?'

'This only came up today. We haven't had a chance yet. I'm going there tomorrow.'

'Your ME might have something, but that'll depend on what you find at the scene. If the guy is a real kink, there'll be other stuff around.'

'Stuff?'

'Sex toys, magazines, more paraphernalia. The kind of things that you keep under your bed and you don't want your mom to find out about.'

She made a note to look under Brendan's bed the next time she visited his flat. 'But do you see anything out of place?'

'The position of the chair isn't quite right, but that kind of thing can happen. No,' he flicked through the photos again, 'it looks like the guy was trying to get off by asphyxiating himself.'

'Fat lot of use you are.' She slapped him on the head.

He stood up and grabbed her around the waist. 'Who the hell can concentrate on a crime scene when there's a woman with an ass like yours around?'

'What about your precious email?'

'To hell with the email,' he said picking her up and heading for the bedroom.

CHAPTER THIRTEEN

W ilson parked his car in his appointed slot at the station. Despite the end of the 'Troubles', the station still had the air of a fortress. The powers that be had tried to get rid of some of the fortifications in an attempt to soften the image of the PSNI, but the project foundered when their budget ran out. Or so they said. In a way, Wilson was glad, as there was no way his car could be interfered with behind a six-foot, thick wall of concrete. He had spent the previous evening finding out what was at the bottom of a bottle of Jameson. There hadn't been any solution in the booze and his head was pounding. He'd found the bedroom door locked and managed to stagger to the third bedroom where he fell into a comatose sleep. Kate was gone when he woke and there was no sign of Helen. He drank four cups of coffee before he felt human enough to pilot a motor vehicle. Had he been stopped he was in no doubt that he would have been proven over the limit.

The Desk Sergeant's brow creased as he saw Wilson enter the reception area of the station. 'Boss,' he said. 'Canteen is serving that muck they call coffee. I could have one sent up.'

Wilson ignored the remark and headed straight to the squad room. He didn't see the Desk Sergeant pick up the telephone to inform the boss of the station, Chief Superintendent Spence, that Wilson was on the premises.

Wilson pushed in the door of the squad room.

'Morning, Boss,' Eric Taylor looked up from his desk. 'How did the Police College go? The female members of the class wet themselves, as usual.'

'No, I've ascended into the old fart club. Time flies, or hadn't that fact got through to you.'

'You're a cynic, Boss,' Taylor said.

'Where are the rest of them?' He nodded at the empty desks.

'The DS and Harry have gone to Grant's house. Peter was working late last night. He called in to say that he'd be late.'

Wilson could have kicked himself. He should have called Moira. He needed to see the scene himself.

'A wee piece of news from Peter that'll interest you,' Taylor said. 'Jock McDevitt's back in town, he's returned to the *Chronicle*, on the crime beat.'

'That should stir things up a bit. Jock's not known for abiding by the niceties.'

Wilson's office was at the end of the room. It was cordoned off from the rest of the room by a glass partition into which a glass door had been inserted. He looked around the small space. Maybe it was just a little too early for the pipe and slippers. This is the place that his dead wife referred to as 'the womb'. He realised that he seldom thought of Susan these days. It was the same with his father. He had adored his father, but the memories fade. You think about the departed only when they force themselves into your memory through something they said, or regularly did. Like the word 'womb', it was used so often that he associated it with his departed wife. But the dead were dead, and he would leave them like that. Grandparents, father, wife, they no longer existed except in his memory, and then only fleetingly. He looked at the computer on his desk. It was time to wrestle with the contents of his inbox. He switched on his computer and waited as the machine warmed up. Then, reluctantly, he pointed the curser at the email icon, and pushed the left-hand button on the mouse. The screen instantly filled with a continuous stream of unread emails. So this was the technology that was going to make humans redundant. He looked at the bottom of the screen – '123 unread emails' stared back at him. Given his normal rate of dealing with emails, he reckoned it would take him a week to get rid of that lot. There was only one solution. He selected all the unread emails and pushed the delete key. He was working on the premise that any urgent unanswered emails would be followed up on. The rest were nonessential. Wilson had just finished his cleaning operation when his phone rang.

'I heard you were in the house.' Chief Superintendent Donald Spence's voice was friendly but businesslike. 'My office, five minutes.'

Wilson knocked on CSU Spence's office door exactly five minutes later. Spence was Wilson's boss and sole supporter for the past five years. The two men stood shoulder to shoulder in all of Wilson's trials with the hierarchy of the PSNI.

'You look buggered,' Spence said, as soon as Wilson entered his office. 'I'd offer you the hair of the dog but it's too early in the day. What's the problem?'

Wilson took the seat directly across from his superior. 'Nothing for you to concern yourself with.'

'That's what they pay me for, to help people solve their problems. When you get to my exalted level—that is if you ever get to my exalted level—you'll find that aside from lots of administration, there's no real work to do. So I have to stick my nose into everybody's business.'

Spence's secretary entered carrying a tray containing two coffee cups, a milk jug and a sugar bowl.

'I hope they're strong,' Spence said as she deposited the tray on his desk.

'The usual,' she said and departed.

Spence passed a cup to Wilson. 'I suggest that you take it black.'

Wilson took the cup and sipped the dark liquid. It was at least ten times better than the crap they served in the canteen. 'I've already had a barrelful.'

'This is you after a barrelful. I'm glad I didn't wake up next to you. You're a sad case, man.'

'Kate hasn't quite got over the miscarriage.' Wilson sipped the coffee.

Spence remained silent.

'At the moment I'm wondering whether she ever will,' Wilson continued.

'Time is a great healer.' Spence was staring into his coffee cup. 'We've all been down roads like the one you're going down at the moment. All things do pass.'

Wilson drained his cup. 'And that's your idea of help.'

'It's all I've got for the moment.'

'How's the run in to retirement?' Wilson asked trying to get off the subject of his problem.

'Six months to go, that is if *you* don't fuck up so badly in the meantime that it costs me my pension.'

'Speaking of which,' Wilson said leaning forward. He brought Spence up to date on the phone call from Reid, the autopsy and his meeting the previous day with Moira.

'Christ, I was hoping that the McIver and Cummerford trials would keep you busy until I clear this desk for the final time. Have you any idea what'll happen when the Press get a whiff of murder and sex? It's the perfect combination. They're almost in a feeding frenzy on the sexual aspect alone.'

'It might get worse than that,' Wilson said. 'Jock McDevitt is back in town. Apparently, the *Chronicle* dragged him back using a trail of peanuts so he can cover the Cummerford and McIver trials.'

'Just what we don't need. What's your initial impression on David Grant's death?'

'I'll know more by the end of the day. But from what I saw and heard at the autopsy I would be inclined to believe that he was murdered.'

Spence ran his tongue along his lips. They seemed to have gone instantly dry. He was already under the gun over the fact that one of his officers was about to go on trial for murder. A murder investigation involving a minor politician and kinky sex was something he didn't need right now. 'I want you to go very quietly on this one and for God's sake make sure that the photos Reid took are locked away. I don't want anything to get to the Press until we're good and ready.'

'McDevitt will have every tout in Belfast in his pocket. That means that he'll know pretty soon that we're up to something. Don't count on having much in terms of a period of grace.'

'I don't know whether it's this city or you, but you do attract murder like honey attracts bees. I need to be completely informed on this one.'

'Yes, Boss.' Wilson stood up to leave. 'Let's just hope that for once Professor Reid has got it wrong.'

CHAPTER FOURTEEN

Stephanie Reid woke late. The previous evening, she had taken a hot bath and finished a half a bottle of Sauvignon Blanc as she lay soaking. She had a slight headache but nothing a Solpadeine wouldn't cure. The details of the last autopsy came back to her slowly. Brian Malone, twenty-six, heart attack. Body of an athlete, fantastic shape, should have lasted another sixty to seventy years, bar an accident or cancer. At first, she had believed she was looking at a case of sudden death syndrome. After all, marathon runners and professional athletes had simply dropped out of their standing, and that footballer who collapsed at White Heart Lane probably wouldn't have made it if a famous heart specialist hadn't been in the stand and instantly available. She was always pissed off when she couldn't discover the cause of death and as far as she was concerned there was no obvious reason why Brian Malone's heart should suddenly stop beating. Maybe the toxicity screens she'd ordered would lead to some conclusion. She needed coffee and maybe a few more headache tablets. Thinking about her work wasn't possible in this condition. She slipped out of bed, and after a short visit to the bathroom made her way to the kitchen, first for the tablets and then the coffee.

Ten minutes later, the pills were taking effect, and she was enjoying a large coffee with a croissant she had heated in the oven. She had thought about calling Wilson the previous evening to discuss the Malone autopsy but changed her mind. She was wondering whether she was turning every autopsy into a possible murder scenario so that she could be in constant contact with him. That was ridiculous. She was a professional. She wasn't about to change her mind on David Grant's death but she would have to think again about Malone. Then it clicked with her. The mark on the side of Malone's head, it was almost exactly the same mark she had noticed on the side of Grant's head. Perhaps it was a coincidence. But how much of a coincidence was it that two relatively young men had died on the same night and that both had a mark on the same spot on their temples? She finished her coffee and made her way back to the bedroom. She needed to get to the Royal as soon as possible. She would review the autopsy. After all, she'd been out on her feet when she carried it out. Perhaps she should have waited until today when she would have been fresh. If the marks matched, she would have to inform Wilson.

CHAPTER FIFTEEN

Moira McElvaney and Harry Graham were standing in front of the door of the house that had been the home of David Grant. The front door had been given a temporary patch job that didn't look overly secure. The lock had been replaced, and Moira had managed to collect a copy of the key from the firm that was employed to carry out the repair. The door hung uneasily on its hinges as soon as Moira pushed it in. She stood for a moment in the opening and stared into the hallway reminding herself of the photo that Reid had taken from this position. In her mind's eye, she could see the body of David Grant hanging from the rope tied to the bannister of the stairs. The ambulance crew had cut the rope in order to retrieve the body but the knot that had been tied at the top of the stairs was still intact. She moved carefully into the hallway. She knew that the scene had already been compromised by the attending officers, Reid and the ambulance men, and she would have been naïve to think that the workmen who had done the door job hadn't entered the house. Still she tried to leave as little trace as possible. Although it was a long shot, there was always the possibility that the forensics team might be able to find some useful evidence.

'Spooky,' Graham said moving beside her. 'I've been in dozens of houses where people have died violently, and I always get this cold feeling, like the deceased is still about somewhere.'

Moira looked at him. 'You'll be telling me you're psychic next. Living room to the right, give it a good search. We're looking for something that'll confirm that Grant was into any kind of kinky sex. Look for DVDs, sex toys, outfits, that kind of thing.'

Graham smiled. 'You're well up on the kinky stuff. Speaking from experience, I suppose.'

'Get on with it,' Moira said and moved further down the hall. She walked to where the body had been hanging and looked at the ground. There were a variety of footprints on the carpet. Forensics would have a field day with them. Then she noticed the smell. It was a combination of the ammoniacal smell of urine and the acrid smell of shit. She could see, just beneath the hanging rope, a series of fresh stains. Again, a job for Forensics but she could imagine that they would prove to be a combination of semen, urine and faeces. The upturned chair had been left where it was when the body was discovered. She moved back and tried to picture Grant standing on the chair, connected to the rope. The chair was of the solid wood variety. It would have been difficult to overturn, but she supposed it would have been possible. She was beginning to see what Brendan had said about the position of the chair. It had tumbled sideways rather than backward or forward. She thought that odd, so she made a note in her daybook. She left the hallway and moved into the small kitchen at the rear. It contained the bare essentials. The fridge and cooker had seen better days, and she fancied she had seen a table similar to the one at the back wall in an IKEA catalogue. There was one chair at the table, and a space where the other chair had stood. She moved to the fridge and opened the door. It was what she expected. David Grant led a busy life as a lawyer and a councillor. Food was a secondary consideration, something he grabbed on the go. There were a couple of foil containers with some kind of brown goo still visible in the bottom. From the smell, it was the remnants of a half-eaten Indian meal. Grant wasn't one for the high life. She went through the various cupboards and found nothing out of the ordinary. She was just finished when Graham poked his head around the door.

'Not a sausage,' he said. 'Lots of books, papers, journals. No skin mags and certainly no sex toys.'

'Let's do upstairs but go easy, just in case there's some forensic evidence.'

They left the kitchen and made for the stairs. Moira climbed the steps first, taking care to stay away from the middle of the steps. She stopped at the top and examined the knot in the rope.

'It's a bowline,' Graham said from behind her.

'A what?'

'Bowline. One of the best knots you can tie. My dad took me sailing on Lough Neagh when I was a kid and taught me a couple of knots. I had so much trouble with that one I still remember it. There's a rhyme about a rabbit and a hole to help people remember how to tie it.'

'We need to find out if Grant did any sailing. That's a pretty sophisticated knot for someone who isn't in the know.'

The first floor was laid out in a traditional fashion. There were two bedrooms and a small bathroom. The house had been built before en-suites had become standard. Moira entered the main bedroom. The furniture was sparse and functional. The bed was queen size and was covered with a multi-coloured duvet. The duvet was a departure from the drabness of the rest of the house. The bed was the dominant feature in the room and left scarcely enough space for a small chest of drawers standing under a window that looked out on the street below. An old closet stood facing the bottom of the bed. She opened the closet door and saw three dark business suits, a series of similar white shirts and five ties. David Grant was obviously not into flash clothes. The drawers of the chest contained underwear, socks and sweaters. No sex toys, Moira noted. A book on Africa sat on a nightstand along with a reading lamp. Moira had been resisting looking under the bed, but she got down on her knees and peered underneath. Nothing. They moved to the second bedroom and found it filled with miscellaneous junk.

'Check this out,' Moira said. 'I'll do the bathroom.'

Graham shook his head. 'I always get to deal with the junk,' he said entering the room. It looked like Grant stored a lifetime of trash there. Magazines and books formed mountains supported by sporting goods and work-out machines.

The bathroom was small and contained the usual soaps and shampoos. Nothing fancy. It was a bachelor's bathroom that had never had the touch of a female hand. It appeared with David Grant that what you saw was what you got. She stood at the door of the second bedroom and watched Harry Graham rifle through the various items and bags of rubbish.

'Not a sex toy or a studded bikini in sight,' he said tossing a plastic bag back into the place it had previously occupied.

'One last look at the living room and we're out of here.' Moira started down the stairs trying as best she could to step on the same area as when she ascended.

She took a quick look in the living room. 'Computer,' she said turning to Graham.

'Yeah,' he said.

'Where is it?'

'Didn't see one,' he replied.

'See that thing in the corner.' She nodded to the area beneath a small desk. 'That's what they call a router. There was an Internet connection in the house, and that means he had a computer. So, where is it?'

'Maybe he left it in his office.'

Moira took out her notebook and made a note. 'Okay, we're done here,' she said.

It had started to rain, and they both got a soaking as they struggled to put the door back in its original position. As soon as they succeeded, they sprinted for the car. Neither of them took any notice of the man sheltering in the doorway across the road.

Jock McDevitt watched the young woman and the older man exiting the house, struggling with the door and making a mad rush for the car. He didn't recognise the woman. She must have been added to the roster since he'd left. But the man he'd seen before at Tennant Street and around the Shankill. The name rambled around in his head and then tumbled out – Harry Graham, Detective Constable Harry Graham. The rain had extinguished the cigarette in McDevitt's mouth, but he hadn't dumped it. His mind was too busy concentrating on the visit of the two plods to David Grant's house. For a second, he contemplated pushing the door in and taking a look around. Maybe he could get a photo of the hallway, and some genius at the *Chronicle* could Photoshop a picture of Grant hanging from the bannister. A plan like that could land him in jail, and someone like Ian Wilson would be happy to put him there. He hunched his coat around his shoulders and neck. Sex and murder sold a hell of a lot of newspapers, all of them with McDevitt's name on the front page. He needed to know what was going on.

CHAPTER SIXTEEN

Stephanie Reid had spent the previous hour reviewing the Malone autopsy. She was convinced that she had done a professional job, but she was troubled that she had been unable to discover the cause of death. On the table before her were two blown-up photographs. The first showed the mark on Malone's temple and the second the mark on Grant's temple. They were remarkably similar. So remarkably similar that they must have been made by the same implement or hand. She was not an expert on martial arts, but it looked like some kind of Karate blow. She picked up the telephone handset and put it down again. She sat staring at the photographs then made her mind up. She picked up the phone and dialled Wilson's mobile number.

'It's your favourite pathologist,' she said when he answered. 'Where are you?'

'At the office.'

'Busy?'

'I've just dumped a couple of hundred emails instead of reading or answering them.'

'An act of rebellion?'

He laughed. 'I don't see myself as an outlaw, just someone

who's trying to run away from a technology that can follow me anywhere. What can I do for you?'

'Now let me think.' She laughed. 'What's happening with the David Grant business?'

'I just got in this morning. Moira and Harry Graham have gone to Grant's house, and Peter Davidson is out and about. I'm sitting here twiddling my thumbs until everyone gets back and reports.'

'Fancy a visit to the Royal?'

'Don't tell me that you screwed up and I've been wasting police time on the Grant death.'

'No, I'm pretty sure on that one.' She hesitated. 'It's just that I autopsied a body last night and there's a similarity with Grant.'

'What kind of similarity? Another asphyxiation?'

'No, I have no idea of the cause of death. The man's name was Brian Malone, twenty-six years old and in perfect condition. It appears that his heart just stopped. But he has a mark on his temple remarkably similar to the mark on Grant's temple.'

Wilson sighed. 'Look Stephanie, that's just too much of a stretch. I'm willing to buy your conclusion on Grant, but you're beginning to get murder-prone. Not everyone who dies in Belfast is a murder victim, although there have been some periods when I've believed that myself.'

'I knew this was going to sound like murder paranoia, but I can't shake the feeling that these two men received similar blows to the head.'

'You're the scientist. You don't have hunches. That's my area. You look for facts and draw conclusions from them. I'm the one who looks at facts and hypothesises.'

'But what if I'm right?'

'We're investigating Grant's death. If some connection to this Malone character comes up during the investigation, we'll examine it.'

Reid knew that he was right. It was far-fetched, yet she still felt uncomfortable. 'Okay. I take your point. I'll be in touch.' She shut off the communication and looked at the photos again. It was too much of a coincidence. She picked up the phone and dialled the extension of her assistant. 'Bring Malone back in,' she said. She was too tired last night. She'd missed something, but she was going to go over that body with a fine toothcomb. Malone didn't just drop dead. Something killed him, and she was going to find out what.

CHAPTER SEVENTEEN

Wilson put the phone down and leaned back in his chair. What was going on with Reid? To spot one suspicious death was acceptable, two in the one week really was bordering on the hyper-vigilant. Despite the constant sexual innuendos, she seemed to have a good head on her shoulders. Davidson had returned a half hour earlier, but Wilson had delayed speaking to him in order to bring the whole team together. Just at that moment Moira and Harry walked into the squad room. Moira dumped her satchel at her desk and made for his office.

'Like your new office?' she said from the doorway.

'I suppose the clean-up is down to you.' He didn't want to answer her question.

'Things have been slack.'

'A temporary lull, I can assure you. Briefing in ten minutes. I want to see that whiteboard covered in information. I passed the message to Spence; as usual he's already put on his worry hat. In six months he gets to raise roses in Portaferry or wherever he decides to retire. The McIver case is going to shine enough light on him and me. The Grant investigation, if it happens, will intensify the media interest in what we're up to.'

'You're not usually too bothered about what people think,' Moira said.

'I'm fond of Donald, as you might have gathered. I'd like to see him out of here with the minimum of hassle. That's it.'

'I supposed it might have been a newer, gentler Wilson.' She smiled.

'Bog off.' He glanced at his watch. 'You've now got ten minutes to get that whiteboard prepared.'

He took out his mobile phone and looked at his messages. He had texted Kate earlier and asked whether she might be free for lunch. His message box was empty. He was left to draw the obvious conclusion. He didn't like the direction in which things were going. It appeared that he was now banished to the third bedroom. That was a major step. He would have to put a stop to the escalation, but he was at a loss as to how to do it.

Five minutes later, Wilson stood before the whiteboard to which a photo of David Grant had been affixed. Beneath was a short biography, including details on family and education as well as his political career. Moira had printed off two of the photographs taken by Reid at the scene. 'Peter, any news from the BDSM circuit?' Wilson asked.

'I hit a few of my contacts yesterday. Nobody has ever seen him or heard a word about him on the circuit. That's not to say that there isn't some off-scene bordello where his fantasies could have been satisfied.'

'So there's no definitive answer?'

'Sorry, Boss,' Peter said. 'The word is out. Someone might get back. I also checked with one of my old colleagues who's still up to date with the BDSM scene, and he's never heard Grant's name.'

'Eric, any next of kin?' Wilson asked.

'Parents dead,' Eric Taylor said. 'One brother works for

some charity or other helping children in Burma. He's been informed, and he's on his way.'

'Moira,' Wilson said.

'I interviewed the two attending officers yesterday. They were responding to a call made by one of Grant's colleagues who was concerned he hadn't turned up for a meeting.'

'Anything of interest?'

Moira shook her head.

'What about the house?' Wilson asked.

'Clean as a whistle on the surface,' Moira said. 'We gave it a once-over, but maybe you should ask Forensics to take a look. The place looks like a herd of elephants passed through. A couple of things: one, the knot on the bannister was, according to Harry, a bowline. Not everybody's choice of knot and apparently a bit of a favourite with the sailing crowd. We should find out whether Grant was into sailing. If not, how did he know how to tie a bowline. Two, there was a router but no sign of a computer. Three, and maybe most significant of all, there's no sign of any interest in unusual sexual practices. No magazines, no sex toys, no sex DVDs, nothing.'

'She even looked under his bed,' Graham said smiling. 'There's a lifetime of trash, books, papers, old sporting junk but nothing remotely kinky. If this was his first try at erotic asphyxia, he was one unlucky man. When we locate his computer, we should be able to find out if he Googled the methodology.'

'We need to decide here and now whether this investigation is worth our while,' Wilson said. 'The big question is, was David Grant murdered?'

'There are enough discrepancies to look into the case further,' Moira said.

'Agreed,' Graham and Davidson said together.

'Okay,' Wilson said. 'We need a timeline of his movements for the day in question. We also need to check the CCTV in the area for the time of the murder. I'll get Forensics and see whether something can be done at the scene. At the very least, we might be able to get something about the rope. Moira, I want you to interview this colleague who made the call. Everything we just discussed goes on the whiteboard. No photo goes outside this office. This investigation is to be kept as low-key as possible.'

'Boss,' Davidson said. 'We might get a day's start. But when we involve Forensics, CCTV, questions to establish the timeline, the cat is going to be out of the bag.'

Wilson frowned. Peter was right. 'Okay, let's just make sure the information we generate stays here. I don't want to see anything in the Press that we don't put there. Okay, Moira will divide the tasks.'

Graham, Davidson and Taylor returned to their desks.

'No sign of a replacement for McIver?' Moira asked.

Wilson thought of the emails he'd dumped. 'Not so far.'

'We need another body.'

'The stuff about the paraphernalia, the sex toys and such, you came up with that on your own?'

'Of course,' she said.

'Yeah, sure,' Wilson said, and he headed off in the direction of his office. He was just in his chair when his mobile rang.

'Deane's at twelve thirty for lunch?' the female voice said.

He smiled. Kate had cracked. 'OK,' he said. Then something about the voice hit him. It wasn't Kate. It was her mother.

CHAPTER EIGHTEEN

Deane's restaurant in Howard Street in the centre of Belfast was the city's only Michelin starred restaurant. Although the single star rating had been lost, the clientele still reflected that cachet. Wilson arrived a few minutes after the appointed time and found Kate's mother already ensconced at a table. Those at the surrounding tables represented the great and the good of the city and the Province. Helen McCann was comfortable in such elevated company and was being fussed over, not by a waiter, but by the owner.

The privilege of wealth and position, Wilson thought, as he joined her.

'I hope you don't feel like you look,' Helen said as Wilson took his seat.

'No. Worse.' He looked around the room. He noticed that half of the diners were glancing in their direction.

'Something to drink?' she asked.

'An Alka-Seltzer would go down well.'

She laughed. He really was quite charming. For someone who had been a sporting hero and was a senior police officer, he was genuinely humble. He was also quite handsome. She could see how Kate had fallen for him. She motioned to the waiter. 'Large bottle of still water for the gentleman, please.' She turned to Wilson. 'Water is the best remedy for dehydration.'

'Thanks for the advice. I normally go for a run in the morning to banish a hangover, I just wasn't up to it today. What's the agenda?'

'Don't look so apprehensive. It's just a friendly lunch.' She picked up the menu.

Wilson followed her lead. His apprehension was increasing by the minute. Helen McCann didn't look like the kind of person who did 'friendly lunches' very often.

A waiter came and stood beside their table. Helen chose the weight-watchers lunch of roast tomato soup, no main course. Wilson asked for a grilled sirloin.

'Things between you and Kate have certainly taken a turn for the worse,' she said when the waiter disappeared.

'You could say that.' Wilson drained a glass of water. He wondered why people drank alcohol when water tasted so wonderful.

'Kate is very fragile at the moment. Her response to losing her child is a classic one. She is angry, depressed, guilty and even doubts her own femininity. She is also involved in two very difficult cases. Maggie Cummerford insists on going to trial with a not-guilty plea. Kate is struggling to develop some sort of justification for what most juries will consider serial killing. Apparently, Cummerford is getting pretty rough treatment from some of the prisoners in Hydebank. Sammy Rice is pulling some strings to avenge his mother's death.'

'That would be Sammy.alright,' Wilson said.

'Then there's your friend McIver.'

'Not friend, colleague.'

'Whatever. He wants to plead guilty and throw himself on the mercy of the court.'

'That doesn't sound too clever.'

'Kate thinks that he won't get much leniency for the

McIlroy murder. He brought a gun to the meeting. The Prosecution will paint that as premeditation. The man's apparently a mess psychologically. Kate thinks prison will finish the job. She doubts he'll last a year. She wants you to go and see him.'

Wilson smiled. 'Is this our new mode of communication? Kate won't talk to me directly, and you're going to be the conduit.'

'For the moment that seems to be the situation.' She leaned her hand across the table and touched his hand. 'But things will change. Kate's a strong woman. She'll rebound.'

Wilson looked at Helen's hand. There was a large diamond ring on her third finger that, if cashed in, would keep a family of four for a year. Wilson glanced around the room. The tables were for the most part occupied by groups of four, and all were talking animatedly. He screwed up badly with McIver. He'd seen him coming apart, and he did nothing about it. What happened had a lot to do with him whether he liked it or not. And it wouldn't be forgotten in HQ.

'Ah lunch,' Helen said as the waiter arrived with her soup and Wilson's sirloin.

'I'm to convince McIver to go for murder while the balance of his mind was disturbed?' Wilson said cutting a chunk off his steak.

Helen raised her head from her soup. 'That would reduce the pressure on Kate.'

Wilson's steak tasted bitter in his mouth. He knew it had nothing to do with the food. Guilt coursed through his body. What kind of person was he? He didn't bother visiting McIver in the three months he'd been incarcerated. For God's sake, he had worked with the man for the past four years, and he had just cut him off. 'Tell Kate, I'll go to see him.'

'Mr W.'

Wilson turned and stared into Jock McDevitt's face. He turned slowly back to his food.

McDevitt turned to Helen. 'And the gorgeous Mrs

McCann.' He smiled exposing a top row of stained teeth. He stood for a moment waiting for a reply that never came. 'A little bird dropped me the word that the Detective Superintendent was lunching here.' He looked directly at Wilson. 'I wanted to run something past you.'

'I'm eating my lunch, Jock,' Wilson said without turning around. 'Why don't you just piss off before I have you removed unceremoniously?'

'That's harsh, Mister Wilson. I don't mean to interrupt your meal. It's just that I have a story in tomorrow's *Chronicle* that might interest you. It seems that David Grant didn't die by accident, as far as I understand it a police investigation into his death is currently under way, led by your good self.'

'I look forward to reading the article,' Wilson said without taking his eyes from his plate.

'No confirmation?' McDevitt asked.

'Not today, Jock, now I really mean it, piss off.'

'Madame, Mr Wilson.' McDevitt did a mock bow and retreated towards the door.

'Who was that distasteful little man?' Helen asked.

'He's the crime reporter for the *Chronicle*,' Wilson answered.

'And that story about David Grant. Is it true? Are you really investigating his death?' Helen asked.

Wilson was surprised to see Helen so animated. 'Yes, well sort of. We can find no evidence of his having been involved in any kind of deviant sexual activities.'

'What do you mean sort of?" Helen asked. 'An investigation is like being pregnant; you're either investigating or not. Which is it?' She was now quite animated.

Wilson finished his steak. 'We're following up on the pathologist's report. She's going to present her finding to the coroner that the death was at the hand of person or persons unknown. We're looking into whether the physical evidence supports that theory.'

Wilson was about to ask why Helen seemed so interested in David Grant when his mobile phone made its funny sound. He removed it from his pocket and smiled when he saw two other men at different tables do the same. The jingle he'd chosen wasn't just funny, it was also popular. He looked at the screen. The message was from Stephanie Reid. She wanted to see him urgently, and it was important.

CHAPTER NINETEEN

The body of a man was laid out on the steel table when Wilson entered the autopsy room. His chest looked like a patchwork quilt where Reid had sown him up. On the drive to the Royal Victoria, Wilson had been mulling over the fact that McDevitt was about to make public the investigation into Grant's death. In less than twenty-four hours that particular cat would be out of the bag. It meant that the clever dick who had set up the perfect murder would know they were after him. The killer had gone to considerable pains to hide the fact that Grant had been murdered. Which meant that there was possibly a deep secret behind the death. The fact that his plan had been rumbled so quickly would upset his applecart. The question was, how would he react? The secondary question was, why had it been necessary to murder Grant? What was the deep dark secret that had to be protected? Now there was the urgent summons from Reid. It was all getting very complicated. He tried to ring Reid from his car, but the call went straight to voicemail. His message was curt; he was on his way to the Royal. There was no one around when he arrived. He assumed that Reid and her assistant had taken a late lunch. He moved to the table and looked at the tag attached to the man's toe. This was Brian Malone. Despite being kept chilled, Malone's body had taken on a distinctly blue tint. He could see that Reid had done a more than professional job, and the undertakers would have to be equally professional in ensuring that Malone's family would be spared the sight of the results of the autopsy. He was about to carry out a closer examination of the body when the door to the room opened, and Reid entered like a white-coated whirlwind. The buttons of her white coat were undone exposing a white blouse tucked into a knee-length black skirt. Her blonde hair was tied back with two ringlets freed on either side of her head and hanging in front of her ears like sideburns.

'I just got your voicemail,' she said joining Wilson at the autopsy table. 'The bloody mobile is acting up, or my provider is delaying my messages. Hope I didn't spoil your lunch.'

'It's OK,' he said. 'Your text allowed me to slip away quietly.'

'I hope that I can make the intrusion worth your while,' she smiled, but it was a tired smile.

'You look beat,' he said.

She nodded at the corpse on the table. 'Remember I spoke to you about Brian Malone.'

'Remember I told you that you were becoming paranoid.'

'Yes and that pissed me off. So I've spent this morning going over the autopsy again and when I still couldn't find why his heart stopped, I took a magnifying glass, and I went over the body inch by inch.'

'And?'

'I found this.' She opened Malone's mouth, pulled out his tongue and held it back. 'Take a look.' She nodded at the magnifying glass that was on a tray upon the table.

Wilson lifted the glass and held it over the area beneath her fingers. He saw the red dot. 'Looks like a needle mark.'

'It is a needle mark.'

'And it's important because?' he asked.

'There isn't another needle mark on the body. Malone wasn't an intravenous drug user. Even if he had been, he wouldn't have used his tongue. There are no veins. I found his GP through the patient register and asked whether he'd had an injection lately, and the answer was negative. The question now poses itself how did Malone get the needle mark?'

'You did a toxicity screen?'

'Yes.'

'And?'

'Nothing. They found no toxic substance in Malone's blood.'

He saw a smile on her full lips. 'But you expected that.'

'They did find something.' She dropped Malone's tongue back into his mouth. 'An elevated reading of NaCl.'

'I failed chemistry at school,' Wilson said putting down the magnifying glass.

'Sodium chloride, or common salt. We all have a level of salt in our blood and normally I wouldn't have taken any notice of this reading.'

'And the significance of this elevated level is?'

'I'm pretty sure that someone killed Brian Malone by injecting potassium chloride into his tongue. The compound breaks down into both potassium and chlorine. The chlorine binds with the human body's naturally occurring sodium to create the NaCl. Too much potassium in the body causes tachycardia which leads to ventricular fibrillation and a resultant fatal heart attack. The fact that it's undetectable means whoever injected him didn't want us to know that he was murdered.'

'But he only had a heart attack. People survive heart attacks.'

'Ventricular fibrillation requires immediate defibrillation. Cardiac arrest is an emergency that demands speedy intervention. CPR has to be carried out in order to circulate oxygenated blood by external mechanical means. If CPR is withheld from the victim, death is assured.'

'You're reading too much Sherlock Holmes,' Wilson said. 'You have me buying into the David Grant theory but this is taking it a bit too far. There's a level of sophistication here that we don't normally get in Northern Ireland. Even when MI5 took people out, they used the 'sledgehammer' technique. Collateral damage is the name of the game in Ulster. You're talking highly organised professional killers. I couldn't name one person in this Province with the finesse used in this case.'

'But such people do exist, and they can be employed.' She moved closer to him. 'I don't normally buy into conspiracy theories, Ian, but these two men were murdered within hours of each other. I'll stake my professional reputation on it.'

He smelled her perfume and looked into her blue eyes. They were wet. He wondered whether she was afraid, but from what he knew of her, she didn't do fear easily. 'The *Chronicle* is going to run a headline on the David Grant investigation tomorrow morning. If there is a murderer out there, he's going to know that his ploy with Grant didn't work. If the same man killed Malone, he's going to wonder whether we're on to that one as well. I don't like it. It sounds political, and that means messy.' He made up his mind quickly. 'We'll investigate Malone as part of the Grant case. We can look at commonalities between the two men. Maybe we can develop a hypothesis for a motive. However, we'll have to tread softly. The kind of people who kill like this are best left sleeping. The more they think we'll never get them, the safer we can sleep.'

'Talking of sleep.' She wanted to let herself fall into his arms.

He seemed to anticipate her body movement and held her shoulders with his hands. 'Take a break. You've done a fabulous job. You can leave it to me now.'

'Careful as you go, Ian. I really do care.'

Wilson let her go and moved towards the door. So do I, he thought, but he didn't say it.

CHAPTER TWENTY

Jackie Carlisle lived with his wife in a converted coach house in the Hillsborough, an exclusive residential area to the south of Belfast. It was a fine stone building that had been updated with style and was a residence befitting a man who had worked tirelessly for the people of the Province. Since his retirement, Carlisle tended to spend the greater part of the day in the conservatory that had been added to the rear of the original property. He had installed a wood-burning stove so that even on the coldest of winter days the glass room was warm and welcoming. He was seated on his favourite couch, which gave him a view of his garden as well as the driveway. He heard the car crunching on the gravel before he saw it pull into the area beside the house. He stood up slowly, made his way to the front door and opened it. He watched as Helen McCann exited from the rear seat of the Mercedes Saloon. He'd known her for more years than he cared to remember, but he always smiled in admiration when he saw her. She was approaching sixty but she had maintained a beauty that still caused men to turn their heads when she passed. The light tan she continually sported perfectly set off her blonde hair and her Scandinavian good looks.

'Helen.' He held out his two arms and embraced her.

Helen air-kissed his cheeks. 'It's good to see you.'

'Will you ever age?' Carlisle asked standing aside to let her enter.

'You ought to be in this poor old body.' She entered the house and looked around. The place had been modernised since she had seen it last. As she passed, she looked into a kitchen. There was so much brushed metal it could have passed for the deck of the Starship Enterprise. 'I see you've been busy,' she said.

'Sure it makes Agnes happy, and an auld man has to spend his money somewhere.' He took her by the arm and led her away from the kitchen. 'Let's go through to the conservatory. I need the warmth these days.'

They walked to the rear of the house, and Carlisle led her to an easy chair before taking his customary seat on the couch.

Helen McCann sat and crossed her shapely legs. She smiled when she saw the way Carlisle looked at them. 'There's still an old rake in there somewhere, Jackie,' she said. But that wasn't what she was thinking. Carlisle was only half the man she remembered. She hadn't seen him in over a year, and she was taken aback at the rapidity of his aging. His trousers hung off his skeletal body, and bony knees protruded through the fabric when he sat. She noticed a slight tremor in his hands. He was a man in serious decline.

'Don't tell Agnes that. She's of the opinion that I'm dead downstairs. Can I offer you tea or coffee?'

'No thanks, I don't have much time. I've a board meeting at four o'clock.'

'Always intent on the business.' He smiled. 'So, to what do I owe the pleasure?'

'I just had lunch with Ian Wilson at Deane's,' she began.

He interrupted. 'A dangerous man, Helen, a dangerous man to those that love Ulster.'

'Our meal was disturbed by some journalist or other,

McDevitt I think his name is.' She could see that Carlisle recognised the name. 'It seems that he's written an article that will appear in the *Chronicle* tomorrow morning on the police investigation into David Grant's death.' She watched him turn a whiter shade of pale. 'It seems the pathologist has concluded that Grant was murdered, and she's passed that message to Wilson who, being the good little terrier that he is, has taken the bone and is heading off to play with it. I don't have to tell you that when he gets stuck into something, he follows it to the end.'

Carlisle was well aware of Ian Wilson's capabilities.

'You're shocked,' she said.

'The job was given to specialists. They guaranteed that the deaths would go unnoticed.'

'But Grant's hasn't.'

Carlisle tried to pull himself together. 'Jennings will put a stop to the investigation. Once we get Wilson off the case, we can bury it. It won't be the first time we've had a murder investigation quashed.'

'What about the pathologist?' Helen asked. 'There'll be an inquest. She'll stand up in front of the coroner and insist that Grant was murdered. The Press will be on hand and maybe a few concerned citizens will wonder why the police are doing nothing about it. The response has to be two-pronged. Jennings will have to put pressure on to have the investigation quashed, but we absolutely need to get the pathologist to revise her opinion.'

'I'll get on it immediately.' Carlisle made to rise but was having some difficulty and sat back instead.

'Things are getting untidy.' She straightened her skirt. 'It should never have come to this. Rice and his organisation are a risk to us. They act without thinking, and that has never been a trait that the Circle has endorsed.'

'They've had their uses,' Carlisle said.

She looked at him. She normally didn't feel empathy with

people she did business with but Jackie Carlisle had been more than a business acquaintance. He had played an integral part in helping her and her husband create a business empire, and as such he had almost passed into the prized category of friend. She was sad to see that he had disintegrated so much. She wondered whether he could be trusted to derail Wilson and his pathologist friend. Inside, she didn't think so.

'We must preserve the Circle at all costs,' she said. 'We are where we are right now, there's no point crying over spilt milk. We need to consider whether someone might have to be sacrificed.'

A smile flitted across Carlisle's lips. My God, what a woman, he thought. Whoever said to shoot the women first had certainly got it right. Helen McCann was as tough as they come. She would be prepared to sacrifice him and many others like him to preserve her precious Circle. 'Word on the street is that Rice has become a cokehead since his mother's murder. If we decide to jettison him, there may be consequences.'

'I've studied the man,' she said. 'He'd squeal like a stuck pig.'

'Let's just think about it as a back-up plan. Rice has resources that we need for the moment. I'll get on to Jennings, and I'll try to have the pathologist woman silenced. If that doesn't work, we'll look at other possibilities.'

She glanced at her watch and stood up. 'You should have passed this one upstairs. There's no way we would have sanctioned murder until all other avenues had been explored. It was a mistake and now we have to put it right.'

Carlisle stood with difficulty and faced her. 'My knees are giving me trouble,' he said by way of explanation. 'I'll make the calls immediately. This investigation has to be nipped in the bud.'

'I know, old friend.' She patted his hand. 'When this is over, we'll talk again.'

They walked through the house to the front door. 'It's a

lovely place you have here,' she said looking around the well-developed garden. 'It's a grand spot to spend your reclining years.' She air-kissed his cheeks and strode purposefully towards the waiting Mercedes.

Carlisle watched her as she seated herself in the rear of the Mercedes. She was the most formidable woman he had ever met, the First Minister the Province should have had. He had spent his life climbing the greasy pole. On his way up, he was admitted to many rooms. He always thought he had reached the top room only to find that there was a room above to which he was not yet permitted entrance. He knew Helen McCann had admittance to the room above the one he was currently in. He wondered whether there was a room to which even she could not gain access. He couldn't even speculate on who might inhabit such a room. He would never find out. He had reached his peak; all he could do from here was fall. Killing Grant and Malone had been a risk. However, he had considered it a calculated risk. Maybe that had been a mistake. His faith in Rice had been undermined. Maybe Sammy would have to be thrown to the wolves, and maybe he wouldn't be alone. A shiver ran down his spine.

CHAPTER TWENTY-ONE

A s soon as Wilson returned to the station, he called Moira to his office. He told her of his visit to the Royal Victoria and Reid's suspicions.

'Come on, Boss,' Moira said. 'You're not buying this.'

'Maybe she's right.' He didn't want to believe it but he had to admit the possibility. 'It won't cost anything to have a look. Check out Malone and see if there's any possible connection between him and Grant. Two men dying on the same night, in suspicious circumstances, maybe there's something that connects them.'

'We're already overstretched, and the Grant investigation is heading nowhere fast. I've been on to Forensics; they had a good laugh at me. In the end, they agreed to have a look, but they're not holding out much hope.'

'Humour me. Take a look at Malone's background. See if you can turn up some connection between the two men. He was found at home. Visit his place. If nothing turns up in the next few days, we'll drop it.'

'You're the boss,' she said making for the door.

'That's what they tell me.' Wilson eased back in his chair. McDevitt was a pest and a dangerous one at that. Sex and murder was an explosive cocktail and grist to the mill for a newshound like McDevitt. For as long as he could fan the flames, he would be assured the front page, and he was adept at keeping the fire going. If Reid were wrong, there would be hell to pay. His thoughts moved to McIver. He hadn't visited him since he had been incarcerated. Now he had both Kate and the Police Federation on his back to help with the defence while he was preparing the evidence for the Prosecution. It placed him in a difficult position. He picked up his phone and called one of his friends in the Prison Service.

'I need to see McIver,' he said as soon as they were through with the pleasantries.

'He's being assessed at Holywell tomorrow morning at ten a.m. Be there at eleven o'clock, and I'll arrange for you to see him. Eleven tomorrow, okay.'

'Thanks, I owe you one.' He put down the phone. He started to lean back in his chair when the phone rang.

'What the fuck have you done now, Ian?' Spence almost shouted. 'I've just had Jennings on the line and he was apoplectic. We're wanted in HQ immediately.'

'Calm down, Sir,' Wilson said. 'I haven't done anything, so I haven't had the chance to fuck up. Let's not get ahead of ourselves. By the time we get there the storm will have blown itself out. Then we might be informed of what bee is in the DCC's bonnet.'

'Downstairs, five minutes. It gets boring being pulled over the coals for you.'

'Only a few months more.' Wilson put down the phone and reached for his coat.

WILSON AND SPENCE rode in silence in the rear of Spence's official car for the entire fifteen-minute journey to Castlereagh. PSNI Headquarters was a collection of buildings off the Knock Road. Spence's uniformed driver dropped them at the front door before proceeding to the car park. The Chief Super-intendent straightened his uniform before entering the main door. The officer on reception called up to the DCC's office, and they proceeded to the lift. When they reached the fifth floor, they walked briskly to Jennings' office. Once there, Spence hesitated.

'Whatever it is, Ian. Don't make it any worse,' he said before entering the outer office.

The secretary immediately hit a buzzer, and the door to Jennings' office opened.

Deputy Chief Constable Jennings was seated on the raised dais behind his desk. At five feet seven inches, he was shorter than most of the officers under his command. To make up for the absence of height, he habitually wore platform shoes and had had a raised dais built under his office chair so that he did not have to look up to officers seated on the far side of his desk. Wilson and Spence were both over six feet tall with Wilson touching six feet and three inches.

Jennings looked up as the two men entered. Dark-red lines stood out on his face. 'Who am I?' he asked.

Wilson and Spence looked at each other. 'Deputy Chief Constable Jennings, Sir,' Spence took the lead.

'And do both of you work directly for me?'

'Yes, Sir,' Spence said.

'And yet both of you take me for an idiot.' Jennings held his two hands in front of his chest, palms together as though praying.

Wilson suppressed a smile.

'That is not true, Sir,' Spence said.

'Then why will I find out in tomorrow's *Chronicle* that you two idiots have launched an investigation into the death of David Grant.' Jennings' voice had a quiver in it. 'Are either of you unaware of the reporting channels in the PSNI?'

'No, Sir,' Wilson and Spence answered together.

'Then why wasn't I informed that you intended to launch

an investigation? Note that I should have been informed before any such investigation was launched.'

'The evidence to support the investigation into Grant's death is only being collected as we speak,' Spence began. 'Superintendent Wilson informed me this morning that his team were looking into the death of David Grant, principally because the pathologist had reported that she considered it a suspicious death.'

Jennings glared at Wilson. 'And the *Chronicle* has the story within hours of this so-called investigation being launched. Your team leaks like a sieve. It was my understanding that David Grant died accidentally while practising some perverted masturbatory act. I was not aware that there was any evidence to the contrary. Perhaps Superintendent Wilson could enlighten me as to the nature of the evidence of foul play.'

'There are several discrepancies in the facts surrounding the death,' Wilson began. 'The pathologist has serious reservations concerning an accidental death. Aside from that, we can find no evidence that Grant was involved in the BDSM scene in Belfast and there was a total absence of sexual paraphernalia in his house.'

'That is all conjecture. Where's the direct evidence? What are you investigating? Are there suspects? This investigation has its basis in the possibly mistaken autopsy conclusions of a pathologist.' He moved his gaze to Spence. 'Superintendent Wilson has, as usual, run off like an out of control elephant, and you have done nothing to restrain him. The result is that the Press will have a field day with speculation. We, as usual, will look like a group of fools who have failed to bring to justice the supposed murderers of David Grant. This folly will eat up thousands of police hours and end up costing millions of pounds. And I tell you, I will not have it. That man', Jennings pointed his finger at Wilson, 'is in the business of wreaking havoc. McIver, one of his own men, is up on a double murder charge, and I don't want to think about the Cummerford business. I want this investigation terminated, forthwith.'

'Sir,' Spence said.

'If I may, Sir,' Wilson said. 'The pathologist will advise a conclusion of death at the hands of person or persons unknown at the inquest. If you think it's an embarrassment to the Force at the moment, imagine what the Public will think if it transpires that we could have investigated the death from the beginning but decided not to do so.'

Jennings' mind was racing. He had promised Carlisle and Lattimer that he would quash any investigation. If he did so at this point, he could be accused of incompetence when the coroner's inquest did indeed stick with a verdict of unlawful death. Wilson jumping the gun put him between a rock and a hard place. Carlisle was insistent on the phone. The investigation was to disappear. If he reneged on his promise to Carlisle, he could kiss his chances of becoming Chief Constable goodbye. On the other hand, if the Chief Constable learned that he had stopped a valid investigation, the result could be worse. 'Superintendent leave us please,' he said finally.

'Chief Superintendent,' Jennings said when Wilson had left the office. 'I am aware that you will be leaving us shortly. After such a distinguished career, it would be unfortunate if you were to leave under a cloud. I respect the support you have given Superintendent Wilson in the past. It's admirable to support one's staff. However, we both know that Wilson treads a fine line. I'm entrusting you with making sure that this investigation peters out. I'm already considering cutting the resources allocated to your station. I'll be considering those cuts in the next week or so. They may also concern Superintendent Wilson's team.'

'I am cognisant of my duties, Sir,' Spence said.

'I'm sure you are. It would be sad if your legacy were to be destroyed by flagrant disregard for the proper channels. You may leave, but I want a blow-by-blow account on this investigation. You understand?'

'Perfectly,' Spence said.

'Do we still have jobs?' Wilson asked when Spence left Jennings' office.

'Just about,' Spence said putting on his cap. 'That jumped-up little bastard is going to get his comeuppance one of these days. How the hell did the *Chronicle* get hold of the story?'

'You know Jock McDevitt; he adds one and one and arrives at three. Peter Davidson talked to a few of his old vice contacts about whether Grant was on the BDSM scene, they're the kind of people McDevitt has in his Rolodex.'

'People still have Rolodexes?'

'I was speaking metaphorically.'

'That's a big word, like arsehole. That barrister lady of yours must be improving your vocabulary. Anyway, I'm to keep a tight hold on you. And then there's the threat that he's going to cut staff and overtime.'

'I'd given up on a replacement for McIver, but I can't operate if even one more member of the team is cut.'

'Maybe that's the intention.' Spence pushed the button on the lift. 'I don't like what just happened in there. Grant is a high-profile individual. You don't just dump an investigation into his death because it might cost police hours or money. I don't know why Jennings wants the investigation killed, but he does.'

'The guy is about as transparent as a pane of glass,' Wilson said. 'Jennings does nothing without there being a good reason. So there's a motive for wanting this investigation killed. The question is, what's that motive?'

CHAPTER TWENTY-TWO

Professor Stephanie Reid concluded her lecture to the student doctors in the Royal Victoria Hospital. She had to admit that she was dissatisfied with the level of preparation she had given to this particular lecture. At least the students didn't seem to mind. She put her lack of enthusiasm for lecturing down to the long hours she was working, and the fact that the Grant and Malone autopsies had dominated her thinking. She grabbed a quick cup of coffee in the cafeteria. It might not have been so quick if she hadn't had to fight off the advances of one of her sleazy male colleagues. She removed her white coat as soon as she reached her office and threw it at the coat hanger in the corner of the room. Her aim was good and it landed on one of the hooks. She sat down behind her desk and started to work through her files, reminding herself that she needed to be better prepared for her next lecture. She had just finished writing up the autopsy result of a woman who had been struck by a drunk driver when her assistant popped his head around her open door.

'How did it go?' he asked.

'You know student doctors they lap up any old crap.' She welcomed the intrusion.

'You are so bloody smug,' the assistant said. 'You know damn well you're one of the star performers. All the students want to become pathologists so they can emulate you. Anyway, the Head of Administration wants to see you. Been fiddling your expenses again?'

'Fat chance,' she said standing up. She hadn't much time for hospital administrators. She happened to think that hospitals should be staffed by doctors, not by pen pushers. The salaries of the administrators had been leaked recently, to public outcry. She hoped they were one day closer to getting rid of the bloodsuckers. Still, she was so far behind in her work that she resented the call from above. She drank the dregs from an almost empty beaker of coffee and prayed that the meeting, whatever it was about, would be relatively short. She put her white coat on. When dealing with the administration it was important to look like a doctor.

While her office consisted of a glass cubicle in the bowels of the Mortuary, the administration offices on the third floor of the hospital proper could not have been more palatial. The corridors were covered with pieces of signed original art and even the secretaries had been provided with the most modern computers and flat monitor screens. She thought of the six-year-old lump of electronic crap that sat on her desk. She had always assumed that the money was going into patient care, but she was beginning to revise that assumption.

Charles Grey perfectly suited his name. As she was announced, he came to meet her at the door dressed in a Prince Charles checked grey suit that entirely matched the pallor of his skin. A bony hand extended from the cuffs of the suit. Reid took the hand, and despite the preponderance of bone felt something soft and gooey. She withdrew her hand as quickly as possible and rubbed it off her white coat. She stared into Grey's brown eyes and saw no flicker of life. His head was completely bald, as in every hair had been removed by shaving. He had no eyebrows, and the false smile on his lips displayed two rows of small but perfect white teeth.

'Professor Reid.' He stood aside indicating that she should enter. 'We very rarely get to see you in this part of the building.'

'I'm impressed,' she said entering an office that was easily four times the size of hers. The wooden floor was covered in places by oriental carpets, possibly Persian, or perhaps Turkish. She was sure that Grey would know their provenance. The walls of the office were covered with tasteful pictures of the hospital and Grey standing with groups of what were obviously influential people. There were two framed diplomas on the wall behind Grey's desk, each attesting to his prowess in financial management. 'It's just as well I don't come here too often.' She glanced round the room. 'It might make me unhappy to sit in the Mortuary basement in my little glass cubicle surrounded by dead bodies.'

Grey moved to his desk and sat slowly into his seat. 'The trappings are unfortunately necessary. When one is dealing with individuals from the private sector, one must be careful to project the same kind of image and professionalism. Of course, you and your colleagues project your professionalism in a different manner, through your concentration on your patients.'

Reid sat in the chair across from him. 'My clients very rarely get to observe my professionalism since they are already dead by the time they reach me.'

'How very droll,' Grey said and a smile flicked at his lips. 'Graveyard humour, yes very droll indeed.'

'Well I've enjoyed the visit, and since we're both incredibly busy ...' Reid said.

'Droll and direct, an impressive combination.' Grey leaned forward. 'As you are well aware, there is a great deal of pressure on hospital trusts not only to act responsibly in terms of financial rectitude and medical professionalism, but also to be socially responsible.'

Reid was already bored but feigned an interested look.

Grey sighed theatrically. 'I have been contacted by a number of our Trust members who are concerned at the role you may have played in making a spectacle of David Grant's unfortunate demise. I don't know whether you are aware, but the *Chronicle* intends to print a story tomorrow that a police investigation into Grant's death has been launched on the foot of allegations emanating from this hospital that he was murdered. The only person in this hospital who dealt with Grant was you. So we must assume that you are the instigator of this vicious rumour. I assume that you discussed this issue with your colleagues before you rushed to the Press, as it were.'

'I did my job and the only people I informed were the police,' Reid said. She was intrigued by the unexpected direction the conversation was taking. 'And no, I didn't discuss my findings with my colleagues. And I certainly did not speak to anybody at the *Chronicle*.'

'And if your conclusions are wrong.'

'To err is human.'

'Ah yes, it may be human but the Trust cannot afford to be publically humiliated if one of our staff not only has displayed poor professionalism, but also is subsequently charged with wasting police time.'

Where the hell was this coming from, or more importantly, where was it going? Reid wondered.

'The Trust has decided that you should reverse your opinion. We've examined your workload over the past month, and we realise that you must be suffering from exhaustion. Perhaps a short holiday might be in order. Adverse publicity on this matter might not impact on the Trust alone. It may impact on you, and your position with the Trust.'

Reid could feel a cold sensation in her brain. She took a deep breath. 'Have you every heard of a place called Kasika?'

'No.' Grey affected a puzzled look. 'Should I have?'

'Of course not,' she said. 'There's no reason that you should have. It's a small town in South Kivu. I was stationed there when I worked for Doctors without Borders. It's one of those shitty little places that changed hands every couple of weeks during the fighting in the Congo. I was there once when the Mai Mai, who for the record are the greatest load of vicious bastards on this planet, overran the town. As soon as they hit the town, I made for the bush and stayed hidden there for three days. No food, no water. Of course, they eventually found me and dragged me off to a hut, four of them. We were all set up for a bit of gang rape and a slow death for me. I should add that they were off their heads with drugs. To cut a long story short, they stripped me and the most vicious thug among them took his Kalashnikov and inserted the muzzle into my vagina. He and his friends had a short discussion about whether they should rape me first or would it be more fun to pull the trigger on the Kalashnikov.'

Grey was watching her in astonishment.

'Just when they decided they could rape me and then have fun with the Kalashnikov, two French Legionnaires from the UN contingent pushed the door open and shot the four of them dead.'

'That's some tale, but what's the relevance?' Grey said with a catch in his voice.

'The point is, I've been threatened by the best, or the worst if you prefer, and I'm still here. So I'll take my chances with the venerable Trust, and if we have to part company, then so be it.' She stood up. 'Now I really do have to return to my work. It's been so pleasant visiting with you here in your sumptuous office. I'll tell all my dead clients about how well the hospital administrators live. Don't get up to see me out.' She wheeled around in a swish of white coat and made for the door of the office.

Grey was breathing with difficulty when she left the office.

He felt as though he had been punched in the stomach. He picked up his telephone wondering whether Carlisle and his friends knew who they were dealing with.

REID PULLED out her phone as soon as she was in the lift. The message to Wilson was simple – we need to talk.

CHAPTER TWENTY-THREE

'No can do,' Denis Brennan, the editor of the *Belfast Chronicle*, said into the phone at the same time as he took a slug of coffee. 'The story's too big.' It wasn't the first time some bigwig had phoned him asking to kill a story, but Jackie Carlisle wasn't any ordinary bigwig. Although Carlisle was a blast from the past, he was still a big player in the Province. Brennan put down his cup and started waving his arms frantically at his assistant while pointing in the direction of Jock McDevitt. The dozy bitch finally got the message and ran to McDevitt's desk. As soon as he caught McDevitt's eye, he beckoned him into his office.

McDevitt pushed himself from his swivel chair in the newsroom and made his way to Brennan's office. As soon as he entered, Brennan motioned him to close the door, and placed a finger vertically against his lips in order to keep McDevitt quiet. He then flipped the switch to put Carlisle on speaker.

'The story checks out,' Brennan said. 'The police have launched an investigation into David Grant's death. Someone has decided that he could have been murdered. And we understand that Detective Superintendent Wilson has been tasked with discovering why David Grant was found hanging from his bannister. This story has everything; the combination of sex, murder and politics equals lots of newspapers sold.'

'David Grant was a minor politician,' Carlisle spoke calmly. 'I am well aware of the salacious nature of the death. However, you can imagine that airing this particular piece of dirty linen in public could damage the image of politicians in the Province. Public opinion of politicians is already on the floor. The death of a politician in the performance of a depraved sexual act will only serve to accentuate the decline in confidence.'

'Like I said before,' Brennan said. 'No can do. It's too big.'

'I would consider it a personal favour,' Carlisle said.

Brennan hesitated. Carlisle had been to the *Chronicle* in the past. He looked at McDevitt who was staring at the ceiling. 'Sorry,' he said.

'That's the gratitude I get for supporting the *Chronicle*. You have a very short memory.' Carlisle's reedy voice reverberated around the room. 'I will be speaking to some of my friends about advertising in your paper. Maybe the owners will have a different opinion.'

'Like I said,' Brennan said. 'I'm sorry.'

'You will be.' The line went dead.

Brennan pressed the button to cut the line. He looked at McDevitt 'What the fuck is going on?'

'Something bigger than the Cummerford trial, that's for sure.' McDevitt picked up Brennan's coffee cup, put it to his own lips and drained it. 'First it was about sex, now it's about murder. God knows what it'll be about tomorrow. Carlisle doesn't want to kill the story because it reflects badly on politicians.'

'So why does he want to kill it?' Brennan asked. 'The police are examining the circumstances surrounding David Grant's death, so fucking what.'

'There's something more to it,' McDevitt said. 'I've been looking into Grant's life. The man was a straight shooter, probably too much of a straight shooter for the game he put himself in. I've been at this business for the past thirty years; I've got a feeling in my bones that we're at the start of something big. I've only had this feeling a few times in my life and it paid off.'

'So where do we go from here?'

'We dig. Wilson will be digging as well, and he probably has greater resources than us. But we can go places and get things from people that he can't. Then we'll be in a position to trade.'

'In the meantime Carlisle is going to drop a sackful of shit on my head.'

'In the meantime you should start contacting your colleagues on the mainland. If this story goes where I think it may, there's going to be a lot of traction in what we can offer.'

'You're sure we're on solid ground.'

'It's in my bones. I may need help.'

'To hell with you and your bones. You hang me out to dry on this one, and you won't even get a job as a copyboy.'

CHAPTER TWENTY-FOUR

Wilson had chosen McHugh's Bar in Queen's Square for his rendezvous with Reid. Although the Crown was his habitual watering hole, the terseness of Reid's message made him opt for somewhere he might not be as well known. It was unfortunate that his rugby career had made him a recognisable face, not a good trait for a policeman. However, as his sporting fame had receded into the past, so had the chances of recognition by members of the general public. As a young man, he had often visited McHugh's. It had the magnificent advantage of having a back bar with an open fire, and comfortable armchairs where people could converse in private. He was already seated by the time Reid arrived. She looked tired.

'Drink?' he asked as she collapsed into the armchair beside him.

'Double Scotch, ice and soda.' She dropped her bag on the ground between them.

'We have to stop meeting like this,' he said before heading for the bar.

He returned with two glasses and a small bottle. He put all three on the table in front of Reid.

'I'd go to your office except the Rottweiler would be

hanging around.' She dropped four pieces of ice into the Scotch and filled the rest of the glass with soda.

He flopped into the armchair. 'You've got to stop calling Moira the Rottweiler. She's an outstanding police officer.'

'And I suppose she doesn't have a nickname for me.' She sipped her drink and smiled.

'What's so urgent?'

She sat forward and recounted her interview with Grey. 'It was definitely an attempt to get me to retract my opinion. The bastard more or less threatened me with my job.'

'Snap,' Wilson said.

She looked at him quizzically.

He told her the details of his and Spence's trip to HQ. 'It looks like you have upset someone's applecart by spotting that Grant was murdered. The question is, whose applecart?'

'Someone with considerable juice as the Americans would say. You don't get a Deputy Chief Constable and the number two in a hospital trust the size of Belfast's to threaten their staff unless you have power.'

Wilson took a sip from his pint of Guinness. 'We've looked into Grant. He was strictly small-time. He was on the way up but he hadn't arrived anywhere that could have ruffled someone's feathers.'

'Don't forget Malone,' she said.

'Malone was the quintessential nobody. He was some kind of minor functionary in the Infrastructure Agency. He stamped forms or something like that. I respect you, but you might have got that one wrong.'

'I haven't,' she said. 'There's a link. You just need to find it.'

'You'd better be careful.'

'How so?' she asked.

'If Grant was murdered, and I said if, whoever is behind his death obviously thinks that you're the key to having the investigation dropped. You change your mind on the autopsy, and we can all go home and forget about Grant.'

'I'm not about to do that.'

'I didn't think so.' Wilson looked at his watch.

'Somewhere to go, someone to meet?' she asked.

Wilson hesitated. He was thinking of going back to the apartment. But now that he thought of it, he realised that it might be better not to. He realised that he had nowhere to go. 'No just wondering about the time.'

'Ms McCann not waiting anxiously for the sound of your size elevens on the hallway? One for the road then, I haven't paid my round.'

He stood up. 'Sorry.' Two men looked into the back bar, their eyes staying on Reid. They would both jump at the invitation he'd just received. He could go to the apartment and face Kate's wrath or silence. He made his mind up and sat down again. 'Guinness, but no shop talk.'

She was about to open her mouth. 'And no personal stuff,' he added quickly.

'Is this a date?' she asked.

He laughed. 'You're hopeless. No it certainly isn't a date. And if you don't start talking about rugby or some related topic then I'm out of here.'

'Tell me what it's like to play against fifteen devils in black jerseys.' Reid sensed that something more serious was going on in Wilson's relationship. He wasn't just tired because of work. He was stressed out. He started to tell her what it felt like to stand facing the All Blacks and the Haka, and she feigned interest. She needed to know what was going on but she couldn't think of how she might find out. She signalled to the barman to replenish their drinks and turned her full attention to Wilson.

CHAPTER TWENTY-FIVE

W ilson reached the station at eight o'clock the following morning. He'd arrived back at the apartment after midnight and found himself locked out of the main bedroom for the second time. He had to admit that he had enjoyed the evening with Reid. He had been with more women than he could count, but Reid had a sense of fun and an enjoyment in living life that was hard to find. He had piled her into a taxi despite several attempts on her part to entice him back to her place. As the taxi sped away, he started walking in the direction of the apartment where he had been so happy with Kate. He felt like a skier who hears the rumble of an avalanche in the distance. He knows something is coming, and he prays that it won't come in his direction. Wilson didn't have much faith in the power of prayer. There was an avalanche coming in his life and it was going to hit him whatever evasive steps he took. As he walked through the door of the station, he banished his personal thoughts and concentrated on the task at hand. After the meeting with the DCC, he was under no illusion that both he and Spence were under the gun. If Reid was wrong, and Grant really had managed to kill himself, he'd better prove it damn quick. This was not one of those investigations that could just stumble along. He would have to set the pace from the beginning. That would mean everyone on the team would have to be singing from the same hymn sheet. He was aware that there was no possibility of a replacement for McIver. His reading of the smoke signals was that the cuts to his team were not over. It was only a question of who Jennings would pull out. Add to the investigation the need to prepare for two capital trials, which would involve evidence from his team, and you had a toxic cocktail.

'Boss,' the Desk Sergeant said as soon as Wilson entered. 'The gent over there is here to see you.'

Wilson followed the Desk Sergeant's eyes and saw a well-dressed man sitting on the bench just inside the door. He was engrossed in a copy of the *Belfast Chronicle*. Wilson walked over and stood above the man. 'I'm Detective Superintendent Wilson,' he said. 'I understand you've been waiting for me.'

The man looked up from his newspaper then stood up. 'I'm Councillor Michael Eaton. I was a colleague of David Grant's.' He folded the newspaper with the front page exposed, and held it towards Wilson. 'I was the one who phoned the police when David didn't turn up. I understand that your sergeant has been trying to contact me.'

Wilson saw his picture placed prominently on the front page beside a portrait photo of David Grant. Jock McDevitt's name was in large letters in the byline, indicating that this was only the first of many articles on the subject. It was just what he didn't need. He imagined the scene in Jennings' office; an apoplectic DCC bouncing off the walls. Anyone who ran across him this morning would get the full blast of his anger. Wilson smiled. He liked the idea of Jennings' blood pressure heading through the roof. He turned to the Desk Sergeant. 'The soft interview room vacant?' he asked.

The Desk Sergeant nodded.

'Please come with me,' Wilson said, and led the way as Eaton followed.

The soft interview room was another feature of the new kinder image that the PSNI was endeavouring to portray. It was reserved for interviewing witnesses who were not thought to be involved in a crime. Unlike the interrogation rooms that normally contained a table and four hard chairs, the soft room was furnished in the fashion of a normal living room with easy chairs and a sofa arranged around a coffee table.

'Please sit.' Wilson pointed at the sofa and sat in an easy chair himself. 'What can I do for you?' he asked.

Eaton cleared his throat. 'Until I read the *Chronicle* this morning, I thought that David had killed himself by accident. Right now, I'm not very proud of myself for thinking that someone I worked with for five years could have been so totally different from the man I knew. I should have guessed that something was amiss when I heard the manner in which David died. A man wearing women's underwear hanging from the stairs was not consistent with the David I knew. I came today to tell you that I'm glad you've decided to investigate David's death.'

'Don't beat yourself up,' Wilson said. He was thinking of his own experience with his former colleague Ronald McIver who was currently banged up accused of a double murder. 'We very rarely know what's going on in people's heads. It's easy to look at the evidence and jump to conclusions.'

'You didn't.'

'The pathologist didn't,' Wilson said. 'She's the one who will ultimately deserve the credit, if we find that Grant was indeed murdered. Let's go back a bit. You called in and asked the police to check out his house. Why?'

'David and I are both independent councillors. We had a meeting every week to discuss tactics and since I've known him, David has never missed that meeting. Meetings with him were like religion. He always turned up, or called if he was going to be late. It was so out of character that I was instantly worried. I thought that maybe he was in an accident, or had been mugged. I never imagined he might be dead.'

'Tell me about him.'

'He was intelligent, honest, a good friend but a bad enemy. He was on his way up. At the next General Election, he would've gone very close to winning a seat on the Assembly. If he hadn't made it next time, he would've been elected the time after. He was already marked out as a future "comer". The organised parties were courting him like crazy. Behind a soft exterior, he could be hard and very tough. He hated corruption to the extent that it was like a crusade for him.'

'What about the sex thing? Could he have hooked himself up?' Wilson asked.

'I hate myself for believing that he could. It wasn't part of his make-up. OK, he wasn't a lothario, or a man about town. I think he'd put his emotional life on the back burner until he'd made it politically. Women liked him principally because he came across as himself, I think.'

'But he didn't have a girlfriend or partner?'

'Not that I knew of.'

'How was he lately? Any change in behaviour?'

'He was preoccupied, and sort of excited. He was one of the best listeners I ever met but lately his mind seemed to be somewhere else.'

'Any idea what might have been bothering him?'

'I haven't a clue. It was nothing to do with Council business. We're in a bit of a quiet period now. The organised parties are playing out the main issues. It's all about flags and marches, and crap like that. David and I were more interested in what was happening to people on the ground. You can't eat a flag and marching does nothing to improve the quality of life. Politicians here deal in distractions.'

'Any idea where we can look for the source of his preoccupation?' Wilson asked.

'Maybe his private work, he sometimes handled clients who were less than honest. Perhaps he crossed one of them. I really can't say.'

Wilson removed a card from his pocket. 'If anything else occurs to you, I'd be obliged if you'd contact me.'

Eaton took the card and produced one of his own. 'You can contact me anytime if you think I can help.'

THE MURDER SQUAD team stood in a semicircle around the whiteboard which was now covered with photographs and writing.

Wilson gave a quick rundown on the meeting with the DCC but omitted any details of his meeting with Reid. 'So,' he said. 'It's apparent that the DCC wanted the investigation stopped. That may be because of the political or sexual overtones, or he's receiving instructions from higher up. It wouldn't be the first time that an investigation would have been buried for political reasons, and it certainly won't be the last. The problem for HQ is that the cat is out of the bag. You've all seen the *Chronicle* this morning and those of you who have been around for a while know that McDevitt is a formidable reporter. Especially when there's some dirt to be dished. Harry, the timeline?'

Harry Graham took his place in front of the board. 'Grant was the kind of guy you could set your watch by. He left his house in Ashley Avenue at exactly eight thirty every morning. He stopped at Starbucks in Queens University for his breakfast and normally left with the remainder of his coffee in hand. Most of the staff in Starbucks knew him by name. Apparently, he was pretty popular with them, but always breakfasted alone. His office is in Central Belfast, and if the weather was kind, he liked to walk. On the day of his death he walked. He arrived at the office at nine o'clock and worked through lunch. He sent out for a sandwich and coffee at two p.m. I have a copy of his agenda for the day and I've spoken to all the clients. They're a bunch of normal citizens with minor legal problems, nothing out of the ordinary. Nobody was aware of anything strange in his demeanour. In fact, several of them had never even met him before. He had the habit of working late. Except when there was a Council meeting. On the day of his death the Council meeting finished at eight o'clock. He had a meeting in his agenda for ten o'clock that we now know he never made. We have to assume that he arrived home sometime around eight thirty, although I found nobody who could confirm an exact time. Since our two officers kicked the front door in at eleven thirty, we have a pretty good window for the time of death.'

Wilson thanked Graham and gave a short version of his interview with Eaton which appeared to tie in with the timeline already established. 'We need to know what happened at the house in Ashley Avenue between eight thirty and eleven thirty. I know it's a pain in the butt, Harry, but I want you to canvas the area, see if anyone saw anything strange. What about CCTV?'

'None on Ashley Avenue, Boss,' Graham said. 'But there may be some in the surrounding streets.'

'Peter,' Wilson said. 'Anything new from your contacts?'

'Not a sausage, Boss,' Davidson replied. 'If Grant was into the kinky stuff, he kept it in house.'

'Boss,' Moira interrupted. 'I thought we'd already established that Grant wasn't a perv, the absence of toys, magazines and the like.'

'I think we can drop that element of the investigation,' Wilson said. 'I'd like to know where the ladies' undergarments came from.' He was staring at Moira. 'Call the Mortuary and get them to send the clothes over. Forensics will want them but maybe you could examine the labels and see where they might have been bought. Then look at Grant's credit card purchases and see if he bought any ladies' underwear lately.'

'Yes, Boss,' Moira said, not trying to hide her displeasure at being given what she considered donkey work.

'We need to find out everything about this man's life. Peter, get to the law office and go through all his files. The head buck lawyers will put up a fight on the files, but the article in the *Chronicle* will at least take some of the stain away from them professionally. Establishing that the death has no connection to his legal work will be to their advantage. Also, I want his diary for the past few weeks. Let's see if there's someone in it who shouldn't be there. Eric, get a list of everyone that knows this guy. Right now he looks like a grey man but I want to see what colour comes out when his friends and colleagues talk about him.' Wilson glanced at his watch. 'I'm busy this morning but I should be back well before lunch. If you need me, I'm on the mobile. Moira, with me.' He turned and walked to his office. As soon as Moira and he were inside, he closed the door. 'Anything on the Malone business?'

'Not so far but I haven't had time to follow it up,' Moira said. 'Reid thinks he might have been murdered as well?'

'She has some suspicions,' Wilson said.

'How?' she asked.

'Injection of potassium chloride on the underside of the tongue.'

'What!'

Wilson explained the delicate balance of potassium in the body, and the effect of even a small increase.

Moira threw up her hands. 'This is a fantasy, that damn woman will do anything to get close to you. Every corpse she handles from now on will be a possible murder victim. Wake up and smell the coffee, Boss.'

'Humour me. If there's nothing there, we'll drop it. After the way Jennings reacted yesterday, I'm not about to take a flier on launching another murder investigation. That's why it's just you and me for the moment.'

'OK, Boss. But this might be considered as a waste of police time. Not so good when we're undermanned and facing a difficult investigation.'

'Humour me.'

CHAPTER TWENTY-SIX

Holywell Hospital was situated on high ground off the Steeple Road, two miles north of Antrim town. In 1891, the Holywell site of 100 acres was selected as the location for a County Antrim Lunatic Asylum. Built primarily to alleviate serious overcrowding at the Belfast Asylum, it provided a separate asylum for Country Antrim and was opened in 1898. The hospital's prominent features included a clock tower and gargoyles at the front entrance. The clock tower was lit at night and used by boaters on Lough Neagh as a guide to the mouth of the Six Mile Water. It wasn't Wilson's first visit to the facility, and as he drove in through the front gate, he thought the choice of sculptures at the entrance to be particularly apt. Some of the people he had interviewed here had minds that would have fit perfectly with a gargoyle. He followed the signs for the Assessment Centre and steered towards a small red-bricked building set to the side of the central building. The drive from Belfast to Antrim was not a long one, and it passed through some of the nicest countryside in Ulster, culminating in the town of Antrim on the shores of Lough Neagh. He would normally have enjoyed the ride, but he spent most of the journey thinking over the Grant case.

Although the whiteboard was beginning to fill up with information on Grant and his movements, there was little or no evidence of a crime aside from Reid's misgivings, and no evidence at all pointing to the perpetrators. Just outside Antrim, he decided to put the Grant business out of his mind and concentrate on the meeting with his former colleague. The Assessment Centre was showing its age. A hundred and thirty years of wind and rain in the Irish climate was apt to weigh heavily on Victorian construction. The Centre was the smallest of the buildings, and the outer wall was overgrown concealing whatever structural defects might be hidden behind the shrubbery. Wilson noticed some debris dumped at the side of the entrance. While Holywell wasn't exactly Bedlam, it was in need of a serious makeover. The reception area of the Assessment Centre accentuated this conclusion. The plaster on the walls was cracked and peeling, and there was a musty smell in the air. Wilson removed his warrant card and showed it to the receptionist. 'I have a meeting at eleven,' he said simply.

The receptionist examined a clipboard. 'Take a seat and I'll see if they're ready.'

Wilson sat on a bench in the corner of the room. A half dozen dog-eared magazines sat on a battered coffee table in front of him. Two golf magazines displayed the interest of some of the senior staff, while a couple of ancient copies of *Hello* and *Heat* might have owed more to the female receptionist. He didn't bother with the magazines but continued to visualise his approaching interview with Ronald McIver. He'd been McIver's superior for more than four years, but did that really mean that he knew the man? He should have known enough to see that the job had taken its toll on McIver. Police work eats people up. The toxicity doesn't just come from the long hours and the discipline. There's also the fact that everyone you meet is in trouble, or about to land in trouble. Policing can be equated with a swim through a sewer.

Inevitably some of the shit sticks. There's very rarely light at the end of the tunnel, and if there is, it's usually in the form of a train heading in your direction. That's police work in general. Being a member of the Murder Squad was another matter entirely. He often wondered how he slept having stood over the broken bodies of men, women and children. And then there were the clients, the scum of the earth, men and women with serious mental defects who would maim and kill without a second thought. It was a wonder that policemen and women remained sane for the thirty or so years required to take retirement. One thing was clear. Despite the drawbacks Wilson loved the job. He knew that it ate away at some people, but in a way it charged him. He had always loved solving problems, and over time, he had added to that the high he got from putting bad guys behind bars. He *was* the job. He didn't have a hobby. When he'd been forced to give up rugby, he decided that was the end of it. Did he miss rugby? Only every day; there was a hole inside him that rugby once occupied, which would be forever empty. He could have taken up coaching. There were plenty of offers. Radio and TV people pursued him for months with offers to become a pundit. But he had already decided that the rugby part of his life was over. He dragged his mind away from himself. The job had a lot to answer for in McIver's situation, and so had he. McIver was going on trial for the killing of Ivan McIlroy, a member of a criminal gang headed up by Sammy Rice. A secondary indictment had been the mercy killing of his wife who had been sliding into dementia. Although former detective constable Ronald McIver had taken two lives, he was no murderer. Both crimes had been committed when the balance of his mind was affected. That was the defence Kate had established for him. He heard a door open in the corner of the reception area and looked up. 'Superintendent Wilson?'

'Aye,' Wilson said standing.

'Dr Liam O'Neill.' A man of sixty or so years thrust out his hand. 'I'm one of the resident psychologists. You're here to see Ronald McIver?'

Wilson took the outstretched hand. 'Yes, how is he?'

'I would not consider him to be a well man,' O'Neill said. He had the soft accent of County Tyrone. 'We've diagnosed him to have severe psychotic depression. It may be enough to get him out of the legal mess but I'm afraid that he's going to spend an extended period in hospital. The question is whether he'll last long enough for us to get him there. We're going to put him on suicide watch when he goes back to prison.' They walked down a corridor. 'I've spoken to him at great length in formulating a diagnosis. You're one of the few people he respects. You could have a very positive effect by convincing him not to give up hope. He thinks his life is over, but I'm sure that with the right help, he'll make a full recovery.' They stopped at a door. O'Neill knocked and opened it. 'Do your best. If you need anything from me, get through to reception.'

Wilson entered the small room. He wasn't easily shocked, but he did a double take when he saw McIver sitting at a small table. His former colleague seemed to have disappeared into himself. In a few short months, his hair had turned completely white and the skin hung on his cheeks. He'd lost weight and his shoulders slumped. He glanced up when Wilson entered, but his eyes had a faraway look, as though he was concentrating on some point beyond Wilson's head. The room was smaller than the interrogation areas at the station but it had the same feel. It was sparsely furnished with only the small table and two wooden chairs. It smelled of depression and desperation. He noticed a uniformed prison warden standing at the door and nodded. 'Do you mind if I handle this myself?'

The prison officer looked at him and nodded, then silently left the room.

'Hello, Ron,' Wilson said sitting down on the seat across from McIver.

McIver lowered his eyes and blinked. He stared into

Wilson's face. 'Boss?' he said as though seeing Wilson for the first time.

'How are you, Ron?'

'They say I'm mad, Boss.' He laughed. 'The Doc says that I have psychotic depression, whatever that is. I suppose you've got to be mad to kill two people.'

Wilson leaned forward and put his two hands on the table. 'It wasn't your fault. The job eats people. You can blame the job, and me.'

McIver's brow furrowed. 'Why should I blame you? I killed them on my own. It was our job to put people like me away.'

'It was my job to take care of you, and I didn't do my job properly. So in a way I'm responsible for you being here.'

McIver laughed. 'You have a weird sense of humour, Boss. I'm going down, and I deserve it. They want to believe that I was hearing voices and shit like that. I don't know whether they're right or wrong about the voices, but I know I did wrong, and I'm ready to accept the punishment. I'm only sorry that they can't hang me.'

'You can't go to prison, Ron.'

'Why not, Boss? My life is finished. I have no job, no wife. I can't go back to the house. For Christ's sake why don't they just help me finish things?'

'The doctors are right. You're ill. I don't know about the psychotic depression, but you are certainly ill. They'll make you better. You'll be able to return to some kind of life. You won't be back to the job, but we'll make sure that you get whatever you're entitled to. There is a future.'

'Will they bring Mary back?'

'They're doctors not Gods,' Wilson said. 'But they will heal you. The person you killed wasn't Mary. She was already gone from that body.'

Tears started to roll down McIver's face. 'Help me, Boss. Help me.'

Wilson stood up and moved to the other side of the table. He lifted McIver out of his seat and hugged him. 'I'm sorry, Ron. I'm sorry I let you down. Let me make it up to you. Let Kate organise the hospital. Get better. If you don't do it for yourself, then do it for me.' McIver convulsed in his arms, and he could feel wet tears on his shirt.

There was a knock at the door.

'Will you let Kate handle it?' Wilson asked. He stood back and McIver's head came away from his chest. He looked into his former colleague's eyes. 'Just do what she tells you.'

'OK, Boss. I'll try.'

The door opened, and the uniformed officer entered. 'The van's outside. Time to go,' he said coming forward to handcuff McIver.

'I won't let you down again,' Wilson said.

McIver didn't reply but smiled wanly. He followed the officer out of the room.

Wilson sat heavily on the wooden chair. He didn't like the psychological stuff, and he wondered whether he had hit the right note with McIver. Whatever the future was he had tried his best. He stood up and left the small room. His feet felt heavy as he walked down the corridor towards the reception area. He thought about Kate and their new means of communication. What would happen when Helen wasn't there?

CHAPTER TWENTY-SEVEN

Moira McElvaney had spent the morning on social media trawling through the trivia that was the life of Brian Malone. She had already spoken to Reid's assistant and arranged for the clothes Grant had been wearing to be sent to her. She had learned that Malone was not a complicated individual. He was born in Omagh in County Tyrone. After school, he had attended Omagh College of Further Education and left with a degree in Business Administration. He had obtained a job at the Infrastructure Agency and that was pretty much it. He played football on the weekend. She had managed to construct a list of people who might have been considered his friends. By the time she finished, the file on Malone already contained about twenty pages of official documents; his birth certificate, college diploma, school reports, tax forms. She knew the official Brian Malone, but it would take a series of interviews with his friends and family to find out who the person really was. She wasn't sure that Wilson wanted to go that far. His parents might wonder why an officer from the Belfast Murder Squad had just dropped by to have a chat about their son. She needed a coffee, and her eyes hurt. She hadn't been sleeping well. The business with Brendan was affecting her. The long-awaited email had finally arrived, and the news was not good. There was no possibility of Harvard extending Brendan's sabbatical, and he was expected back in Boston for the new college year. His courses had already been included in the college catalogue, and the die was cast. She had brought Brendan to meet her parents in Dungannon the previous week, and the visit had gone ten times better than she anticipated. Brendan and her dad had hit it off while her mother thought that he was a much sounder fit for her than her ex, who both of her parents had hated. So the problem was exacerbated. She wondered what would have happened if they'd hated Brendan. The question was moot. Now the decision was up to her. If she went to Boston with him, it would be the end of her career in the PSNI. If she didn't go, she would probably regret it for the rest of her life. She sleepwalked her way to the cafeteria and got a coffee and a chocolate muffin, and she was on her way back to the squad room when a uniform stopped her.

'Your Boss about?' he asked.

'Probably not before lunch,' she answered through a mouthful of muffin. 'Why?'

'Man in reception to see him.'

'Name?'

'Nathan Grant. Who these days has a name like Nathan?' The uniform smiled.

'Check if the soft room is available, and if it is, and ask him to wait there. Rustle up a coffee for him. Ring me when he's ready.' She went back to the squad room. The information on Malone was still on her screen, and she didn't want to leave it that way. She had just turned off her computer when her phone rang. Nathan Grant was waiting for her in the soft interview room.

The man seated at the coffee table looked up as soon as

Moira entered the room. He looked like someone who had been put through the wringer. His dark hair was dishevelled. His face was a light brown colour, with signs of tiredness clearly visible. There were black rings beneath his eyes. He stood when she entered. He could have doubled for his younger brother both in looks and in stature.

Moira deposited her coffee on the table and extended her hand. 'Detective Sergeant McElvaney,' she said simply.

'Nathan Grant, pleased to meet you.'

She noted the accent, not a trace of Northern Ireland. 'Please sit, you look like you're about to collapse.'

He didn't wait for a second invitation. 'When I heard about David's death three days ago, I was in the middle of nowhere in Northern Burma. Since then, I've trekked through a forest, travelled down a swollen river in a boat only slightly bigger than a kayak, travelled on a rickety bus for twelve hours over roads normally used by pack animals and all that was just to get to Yangon. I wanted to get here before the funeral. When I finally arrived in Belfast this morning, I was greeted by this.' He removed a copy of the *Chronicle* from the pocket of his coat and tossed it on the coffee table. 'I rang this guy McDevitt who wrote the article, and he suggested that I talk to Detective Superintendent Wilson. So I'm here.'

'Superintendent Wilson is not available right now.' Moira set her coffee on the table and sat facing Grant. 'I'm working this case with him. I'm sorry that you have to come here under such circumstances. Your brother appears to have been a very nice person.'

'That's only the half of it.' There was a catch in Grant's voice. 'He was the finest person I've met, and I'm not just saying that because he was my brother.'

'I understand,' Moira said. 'When was the last time you saw him?'

'Last year, I try to get back every year, and we're on Skype whenever I'm somewhere there's Internet.'

'You're close?'

'Very, our parents died in an accident when David was at college, and I was working in Africa. We're all we've got. We would have been closer except that work for the agency sent me all over the world.'

'What do you do?'

'I'm with UNHCR.' He saw the look on her face at the use of the acronym. 'The United Nations Human Rights Commission, we mainly look after refugees, but we're generally around when anyone's human rights are being infringed. What about this article in the *Chronicle*? There's an implication here that David was some kind of sexual pervert.'

'We'll get there,' Moira said. 'When did you last speak with David?'

'A month ago when I had decent Internet.'

'Did he mention anything in particular?'

'Most of our conversations wander around the trials and tribulations of Manchester United. We're both avid fans.' He cleared his throat. 'I have to get used to saying the past tense when I talk about David. I'm just not used to it yet.'

'And work?' she asked.

'Yeah, sometimes. I'd rattle on about the venal bastard politicians who use their own people to enrich themselves in the Third World.'

'And David?'

'He'd rattle on about the venal bastard politicians who use corruption to enrich themselves in places like Northern Ireland. I want to talk about how he died. David didn't fix up a noose and stick his head into it. He didn't dress in women's underwear, and he didn't use, what did they call it, erotic asphyxiation to get off.'

'You know a lot about David's sex life?'

'I know a lot about David, and that means I know for sure that someone did this to him.' He held up the *Chronicle*. 'And now I know that someone else agrees with me.'

'We're currently looking at this case,' Moira said trying to be sensitive, but she didn't want to give too much encouragement to the notion that David Grant was murdered. 'It's early days, that's why I was asking about your contact with David. Right now, we have no idea why someone wanted to murder your brother. The pathologist is convinced that David's death was due to foul play. We haven't as yet confirmed that, but certainly a motive for murder would assist us.'

Nathan Grant sat back and thought for a moment. His brow furrowed, and it was almost possible to see the wheels turning within his skull. 'I'm trying to replay our last conversation. David was excited. He was very up. Things were going well for him both politically and in work. The main parties were courting him, and he looked odds-on to get an Assembly seat in the next election. Then he would be in line for a shot at Westminster.' He slipped into thought again. 'Sorry,' he said finally. 'The travelling has caught up with me. My brain has turned to mush.'

'It's OK,' Moira said. 'We can go through this again when you've had a chance to rest.'

'I want to see David.'

'We can arrange that. Maybe it would be better after you've had some rest.'

'I've got to make some arrangements. I've got to locate a Chevra Kadisha. David wasn't particularly religious. In fact, I know it had been years since he had attended synagogue. It's the right thing to do.'

Moira had an instant liking for the man sitting across from her. 'Where are you staying?' she asked.

'I normally stay with David. I phoned from the airport and I got a room in the Old Rectory Guest House in the Malone Road.'

Moira made a note in her notebook. She withdrew one of her business cards from the back cover of the book and handed it to him. 'My mobile is on the card. You can call me anytime. My boss will probably want to speak to you himself, but I'll make sure he doesn't cover the same ground. In the meantime, if anything comes to mind about your last conversation with David, I'd be grateful if you would give us a call.'

CHAPTER TWENTY-EIGHT

Wilson's lunch consisted of a ham sandwich and a cup of coffee, both of which had been procured from the cafeteria. After taking one bite of the sandwich, he parted the two slices of white bread to find a morsel of ham inserted between them. It appeared that the budget cuts had reached as far as the cafeteria. He decided that in future, he would forgo the pleasures of station food. The report on the forensic examination of Grant's house was in and it didn't create an atmosphere of confidence in him. There was precisely nothing to report. The knot was certainly a bowline, and they would have to determine whether Grant was able to construct what was a reasonably difficult knot. The rope was bagged and was currently being examined in terms of its provenance. He doubted if the examination would lead anywhere, but it would be thought thorough to pursue it. There were no labels on the ladies' underwear. That begged the question, if Grant had removed the labels, why had he done so? It didn't sound logical. On the other hand, if a third party had procured the items, and didn't want their provenance to be discovered, they might have removed the labels. The house was awash with finger-prints. The attending officers and the ambulance crew were already eliminated. Reid's fingerprints were on file and she would be eliminated also. He read the two-page report with increasing gloom then turned to the four pages of inventory appended to the report. Grant was an avid reader and not just of trash fiction. He was obviously fascinated by the financial crisis and Wilson counted twelve different books whose titles indicated that they had the inside track on why the world's bankers had managed to bring the financial system to the brink of failure. Another section of books was dedicated to the memoirs of whistle-blowers. Wilson recognised one of the titles from a recent visit to Waterstones. He flicked through the pages. The forensics team had been thorough. He tossed the remnants of his ham-less sandwich into the wastepaper basket and took a gulp of his now tepid coffee. He was alone in the squad room. He wondered whether the rest of the team were drawing blanks on their elements of the inquiry. He glanced through the single window of his office at the dark skies enveloping Belfast. The darkness seemed to exemplify the state of the investigation. There was not one single ray of light. It was police lore that the first forty-eight hours were the most important in any investigation. There was some truth to that, but it wasn't always the case. He felt a pain in his stomach. It was caused by either hunger or the nagging feeling that David Grant's death would be added to the three thousand plus unsolved murders in the Province. Wilson's crime clearance record was among the highest, but too often all the method and all the intuition in the world are not enough to crack a case. Sometimes the murderer is too damn clever for the plodding policemen, and sometimes the killer got just plain lucky. For Wilson, murders fell into two categories. Either they were random or they had a strong motivation. Random murders were obviously the hardest to solve. The majority of open cases in Ulster were of this variety. There was no direct link between the victim and the murderer. The crime was motiveless, or the motive could simply be one of religious or racial hatred. These crimes depended on the murderer leaving enough of himself at the scene to track him down. Wilson by far preferred a crime with a motive. His great skill as a detective was in sifting through reams of information and putting his finger on the factor that linked victim and murderer. Someone went to a lot of trouble to murder David Grant and to make it look like an accident. The removal of the labels from the underwear seemed to add to that conviction. But the killer had left nothing of himself at the scene. Wilson therefore drew two conclusions. First, there was a strong motive for the killing and, second, the killer had carefully planned the murder. To solve this case, he would have to find the motive. That meant examining the minutiae of David Grant's life. At some point, he had interacted with someone or something that had got him killed. When Wilson found that someone or something, he would find the killer.

THE MEMBERS of the Belfast Murder Squad assembled for the two o'clock briefing. Just as Wilson had taken his place in front of the whiteboard, Chief Superintendent Donald Spence entered the room. The team shuffled on the spot and made room in the centre for Spence to stand.

'Please,' Spence said. 'Continue as though I'm not here.'

Wilson smiled. Spence's remark was typical hierarchy-speak. There was no possibility that his team would have the ability to speak their minds with the big boss in attendance. He started the meeting with a short briefing on the forensic report finishing with his two conclusions.

'That doesn't sound promising,' Spence said.

'Of course, we'd prefer to have a whole lot of forensic to work on,' Wilson said. 'But we have to go with what we've got.'

'And that appears to be nothing,' Spence said.

Moira raised her hand, and Wilson nodded at her. She gave an account of her interview with Nathan Grant. 'The brother is adamant that Grant was not involved in any perverted sexual practices. He fully supports the contention that his brother was murdered.'

'It has been my experience', Spence interjected, 'that people rarely expose a distasteful side of themselves. Even to their closest friends or relatives.'

'I'll want to speak with the brother myself,' Wilson said. 'What about the underwear?'

'Like you already said the labels had been removed,' Moira said. 'I've taken photos of the individual pieces, and I'm meeting a buyer at House of Fraser this afternoon.'

'Good.' Wilson knew that he was grasping at straws. 'Harry, anything to report?'

'We did a house-to-house in Lawrence Street,' Graham said. 'Most of the houses are occupied by students so it's been a bit hit and miss. We left a note where we weren't able to contact the resident. So far, we have nothing. The type of people living in that area are used to strange goings-on. There's no CCTV on the street, but we're checking what there is in the area. We'll get a picture of Grant somewhere on the night in question. But in the meantime, we're going to have a mountain of disks to go through.'

Wilson noted that Peter Davidson and Eric Taylor were singing dumb. It was an old copper tactic used when the top brass was present. If you said nothing, then you couldn't say something stupid. He wanted to continue the briefing, but he realised the further he went the more it looked like they had nothing. 'Peter.' He stared at Davidson with his most for-God's-sake-give-me-something look.

'I'm working my way through Grant's agenda.' Davidson shuffled. 'He was a busy man what with the legal practice and the political activism. He met with lots of people, and I'm running them down.'

'Eric,' Wilson said. 'I want you to work with Peter. We

need to speak with everyone on his agenda. Go back as far as you can. Next briefing, six o'clock this evening.'

Wilson turned and headed for his office. Spence fell into step beside him. They both entered the office, and Spence closed the door behind him.

'I'm worried.' Spence sat in the seat directly facing Wilson's chair.

'Tell me about it,' Wilson said.

'You have precisely nothing.'

'It's early days.'

'When I go upstairs, I've got to ring HQ and report to Jennings. I don't have to tell you the reaction I'm going to get.'

'What do you want me to do?'

'Consider following Jennings' instruction. Three months down the line, you might be looking at exactly what you've got right now. Then Jennings will have the ammunition to haul us both over the coals. Possibly hundreds of thousands of pounds' worth of police time expended for nothing.'

Wilson wasn't about to abandon the investigation. 'There'll be pressure on the other side. The brother won't accept us walking away, and neither will Grant's colleagues. And there's always McDevitt.'

'Give me a time limit that I can discuss with Jennings.'

'One month,' Wilson said. 'With unlimited overtime.'

Spence sighed. So like Wilson to push the envelope. 'How was your visit to Holywell?'

'You're very well informed,' Wilson said.

'It goes with the job.'

'McIver's been diagnosed as a psychotic depressive. He's ill and he looks it. Kate is working at avoiding a trial and getting him into hospital so that he can get some help. The DPP are keen on the trial option. They like to display to the public that even police officers are not above the law. The no-trial option would suit Jennings and his friends at HQ. But Kate still has a lot of work to do to get the DPP to back off.'

'And your involvement. You're not guilty. What McIver did he did alone.'

'Tell me that when I wake at two o'clock in the morning. I watched one of my team unravel. I don't think that I can run away from that one.'

Spence stood and sighed. 'Working with you can be a trial sometimes, Ian. Do you know that?'

MOIRA WAITED until Spence had left before knocking on the door of Wilson's office.

He motioned her to enter.

'It doesn't look good,' she said.

'Early days.' It was beginning to sound like a refrain.

'Everything points to murder, but there's a distinct lack of evidence.'

'Someone has been very bloody clever. This is not your usual Belfast hit. The locals have never eschewed the sledge-hammer when a tack hammer would do. Finesse isn't their style. Whoever killed Grant knew what they were doing, that means they've done it before. We know all the local players, so we can dismiss them. We'll check the National Crime Data-base, just in case there's a similar murder elsewhere. Also, check the suicides by erotic asphyxiation in the recent past, especially on the mainland. Now what do we have on Brian Malone.'

'I could almost put it on the back of a postage stamp.' She quickly ran through the information she had pulled from the various databases she had interrogated.

'No connection between Malone and Grant?' he asked.

'On the surface, none. Malone was a drone in the Infrastructure Agency. His only hobby was playing football. Grant's sole interest in sport was as a spectator.'

'No reason why someone should murder him?'

'Like I said you could write his life story on the back of a postage stamp. Why bother killing someone like that.'

'What job did he do at the IA?'

'Something to do with the accounts. If we go any further with the investigation, I would want to talk to his boss. But that might lead to another article in the *Chronicle*.'

'That we need to avoid at all costs. You're not totally onside with this?'

'My energy levels are a bit low.'

'You feeling OK?'

'No,' she said quickly. 'Brendan's been called back to Boston, and he wants me to go with him. I don't know what to do. Also I'm not sleeping well.'

Snap, he thought. What a pair they were? He couldn't sleep because his relationship was falling apart. She couldn't sleep because she had a choice she couldn't make. They were both pitiful.

'You're not giving any advice?' she asked.

'It would be redundant because I can't put myself in your shoes. However, I am open to listening.'

'I think I love Brendan, although I'm wary after my initial run-in with marriage. But I love this job. The problem is I can't have both. I can only have one or the other.'

'And Brendan?'

'Similar problem, he has a prestigious professorship in one of the top universities in the world. He's a consultant to a whole host of crime-fighting agencies. Belfast would be small beer to him.'

'That's some tough choices for both of you. All I can tell you is that you are a talented police officer, and a bloody good detective. You'll go far in the PSNI. However, it may cost you your private life.' He had the feeling that he shouldn't get too close to home. 'In my life I've seen more than one officer head down the road to destruction.' He thought about his meeting with McIver, but the image was immediately replaced by the memory of his father's brains spread across the rear of the garden shed. 'Think about Ronald McIver and be careful of the life you choose.'

She saw the look on his face and wondered about its genesis. There was a sadness in him that rarely came to the surface. 'That's clarified things for me,' she said smiling.

'Your dilemma, so it's your decision. Do you think that in your sleepless hours you'd have time to look over some CCTV?'

'You want me to help Peter and Eric?'

'No, I want you to collect CCTV from around Malone's flat. Check the movements on the night of his death. Find something that's out of the ordinary.'

'But don't tell anyone why I'm doing it.'

'Precisely.'

CHAPTER TWENTY-NINE

Jackie Carlisle drove to Sammy Rice's house in Ballygomartin Road along the Shankill Road. The Shankill wasn't the most direct route from Carlisle's residence in Hillsborough, but he hadn't been down the Protestant thoroughfare for more than a year. He looked at the faces along the side of the road. They were all good Loyalist faces, the salt of the earth that was Northern Ireland. Their ancestors had arrived with William of Orange to fight the papists at the Battle of the Boyne and had stayed on. Or maybe their ancestors were Scottish Presbyterians who were imported to displace the papist Gaelic population. Wherever they came from, they had been Jackie Carlisle's people for more than fifty years. He drove slowly so that his people could see and recognise him. He had often driven down this road and found his progress impeded by the crowds who strayed off the footpath in order to shake his hand. He looked for that level of recognition today. However, there was no one impeding his progress, and the faces that streamed past showed no sign that they recognised him. He glanced at the rearview mirror and saw that time and the disease that was gradually eating his body had not been kind to him. He had always been on the slight side but both his features and his body were now cadaverous. Maybe he was asking too much of his people to recognise their diminished hero. The Shankill was the same, but it was also in the process of change. The murals depicting scenes from Protestant mythology were still there. He passed one portraying the great Protestant leader Edward Carson signing the Convention. The painter didn't do his subject justice. However, the Union Jack painted beneath the mural was a reasonable representation. The predominant shop-front colour was still royal blue; he smiled because the façade of every shop from the local chemist to the Indian takeaway was painted the same colour. The Union Jack predominated and was matched in many cases by the Red Hand flag of Ulster. He passed a shop with a large sign above it offering camouflage uniforms. A vestige of the time when every young Loyalist was dressed as though he was on leave from the British Army. The car behind hooted and he reluctantly pressed the accelerator. There was something in the air of the Shankill that was missing in Hillsborough. It was something visceral; this road running through the centre of Belfast was the heart of Protestant resistance. He was part of creating that heart. He worked all his life to preserve the culture of his people. He was at their head during the riots and was their chief negotiator with the British government. He represented them locally, in Westminster and in Europe. His legacy was secure. In years to come, there might be murals depicting the highlights of his career. Thankfully, only he and his associates knew some of those highlights. The preservation of Protestant Ulster could not be attained without the spilling of blood. As a leader of the Protestant paramilitaries, he was prepared to shed Fenian blood. That was before he morphed into a politician. He was lost in thought and suddenly found himself on the Woodvale Road. Away to his left were the Catholic enclaves where the papists were breeding like rats. He felt a sharp pain in his abdomen. The rats would have a field day when he died. His people would parade behind the hearse bearing his body, and he would be laid in the grave with a hero's oration. On the other side of the Peace Wall, there would be celebration. And yet he wanted to live. He was too young to die. He had too much to offer Ulster to just fade away and be eaten by worms. He was a hero, and heroes died glorious deaths. He had almost reached Sammy Rice's house. He smiled when he thought of his acolyte. He was Sammy's mentor during his days as a hellion leader. But Sammy, like his father, had a bad streak in him. While Carlisle morphed into a politician, Sammy transformed into a criminal. They both continued to serve Ulster, but in their separate ways. Carlisle pulled into the driveway of Rice's house. George Carroll, one of Sammy's men, stood by the front door.

Carroll moved slowly towards that car. His walk was like that of an automaton. He recognised Carlisle and bent to open the driver's door. 'Afternoon, Mr Carlisle.'

'Afternoon, George.' Carlisle stepped out of the car.

Big George Carroll stepped to the side. His face registered satisfaction at being recognised. 'The Chief is inside.'

Carlisle walked behind Big George as he led the way to the front door.

Big George opened the front door with a key he removed from his pocket. He stood aside, and Carlisle entered the house. The first thing he noticed was the smell. Someone had neglected to take out the rubbish. The house looked, and smelled, like a tip.

'Jackie.' Sammy Rice appeared from the living room. He was dressed in a filthy tee-shirt and grey training bottoms.

'Hello, Sammy.' Carlisle was shocked at Rice's condition. He sported three days' growth of beard and looked like he needed a good wash. The normal blond pompadour was lank and greasy. Rice always prided himself on his tan. It was faded, and his skin was pale and blotchy. Carlisle didn't like what he saw. Sammy Rice knew too much to be allowed to go to seed.

'Come into the living room.' Rice pinched the base of his nose and led the way. 'Long time since we've seen you in this neck of the woods. Last I heard you'd buried yourself in Hillsborough waiting for a visit from the Grim Reaper.' He laughed.

'I've a bit to go yet,' Carlisle said taking the only seat that wasn't strewn with rubbish. He wondered how Rice knew of his medical condition. He looked around the room. 'This place used to be nice. I see you're trying to go for the rubbish heap look.'

Rice gave a hoarse laugh. 'I used to have a wife who looked after the place.'

'Take my advice and get her back.'

'Drink?' Rice asked moving to a drinks cabinet.

'I'm off the booze,' Carlisle said.

Rice poured himself a large whiskey. He turned and faced Carlisle. 'What are you doing here?'

'Did you see today's *Chronicle*?'

Rice brushed some DVD boxes off a chair and sat down. 'I don't have time to read the newspapers.'

Carlisle looked at the boxes on the floor. The pictures on the covers were indicative of the contents. 'Maybe you should find time. The police have launched an investigation into Grant's death. Ian Wilson is the senior investigating officer.'

'That bollocks.' Rice took a slug from his glass. 'At least he caught the cunt that killed my mother.'

'He's persistent and some people are getting anxious. There's a worry that you didn't clean up as well as you promised.'

Rice took another drink from his glass. 'I thought that you people had all the bases covered. Don't you own that little prick Jennings? Get him to put the break on Wilson. What's the point of having a dog that can't bark? Anyway, the mechanics left nothing behind. It'll be one of those unsolved murders that we read about.' Rice stood up and started pacing the room.

'It should never have gone this far.' Carlisle leaned forward. 'This should have been passed up the tree. It would never have been sanctioned.'

'You know Willie, my old alcoholic father?' Rice shoved his face into Carlisle's.

Carlisle nodded. 'Of course I do.' He was beginning to wonder where Rice's head was. He noticed the redness around his nose and hoped that it was the result of a cold. He doubted it, though. What they didn't need right now was a coke addict.

Rice pulled his face away and continued his pacing. 'Well auld Willie filled my head with a load of old shite, but he did tell me one thing.'

Carlisle waited.

'You always find the biggest monkeys near the top of the tree.' Rice descended into a fit of laughing. 'That was the only thing the auld bastard said that I took on board.' His face suddenly reddened. 'You can go and tell the big monkeys who are getting anxious that the Peelers are no risk. Everything is in hand.' He pointed at two bin bags in the corner of the room. 'That's the crap that was picked up at Malone's and Grant's, computers, papers, briefcases. Nothing was left behind. You can sleep safely in your beds on top of the piles of money you have made from me and people like me.' He decided there was no need to mention that Grant had contacted an accountant friend.

Cocky bastard, Carlisle thought. He hoped Sammy was right. There was a lot riding on him being right. Looking into Rice's face, he was doubtful.

Rice was suddenly in front of him. 'Problem?' he asked.

'No problem, Sammy.' It wasn't the time to argue with a hopped-up Rice. Carlisle stood. He would have to get in contact with the others. He prepared to leave. He moved slowly towards the door. As he passed a coffee table, he saw a small smear of white powder and knew that his worse fears were probably confirmed. Sammy Rice was a drug dealer who had become one of his own customers. It wouldn't be long before he wasn't to be trusted. The Circle didn't like people it couldn't trust.

As soon as CARLISLE left, Sammy Rice spread some cocaine on the coffee table and chopped it into three lines with a credit card. He rolled up a fifty-pound note and snorted the first line. His head shot up as the cocaine rushed to his brain. Fuck Carlisle and fuck Wilson. He bent and snorted the second line. His head shot up again and he beat his chest with his fists. He would fuck them all. Some people were getting anxious. He laughed. He should care about the big monkeys at the top of the tree. Their day was done. 'Georgie, get your fucking arse in here,' he shouted before snorting the last line. He stomped around the room.

Big George Carroll walked quietly into Rice's living room.

Rice put his arm around Carroll. 'It's time,' he said, a wide grin on his face. 'It's time to show the fuckers. You and me are going to pay a visit to that Taig, O'Reilly, this evening. I'll show the fuckers.'

CHAPTER THIRTY

The six o'clock briefing was low-key and, for Wilson, depressing. The team were working their socks off but there was no forward progress in the investigation. It would be a late evening for Moira, Harry, Peter and Eric. He would fare slightly better. He had arranged to meet Nathan Grant at the Crown at six thirty. He had set the time in the knowledge that the briefing would yield no progress. He was seated in one of the snugs when a young man bearing a remarkable likeness to David Grant entered. Wilson stood and beckoned the young man over. 'Nathan Grant?' he asked.

The young man nodded.

'Detective Superintendent Wilson,' he said holding out his hand. 'I'm sorry for your trouble.'

'Thank you.' Grant's handshake was firm.

'Over the jet lag?' Wilson asked.

'Not quite, but there's a lot to do. I'll sleep when David has been laid to rest.'

'Can I offer you a drink?' Wilson asked as he sat down again.

'Beer, please.'

Wilson nodded at the barman and ordered a pint of beer. 'DS McElvaney briefed me on your conversation.'

'She seemed very competent.' Grant sat facing Wilson.

'She is. I know you're busy, so I won't take up a lot of your time.'

'Can you tell me when I can see David?' Grant asked.

'I've spoken to the pathologist, and they're expecting you at the morgue in the Royal Victoria at nine tomorrow morning. Do you want one of my officers to attend?'

'That won't be necessary.' He moved his left hand over his mouth. 'I never thought that I'd see this day. David was so full of life. He was like a whirlwind.'

'So it couldn't have been suicide?' The barman had returned with Grant's drink, and Wilson motioned him to place the drink before his guest.

'Not a chance.' Grant took a long drink of his beer. 'You people take photographs of the crime scene, don't you?'

'We do.'

'Can I see them?'

Wilson thought for a moment. 'They're not especially pretty.'

'Don't worry, Superintendent, I won't freak out. I've seen some sights in my life. I'm sure I can handle whatever that look on your face said.'

'I'm sure that you're toughened, but this was your brother.'

'I need to see them.'

'Come to the station after the morgue, and we'll let you see the photos. Nothing leaves our office, especially the photographs. So if it wasn't suicide, how did David die?'

'I thought that you're of the opinion that he was murdered.'

'That's one hypothesis.' Wilson's voice was low. He had chosen a snug in a part of the bar that was empty, but the after-work crowd were already filling the pub. He removed a sheaf of paper from his inside pocket. 'I have only two questions.' He passed the sheaf of paper to Grant. 'That's an inventory of everything that was found at your brother's house. Is there anything missing?'

Grant took the papers. 'It's been some time since I stayed with David. He could have bought something in the meantime.'

'I understand. But is there anything you know of that's definitely not there?' Grant sipped his drink and stared at the list.

Wilson watched as he flicked through the pages.

'I bought him an expensive crocodile briefcase when I was in Madagascar. He always carried it with him to work and meetings. If he was at home, it would have been there as well.'

'Anything else?'

'His computer, David was addicted to his computer. His whole life was on that machine.' He handed the pages back. 'That's all I can think of.'

'Last question,' Wilson said. 'Was David interested in sailing?'

Nathan Grant laughed. 'You're kidding.'

Wilson smiled.

'David got sick if he even looked at the sea. When we were kids, he wouldn't even go out in a pedalo with me on a flat calm.'

'So he had no knowledge of knots a sailor might use?' Wilson asked.

'David could barely tie his shoes,' Grant said. 'Of course, I can't be sure but David had no idea about knots.'

Wilson bundled up the inventory pages and put them back into his inside pocket. 'I've taken enough of your time. I'm sure you have better things to do. You've been very helpful.'

'The photos?' Grant asked.

'At the station tomorrow morning.'

CHAPTER THIRTY-ONE

W ilson had had a habit of getting sick before important rugby games. The apprehension used to find its way directly to his stomach, and he would be obliged to leave the team talk in order to vomit. And he wasn't alone. At the time, he had decided that the sick feeling was simply a response to the tension. But that was positive tension. His stomach was rumbling ominously as he pushed in the door of the apartment that evening. He struggled with the fact that he had relished the thought of facing a fearsome South African pack, but he was uneasy about facing his partner. He had come directly from the Crown and was aware that there was the smell of booze on his breath. Both the McCann ladies were seated in the living room. Their conversation stopped abruptly as he entered the room.

'Hi,' he said walking to Kate and bending for a kiss. She presented her cheek, and he kissed it. He moved to Helen and got the traditional air kiss.

'Have you eaten?' Helen asked.

'No, I'm ravenous.' He went to the drinks' cabinet. 'Can I get either of you ladies a pre-dinner drink?'

'Gin and tonic,' Helen said quickly. 'Make it two.'

'I saw McIver today.' He thought the subject was the most anodyne he could bring up. 'I think I managed to get him onside. I suggested that he take your advice, Kate.' He carried two gin and tonics to Kate and Helen. They nodded rather than thanked him. He returned to the cabinet and poured himself a stiff whiskey.

'Well done,' Helen said raising her glass in a toast.

'Yes, well done,' Kate said and the temperature in the room rose appreciably.

'Kate and I were just discussing the hiring of a maid,' Helen said.

Wilson noted that he hadn't been part of the discussion. It didn't worry him. He was a guest in Kate's apartment. Despite his protests, she insisted that she pay for everything. He thought about the money he had sitting in the bank. The sale of the house in Malwood Park netted him a profit of two hundred thousand pounds. It ranked as the best investment he'd ever made. Correction, the best investment his dead wife had ever made. 'And what conclusion did you come to?'

'I have several difficult trials coming up,' Kate said. 'And Helen has found this wonderful woman from the Philippines who will take care of the apartment.'

'Great,' Wilson said. 'When does she start?'

'She already has,' Kate said.

Wilson sucked on his whiskey and looked at Kate. She looked drowsy. He wondered whether she had taken, or was taking, something. The change from her usual belligerence was striking. Her moods were oscillating wildly these days. He decided to play along. 'Great,' he said.

'She's made us some dinner,' Helen said. She finished her drink and went into the kitchen. 'I'll just heat it up.'

'I've never tried Philippino food,' Wilson said. He took advantage of Helen's absence to sit beside Kate. 'How are you, darling?' he said.

'Tired, Ian, oh so tired. Everything has changed. I feel so wretched.'

'Maybe you should take some time off work.' He tried to hold her hand but she removed it.

'How can I? The Chambers is generating more business than I can manage.'

'Take on another partner.'

'Chicken inisal and rice,' Helen said from the kitchen. 'I have no idea what it is, but it smells divine.'

Kate stood up slowly. 'Let's not talk shop.'

He saw that she barely touched her drink.

'I'M WORRIED ABOUT KATE,' Wilson said. It was only eight o'clock, and Kate had already retired. There was no indication either during or after the meal that the sleeping arrangements had changed.

'How so?' Helen asked.

'She was very different this evening. She couldn't even raise the energy to fight with me, and she looked drowsy. Is she on something?'

'The doctor gave her something to help her sleep and a painkiller as well. Do you want me to broach the subject?'

'Just keep an eye out. It's easy to become hooked on drugs like Lunesta, Ambien and Sonata and barbiturates like Seconal and Amyta. See what the doctor prescribed.'

Helen nodded. 'How's the investigation into David Grant's death going?' she asked.

'It's going nowhere.' Wilson didn't like making the admission.

Helen shook her head. 'Perhaps your pathologist friend made an error.'

'Could be.'

'And if she did, won't the PSNI and you be embarrassed?'

'Won't be the first time.'

'Wouldn't it be wise to drop the investigation before that happens?'

Something was trying to break through the cotton wool in Wilson's brain. Jennings had tried to make him drop the case, the chief administrator at the Royal had tried to get Reid to change her opinion and now a concerned citizen had stuck her oar in. What had all these people in common? They were all part of the establishment. The thought flew through Wilson's head and then left.

Helen stood up. 'I'm off to bed. Sweet dreams.'

Wilson picked up the TV controller. Yeah, sweet dreams, he thought.

CHAPTER THIRTY-TWO

Big George Carroll spent the early evening sitting in Cosgrove's Bar waiting for Mark O'Reilly's car to show up. The March air still bore the vestiges of winter. Carroll was a non-smoker, but he was obliged to pretend to be one in order to stand watch in the alcove at the front of the pub. The light was fading rapidly when he saw O'Reilly's black Volkswagen Golf turning into Francis Street on its way to the multi-storey car park. He took out his mobile phone and sent a text message to Sammy Rice. His phone buzzed one minute later and then stopped. It was the signal that the Boss was on his way. Carroll tossed away his half-smoked cigarette and re-entered the pub. He enjoyed the rush of warm air that surrounded him before stationing himself in plain view of the door and waited.

Twenty minutes later, Sammy Rice pushed in the door of Cosgrove's. He was wearing a black beanie down to the edge of his eyes. He nodded at Carroll and left. He was waiting on the footpath at King's Street when Carroll exited the pub. The junction wasn't busy. The evening rush hour had ended an hour ago. Without speaking, Rice led the way down Francis Street. They passed the taxi station beneath the multi-storey car park. They walked on until they came to the rollover doors leading to the car park. Rice removed a remote control from his pocket and pointed it at the door. He operated a fleet of black cabs, and his contacts in the business had been happy to provide him with the means of entry. The steel door rolled up, and the two men entered. As soon as they were inside, the door closed. They located the emergency stairway and started their climb to the fifth floor. The apartment section of the building was separated from the car park by a stout door with an electronic control. Carroll removed an iron jimmy from inside his coat and slipped it into a gap at the door jam. He wedged the jimmy into place and then pushed. The door creaked. He increased the torque, and the door gave way. They were on the fifth floor of the apartment complex. Rice removed the hat and straightened his hair. They went to the door of O'Reilly's apartment and knocked.

MARK O'REILLY WAS no dab hand in the kitchen. When he did prepare dinner for himself, it generally came out of a packet and was cooked by the microwave. He'd had a substantial lunch so he decided on a bowl of soup as his evening repast, and the contents of a can of Scotch broth were already in a saucepan. Manchester United were playing in the Champions League, and UTV was tuned in. Everything was set up for an evening in front of the box. He heard the rapping on his front door and was taken aback. There was an intercom in the entrance hall and that was supposed to be the only method of entry to the apartments. He went to the front door and looked through the peephole. A blond-haired man, looking confused, was standing at his door. The rapping started on the door again. The bloody ass must be lost, O'Reilly thought. He released the latch on the door and opened it a crack. The door flew into his face, and he fell back onto the floor of the hallway of the apartment. By the time he got his senses back, there was a giant of a man standing over him.

'What the hell,' he said pushing himself up with his hands.

Big George Carroll bent down and lifted O'Reilly off the ground.

Rice pushed the apartment door shut. 'Shut the fuck up,' he said. 'Bring him into the living room.'

Carroll half-carried half-walked O'Reilly into his living room. The man was shaking so hard he had to hold on tight to his arm.

'Take whatever you want,' O'Reilly said. 'You can have my Barclaycard, and I'll give you the pin number.'

Rice grabbed O'Reilly by the throat. 'Fuck your Barclaycard. David Grant sent you some files.'

O'Reilly did a double take. This wasn't a robbery. It was something much, much worse. He had already examined the files that David sent him and was aware of the contents. They exposed a major corruption. The men who had invaded his apartment were obviously part of the criminal conspiracy that David had uncovered. The *Chronicle*'s story about David's death caused a shiver to run down his back. He stared into the face of the man holding him. He was certainly a thug. The only possible way out for him was to give them whatever they wanted. 'David did send me some files, but I haven't had time to get around to them. If you want, I could delete them.'

Rice smiled and released his grip on O'Reilly's throat. He could give lessons to the FBI on spotting liars. 'Get your computer,' he said.

O'Reilly scurried away to a corner and removed a computer from its bag. He placed the computer on a coffee table and opened the lid. He pressed some of the keys and brought up his emails. 'See.' He lied. 'I haven't even opened the files.'

Rice came over and stood behind him. He knew fuck all about computers, but he knew enough to see that the email had indeed been opened.

'Look,' O'Reilly said. 'I'll dump it.' His fingers flashed over the keys again, and the email from David Grant disappeared. The television suddenly burst into life as the music announcing the start of the football game reverberated around the room.

'Good boy,' Rice said and moved to the large window in the living room. The apartment looked directly down on Francis Street. At this time of the evening, the street was relatively empty. He opened the window wide and looked out.

O'Reilly was trying to remain calm. Maybe he would get out of this after all. It was a victory of optimism over experience. He had blanked from his mind the fact that David Grant was murdered.

'Rice turned to Big George Carroll. 'Fuck him out the window,' he said simply.

NORMAN WHITE WAS PISSED OFF. The bloody match was live on TV and yet his wife had insisted on him driving her to meet a colleague from her company's office in Glasgow. He dropped her at the Ibis Hotel and decided not to bother heading home. There was a television in Cosgrove's Bar, and they'd surely have the match on. He was driving his company BMW 520 so there was no way he was leaving it on the street. He'd put it in the multi-storey across the road from Cosgrove's. That way it would be safe, and he would be ready to pick up his wife as soon as she was through. What the hell had been wrong with a taxi anyway? He turned into Francis Street and was approaching the car park when there was an almighty thud on the front of his car. His windscreen turned red as though someone had thrown a bucket of paint over it. He stopped and turned on his windscreen wipers. The red liquid was viscous and spread as the wipers gradually assisted it in covering the entire windscreen. Through a gap in the liquid, he could see what he took to be a man's head. It looked like he wouldn't be seeing the match after all.

CHAPTER THIRTY-THREE

Professor Stephanie Reid was attending a dinner for the British Medical Association hosted by the chairman of the Northern Ireland Council. It was held in the members' dining room at Parliament Buildings, and the great and the good of the medical profession in the Province were in attendance, along with representative Assembly members from each of the five major political parties. Invitees included the chief officers of the Association, the Northern Ireland members of the UK Council, the local committee chairs as well as key stakeholders from across the health service in the Province. The occasion was announced as an excellent networking and influencing opportunity for all concerned. Except that Professor Reid was bored out of her tree. She loved being a doctor, and she was sure that she was an excellent pathologist, but she abhorred having to prostitute herself at these events in order to promote the reputation of the Royal Victoria. She noted the predominance of men in the official photographs. Although it was an acknowledged fact that women were superior in fields requiring caring and empathy, men dominated the upper echelons of the profession. Unfortunately, women were not good golf companions;

they didn't appreciate lewd jokes or understand the finer points of rugby. So while a great many men fawned over her during the rubber chicken dinner, she was in no doubt that were she to run for office, votes from her male colleagues would be thin on the ground. The hospital required her to attend such events in order to ensure its position as the primary care and teaching establishment in the Province. It was with a sense of relief that she responded to her beeper during one of the long-winded and extremely boring speeches. She excused herself from her table, and as soon as she was outside the dining-room she called her office. The news ensured that her evening was over and she made her way to the car park. There was no point in heading home to change, so she drove straight to Castle Street. Two police Land Rovers had already arrived and a traffic diversion had been set up. She pulled in before the crime-scene tape and identified herself to the officer manning the entrance to the scene. She removed her crime-scene suit from the back of her car. She had dressed conservatively for the Association dinner, but she was aware of the spectacle her bare legs made as she was required to hitch the black dress up in order to get into her plastic suit. Spending four years in Africa where one was required to squat in front of whatever group was around in order to perform one's toileting had removed most of her inhibitions. In any event, she was sure that she wasn't showing the onlookers anything that they hadn't seen before. She ignored the stares of the men gathered at the edge of the crime-scene tape and their jibes as she strode forward carrying her black bag.

The jumper had landed with some force on the bonnet of a passing car. The only person inside the police cordon wearing civilian clothing was sitting on the edge of the pavement holding his head. Reid concluded that this was the driver of the car. The body lay sprawled across the bonnet. The head had impacted with the windscreen and had been opened like a coconut on a fête booth. Frothy cranial blood covered the shattered glass.

'Ma'am.' A police officer came forward. 'Can we help?'

'Thanks,' Reid said. 'But it would be best if you just stay out of my way for the time being. I'll get through as quickly as I can, and we can close off the spectacle.'

'The ambulance crew is already here.'

She looked to her left and saw a man and a woman in paramedic gear standing beside their white and orange vehicle. Beside the crew, spectators were pointing mobile phones in her direction. The whole scene would be on YouTube this evening. The police had already set up a screen, but the early spectators would already have their pictures of the man spread across the bonnet of the car. It was the new availability of instant news. There was certainly no dignity in death, and the mobile phone had added to the lack of dignity. She walked to the body. A police photographer was just completing a series of photos that covered the body from every angle. She didn't see any point in a detailed examination. The man had died on impact. There would most likely be bodily injuries, broken limbs and ruptured organs, but death was certainly occasioned by the injuries to the head. She examined the body from every angle before signalling to the ambulance crew. She could leave it to the police to deal with the driver and his car. She could hear him in the background repeating ad nauseam 'He just fell out of the sky'. She crossed the road and looked up at the Tannery Building. She could see a window open on the fifth floor. 'Is this exactly where the impact took place?' she asked the officer who had offered her assistance.

'Pretty much,' he said. 'The driver slammed on the breaks as soon as the body hit. He was making for the entrance to the car park, so he wasn't travelling at speed.'

She walked across the road and looked up at the open window. Strange, she thought. She would have guessed that if he had jumped, he would have hit the footpath. The car had been in the roadway, so he would have had to jump outwards in order to land on the bonnet as he had.

'Has anyone been upstairs?' she asked.

'We called it in so I would expect they'll send someone along,' the policeman said. 'We've sealed off the apartment until the Murder Squad guys arrive.'

AROUND THE TIME Reid had been digging into her rubber chicken in the members' dining room, Moira McElvaney was at home ploughing through CCTV footage from the area around the apartment where Brian Malone had lived. Her boyfriend, Brendan sat in the corner of her living room watching a Champions League match on the television. Although he had never watched soccer in the US, since arriving in Belfast he had joined the local population in supporting the premier Manchester club. His arms were folded which was a clear sign that Brendan was not very happy.

He stood up and walked up behind Moira. 'Boring,' he said looking over her shoulder at the grainy black and white images of time-elapsed cars going up and down a street. 'You work ridiculous hours, and you even bring the boring stuff home with you.'

'Sit down and watch your match.' She continued to scan the image on her computer. 'Your team is winning and if you're a good boy, we can go for a drink later.'

'You know I've got a feeling that you're trying to avoid discussing some issues with me.'

She hit the pause button and looked up into his face. 'We can't all have nice nine-to-five jobs like some university professors I could name. This is my life, and you knew it.' She didn't want to answer the remark about avoiding the issues because she was afraid that that was exactly what she was doing. She knew she wasn't being fair to Brendan, but she was still churning inside trying to come to a decision. Her parents were not being helpful. Yes, they loved having her around but sure wasn't Boston just a few hours away by plane, and hadn't they always wanted to visit New England. For them, the decision was already made. Her mother's last comment during their phone conversation that day was 'don't be a fool'. The problem was that she had already been a fool once, and she didn't feel like repeating the error.

'We really need to talk,' Brendan said. 'Whenever we try, we always end up making love but not coming to any conclusion.'

She was about to speak when her mobile phone rang. She grabbed it and pressed the green button. She listened for a few moments and then said, 'I'm on my way.' She turned to Brendan and kissed him on the cheek. 'Sorry, baby, but we have a jumper.'

Brendan picked up the remote control and killed the television picture. 'I always wanted to go on a ride-along here.' He picked up his jacket.

'No can do,' she said.

'Let's assume that we were in a restaurant, and you got that call. You wouldn't just leave me there. You'd take me along. Same difference.'

She picked up her jacket and put it on. 'OK, but for God's sake let's make it a silent ride-along.'

'You got it.'

When Moira arrived in Castle Street, Reid was putting her black bag into the boot of her car. The two women noted each other but didn't speak.

Reid saw that the DS had a young man in tow. She smiled at Brendan and he returned her smile as he was borne along in Moira's wake.

Moira went immediately to the car. The ambulance crew

were carefully removing the corpse from the bonnet. The windscreen was covered in blood.

A policeman approached Moira.

She produced her warrant card. 'DS McElvaney,' she said.

The policeman looked at Brendan.

'He's with me,' she said without adding any detail. 'What have we got?'

'Looks like he jumped from the open fifth-floor window. Landed smack on the car of a poor bugger driving down the street.' He nodded in the direction of the man seated on the side of the road. 'Pathologist said he died instantly.'

'Has anyone been upstairs?'

'I sent one of the boys up, and we've sealed the apartment off. But we haven't been able to locate keys. You'll have to instruct us to break in. We don't want to screw up any evidence.'

'Good man.' Moira led the way into the building.

Each level of the building had four individual apartments. A young officer was standing before the door of one on the fifth floor.

Moira checked the door and saw that it wasn't forced. 'Break it,' she said to the young officer.

The door shattered by the first impact, and the officer tumbled through the shattered door.

Moira and Brendan entered the living room. The first thing they noticed was that they had to bat their way through a wall of smoke. An alarm was wailing somewhere in the apartment. The second thing was the smell of burning.

'Turn that bloody noise off.' Moira shouted at one of the uniforms as she made her way quickly into the kitchen where a pot was emitting a spiral of black smoke. She switched off the electric cooker and wafted away some of the smoke with her hand. She saw an empty soup can on the counter top beside the cooker. The kitchen was of modern design with both high and low units and had its own small dining area.

'Looks like he didn't wait for his supper,' Brendan said.

Moira looked sharply at him. 'I thought we agreed to a silent ride-along.' She exited the kitchen and went into the living room. Despite the smoke, she was able to see that Manchester United still had a one goal lead. The living room was about twelve metres squared and outfitted by IKEA. It was only a guess, but she was fairly sure that the man currently on his way to the morgue was the tenant. She moved to a small wooden bookcase on which a number of letters were scattered. She picked them up and saw that they were addressed to 'Mark O'Reilly'.

Brendan looked over her shoulder. 'I don't think that Mr O'Reilly jumped. Maybe you should call it in and have Forensics give this place a going-over.'

She knew that Brendan was probably right but was miffed that he had said it first and especially in front of one of the uniforms. 'Maybe you'd like to wait for me downstairs. You'll need to come to the station tomorrow to give elimination fingerprints.'

Brendan nodded and left the room.

Moira took out her mobile phone.

WILSON WANDERED around the living room of the apartment in the Tannery Building. It was a typical yuppie pad. The living room was sparsely furnished, and the smaller of the two bedrooms had been turned into a storeroom for packed cardboard boxes and miscellaneous sports equipment. The boys in the white plastic jumpsuits were already there and were busy photographing everything, and bagging samples. On his arrival he had said hello to Brendan Guilfoyle, who he found sitting forlornly in Moira's car. It was safe to assume that Brendan was a bit pissed at not being part of the action.

'Mark O'Reilly,' Moira said. 'Works as an accountant at

Watson Accountants, they're located in Windsor House in Bedford Street.'

'And he didn't jump?' Wilson asked.

'It doesn't look like it,' she said.

He continued to look at her.

'There was a pot of soup on the cooker, and the Champions League match was on the TV,' she said. 'It's a bit unusual for someone who has just prepared a meal, and is settling down to watch a match, to suddenly decide to throw themselves out of a window onto a passing car.'

'So tell me. Has Brendan been up here?'

'He'll pass by the station tomorrow to give elimination prints,' she said defensively.

'I've been noticing more inputs from Brendan lately. Like your idea on the sexual paraphernalia at Grant's place.'

'OK, Brendan thinks that O'Reilly didn't leave the room under his own steam. He thinks he was helped through the window.' She glanced inadvertently at the open window.

'We need to find out whether any of the neighbours saw or heard anything. Get on to that straight away, and get some of those uniforms who are standing around to carry out a house-to-house.'

Wilson moved around the room and went into the kitchen. He picked up the soup pot and examined the blackened mess on the bottom.

'We're all set,' she said rejoining Wilson. 'Three of the uniform officers are starting a house-to-house enquiry.'

Wilson walked to the sink and dropped the pot into it. 'Three relatively young men die in strange circumstances. Even for Belfast, that's a bit too much of a coincidence.' His phone rang, and he saw that it was Reid on the line. He hit the red button and put the phone in his pocket. 'Was Reid here?'

'She was just leaving when I arrived.'

'We might just have to eat our pride and admit that she

could be right about both Grant and Malone. The problem for us is locating who's behind this mini murder spree.'

'You think they're all connected?' she asked.

'Why don't we ask Brendan what he thinks?'

She didn't know whether he was being serious or facetious. She felt her face colouring, but didn't reply.

'There's nothing more for us here,' Wilson said smiling at her discomfort. 'Cosgrove's is across the road, and we might just catch the end of the game. Let's pick up Brendan on the way. He looked like an errant schoolboy sitting in the car.'

They sat in the only quiet corner of the pub.

'So,' Wilson said looking pointedly at Guilfoyle. 'You think he didn't jump.'

'I'm sure of it,' Brendan said. 'The meal, the TV, it all points to an evening in with the football game. Anyway this method of suicide is relatively unusual. The latest statistics recorded show that firearms made up fifty two per cent of all suicides, hanging twenty three per cent and poison eighteen per cent. Many people who die by suicide, as best we can determine, may have had some level of ambivalence right up until that final moment. If you use a less lethal means like an overdose, there's still the possibility of taking it back. You need to find out whether O'Reilly has threatened suicide before. Check his phone records for calls to the Samaritans, and check with his friends. If he committed suicide, and I seriously doubt it, then you'll find something to corroborate it.'

Wilson nodded. Brendan Guilfoyle certainly knew his business. 'We'll follow your advice,' he said. Given the resources he had it would be a bit of a stretch. 'The uniforms discovered that a door from the garage to the apartments was forced. Unfortunately, the Property Management Company didn't bother to install CCTV so there are no pictures. If someone assisted him through the window, he let that someone in. Moira confirmed that the door was closed properly and an officer had to break it down. Whoever was inside was long gone.'

'So he might have known his assailant,' Brendan said.

'It's possible,' Wilson sipped his Guinness. 'Either that or he was scammed. You saw the body?'

'We did,' Moira answered before Brendan could speak.

'Height and weight?' Wilson asked.

'Come on, Boss,' Moira said. 'He wasn't in a great situation to assess his height and weight.'

'OK then,' Wilson said. 'Was he small, medium or large?'

Moira and Brendan looked at each other. 'Medium,' they said together.

'That means if he was pushed it would have required someone larger to do the pushing,' Wilson said.

'Unless whoever pushed him convinced him to lean out of the window,' Brendan said. 'Or maybe there was more than one assailant.'

Wilson was about to comment when his phone rang. He removed it from his pocket and saw Reid's name on the screen. He decided to take it.

'Yes,' he said.

'You're obviously at home,' Reid said.

'I'm in Cosgrove's in Castle Street,' Wilson said.

'So, the Rottweiler worked it out.'

'DS McElvaney did indeed work it out and she's sitting next to me right now.'

'Lucky girl. By the way, he didn't jump. Your people measured the distance of the car from the Tannery Building. You'll find that the deceased was propelled through the window. Autopsy tomorrow morning at ten, are you coming?'

'Perhaps DS McElvaney will attend.'

'Spoilsport.' She cut the connection.

'Reid, I assume,' Moira said.

'The autopsy is at ten tomorrow morning,' Wilson said. 'Think you can make it?'

Moira sighed. 'I'm up to my tonsils.' She stood up. 'I need the loo.'

Brendan waited until she had disappeared. 'She's not sleeping.'

'So I hear,' Wilson said. 'Any idea why?'

'The case?'

'I don't think so.'

'Ah Jeez.' Brendan rubbed both sides of his temples with his fingers. 'I know I'm the problem. I was supposed to go back to Boston a month ago, but I extended. Right now, one of my colleagues and a teaching assistant are taking my classes, and the goddamned head of department is putting the screws on me. I have a ticket for the week after next.' He leaned forward. 'I love her, and I want her to come with me. She respects you. What do you think?'

'I don't know but I think she would be bloody stupid not to go with you.'

'She loves the damn job. If it wasn't for the job, I'm sure she'd come.'

'It's been my experience that the job won't keep her warm at night. In fact, I know more than one person that this job has destroyed. Personally, I got tired of shovelling other people's shit years ago.'

'But you still stay on.'

'As they used to say in the Westerns, 'it's what I do'. There are lots of times when I wished it wasn't what I'm good at but unfortunately we don't get to choose our talents, and mine appear to be centred on cleaning up crap in this city.' Wilson was pleased to see Moira exiting the Ladies. Talking with Brendan was getting dangerously close to a bleating session. He could imagine Brendan being a good psychologist. Maybe he should have spent more time talking to him, or maybe not.

'You two boys getting along without me?' Moira asked sitting down.

'Manchester United managed to lose so we were commiserating,' Wilson said.

She raised her eyebrows. 'Strange, Brendan hasn't managed to pick up the niceties of kickball, or whatever they call football in the States.'

Brendan gave her a tap on the top of her head. 'There's only one football and it's played by the New England Patriots. Manchester United play soccer.'

'Tomorrow.' Wilson finished his drink and stood up. He'd had enough for one day. As he stood, he looked along the bar, and his eyes were drawn to a slight man dressed in a light-brown safari jacket who raised a glass in his direction.

Jock McDevitt smiled at Wilson.

'Enjoy the rest of the evening.' Wilson turned to Brendan and extended his hand. 'You and I should have a drink again soon.'

'I'd love to.' Brendan grasped his hand and they shook.

Wilson walked slowly in McDevitt's direction.

'Mr Wilson,' McDevitt said. 'Can I buy you a drink?'

'I've had my quota for the night,' Wilson said.

McDevitt laughed. 'I can't imagine a copper pulling in the famous Detective Super. It'd be more than his job would be worth. Guys like you are Teflon.'

'OK, Jock, suppose I ask you what you're doing in this neck of the woods?'

'I love old pubs. Cosgrove's is one of my favourites. All that wood and shiny old mirrors, and you never know who you'll meet.'

'Cut the crap, Jock. I don't believe in coincidences.'

'Like people taking swallow dives out of fifth-storey windows.'

Wilson sighed. 'Like people taking swallow dives out of fifth-storey windows.'

'Any news on the Grant murder?'

'We haven't decided it was murder.'

'I've got something to trade.' McDevitt finished his whiskey. 'Sure I can't offer you something.'

Wilson shook his head. 'What do you mean you have something to trade?'

McDevitt motioned to the barman for a refill. 'I've come by a morsel of information from my contacts in Glasgow. I'd be happy to trade it for something on the guy who just took a dive.'

Wilson watched McDevitt's drink arrive and wished he had asked for one. 'Impeding a police enquiry is an offence.'

'Let's say I never spoke,' McDevitt saluted Wilson with his glass.

'What would I have to trade?'

'Did the guy jump or was he pushed?'

'OK, show me yours, and I'll show you mine.'

'Two mechanics from Glasgow did a job here some weeks back. Might have been Grant.'

'Any evidence?'

'These people don't leave evidence and they've already skipped Glasgow. Apparently, my article in the *Chronicle* spooked them.'

'Names?'

McDevitt shook his head.

Wilson tried to assimilate the news. Grant's murderers weren't local, and were already on the run. However, someone local must have hired them. That meant that the motive must be local as well. 'I don't suppose your informant has any idea who was behind them.'

'End of the information trade on my side, now what about the guy who landed on the car?'

'He might not have jumped.'

'Check out the *Chronicle* tomorrow. I've got a peach of a photo of the scene. It's amazing the clarity you can get from a mobile phone these days.'

Shit, Wilson thought. They should have thought of

canvassing the watchers for photos. He reminded himself to mention it at the briefing. He turned to leave.

'Mr Wilson,' McDevitt held his arm. 'We have complementary information sources. We can help each other.'

Wilson looked at McDevitt's hand on his arm, and McDevitt removed it. 'Tread carefully, Jock.'

'Always Mr Wilson.'

Wilson turned and left the pub.

CHAPTER THIRTY-FOUR

Wilson woke at six o'clock. He pushed aside the covers and stood up. He needed to clear his head. So after he finished his toilet, he slipped into his running gear. Light was just dissipating the darkness and there was a chill in the air when he closed the front door of the apartment building behind him. There was also a smell of salt which indicated that the tide was pushing up along the river. He suddenly realised that this was the first time he had a run in over a week. If he kept this up, it wouldn't take long for his paunch to reappear. He started off at a good lick filling his lungs with the cold air. His leg was apt to give him some gip during the winter, but spring was in the air so the nagging pain was at its most bearable. He loved these early-morning runs. They invigorated him for the day ahead. He had always been a good trainer. Maybe he should have taken up the coaching jobs he had been offered when he left rehabilitation. The morning run was his equivalent of meditation. As his feet beat the pavement, his mind could banish all external thoughts and concentrate on his priorities. Three young men had lost their lives and he wanted to know why. His feet pounded the concrete path running alongside the river. He passed several slow-moving runners dressed in all black running outfits of skin-tight pants and matching hoodies. He took no notice of them as he tried to establish his normal rhythm. He had an effective staff of four and three possible lines of enquiry, one for each murder. That gave him one and one third officers for each murder. That was a sick joke. Add to that Jennings' threat to cut his staff by one, and the impending departure of Moira, and it was more and more certain that three deaths would go unpunished. He hit his rhythm, and his feet pounded the ground as he turned and headed back to the apartment pushing hard. It was becoming clear that Jennings meant to disband the Murder Squad. This may be the last case he worked on for the PSNI. Well if that was so, he would give it his best shot.

THE CHILL in the apartment was several degrees lower than that outside. Kate and Helen were both up and considering the early hour, that was first. As was now usual, the buzz of conversation died as soon as he appeared.

'I need a shower,' Wilson said and headed for the bathroom. He stood under the hot water. There were two options. He could be patient and ride out the storm, or he could grab the bull by the horns and demand that he and Kate sort out their problems. He wasn't a great fan of counselling but if that was what they needed. Whatever it was, something would have to break, and it would have to break soon. Their relationship had turned into a festering sore that needed treatment. He towelled off and selected some clothes from his part of the closet. He made his mind up. Kate and he would have a long talk and try to work things out. He strode towards the kitchen with that new resolve. Helen was sitting alone at the breakfast bar cradling a cup of coffee in her hands.

'Where's Kate?' He knew there was an edge to his voice.

'Off to work,' Helen said.

'Shit,' Wilson said under his breath.

'Have you and Kate thought of taking a break from each other?' Helen asked.

'Kate and I are not on speaking terms.' Wilson made himself a cup of coffee. 'Or hadn't you noticed?'

'It's a pity that Kate is so busy. It's beautiful in Antibes this time of year. Can't you take a break?'

Wilson thought of the bodies piled up in the morgue and laughed.

'What's so funny?' Helen asked.

'Yesterday, I was investigating two possible murders.' He sipped his coffee. 'Today, it might be three.'

'What?' Helen shuffled uneasily on her stool and spilled some of her coffee.

'Guy took a flier out of a fifth-floor window in the Tannery Building. We don't think he did so on his own volition. Anyway, you can read all about it in the *Chronicle* this morning. Jock McDevitt was on the scene.'

Helen looked at her watch. 'Gosh, is that the time?' She climbed down from the stool and left in a hurry.

Wilson surveyed the empty kitchen. It was kind of a 'where did it all go wrong' moment. He hadn't missed the point of Mrs McCann's message. The whispering and colluding was heading in one direction. Kate and he should take a 'break'. Whatever was going on in Kate's head wasn't going to be solved by him being patient. The resolve he'd had in the shower might be fleeting. Or it might lead to an explosion. He had learned in life to expect the unexpected. Something was coming down the line, and whatever it was, his life was going to change, again.

CHAPTER THIRTY-FIVE

W ilson had divided the whiteboard in the murder squad room into three sections before the briefing began. He had also locked the door to the squad room.

'For a start no information on these briefings is to go outside this room,' he started. 'Moira, briefing on the events of last night.'

Moira explained the scene at Francis Street the previous evening. She had already obtained a photo of the body on the car, and it was appended to the whiteboard.

'You'll note that I've divided the whiteboard into three sections. One is for the Grant murder, the second is for last night's victim Mark O'Reilly, and the third is for a young man named Brian Malone. Moira, sketch in what we know about Malone.'

Moira came forward and picked up the felt pen. She outlined what she had learned about Malone, and wrote it beneath his name on the board.

'Boss,' Harry Graham interrupted. 'Why haven't we heard of this Malone guy before?'

Wilson explained that Reid was certain Malone had been

murdered, but that he hadn't been convinced. He'd asked Moira to take a look at the case unofficially.

'And now you believe her?' Graham asked.

It was a question that Wilson didn't want to answer. 'We have three lines of enquiry. I'd prefer less but maybe there's an advantage here somewhere. The lives of these three people, one an accounts analyst in the Infrastructure Agency, another a Belfast Councillor and the last an accountant with a prestigious Belfast accountancy firm, have intersected at some point in time. The reason behind that node is possibly the reason why they had to die. We need to find what binds these men together, then I'll answer Harry's question.'

Peter Davidson shuffled uneasily. 'How far back do we go? Three lines of enquiry means lots of hours looking through agendas, timelines, phone calls. These people might not only have met socially. They could have seen something they shouldn't have seen, heard something they shouldn't have heard. You know better than all of us, Boss. This is like looking for a needle in a haystack.'

'One last piece of information,' Wilson said and gave the team the information McDevitt had given him.

Eric Taylor whistled. 'Interesting. Someone didn't trust the local deadheads. Moving upmarket costs money, and there are only a few locals who have the ability to go to the mainland for hitters. But it means we're dealing with some pretty serious people. There might be connections that were made during the "'Troubles'".'

'Someone should thank Reid,' Graham said. 'They might have got away with it, if she hadn't spotted that Grant had been murdered.'

'You can thank her yourself Harry,' Wilson said. 'I want you to go over to the Mortuary at the Royal Victoria for O'Reilly's autopsy. It's due to start at ten. You don't have to be there when it starts, but I'd like to have the result as soon as possible.'

He looked at Moira and saw that she was smiling. There would be no confrontation with Reid today. 'One small conclusion on the O'Reilly death,' he continued. 'It lacks the subtlety of the other two murders. That makes me think that it's a local hit. It's very Belfast to toss someone out of a fifth-floor window.'

The team laughed.

'OK,' Wilson continued. 'We're thin on the ground, and we're going to have to divide our forces. Harry you stick with O'Reilly. After the autopsy, go to his office and find out if he was working on anything special. Then check with Forensics. If it was a Belfast job, there'll be either fingerprints or DNA. Our bad boys tend to be forgetful about traces of their handiwork behind. Timeline over the past few days, emails, agenda, phone calls if possible. Check the CCTV from the Tannery. Look for something that links him to either Grant or Malone, either a contact or somewhere they were at the same time.'

'Moira you stick with Malone, same procedure as for Harry. We look at the timeline, the contacts, agenda and phone records.'

'I'm working on it,' Moira said.

Wilson turned to Davidson. 'Peter, you lucky boy. Put in a travel request. You're going to Glasgow. I know you dealt with the guys over there before. I want you to follow up on McDevitt's tip. See if there's any truth in it, and if so, what do the local guys think about the mechanics. They may have come by plane. Check with Belfast International and get our colleagues there to provide you with photos of everyone who checked in for a flight to Glasgow on the evening of Grant's death and the next day. You can pick up the photos on your way to Glasgow. Eric, you and I are going to concentrate on Grant. His brother says that his computer is missing. Is it backed up anywhere? Can the boffins find out whether he's on the Cloud? What about CCTV? Something tells me he's the central character in this little drama.'

There was knocking at the door to the squad room. Eric

Taylor detached himself from the team and went to the door. The Desk Sergeant was standing outside. He passed a copy of the *Chronicle* to Taylor. The front page had a picture of a man lying over the bonnet of a car. The headline read: Did he jump or was he pushed? The Desk Sergeant was pointing at the ceiling.

'Boss,' Taylor said. 'I think you're wanted upstairs.'

CHAPTER THIRTY-SIX

Deputy Chief Constable Royson Jennings was sitting at his desk examining a copy of the *Chronicle*'s front page. He had been fixated on the lead article for the past half hour. He prided himself on having the best contacts in Belfast. For God's sake, he was both a Mason and a senior member of the Orange Order. He was a member of the Royal County Down Golf Club, although he could barely swing a golf club. He supped regularly with the great and the good, and yet he had the feeling that events that Lattimer and Carlisle had set in motion were going to seriously affect his career and social standing. He could not dispel the feeling of impending doom. He had cancelled the first part of his morning. He looked again at the headline in the *Chronicle*, picked up his phone and dialled Jackie Carlisle's number.

IT WAS a beautiful spring morning in Hillsborough. Although the air outside still had a touch of winter in it, the low sun had already penetrated the conservatory where Jackie Carlisle sat drinking his early-morning coffee. The cancer cells entangling his spine like an anaconda had led him to appreciate even more the magnificent nature of the garden that surrounded his house. He should have been enjoying the view through the windows of the conservatory, but his concentration had been on the front page of the *Belfast Chronicle* ever since the paper had dropped through the letterbox. His wife generally joined him for coffee, but she had seen the black aspect to his normally pallid face, and had discretely disappeared to the kitchen. He couldn't believe his eyes, although he had recently told himself to expect the worst. The events in Francis Street had Sammy Rice's signature all over them. Sammy was out of control. Carlisle's life was draining away and dealing with the likes of Rice would only make it drain away faster. If it hadn't been for his children and grandchildren, he would have left the Province in the hope that a less stressful life might lead to a prolongation of it. For Helen McCann and the rest of the Circle, Sammy Rice and his behaviour would be on him. He had guided Sammy's paramilitary career, and while he wasn't responsible for his descent into criminality, he had used Sammy's skill set and his contacts to further both his own and the Circle's agenda. So, he would have to shoulder some of the blame for creating a hopped-up monster like Sammy. The problem was that Rice wasn't the only monster out there. The futile experience known as the 'Troubles' had created a generation of monsters on both sides of the sectarian divide. The men who created them were dying off, but the Frankensteins they made were still wandering the streets. He wondered whether men like Sammy would be his legacy to Ulster. He hoped not and it hadn't been his intention. He had wanted to preserve Ulster as a Protestant entity within Britain. He chuckled. When he started out in politics, he wanted to be as big as Castlereagh, or maybe even Edward Carson. That's how deluded he'd been. He should have been happy to stand on the shoulders of giants. In comparison to the greats of Ulster politics, he had simply been a pigmy who had been an attendant at a bloodbath. Where was the honour in blowing the legs off women in the Abercorn, or in murdering people on the street in Enniskillen? Where was the honour in tossing some poor fool out of a fifth-floor window in the Tannery? Maybe Helen was right, they should have kicked the decision on Grant and Malone upstairs. But Rice wasn't stupid, and his remark about the biggest monkeys being at the top of the tree had some validity. The die had been cast. There were two main questions. Would there be any more violent deaths, and what was going to be done about Rice? He drained his coffee cup and looked out of the window. Sunlight was spilling over the larch and silver birch trees at the back of the garden; a rowan was showing its spectacular red foliage. Normally, he would have soaked in the beauty of the scene but his mood was dark, and he saw only the ugliness of the world beyond his garden. A man needed to leave a legacy. A tear crept out of his eye as the phone rang.

'Jackie,' Jennings' voice was an octave higher than its normal pitch, 'I assume you've seen the *Chronicle*?'

'Good morning, Roy.' It was anything but, Carlisle thought. Jennings was the quintessential shivershite. He was always the first to run for the hills.

'What do you know about the events at the Tannery last night?' Jennings asked.

'Only what I read in the *Chronicle*,' Carlisle replied. 'The question is, what do you know about it?'

'I'm trying to get both Spence and Wilson, but they appear to have gone dark together. I have gleaned that there is indeed evidence to suggest that this man O'Reilly was assisted on his way out of the window. I never heard his name before. I hope to God he has no connection with the Grant business.'

'This phone call is over,' Carlisle said. 'We were all decimated by what happened to poor David.' He kept his voice calm. That fool Jennings was going to drop them all in it with his panic. 'It's beautiful here in Hillsborough this morning. You really should come and visit sometime.'

There was a silence on Jennings' side of the conversation. 'Thanks very much for the invitation, Jackie,' Jennings said after a pause. His voice was more normal now. The penny appeared to have dropped. 'I'll clear my desk and call back to arrange a time to visit.'

'I look forward to seeing you.' Carlisle cut the communication. He slumped back in his chair. He wondered whether such incompetents had surrounded Castlereagh and Carson.

CHAPTER THIRTY-SEVEN

Harry Graham hated autopsies. It wasn't the sight of dead people. He'd seen enough cadavers in his career not to be freaked out by inert bodies. It also wasn't the sight of blood; he wasn't the sort to fall over at a pool of the red stuff. For him, it was the noise the scalpel made as the incisions cut deep into the chest. It was also the whirr of the saw cutting through the crown of the head and exposing the brain. He wasn't too keen on watching the organs being withdrawn, weighed and eventually put back. He'd watched a programme on the Discovery Channel about how the Egyptians treated their dead. The corpse was eviscerated pretty much as the pathologist would do today. The internal organs were removed and put in a jar, and the organless body was sown up and mummified. It didn't look like medicine had advanced that much in its treatment of the dead. He parked outside the morgue at the Royal Victoria and steeled himself for the performance ahead.

STEPHANIE REID TRIED NOT to show her disappointment when Graham entered the autopsy room. She knew that she was being pathetic, hoping against hope that Wilson would show up. She wanted to get the man out of her mind, but she wasn't succeeding. She always had a healthy sexual appetite, but lately she had been off her feed. Before she'd come across Wilson, she hadn't given up the search for the 'one' but she was getting pissed off at having to kiss so many frogs without having found the prince. Now she had met someone who she considered could very well be the 'one' only to find out that another woman already had her claws into him. And Kate McCann wasn't just any other woman. Reid had been told too many times that she was beautiful not to believe that she was the equal of any other woman. But she would be the first to admit, reluctantly, that McCann was also beautiful. Add to that the fact that she was one of the United Kingdom's top barristers, and the package was pretty complete. She knew she should give up the quest but something inside wouldn't let her. She wanted that damn man, and would have done anything to get him. She greeted Graham coldly and told him to get his scrubs on if he was going to stand beside her. From the way he shuffled around, she got the impression that autopsies weren't his thing.

'You can watch from the observation room if you prefer,' she said. The temptation to make Graham suffer was great, but she was essentially a fair person, and it wasn't Graham's fault that his boss had wimped out.

Graham nodded and made his way slowly to the observation room.

Reid whipped the cover off O'Reilly's body. The professional in her suddenly took over. She pulled down the microphone and spoke. 'The body is that of a male of approximately thirty years of age.' She picked up a scalpel and made the first incision.

DS Moira McElvaney wished that there were more than

twenty-four hours in the day. She looked at the list of things she had to do. Although viewing the CCTV was important, she had shelved it in favour of an interview with Brian Malone's boss at the Infrastructure Agency. She had also arranged to interview one of his friends. She and Brendan had stayed on in Cosgrove's after Wilson's departure the previous evening. The topic of conversation had been the now usual one of whether she was going to join Brendan in Boston. She had put off the decision for as long as she could, but since Brendan's departure was imminent, she was going to have to bite the bullet soon. Brendan had stayed the night, and she had to admit to herself that she was concluding that she couldn't envisage life without him. Where did that leave her job in the PSNI, and her loyalty to Wilson? Maybe she could delay joining Brendan until this case was completed. Then there was the Cummerford business. She would certainly be called to give evidence, and maybe she would be needed if McIver ever came to trial. It was all very complicated. She was still running through combinations and permutations when she arrived in front of the Northern Ireland Infrastructure Agency office. She looked up at the concrete and glass edifice and decided that it was not going to win any architectural prizes. It was shaped like a concrete box with similar-sized windows inserted in both horizontal and vertical rows. It was the ideal government building, designed for function rather than aesthetics. After checking in with reception, Moira was directed to the lifts and instructed to go to the sixth floor where a secretary would meet her. Moira did as she was told and was led to the office of Dr Simon Healy, the director in charge of the accounting function. As she walked along the corridor on the sixth floor, she passed by small individual offices containing one desk, two chairs, one filing cabinet, one lamp and one computer. They reminded her of why she had aban-doned her job in the Department of Social Welfare and joined the PSNI. She was kept waiting in an outer office for ten minutes before being invited into the inner sanctum of the director's office.

Simon Healy stood as Moira entered the office. He was an exceptionally tall man standing at least six feet four. Like Wilson, he towered over her. But unlike Wilson, he was a bag of bones. Knees and elbows stuck out of his dark blue pin-striped suit. His face had the pallor associated with office work, and his attempt at a smile barely opened his small mouth. 'Detective Sergeant McElvaney.' He affected a confused look. 'Please come in. I'm sorry, but I can only give you ten minutes. I'm extremely busy today.'

Moira shook the hand extended towards her. 'I'll try to be as quick as possible.' She sat in the chair Healy indicated to with his hand.

'I'm slightly confused by your visit,' he began. 'We're all extremely shocked by Brian's demise, but we had been led to believe that it was a sudden death occasioned by some genetic problem.'

'My visit is completely routine,' Moira began. 'The pathologist hasn't yet come to a conclusion on the cause of death, and we are simply making enquiries that may help her to finalise her report for the coroner.'

'And how can I help? I have no knowledge of poor Brian's health.'

'So he had a good attendance record?'

'The best, a cold or a flu maybe but nothing out of the ordinary.'

'And what exactly did he do here?'

'And that would be relevant because?' Healy asked.

'It might indicate a high level of stress with implications for the condition of his heart. I wasn't aware that your work here was of a confidential nature.'

Healy thought for a moment. 'I can't image that his work would have overstressed him.'

Moira smiled reassuringly. 'While I'm willing to accept

your assurances, the pathologist must make up her own mind. And I promise you that your opinion will be relayed to her, but I must also present all the facts. I'll be speaking with his football friends later.'

Healy rubbed his pointed chin. 'Brian was involved in working through tenders for infrastructure projects. It's rather mundane work, which involves checking the prices submitted by various contractors, in order that the selection of the contractors can be as transparent as possible.'

'He was very conscientious?' Moira asked.

'Extremely. He went through every tender with a fine toothcomb.'

'I suppose a lot of money was involved.'

Healy's face took on a smug look. 'More than one billion pounds in some years.'

'I could well imagine that managing that amount of money might be stressful for certain individuals.'

'Brian was a drone. He had no direct responsibility for either selecting the contractors or the conclusion of contracts. So in effect he had no responsibility for money.'

Moira was writing in her notebook. 'You've been very helpful, Dr Healy.'

Healy stood. 'We haven't heard any news of Brian's funeral. I assume his parents will let us know.'

'The body hasn't been released yet. I'm sure his parents will be in touch.' She put her notebook in her pocket, shook hands with the man and left the office.

Healy watched her as she walked down the corridor. He thought she was very attractive, and the red hair was spectacular. He'd never heard of the police following up on a natural death, though. As soon as Moira was out of sight, he called his secretary. 'Bring me the files Malone was working on,' he said curtly. Maybe there was more to Malone's death than bad genes.

CHAPTER THIRTY-EIGHT

It was Jackie Carlisle's habit to have a mid-morning snooze. His medication was of the heavy variety. During his days as an active politician, he had slept little, but he now found himself dropping off in mid-morning and early afternoon. The naps were unintentional. He had so little of life left that he resented the period when he was not actively involved in it. His discussion with Jennings had left him despondent. He was in no doubt that Jennings would concentrate all his efforts on ensuring that Roy Jennings survived. Whereas he had employed whatever brainpower he had left to come up with a series of scenarios aimed at extricating them from their predicament. None of them left him feeling confident. He spent a little time sitting in his garden. His wife brought a blanket and wrapped him up against the cold. He was reminded of Don Corleone's death scene in *The Godfather*. Perhaps he would go the same way, asleep in his favourite chair in his garden.

WHEN HE AWOKE from his nap, he was immediately aware

that someone was sitting with him. His eyes gradually focussed and he saw that Helen McCann had joined him in the garden. He smiled when he saw her.

'Welcome back,' she said returning his smile.

'It's a kind of victory every time I wake up these days,' he said. 'It comes with the realisation that someday I won't.'

She flattened her skirt. 'If it's any consolation, it's the same for all of us.'

'I expected someone, but I didn't know it would be you.' He felt a sudden chill and pulled the blanket around him. He could see the edges of a copy of the *Chronicle* on the seat beneath her.

'The day is so beautiful I wanted to come back and enjoy the garden with you.' She picked up a cup that sat on the wicker table between them and sipped.

He knew it was a lie, but he played along. 'Having you here reminds me of the good old days.'

'In retrospect they weren't so good, but we did what we had to do to preserve this Province.'

And your wealth, he thought but didn't say.

'I love this house,' she said.

He laughed. 'You can't have it. Anyway, I can't see you ever living in Ulster again.'

'On days like this I could. But how many days like this are there?'

'Too few,' he said reflecting on the twenty-six thousand days he had already spent on the planet. He had multiplied it out one day. Twenty-six thousand, it didn't seem a lot when you said it like that.

'Your boy is out of control,' Helen said quietly.

'It hasn't been concluded that it was him.' Again the shiver. 'We shouldn't rush a judgement.'

'We agree. But we should have a contingency plan.'

'You have something in mind?' he asked.

'A Belfast solution to a Belfast problem,' she said. 'There's a well-tried option for getting rid of complications.'

Carlisle smiled. People like Helen McCann might use violent men to accomplish their aims, but they could never stoop to talk about murder without using circular language. 'Do we really need to go there?'

'Don't be obtuse, Jackie. The era of the Mad Dogs is over. There's a big picture here and your boy is crapping all over it.'

Carlisle was taken aback by the change of language.

She continued. 'You brought him into our business, and now you have the solution in your hands. Maybe it's about time for another turf war with one major casualty.'

Carlisle pointed at the paper. 'That's only speculation. That boy could have pitched himself out of that window.'

'It has transpired that the murders of Malone and Grant were a screw-up.' She picked the paper from beneath her bottom and checked the lead story. 'This O'Reilly chap was an accountant. It's not a big step for the police to find out that he knew Grant. You and I have already made that step. Wilson will start to connect the dots unless we provide him with an event which leaves him at a dead end.' She looked at the old man wrapped in the blanket. He looked like one of those shrivelled bodies that are pulled out from a bog somewhere, a hollow skin where the inside has disintegrated. He's no longer up to the job, she thought. She was wasting her time.

Carlisle could see her watching him and sensed what she was thinking. Together they had been a part of Ulster's history for more than forty years, but he could see from her flinty gaze that she would sign his death warrant without compunction. 'If it's established that he killed that boy, I'll make the arrangements,' he said.

Helen McCann finished her coffee and stood up. 'I love your garden,' she said looking around at the shrubs and trees that were beginning to bloom. She longed for her villa in

Antibes, the bougainvillea running along the outer walls, the purple flowering of the jacaranda trees, and the heat of the spring and early summer. It was so far from the grimy streets of Belfast, so far away from murder and death.

CHAPTER THIRTY-NINE

Like so many times before, Wilson knew that the case was at a crossroads. Solving a crime depended on momentum. Statistics showed that there were ninety unsolved murders in the whole of England since nineteen seventy. In the same period, there were more than three thousand two hundred and sixty nine unsolved murders in Ulster. There was a population of fifty three million people in England, and one and a half million in Ulster. You didn't have to be a mathematical genius to analyse the data. The chances of getting away with murder in Ulster were considerably higher than they were in England. It could be that the officers of the PSNI were dumber than their mainland counterparts, because it certainly wasn't because Ulster's criminals were smarter. The statistic constantly played on Wilson's mind. It was all about momentum, momentum, momentum. Each day had to produce some piece of the puzzle that moved the case forward. If that forward momentum was lost, the team soon floundered, and the case was heading towards the unsolved archive. He was afraid that was the direction in which the Grant and Malone cases were headed. He'd read and reread the forensic report on Grant looking for any shred of evidence.

There was nothing. There was no evidence of murder except for Reid's assertion. What if Reid had got it wrong? He was spending all his resources trying to solve three as yet unrelated deaths. Maybe Reid was pissed that she hadn't been able to find the cause of Malone's death. A lethal injection of potassium chlorite lacked proof. Young men dropped dead every day of the week. They needed evidence not conjecture. The only point that nagged at him was the efforts of Jennings and Reid's boss to have the investigation shelved. What possible motivation could these two disparate men have to quash a police investigation? He drew three circles on his notepad and wrote the name of a dead man in each circle. He then drew lines between the three circles with arrows going back and forward to each. If the same murderer killed all three, there had to be a connection. So far, his team had found nothing. Grant was a minor politician with aspirations, Malone a worker bee in a government institution and O'Reilly an accountant with a prestigious firm. He continued to doodle on the page running his pen again and again over the lines connecting the three circles. He hated hypothesising. His methodological approach required evidence not intuition. He looked at the last note Moira had sent him regarding her Malone investigation. Brian Malone's parents were collecting his body at the morgue at midday. He looked at his watch. He had half an hour to get to the Royal Victoria. He'd call Reid on the way.

WILSON PARKED in his usual spot in front of the two-storey red-bricked building. An undertaker's car was parked at the side entrance. He made his way to Reid's office, and found the pathologist in conversation with a man and woman dressed in funereal black. Dark lines streaked the woman's normally pale face. It was evident to Wilson that she hadn't slept in days. The man's head was continuously bent forward as though some weight were pulling it down. Wilson entered the office. 'Professor Reid,' he said as he entered.

'Ah, Detective Superintendent,' Reid played her part, 'I'll be with you shortly.' She hesitated for a second. 'Please excuse my bad manners. Mr and Mrs Malone, may I introduce you to Detective Superintendent Wilson. Mr and Mrs Malone are here to collect the body of their son.'

Wilson came forward and extended his hand. 'I'm sorry for your trouble,' he said as he shook both hands.

'I've got some papers to prepare, if you'll excuse me for a few moments.' She slipped quietly out of the office.

'Professor Reid told me about your son,' Wilson said as soon as she left the room. 'It was very sudden I understand.'

Mrs Malone removed a handkerchief from her pocket and started to cry.

'Our lad was twenty-eight years old,' Mr Malone spoke with a pronounced Tyrone accent. 'The boy was the picture of health, a sportsman too. We're trying to find out from the Professor what killed him, but it appears to be unclear.'

This type of interrogation was difficult for Wilson. 'The funeral will be in Tyrone I suppose?' he asked.

'Day after tomorrow,' Mr Malone said suppressing a sob.

'This is a terrible time for you, I know. Young people are so stressed these days. Perhaps your son was worried about something,' Wilson said.

'On the phone every second day he was.' Malone's mother sobbed. 'Only interested in that damn job and his sports, didn't have a care in the world.'

Mr Malone shook his head. 'He never bothered us with his problems.'

'I suppose you're heading directly for Tyrone?' Wilson asked.

They both nodded.

'Do you need any help here in Belfast?' Wilson asked.

The Malones looked confused.

'Maybe you need someone to pack up your son's stuff?'

'We couldn't ask,' Mrs Malone half-stammered.

'I have some contacts,' Wilson said. 'It's the least I could do. I could have your son's effects sent on to you.'

The Malones looked at each other. 'We really couldn't ask,' Mr Malone said.

'You didn't ask. I offered.'

Mr Malone fished a set of keys from his pocket. 'We'll pay any costs,' he said handing the keys to Wilson.

'I'll get the address from Professor Reid, and I'll make the arrangements. I'm sure you've got enough on your plate.'

Reid re-entered the office. She handed an envelope to Mr Malone. 'Brian is ready. The undertaker has already removed him to the car.'

Mr Malone took the envelope from Reid. 'Thank you for everything.' He turned to Wilson. 'And thank you, Superintendent, you've been very kind.' He took his wife's arm and led her from the office.

'How'd it go?' Reid asked when they had left.

Wilson tossed the set of keys in his hand.

'How do you feel?' she asked.

'Shit.'

BRIAN MALONE'S apartment was situated in a two storey with attic red-bricked house in Fitzroy Avenue. Wilson found the key to the main door and pushed it in. Malone's one bedroomed apartment was on the left of the hallway and included the bay window looking out onto the street. Wilson entered the small living room. This was the room where Brian Malone's short life had ended. He felt no reverence. He had too often invaded the space occupied by people who had died violent deaths. He walked slowly around the room. It was the typical bachelor pad. The 50-inch flat screen TV dominated the room. Across from the TV was an L-shaped fabric couch, a small wooden coffee table stood in the space between the TV and the couch. A couple of posters adorned the otherwise bare walls. If the posters meant anything, Malone supported Liverpool Football Club and liked the music of the Arctic Monkeys. Wilson withdrew a pair of surgical gloves from his pocket and put them on. A small bookcase was in the corner of the room across from the entrance. Wilson rummaged among the books on the bookcase. They were a varied lot, basically divided between best-selling thrillers and accountancy manuals. A small photo of Malone's parents looked out from the top shelf of the bookcase. Beside the photo was a British Telecom router. Wilson passed through the living room into a narrow galley kitchen. He opened the fridge and saw the usual staples. He opened the four kitchen cabinets but found nothing aside from crockery and cutlery. He moved on to the small bedroom containing a queen-sized bed, a wardrobe and a chest of drawers. He made a quick search but found nothing of interest. The bathroom, likewise, produced nothing. He made his way back to the living room. While he was not up to the standard of the forensic team, Wilson felt that if there had been anything out of place, he would have noticed it. He was wondering what the hell Brian Malone had done to get himself killed when his eyes fell on the router. If there's a router, there's usually a computer. Wilson found no Internet device. Maybe he missed it. He started to search again, looking for a laptop or a tablet, anything that might have used the Internet. Fifteen minutes later, he concluded that there was no computer, or Internet device, present in the apartment. The search was another dead end in an investigation of dead ends. He felt shit for the way he had duped the Malones out of their keys for nothing. In compensation, he would organise to have Malone's scant personal effects packed up and sent to his parents. It was the least he could do.

CHAPTER FORTY

Sammy Rice spent the morning dealing with business. Big George had driven him to the Brown Bear where he had an office above the bar. Rice ran a diversified business. If all his interests had been in the official economy, he would have been a conglomerate. Aside from his legitimate businesses of taxis, building construction and pubs, he had interests in drugs, protection, prostitution and people trafficking. The legal side of his businesses were necessary to launder the proceeds from the illegal side. Sammy Rice was rich beyond his wildest dreams, but still lived, for the most part, among the people who had made him rich, the Loyalists of West Belfast. Rice hadn't bothered to read the *Belfast Chronicle*. As far as he was concerned, O'Reilly had joined Grant and Malone in the morgue, and all three were no longer a threat to his business. He was more than pissed off with Jackie Carlisle and the toffee-nosed fuckers he represented. He'd been paying tribute to Jackie and his friends for more than twenty years. Theirs was a symbiotic relationship. He had the muscle and the money-making machine. They had the connections with the bankers, politicians and judges. His business was turning over millions and without them he would have had a hard job hiding it all. But he was beginning to be a force himself. Soon, he wouldn't need them and their so-called financial acumen. He had money stashed all over the place, some of it in banks and some invested in legitimate business. So Jackie and his friends were outliving their usefulness. By midday, he had already snorted £300 worth of coke and drank half a bottle of Remy Martin. He was feeling like a Lord of the Universe.

'Boss,' Owen Boyle pushed open the door of Rice's office. Rice's normally blond hair was streaked and matted. His typically tanned face was red and a little bloated. 'We got someone downstairs wants to talk to you.'

'What?' Rice looked at his lieutenant.

'Arsehole called McDevitt is down in the bar.' Boyle tossed a copy of the *Chronicle* onto the table. 'He's the crime guy on the *Chronicle*.'

'I thought he'd flown the coup.' Rice laughed. 'A couple of people wanted him dead very badly. He has one up on them, since they're the ones that are pushing up daisies. Tell him to come up.'

Rice sat back and read the lead article in the paper.

'Sammy.' Jock McDevitt walked into the room. 'Good to see you.'

Rice pushed his chair back and motioned McDevitt to a chair in front of his desk. 'I thought you were no longer with us.' He laughed at the double meaning.

McDevitt smiled. He spent most of his adult life in the company of criminals. If he were honest, he would have to say that he found a lot of them not only interesting, but also charming. Sammy Rice was in the section that made the hairs stand up on the back of his neck. Rice was one dangerous psychotic motherfucker; it was as simple as that. 'I spent a few years on the crime beat in Glasgow.' He decided to keep things down-to-earth with Rice.

'You took over from the bitch that murdered Lizzie.' Rice

spat the words out. He poured himself a large measure from a bottle of Remy.

'It was a bit of an embarrassment for the paper,' McDevitt said. 'They decided to bring back someone who wasn't a serial killer.' McDevitt's mouth was dry, and he ran his tongue over his lips. He was hoping Rice was going to offer him a drink. He had the feeling it was a forlorn hope.

'What do you want?' Rice asked taking a slug from his glass.

McDevitt nodded at the paper on the desk. 'I'm following up on the mini murder spree here in Belfast.'

Rice's brow furrowed. 'So why come to me?'

'Well I suppose I'm really looking for information on the Grant murder.' McDevitt could feel a bead of sweat running down the back of his neck.

'So why come to me?' This time there was an emphasis on 'me'.

'Before I came back, I was crime correspondent on the *Scotsman*. I've got pretty good contacts in Glasgow, and one of them gave me a story about Belfast.' He stopped and watched Rice's face. It was expressionless. 'I hear that a team of mechanics was engaged by someone in Belfast to take out two men. The reason the story was so good was because they decided to make the second murder look like a gasper gone wrong. That rang a very big bell.' McDevitt stared at Rice. He wasn't sure but he thought he could see a residue of white powder at the base of his nostrils.

A slow smile spread over Rice's face. 'You certainly have a pair of balls, Jock. You come here to my place of business with some cock and bull story about Glasgow mechanics, and insinuate that I might be involved. I should be annoyed. Get the fuck out of here and don't come back. You wouldn't like me if you made me angry.'

This wasn't the first time that Jock McDevitt was threatened. But it was the first time that he felt like going to the toilet post threat. 'Can I take that as a no comment?' McDevitt asked trying manfully to control the quiver he could hear in his voice. 'My contact in Glasgow intimated that I should speak to you.'

There was a tick in Rice's right eye. 'Old arseholes like you drop dead every day of the week, you know. I mind my own business, and I advise you to mind yours. Now piss off.'

McDevitt eased himself out of the chair. 'What about that guy who decided to take a leap from his window in the Tannery last night?'

Rice picked up the *Chronicle*. 'Just read about it. Another victim of the fucked-up economy.'

'The Peelers don't think that he jumped. I wonder who might have pushed him.'

Rice stood up and spread his hands on his desk. 'Piss off now or I won't be responsible if anything happens to you. And don't come back. And don't forget we know where you live.'

McDevitt backed out of the room.

Boyle watched McDevitt as he descended the stairs to the bar. Then he pushed open the door and saw Rice in a rage scattering papers all over the room.

'The next time I see that boy, I'm going to fucking kill him.' Rice was breathing heavily. 'He knows about the boys from Glasgow and he's heard my name. I thought you said that those boys were tighter than a duck's arse.'

'They're professionals.' The 'fickle finger of fate' looked like it was going to land on Boyle, and he was aware of what that could mean. 'Anyway they're already on the Costa and they won't be back soon.'

Rice poured another brandy. The bottle was almost empty and he was swaying. 'It's on you if this gets back to me.'

Boyle knew where this was going. He was the one who had made the arrangements with the boys in Glasgow. He had to use Rice's name to get the introductions. But it was him who had paid over the money and placed the contract. There was one degree of separation between him and Rice. The police might conclude that he was acting for Rice, but there was no proof. Other than his word, and a good brief would make that worth a thimbleful of spit under cross-examination. Closing in on the boys from Glasgow meant they were closing in on him.

CHAPTER FORTY-ONE

Moira was having a bad day at the office. She had struck out with Malone's boss, and her interview with his sporting friend had been equally unproductive. She didn't feel like going back to the station, so she was sitting in the window of Starbucks in Victoria Square. It was a typical spring day; what had started so well had become sheets of rain being blown across the city by a howling west wind. Due to its situation in a passageway leading to the Victoria Square Shopping Centre, Starbucks was in a prime position to examine the effects of the weather. There was a steady stream of drenched denizens of Belfast moving past the window. She watched their faces as they passed. They were mostly pale after a tough Irish winter, huddled into their coats or hidden beneath their umbrellas. Ireland was all about weather, and the weather was generally bad. She found herself wondering what the weather was like in Boston today. It had to be better than what she was looking at through the window. Maybe she would Google it when she went back to the office. Or maybe not, since that would be a step in recognising that she was seriously thinking of going with Brendan. But it shouldn't be just about the weather. Would she have a better life in Boston? Would

Brendan be able to come good on his promise that she would get a Green Card? And the big question, could she ever trust a man again? Life was short, and she could spend too much of it as she had that morning. How would Wilson react to her departure? He had survived before she arrived, and he would survive after she left. He was not part of the equation. She had two weeks in which to decide. Or maybe she didn't have to decide right away. She could join Brendan later. She sipped her coffee. It was time to get back to the office. There were hours of CCTV to view.

DC PETER DAVIDSON arrived at Glasgow International Airport at three o'clock in the afternoon. He caught a taxi outside the main terminal for the 13-kilometre trip to the centre of Glasgow. He'd heard the airport being described as ten minutes from the centre, but he had never made it in that time on any of his visits to Glasgow. Davidson had been part of a RUC liaison group with Strathclyde Police during the period when there was a free interchange between Loyalists in Belfast and Glasgow. It took almost twenty-five minutes to arrive at the HQ of Strathclyde Police in Stewart Street. The office, a concrete block painted in two shades of blue with rows of small windows looking out on the street, hadn't changed in the five years since he had seen it last. He paid the taxi making sure to get a receipt that included the one pound fifty tip. He was just closing the back door of the cab when he felt a slap on his shoulder. He whirled around and looked into the face of Detective Sergeant Ross Brown of the Strathclyde Police.

'Welcome to Glasgow,' Brown said pumping Davidson's hand. 'Long time no see.'

'It's been a while.' Davidson stood back to look at his mainland colleague. Brown was one of the few men who could stand up to Wilson. He stood six feet two in his stocking feet and a wild crop of straw blond hair topped his large head.

'I thought you'd at least be a sergeant by now,' Brown said moving in the direction of the concrete ramp which led to the front entrance.

'We're not all ambitious bastards like you,' Davidson said. 'Anyway I don't want to leave Belfast.' In reality he had no interest, other than money, in moving up the line. He liked to do what he wanted and right now that meant staying with the Belfast Murder Squad.

'What about?' Brown rubbed his thumb and forefinger together in the universal gesture for money.

'Man doth not live by bread alone,' Davidson smiled.

Brown pushed in the main door. 'Born again?' he asked.

'Not really.' Davidson laughed. 'It just means I'm happy with what I've got. When I get fed up, I'll move on under my own steam, not because some administrator wants me somewhere.'

'We on for a few pints tonight?' Brown pressed for the lift.

'I'm on the seven o'clock Easyjet, so pints are out of the question.' The lift stopped, and they got on.

'Easyjet?'

'Budgets,' Davidson said. 'We can't even afford an overnight. Anyway we're strapped staff-wise at the moment.'

They got off at the fifth floor and walked down a corridor. Brown knocked at an office door. 'My Chief Inspector,' he said. 'Courtesy call.'

Davidson sighed.

After ten minutes of platitudes to the DCI, Brown led Davidson to his office. 'Correct me if I'm wrong,' Brown said. 'You have two murders carried out on the same evening. And you have information that two professionals from Glasgow were engaged.'

Davidson nodded and removed a thick file from his brief-case. 'Two possible murders.' He took two of the photos taken by Reid at Grant's, and put them on the desk. 'The pathologist doesn't think this was an accident, and neither does my boss.'

Brown looked at the photos. 'Aye, not a case of shit happens.'

'We got a tip that some mechanics from Glasgow were involved.' Davidson opened the file and removed a sheaf of black-and-white photos. 'These are photos of everyone who checked in for flights to Glasgow on the day of the murders, and the next day. It's a long shot but maybe our boys are in here somewhere. If I were them, I would have used the ferry from Larne to Stranraer. It's more anonymous.'

'You said the murders were supposed to look like natural deaths.' Brown laughed. 'If you can call erotic asphyxiation a natural death. They might have used a plane if they were confident enough that they were in the clear.'

Davidson passed over the batch of photos.

Brown started going through the photos turning over those that were irrelevant. He whistled at the photo of a very beautiful young woman. He showed the photo to Davidson. 'Any idea where this one's staying?' He smiled.

Davidson returned the smile. 'You're the detective, it shouldn't be too difficult to find out.'

Brown put the photo aside and continued through the file. He was about halfway through when he stopped. 'Now there's a familiar face.' He turned the photo so Davidson could see it. It was of a tall thin man. 'Frank Baxter, a very bad man, suspected of being involved in contract killings here in Scotland and down south.' He continued through the photos and picked out a second. 'Wee Dougie Weir, small but more dangerous than the most poisonous creature in existence. Dougie and Frank have been known to operate together. We'd really like to get something on either of these two to put them out of circulation, but up to now they've been like Teflon, nothing sticks. These are your boys alright.'

'Only one problem,' Davidson said. 'There's not one iota of evidence at either of the murder sites. Even if you were to pick them up tomorrow, they could stonewall us. There's nothing physical to tie them to the crimes.'

Brown picked up his phone and spoke with one of his colleagues. 'There has been no sign of either man in Glasgow in the last few days,' he said when he put the phone down. 'I'm getting copies of their sheets made up so that you can take them back with you. They're on the national database for pretty minor stuff but we have a more comprehensive file on them here. Given the situation with the evidence, where do we go from there?'

'That's beyond my pay grade. At least we now have a good idea of who the murderers were.'

'It's a pain in the arse but you'll probably never see them in the dock for it.'

'It won't be the first time.' Davidson bundled up his photos. Earlier, he had wondered whether he was on a wild goose chase. At least it was progress, although it was only progress of a kind. They might know who committed the murders but what the hell could they do about it.

A female uniform entered the office and handed Brown a file. He looked at it briefly before passing it to Davidson. 'Everything we think we know about Baxter and wee Dougie. Lots that we can't prove.'

'Thanks.' Davidson took the file and without looking at its contents put it in his briefcase.

Brown looked at his watch. 'Four twenty,' he said. 'You need to be at the airport at six. That gives us an hour and a half to drink a few beers and we might even have time to complain to each other about our bosses.'

CHAPTER FORTY-TWO

Wilson had reluctantly devoted the early afternoon to administrative matters which for him meant that he had to suffer reading the more than fifty emails that had piled up in his 'urgent' file. He had decided to work from the top to the bottom, meaning that he would deal with the DCC's missives first, in an attempt to curry favour with the hierarchy, and then move on to those sent by his immediate colleagues. The latter were generally pitched to show that the solution rate of their team was in the stratosphere. After he saw the title of the first email from Jennings' office, he knew his life was about to become more difficult. Budgets were king but a shrinking commodity. Resources were scarce and would be getting scarcer. So put those two things together, and it spelled trouble for those in the sights of the DCC. The hierarchy had decided to launch a resource analysis exercise which the DCC would chair. Each station, and each section within the station, would be required to justify their staffing levels. The resource analysis exercise would pull together all the information provided by PSNI units throughout the Province and would decide in its wisdom who would gain and who would lose. Wilson wondered whether anyone at the top had reflected on the cost of the resource analysis exercise, in terms of money and manpower. Probably not, he thought. He looked through the glass window into the squad room. The sight depressed him. Eric Taylor was the only member of the team at his desk. Davidson was in Glasgow, and Moira had been a missing person since the morning briefing. Harry was off chasing down information on O'Reilly. He should have been looking out on a room that was a hive of activity. For three murders, there should have been twenty officers chasing down leads or following up on the results of a telephone appeal for information. There was no hive of activity. A single Detective Constable sat at his desk. Wilson leaned back in his chair and closed his eyes. In any investigation the level of resources dictated the results. It was evident that the DCC was starving him of resources. Without resources, the investigation would wither and die. 'Do more with less,' he said as he concentrated on the ceiling above his head. He was close to losing his belief in the investigation. He was going to follow the mantra; he was going to do more with less. He just hadn't worked out how yet. He deleted the email from Jennings, and instantly felt better. He looked at the whiteboard and saw nothing had been added since the morning briefing. There was no momentum whatsoever in the investigation. They were stalled and if they stayed stalled much longer, Jennings would apply the scissors. He looked at the three circles he had drawn on the writing pad earlier. Malone at the Infrastructure Agency, Grant, the crusading rising politician, and O'Reilly, the accountant at a top firm. He continued to draw lines between them. The Infrastructure Agency had large budgets. Could Malone have uncovered some skimming? Would someone kill three men over skimming? If Malone was at the source of whatever got the three killed, it wasn't just a small skim, it was something significant. That meant someone at the top. He shook his head. He couldn't imagine some bureaucrat organising murder. If someone at the top was caught with his hand in the till, he would be required to pack his bags and head into retirement. There would be a gratuity and a nice pension, and the whole affair would be swept under a very large carpet. He signalled for Taylor to join him.

'Boss,' Taylor said when he entered.

'I need to know who the contractors for the Infrastructure Agency are. I want to know how many contracts they have and for how much. Then I want you to check the ownership of every successful contractor. If there's some kind of tangled web behind the ownership, I want you to untangle it.'

'Where are we going on this, Boss?' Taylor asked.

'I don't know. We need to start shaking the bushes to see what falls out.' He tried not to show his desperation.

'What about the timelines for Grant and Malone?'

'Any progress?'

Taylor shook his head.

'Stay with it but follow up on the Infrastructure Agency stuff as well.' He could see the look on Taylor's face. He was dealing with a seasoned copper who knew the ropes and who was aware that he couldn't split himself in half. 'Prioritise the timelines. If we could put Malone and Grant together, at least we'd know we were on the right track.'

CHAPTER FORTY-THREE

Jock McDevitt wasn't a car enthusiast, and for that reason, he drove a black 1990 Mercedes 190e Sedan. He had bought it second-hand when it was five years old and had stuck with it through thick and thin. He hadn't been in Hillsborough in many years, so it took him a little more time than normal to find the Carlisle residence. He drove into the driveway and parked directly in front of the entrance. He switched off the car and sat looking at the house and garden. It was the kind of residence that many people aspire to but never get to own. Not bad for a boy from West Belfast with no education, he thought as he scanned the well-tended gardens. He knew Jackie Carlisle for more than twenty years. Carlisle had ridden the tiger that was the 'Troubles' and instead of being eaten by the beast, he had come out the other side as a relatively astute politician. At least he seemed to care in some way for the people he represented. But politicians weren't supposed to get rich from politics. It was true that Westminster was full of millionaires, but the majority had either inherited it or made it in business. The Carlisle residence spoke of money, but friend Jackie had neither inherited it nor made it in business. McDevitt climbed slowly out of his car and closed the door. He stood on the step at the front door and waited for a few moments. He'd heard that Carlisle was on his last legs. He'd been brought up in a journalistic tradition that said you should push on people when they were at their most vulnerable. He conned his way into this interview with Carlisle by proposing to write a piece for the *Chronicle* on his political legacy. Politicians of whatever colour have one sin in common, vanity. He pushed the bell and waited. A grey-haired lady who McDevitt recognised from a photo as Carlisle's wife eventually opened the door. He introduced himself, and she led him through the house to a conservatory at the rear. McDevitt's journalist eye took in the furniture and art that adorned the rooms. His appreciation of art was not something that was widely known about Jackie Carlisle.

The old man smiled but didn't rise from his chair when McDevitt was led into the conservatory. 'Long time no see, Jock,' he said.

McDevitt turned to thank Carlisle's wife, but she had discretely withdrawn. The withdrawal had been so unobtrusive that it must have been practised over many years. 'Good to see you too, Jackie.' He walked forward, and they shook hands.

'Put your arse on a chair.' Carlisle pointed at a wicker chair at his side.

'You're looking well.' McDevitt sat in the appointed chair.

'You always were a terrible fucking liar.,' Carlisle leaned back. 'What's this crap about you wanting to write a piece on my political legacy? My old doll might swallow that rubbish, but I didn't come up in the last shower.'

'I feel exposed.' McDevitt laughed. Carlisle might be on his way out but he was no fool.

'So what do you really want?'

'Word on the street is that you're very ill.'

'Three to six months, no way out.'

'Sorry to hear it.'

'Don't bullshit me. You didn't come here to commiserate with me about my impending departure from life.'

'You were present at some of the most important events in the history of this Province. We've never had the pleasure of a truth and reconciliation commission, so there are a lot of issues out there that may never be resolved. I was wondering whether you might be interested in clearing up a few points before ...' He left the sentence hanging.

Carlisle laughed. 'You must be desperate for a scoop, Jock. Look elsewhere. I'll make my peace with God. The people of Ulster will have to decide on my legacy based on the information they already have.'

'I've always been amazed', McDevitt continued, 'that there's been so much resistance from all sides to giving the public a detailed explanation of the events of the 'Troubles'. After all, the struggle against Apartheid was equally vicious. Equally large numbers of people on both sides died horrific deaths. How come the participants in Ulster have been so resistant to coming clean about what they did?'

'We've already done our bleating in front of the TV cameras. If you want to see contrition, go to the offices of the BBC or Ulster Television and look at the way we thumped our chests and said that we were wrong. Like I said, I prefer to be judged by God than by television, or by you for that matter.'

'I've been a journalist in this Province for more than twenty years,' McDevitt said. 'I've drank with some of the worst murderers on both sides, and I have the paunch to prove it. And in the process, I've listened to some of the strangest stories. Some were clearly bullshit, but others had at least a kernel of truth.'

'It's time for my nap,' Carlisle said. 'There's nothing for you here, Jock.'

'OK. Let me tell you a little story before I go. Around the 1920s, a group of wealthy Unionists got together and created an organisation they called the Circle. The purpose of the

Circle was to preserve the Union with Great Britain at all costs. They already had the Orange Order and the Masonic Lodges, but they needed a body that could coordinate action. Membership of the Circle was a lot more limited than either the Orange Order or the Masons. It contained the good and the great but at the top were the wealthy. They called themselves the Inner Circle. These people had a different agenda from the rank and file of the organisation. They were concentrated on maintaining their wealth and power. The organisation continued through the Second World War and was still operating when the 'Troubles' exploded in the late 1960s. People have always wondered at how well organised Protestant resistance was, the strikes, the organisation of the paramilitaries, the manipulation of the Westminster government.'

Carlisle yawned.

'The people at the top were still the wealthy, and they saw some potential for them to increase their wealth while giving lip-service to the preservation of union with Britain. Ulster was an embarrassment to both the United Kingdom and the European Community. The EC was established on the rule of law and democracy while terrorists openly walked the streets in a province of one of its biggest members. So major efforts were made to buy peace in Ulster. That meant an influx of money from Westminster, Brussels and, of course, Washington. This was manna from heaven for the Inner Circle. There was so much money flying around to appease the communities on both sides of the sectarian divide that some of it inevitably vanished.' McDevitt smiled. 'Well it didn't so much as vanish as make its way into pockets that were already well lined. Don't worry; the Inner Circle was not unique. What happened here has parallels in Iraq and Afghanistan after the American invasion.'

'Is your fairy tale coming to an end? I'm beginning to drop off.'

'I'm nearly done. The Circle and their bosses in the Inner

Circle will stop at nothing to ensure that their part in siphoning off millions of pounds of aid meant for Ulster does not come to light. They've murdered before but always under the guise of sectarianism. Those who stepped out of line or who had loose tongues ended up with fancy funerals. The big question is, what happened to all that money?' He purposely looked around the interior of Carlisle's house. 'Where did all that money go?'

'I can see a story like that coming out of an excess of the devil's buttermilk. Only a sot could come up with such a fanciful story. Now I really am tired. It's time you were away.'

McDevitt rose to leave. 'Do the right thing, Jackie. They're going to continue bleeding this Province dry. They'll make the bankers who brought us to the brink look like errant school-boys. We have no evidence that the bankers murdered people. But the Inner Circle and the bankers were born of the same bitch, greed.'

'Get out, Jock!' Carlisle's voice was a screech. 'And don't come back until I'm dead.'

CHAPTER FORTY-FOUR

Wilson breathed a huge sigh of relief as he replaced the handset of his phone. He reminded himself to be kinder to Jock McDevitt. The information had proved to be solid, and they now had the first break in the murders of Brian Malone and David Grant. They had their prime suspects, and they had a basis for the investigation. What they didn't have was any real physical evidence. His computer made a pinging noise, and he brought up his emails. It was Peter Davidson, and he opened it instantly. There were two photographs. One of a thin-faced individual who would not have looked out of place in one of the Halloween movies. The second photo showed a bald elfin face, and continuing the movie analogy, he might have been a hobbit in a Peter Jackson film. Wilson printed the two photos and strode into the squad room. He marched up to the whiteboard and pinned the two photos to it. He wrote on the top 'Prime Suspects' and wrote the name of each underneath their photos. Moira had returned and he was aware of her and Eric's eyes boring into his back. They both stood up and walked forward.

'McDevitt's information proved solid,' Wilson said. 'Baxter and Weir, two Glasgow villains, current whereabouts unknown. Both were in Belfast the night that Malone and Grant died.'

Moira and Eric moved forward and examined the two photos.

'Moira,' Wilson said. 'Now we've got something to look for on those CCTV pictures. We'll have surveillance photos of both when Peter arrives back this evening. Until then, we look for the faces. They must have been around Malone's and Grant's places sometime that evening, so find them. Eric, you stay with what we discussed earlier today. Harry should be back shortly, and we'll hold a briefing when he arrives.'

HARRY GRAHAM ATTENDED the whole of the O'Reilly autopsy, but learned absolutely nothing. The conclusion was that O'Reilly had taken a flier from a fifth-floor window in the Tannery Building and landed on a BMW 520. The principal injury was to the head but there were multiple broken bones. So what was new? He followed up with a visit to Watson Accountants where he learned that O'Reilly had never expressed a desire to jump out of a window. The word 'suicide' didn't even appear in his lexicon. The only thing he had learned at Watson was that accountants were indeed the most boring people on earth. It was dead end after dead end. He took out his phone as he left the Watson office and called the chief of the forensic team. 'Anything on the prelim?' he asked.

'We're still processing the evidence from the apartment.' The head of the team answered. 'There are plenty of finger-prints about the place, and we'll run them as soon as we finish collating them. We're processing the fingerprints from the forced door of the garage, but I wouldn't hold out too much hope. I'll let you have the full report as soon as we're finished.'

'Thanks, we're pretty desperate. Anything you can come up with will be gratefully accepted.' He put the phone back in his pocket. He stood for a moment in front of the office building. He could return to the station, or he could check out the forced door at the Tannery. He couldn't see any advantage in going back to the office since there was nothing he could do that would be useful, so he decided to make his way to Castle Street.

Moira went back to her screen. Someone managed to get her a 27-inch monitor, so that at least made watching the CCTV more bearable. She made a note to thank Wilson personally. Her ability to concentrate was something that she had prided herself on, but that ability had been sadly lacking in the past week or so. The news that Brendan would return to Boston was like the Garden of Gethsemane for her. She wished that this chalice would just go away, and that life would go back to the way it was before. But that wasn't going to happen. Life was a forward motion event that was more about change than stability. She looked at the screen and was afraid that she had missed something while her mind was wandering. She wondered whether she should go back to the beginning of the disk. She really was beginning to lose concentration. The business with Brendan was seriously affecting her ability to do her job. That wasn't Brendan's fault, it was hers. It was up to her to make the decision. She had spent far too long weighing up the pros and cons. Life would only get better when she decided to either go or stay. She looked at the screen. Traffic proceeded down the streets around Ashley Avenue. Going back over the CCTV she had already viewed wasn't an option. She would continue and hope to God that they would come up with something.

CHAPTER FORTY-FIVE

Richie Simpson had had better years. In fact, Simpson had been having a bad year ever since Jackie Carlisle had been obliged to give up running the Party due to ill health. Simpson had always considered himself the heir apparent. He had assumed that when Carlisle disappeared into retirement, he would rise chrysalis-like and be embraced as the new Messiah. The opposite was the reality. The Party had proven to be a vehicle for Carlisle and him alone. As soon as the great man had departed the political scene, so had most of the Party members. Simpson had found himself in charge of a political movement that was in terminal decline. He had devoted ten years to cleaning up Carlisle's shit and provided that very necessary quality for his boss, deniability. Carlisle was as dirty and corrupt as any politician in history, but as far as Joe Public was concerned, he was squeaky clean. When the Party died, so did Simpson's source of funding. Under Carlisle's umbrella, he was somebody. After Carlisle's departure, it amazed him the number of people who wouldn't return his phone calls. He was still getting a few pounds from his handlers in British Intelligence, but even that was declining since the information he could provide them was total rubbish. The Brits might be a lot of things, but they weren't dumb, and they weren't about to pay for something they could learn in any pub in Belfast. He had visited a Job Centre, but his lack of specific skills had been an impediment in even getting an interview. It appeared that nobody needed a fixer. Therefore, he was a little surprised when Carlisle called him. First, he didn't expect to hear from his mentor again, and second, he was surprised by the weakness in the voice. The strong booming voice from the slight body was Carlisle's trademark. The meeting was scheduled for his former boss's house in Hillsborough. Money was so tight that Simpson was reduced to the indignity of taking the bus and completing the journey on foot. He had never been to the Hillsborough house and was taken aback as he surveyed the residence from the driveway; at least £800,000 he thought to himself as he took in the red-bricked building and the surrounding gardens. Jackie had done well for himself. He knocked on the front door.

'Richie,' Agnes Carlisle beamed as she opened the door.

Simpson basked in the warmth of the smile that greeted him. 'Agnes, good to see you.'

She opened the door wide. 'You've lost weight, Richie,' she said. 'It doesn't suit you. You need to put a bit of flesh on your bones. He's waiting for you in the conservatory. We're having a procession of people to see him these days.'

Simpson walked through the living room. The wall and tables were covered with the photos that had once adorned the walls of the Party's office in Central Belfast. The Great Man had shaken hands with US presidents, British prime ministers and even with a couple of Irish pop stars who considered themselves the saviours of mankind. Simpson was currently living in a two-up two-down in the Shankill. The Hillsborough house was dreamland for him. He walked into the conservatory and looked around for Jackie. His eyes fell on the shrivelled creature wrapped in a blanket sitting on the sofa. Was this the political giant who he had worked with for more than ten years? The man who had bestridden the Shankill now looked like a monkey wrapped in a blanket.

'What's up, Jackie?' Simpson asked.

'Sit down Richie.' Carlisle could see his wife hovering in the background. 'It's alright, dear,' he said. 'I promise I won't let Richie tire me out.' He waited until his wife left the room. 'You should practise your facial expressions in front of a mirror. I know I look fucked, but I don't need to see it in your face.'

'Sorry, Jackie.' Simpson took the seat beside the sofa. 'It's been a while.'

'You're not exactly looking in the pink yourself.' Carlisle tried a smile.

'Times are hard.'

'Maybe good times are coming.'

Simpson sat back. Getting into bed with Carlisle was like playing with a tarantula. You might survive, but then again you could end up with a poisonous sting. 'So, I suppose you didn't bring me here to admire your house or to note down any famous last words.'

'At least we've established two things.' Carlisle winced in pain. He would need an injection of morphine soon, but the nurse from the hospice wasn't due for another two hours. 'I'm on my last legs, and you're broke.'

'Things didn't go so well after you left.'

Carlisle smiled despite the pain. Richie wasn't the dumbest man in the Shankill, but he'd never really got it. He'd thought it was all about manipulating the hard men. That was because that was his forte. He'd never grasped that it was about appealing to the punters. To survive and prosper, you needed to drag the punters with you. Richie, unfortunately for him, wasn't exactly punter-friendly. It had been no surprise to him that things had fallen apart after he'd retired. 'I may have something for you.'

Simpson was having the typical fight or flight feeling

except instead of fight it was submit. Carlisle had always been able to talk him into doing shit he wouldn't normally countenance. If he kept his arse on the chair, he would be roped into one of his former boss's plots. If he had half a brain, he'd leave now. But he smelled money and he needed it badly. 'Something that's going to drop me in the shit?'

Carlisle's face twisted in an amalgam of a grimace and a smile. He could have auditioned for the part of a gargoyle. 'If you're not interested, say so now. I really don't have the time to waste.'

'How much?'

'Let's say £15,000, not all for you unfortunately. If I tell you about this, there's no road back.'

Simpson thought about the money. He could certainly use it. But he wasn't going to get it for nothing. It was decision time. He was aware that if he agreed to go on, there really would be no way out. Carlisle didn't take prisoners. 'Okay, what do I have to do?'

'Sammy Rice is out of control. He needs to disappear.'

Simpson could feel immediate pressure in his bladder. 'Sammy fucking Rice disappear. You're joking, right.'

Carlisle shook his head. 'No joke.'

Simpson was sorry he hadn't trusted his initial reaction to run. 'Sammy is probably the most dangerous man in Belfast at the moment. He's surrounded by a mass of henchmen all of whom would decapitate anyone who came close to their leader. He is pretty much untouchable.'

'So was Lennie Murray. It needs to be done. The question is, are you the man to organise it?'

'What exactly do you have in mind?' Simpson's heart, which had almost exploded out of his chest, was beginning to return to its normal rhythm.

'Sammy has enemies on two levels. The drugs business is profitable but volatile. There's always some snotty-nosed bastard looking to take the place of whoever is the 'man' of the moment. Sammy has already become one of his own best clients, so it's only a matter of time before someone wants to move up. You know the people around him. Surely one of them wouldn't mind being the boss.'

'And the second level?'

'Sammy and his father were involved in some bad things during the 'Troubles'. There are more than a couple of Fenians who wouldn't mind seeing Sammy paraded down the Shankill in a box. You have contacts there. Use them.'

Simpson felt beads of sweat running down his neck. Maybe he was in an episode of *Mission Impossible*. He'd already been given his mission and his reward for accomplishing it. The only element missing was the plan, and it was dawning on him that he was going to have to come up with something. 'How much time do I have?'

'The sooner the better.' Carlisle was stunned for a second. He still had the power of life or death over people. He remembered sitting in the doctor's office and hearing his own life sentence. He had always considered himself to be a strong individual, but when he heard the fateful word 'terminal' he'd wanted to cry. He loved life and the thought of leaving it filled him with sadness and fear in equal measure. Now it was likely that Sammy would precede him to the pearly gates. Maybe he was doing him a favour. At least Sammy wouldn't have to spend months thinking about dying, and putting up with the pain. There would be no time to settle his affairs. Sammy had lived by the sword, and it was fitting that he should die by the sword. What did that make of his death? His body was slowly killing itself. What did that say about him?

'I'll need money up front,' Simpson said.

Carlisle fished around at the base of the wicker sofa and produced an envelope. He handed it to Simpson. 'That's £5,000 to kick it off. The rest when the job is done.'

Simpson took the envelope, opened it and looked inside. 'I'll let you know when I have it organised.'

'Don't bother. I don't need to know the details. I'll read about it in the *Chronicle*.' Carlisle leaned back and closed his eyes. 'It's been good to see you again, Richie.'

Simpson could see that their meeting was over. He tried to think of some clever parting remark but repartee wasn't his strong suit. He had known Carlisle for a long time, but he realised that they had never really been friends. He was simply his dirty tricks man. 'I'll drop by when it's done.'

'Don't bother. The next place we'll meet is not in this world.'

Simpson looked at the frail figure before him. Carlisle was almost at death's door, but he was still capable of ordering a murder.

Simpson stood and proffered his hand.

Carlisle looked at the hand as though deciding whether to take it or not. He extended a bony hand and gave Simpson a quick handshake.

Simpson turned and walked towards the door. He was thinking that agreeing to kill Sammy Rice could get a person killed. It which case, maybe it would be him that would be standing beside Saint Peter to greet Carlisle.

CHAPTER FORTY-SIX

H arry Graham stood in front of the Tannery Building. There were two entrances, one for the apartment building and one for the garage. He walked slowly around the building. If someone had gained access, there were three possibilities. They could have entered by the front door of the apartment section of the building, but that would have meant buzzing someone in an apartment to open the door. There was a camera system on the door that allowed residents to view their guests before opening the main door. Second, they could have entered from the garage but that would have been seen on the garage CCTV. Third, they could have gained access from the taxi station. The door-to-door enquiry had established that no resident had permitted an entry that evening. The garage CCTV had been checked and showed no unauthorised entries. The process of elimination indicated that the taxi station was the most probable source of entry. He made his way to the office of the taxi station holding out his warrant card as he entered the office. 'Detective Constable Graham,' he said. 'Who's in charge?'

A short fat man with a head of woolly black hair looked up

from the papers on his desk. Every inch of his body that was exposed, excluding half his face, was covered in tattoos. 'Just what we need for a perfect day, a visit from the Peelers,' he said smiling through a mouth full of decaying teeth. 'If it's about the jumper, we don't know anyone living in the building. They don't mix with our sort.'

Graham saw the second man in the office take a quick glance at him before returning to his work.

'Our forensic people found a forced door from the garage to the apartment. Maybe someone got into the apartment building that way. But there's nothing on the garage CCTV. If that's the case, could they have gained access to the garage via the taxi station?'

'They could have but they didn't,' Woolly Head answered.

'How can you be so sure?' Graham asked.

Woolly Head sighed and pointed at a clapped-out computer. 'Look around, man, lots of valuable stuff around here. We'd be out on our ear if we didn't lock up securely every evening. If someone came through here, they'd have to break in. Check it out. No break-in.'

Graham noticed a furtive look from the second man. 'So maybe they had a key.'

'No way,' Woolly Head answered. 'You finished with the questions?'

Graham smiled. 'For now. But I think I may be back, so don't go anywhere. What are your names?'

'Mickey Mouse,' Woolly Head said.

'Now you're really on my radar,' Graham said. 'I think I might be able to find you on the police computer so maybe you shouldn't make me try.'

Woolly Head thought for a moment. 'Mikey Dolan.'

'And?' Graham turned to the other man in the office who had kept his head down.

'Billy Boyle,' he said without looking up.

Graham wrote the names into his notebook. He had just

finished when it dawned on him that Sammy Rice had a lieutenant named Boyle. He put his notebook away and removed
two business cards from his pocket. He placed the cards on the
desk. 'You think of anything give me a call.'

Dolan picked up the cards. 'Definitely,' he said as he tore
the cards in two and dumped them in the wastepaper basket.

Graham turned back to Dolan. 'I'm pretty sure we're going
to meet again.' He turned and walked through the door. He
was going to make a case of Mikey Dolan. And he was going to
check up on Boyle. If it turned out he was connected to Rice's
lieutenant, it might be worth hauling him in.

MOIRA'S EYES HURT. She opened her bag and removed the
mirror she used to put on her make-up. Her eyes were red.
She had spent the afternoon looking at CCTV from traffic
cameras in the streets around Ashley Avenue. She picked up a
cup of cold coffee and drank it. It tasted terrible. She put
down the cup and put her hand on top of the mouse. She
moved the film forward. She stared as the black cab came into
view. Then she stopped the film. There were two men in the
rear of the cab. She used the mouse to close in on the cab. The
driver was so big that he almost blocked the two figures behind
him. She moved the film forward hoping to get a better view
of the rear of the cab. They were heading straight for the
camera which meant the driver was constantly blocking a
clear view of the passengers. She stopped the film and walked
to the whiteboard. She concentrated on the faces of Baxter
and Weir. She returned to her seat and increased the focus on
the passengers. One was tall and one was short but only a fraction of each face was visible. She was suddenly excited. It
could easily be Baxter and Weir. She printed off the best
picture. Unfortunately it was grainy and not very clear. Then
she focussed on the driver and printed his picture. She
changed the focus to the cab's registration number and printed

it off. She took the three pictures and walked to Wilson's office.

'I think I may have something,' she said as she entered the office.

Wilson looked up from the papers on his desk. 'Let's see it.'

'I've been reviewing the CCTV footage from the streets around Ashley Avenue. There's no camera on that street, so I've concentrated on what we've got. Early in the evening, we have a black taxi with two passengers. It's impossible to get a good shot of the passengers. The driver is a giant who takes up most of the front of the cab, so I don't have a real good picture of the occupants.' She tossed a picture of the driver onto the desk in front of Wilson. 'This is the best picture of the occupants that I can come up with.' She put the second picture on the desk. 'You can't really see them, only part of their faces. But I'd bet a month's pay that those two are Baxter and Weir.' She dropped the final picture on the desk. 'That's the registration of the cab.'

'Okay.' Wilson was looking at the three pictures. 'We need to track that taxi for the whole of that evening. Traffic has a mechanism for picking out the registration number from the CCTV footage.' He shouted for Taylor through the open door.

'Boss.' Taylor stood in the doorway.

Wilson passed the picture of the driver to Moira who handed it on to Taylor. 'Who is he?'

Taylor smiled. 'Big George Carroll, they should design a special car just for this guy. He works for Sammy Rice.'

'Now that's interesting,' Wilson said. 'But we mustn't jump to conclusions. If Big George works as a taxi driver, he might very well have picked up two passengers in the course of his job.' He passed the pictures to Moira. 'Get this stuff up on the board. Eric, what do we know about Mister Carroll?'

Taylor passed the picture to Moira. 'He's been associated with Sammy Rice since he was a kid. He's not exactly the sharpest knife in the drawer but what he lacks in brain, he makes up for in brawn. I'll have to check the computer but as far as I can remember we've never had Big George inside but there have been plenty of rumours linking him to demanding money with menace. And it's generally money that was owed to Sammy Rice. Those menaced have a habit of withdrawing their complaint before it gets too far.'

'So we have no problem making Carroll a person of interest,' Wilson said. 'However, we should definitely speak to him. Find out where we can locate him.'

'Locating him may not be the problem, Boss,' Taylor said. 'Getting some sense out of the headful of fluff he carries around on his shoulders might be a little more difficult. People who have interviewed Big George say that it gives a whole new meaning to the phrase "no comment".'

'Moira, Traffic, track that cab,' Wilson said. 'Eric, keep working on the Infrastructure Agency but find out where we can find Mister Carroll.'

Moira and Taylor left the office.

Wilson watched them as they set about their tasks. They were both good coppers. There was hardly a murder squad in the world that could handle three apparently separate murders, but the Belfast murder team was certainly trying. It was strange how one piece of information inevitably led to another. That was what Wilson's theory of momentum was about. That was why forensic evidence was so important and the lack of it a severe impediment. Forensic opened doors, pointed at suspects, created that chink leading to the next link in the chain. He was about to get back to his beloved paperwork when he felt the vibration of his phone in his pocket. He looked at the caller ID but didn't recognise the number. He pressed the green button.

'Good afternoon.' The voice was female and the accent upper-crust Oxford. 'Detective Superintendent Wilson?'

'Speaking,' Wilson said.

'Please hold. I have Laurence Gold for you.'

Wilson cursed himself for taking the call.

'Detective Superintendent,' the voice was the deep bari-tone that Wilson had heard in court on several occasions, 'thank you for taking the call. I was wondering whether we could arrange a meeting.'

'You may have noticed from the newspapers that I'm currently investigating the death of David Grant and then there's the business in Castle Street last night.'

'I fully understand.' Gold's voice dripped like honey. 'However, we really must talk. The Cummerford case is due for hearing within six weeks, and I am reliably informed that the date has already been set. There are still elements of the case that require clarification.'

'What elements?'

'I have an aversion to discussing briefs over the phone. I have a slot available at ten a.m. tomorrow morning. Would that be convenient?'

'I can't say. Events tend to move fast and in all sorts of directions on a murder investigation.'

'I'll expect you at ten. If it's not possible for you to make it, I'm sure you'll let my office know. By the way, how is the Chinese Wall between you and my learned colleague holding up?'

'We don't talk about the case at home if that's what you mean,' Wilson said sharply. He could have added that lately they weren't talking about anything at all.

'I wouldn't expect anything less from professionals like you and Kate. See you tomorrow morning at ten.' The phone went dead.

Wilson put down the handset. What element could Gold be interested in? It couldn't have anything to do with him and Kate living together. His team had already spent considerable resources in helping the prosecution with its case. He was hoping that Cummerford would plead guilty and save them the bother of the trial. They had her bang to rights. There was no doubt that she had murdered the three women she blamed for killing her mother. Now she wanted to waste more of his scarce resources through a lengthy trial. He looked at his watch. It was almost six o'clock and time to review that day's progress with the team.

CHAPTER FORTY-SEVEN

The whiteboard reflected the momentum that was building up in the case. Since he was more confident of the content of the investigation, Wilson had left the squad room door unlocked. As he was leaving his office to start the briefing, Chief Superintendent Spence walked into the room. Wilson wasn't in time to catch Spence before the Chief Super made it to the whiteboard. He stood behind him while Spence examined the information the team had amassed on the murders of Malone, Grant and now O'Reilly. Neither man spoke.

Spence turned and looked at Wilson. 'Your office, now.' He strode towards the office without waiting for a reply.

Wilson turned and looked at Moira. She was shaking her head.

Spence settled himself in the visitor's chair and waited for Wilson to sit behind his desk. 'Explain.'

'Reid thinks there have been three murders, Brian Malone, David Grant and Mark O'Reilly. We've been concentrating on Grant for obvious reasons but looking into Malone on the side.'

'Who the hell is Brian Malone?'

Wilson explained.

'Why didn't I know about this underground investigation? Is this my station or yours?'

'I wanted to give you deniability if things screwed up. Considering Jennings' reaction to the Grant investigation, I thought that we could look quietly into Malone's death, and if it was established that it was murder, I could make the investigation official.'

'Jennings wants a briefing this evening. I'll be lucky to be in this job tomorrow morning if I tell him that we've been running a covert investigation.'

'Tell him that we've just found a connection between the deaths of Malone and Grant. And we are investigating that connection.'

Spence started massaging his forehead. 'What are we talking about here, Ian?'

'Three people have been murdered. It looks like professional hit men from Glasgow, whose names are known to us, were employed to kill Grant and Malone. The killers have disappeared, but they'll surface eventually. Someone local hired them. We have no idea why Malone or Grant had to die, but my guess is that they discovered something that should have remained hidden. We have no idea how O'Reilly fits into the picture.'

'This is excellent police work, Ian. But you should have come to me earlier.'

'Reid was showing two corpses of men, who looked like they died apparently natural deaths, to be murders. I didn't want to make her and me seem like fools without checking it out.'

Spence looked into the squad room. 'Let's go outside, your troops are beginning to wonder what's happening.' He stood up and led the way. 'I think I should stay for the briefing.'

Wilson moved to the whiteboard, now covered with new information. 'Let's start with Malone.' He pointed at the extreme left-hand side of the whiteboard. 'Possible murder suspects Baxter and Weir, Glasgow killers, now missing but in Belfast on the night of the murder. Moira has turned up a CCTV image of a black taxi of which they could be the occupants. The driver is Big George Carroll, foot soldier for Sammy Rice. We've asked Traffic to track the taxi from early evening until midnight. The priority for tomorrow is to pick up Big George and bring him in for questioning. He could be the weak link in the chain.' He pointed at the Grant segment of the whiteboard. 'Depending on what we get from Traffic we might be able to confirm Baxter and Weir as suspects in the Grant murder. If they are, and if Big George drove them, breaking him could be the key.' He pointed at the segment of the board dedicated to Mark O'Reilly. 'Harry, can you fill us in?'

Graham cleared his throat. 'I drew a blank at Watson's. O'Reilly was a bit of a brainiac as far as accountancy was concerned. Despite that, he was friendly and outgoing. No one thought it could have been a suicide. I called his doctor, and he confirmed that O'Reilly was as healthy as a horse and not on any kind of medication. He said he would have been astonished if O'Reilly jumped. Watson's wouldn't let me see what he was working on but claimed that there was nothing that might have led to him being tossed out of a window. He seemed to have been both respected and liked. I checked out the Tannery. The door from the garage to the apartment section took a bit of forcing. The big question is how any intruder might have accessed the garage. I questioned the two boys on duty, a Mikey Dolan and Billy Boyle. I need to check whether the Boyle lad is some relation of Owen Boyle, the man who moved up when Ivan McIlroy was murd...' His voice trailed off.

'So,' Wilson interjected. 'We have a direct connection between the Malone and Grant murders, the suspects are the same and Big George could have been the driver. But Big

George works for Sammy Rice, and Billy Boyle could be a connection there.'

'We might be pushing it there, Boss,' Moira said. 'You know that story that everybody on the planet has six degrees of separation from Kevin Bacon.'

'Who's Kevin Bacon?' Spence asked.

'An actor,' Graham answered quickly.

'The connection may be tenuous, but we need to follow it up,' Wilson said. 'What we don't have is a motive and that I don't like.'

'We know Sammy,' Eric Taylor said. 'And from what I hear on the street he's become a bit unhinged since Lizzie's murder. They say he's spaced out most of the time on drugs and booze. Maybe the new Sammy is just the old Sammy on speed. Anyone who gets in the way has to go.'

'I wish life was so simple,' Wilson said. 'It's like one of those conundrums, what connects a bureaucrat, a rising politician and an accountant. That's what we have to find out and that's what we need to discuss with Mr Carroll. Do we have an address on him, Eric?'

'Several, Boss. You want me to organise to pick him up tomorrow?'

Wilson nodded. 'The man is apparently a human gorilla so take two or three uniforms along. It's been a good day. Peter will be back later this evening we'll meet tomorrow morning to distribute the work.'

'Outstanding work,' Spence said. 'I'll pass the message along to the DCC.'

Wilson watched Spence walk slowly out of the squad room. He seemed to have the weight of the world on his shoulders.

CHAPTER FORTY-EIGHT

'Are you a loyal Ulsterman?'

Wilson was trying to watch the news on the television. It was a report on the disappearance of the Malaysian Airways 777. He was intrigued by mysteries that could not be explained. He heard, in the background the remark made by Helen, and guessed it was addressed to him.

'Are you a loyal Ulsterman?' The question had been raised by an octave as though the questioner thought that the respondent was not only dumb but also deaf.

Wilson looked away from the television and at Helen McCann, who was sitting in one of the lazy boys cradling a gin and tonic. As was now usual, Kate was working late at her office. The situation in the apartment was becoming more strained by the day. He had been thinking about Helen's remark about Kate and him taking a break. He wondered whether the idea was coming from Kate or her mother. Helen would normally have already left for France but was hanging on for some reason.

'How many of those have you had?' he asked.

She held up her glass. 'This is my second. Answer the question.'

He thought for a moment. 'I don't like words like Loyalist or Republican. The sectarian division is bad enough, but words like Loyalist and Republican can lead to fanatics shooting or bombing their neighbours. Rugby was my life but some fool who thought that he could accomplish his political aims with a bomb took it away from me. I ended up losing a sporting career, and I was on the periphery of the blast. Those at the centre lost a hell of a lot more.'

Helen's face hardened. 'Ulster is under threat. A proportion of our fellow Ulstermen would like to join us to the papist South. That possibility obviously doesn't fill you with the same sense of dread as it does me.'

He looked at her. He realised that he knew nothing about her aside from the fact that she was Kate's mother; she was enormously wealthy and lived in the south of France. She had researched him to the extent that she had discovered the whereabouts of his mother. She probably knew the exact amount in his bank account. 'Expressions like Loyal Ulsterman led some of my colleagues to forget their commitment to justice in this Province. I'm not proud of the behaviour of some policemen in colluding in murder during the "Troubles".'

She emptied her glass, stood and walked to the bar in the corner of the living room. 'So you're not a Loyal Ulsterman, interesting.' She made a refill and held up a bottle of Jameson to Wilson.

He shook his head. In general, he steered clear of two subjects, politics and religion. He had been raised a Methodist but only went to church for weddings and funerals. And there had been too many funerals. He had seen a little too much depravity to believe in the all-seeing, all-good entity that had been presented to him in Sunday school. If God knew of the evil acts that were carried out in his name, he would commit celestial seppuku. Wilson's life was dedicated to bringing wrongdoers to justice. He didn't dispense justice. That was the job of the legal system. He simply found the miscreants. Unlike the cop shows on TV, he didn't get himself involved in shoot-'em-ups. He couldn't say that he had never fired his gun but he had certainly never killed another human being, and he had no desire to do so. He was now in possession of another piece of the puzzle that was Helen McCann. She was obviously a very loyal Ulsterwoman. He found it strange that someone who was so committed to the Province should choose to live in the sunshine of southern France instead of the rain and wind of Ulster. He didn't blame her; he just didn't understand her. He looked across as she retook her seat. She was glowering at him.

'Your father was a loyal Ulsterman,' she said slurring slightly.

'What do you know about my father?' Wilson said. Talk about his father was generally taboo for him.

'I know that he was loyal.' A smile passed over her lips. 'And many other things besides.'

'What other things?'

'Maybe another time.' The smile flickered again.

Wilson leaned forward. 'I said what other things?'

'You father displayed his loyalty. He was a fine Ulsterman.'

Wilson relaxed at the compliment. 'You speak like you met him.'

'No, but people mentioned him to me.'

Wilson couldn't see where this conversation was leading. He could see that Helen's face was flushed, and she was looking drowsy. It was time for him to make a strategic withdrawal from a conversation he really didn't want to have. It was time to concentrate on the TV documentary again.

CHAPTER FORTY-NINE

I t was pitch black outside, but the lights were burning in the PSNI Headquarters. Chief Superintendent Spence was sitting in the office of DCC Royson Jennings. He had just spent the last ten minutes bringing the DCC up to speed on the investigations being undertaken by Wilson and his team. He had expected an explosion but the look on the face of the man in front of him did not presage an explosion. Spence was more than a little confused. He had a long experience with Jennings and was well aware of the enmity the DCC bore Wilson. He had not sugared the pill. Wilson had launched an unofficial and unapproved investigation into the death of Brian Malone. He fully expected Jennings to demand some form of reprimand, at the very least a note on Wilson's file. Instead, Spence found himself sitting in front of the proverbial wooden Indian. Considering that Jennings normally had the pallor of a corpse, it was difficult to assess whether the DCC was so upset that he had forced himself into a catatonic state in order to protect his heart. Spence finished the briefing and sat stoically awaiting his punishment. The rain that had threatened all day had started and beat a tattoo on the windowpane. It was the kind of weather he liked to be at home before the fire cradling a whiskey. He was caught between two stools when he thought about his impending retirement. He had spent his life serving the community as a police officer. He was aware of the stress he, his wife and his family had suffered because of the life he had chosen. His retirement day would, on one hand, provide him and his family with the blessed relief that they deserved. However, he was mindful that giving up the PSNI would create an enormous hole in his life. He was now ready to retire, but he had no desire to be pushed.

Jennings cleared his throat as though about to speak but remained silent. He was doing his praying mantis imperson-ation – holding the palms of his hands together in front of his face, not out of habit but trying to hide whatever expression might have been on his countenance. He had no idea what that expression was but he wanted to hide it from Spence that inside he was shocked to his core. Not only was his dream of becoming Chief Constable disappearing down a bottomless black hole, if it ever came out that he had any part in the conspiracy to clean up the mess at the Infrastructure Agency, he might do some jail time. It was never the crime that was the problem, it was always the cover-up. Wilson was inching himself towards Rice. This Big George Carroll would be another nail in Rice's coffin, while Rice could be a nail in his coffin. He knew he should be indignant at Wilson's behaviour, but that was secondary to the fear he was feeling about his own situation. The silence in the room was deafening and was accentuated by the noise of the rain beating on the window. Jennings felt himself in some sort of suspended animation. He knew he should speak, but his mind was totally consumed by his predicament. He needed to get rid of Spence so that he could think in peace. 'Well, Chief Superintendent,' he forced the words out, 'it appears that you have the situation under control. I assume Wilson will launch a warrant for the arrest of Baxter and Weir, although it appears we have no direct evidence against them. If they sing dumb, we have nothing, and if they're professionals, that's exactly what they'll do. The key appears to be this Carroll person.'

Spence nodded. He was wondering whether the DCC was feeling well. The expected tongue-lashing was conspicuous by its absence. 'Wilson intends to pick him up tomorrow. I should be in a position to brief you tomorrow afternoon or evening on progress.'

'Not long left now.' Jennings did his best to put a smile on his face.

Spence shuddered at the look on Jennings' face. It was a rictus that would have done credit to Edvard Munch. Spence was beginning to speculate on the mental state of his superior. 'Yes, just a couple of short months and I'll be tending roses in Holywood.'

'You'll be sadly missed,' Jennings said rictus still in place.

Spence was no longer speculating on Jennings' mental state but had concluded that he had been replaced by an alien. 'I'm sure you're busy, Sir,' he said standing.

Jennings shuffled papers on his desk 'Yes, lots to do. Good evening, Chief Superintendent.'

Spence turned and left the office. The whiskey that he had been thinking about earlier had suddenly turned into a very large one.

DCC JENNINGS STAYED in his seat for a few minutes after Spence left his office. The fact that he hadn't succeeded in stopping the investigation into Grant's death had dealt his immediate chances of becoming Chief Constable a fatal blow. But as the impact of the disappointment had sunk in, he had realised that there was plenty of time to recoup his position. Carlisle and Lattimer were yesterday's men. There was always some smart new blood waiting in the wings when the old elephants finally collapsed. He had time to look around for the comers and attach himself to them. He stood up and walked to the window. He looked out into the darkness. The sky was full of black clouds, and he heard the rumble of thunder coming from the west. Streaks of rain ran down the window. He should go home, but that was out of the question. There was nothing at home for him. He was one of those not so rare creatures who had dedicated his life to his job. There was no wife and no family. He liked to think that his solitary existence had been his choice. He hadn't really tried to find a life partner and despite rumours to the contrary among his colleagues, he was not a homosexual. He simply had no interest in sharing his life with another human being. That wasn't completely true. He had no interest in sharing his life with any other creature, human or animal. He was now about to face the greatest threat in his life as a police officer. He was simply another domino that would fall if Wilson could progress along the line from Carroll to Rice to Carlisle and Lattimer and on to the members of the Inner Circle. If Wilson got as far as Carlisle, there would be no doubt that he would be sacrificed. That wouldn't just mean that his ambition to be Chief Constable would be in tatters. The answer to the problem was to break the chain. No Carroll meant no Rice. No Rice meant no Carlisle. No Carlisle meant he was safe. The solution to the problem was therefore no Carroll. He saw a flash of lightning light up the sky directly over the city. He took it as a portent. He returned to his desk and picked up his phone.

Sammy Rice was sitting in the back room of the Brown Bear when his mobile rang. He had been dealing with his various businesses and drinking since early afternoon, and his humour reflected his tiredness. Despite his initial reaction to tell the caller to piss off, he listened intently without speaking. 'I'll handle it,' he said, resisting the temptation to throw the mobile against the wall. He looked across the room at where Big George Carroll was sitting. As usual, Carroll was staring directly in front of him. Rice had been at school with Big George, and the big man had been one of his crew since he'd left school. There was no way out. 'George, find Owen and tell him I want him. Then stay outside.' Rice took out a small packet of cocaine and looked at it. He wanted to snort a few lines, but he needed Owen to see that he was deadly serious. He would have preferred to be planning to take Wilson out. The man was a thorn in his side since the first day they'd met, and he would never forget the embarrassment of the hand-shake in Kate McCann's office. Nobody disrespected Sammy Rice and got away with it. He put the sachet back in his pocket. It was supposed to be so smooth. That was why they had hired the 'so called' professionals. Wilson had Baxter and Weir's names and sooner or later, he'd pick them up. There was no physical evidence at the crime scenes, so they couldn't be connected to the murders. As long as they kept their mouths shut, everyone would be away scot-free. He was still running over possibilities when the door opened, and Owen Boyle entered. 'Drink?' Rice asked when Boyle took the seat in front of him.

'Why not.' Boyle was pleased that his chief didn't look hopped up.

'Bushmills?'

Boyle nodded.

Rice poured him a large glass. 'Cheers,' he said clinking his glass to Boyle's. 'Death to the Fenians.'

'Aye. Death to the Fenians.'

'Owen, I need you to do something for me.'

'That's what I'm here for.'

'You and Big George are going to take a trip to the Mourne Mountains tomorrow.'

Boyle tossed off half the glass. 'Okay.'

'I have something I need buried.'

CHAPTER FIFTY

Wilson was in a new regime. He was always a light sleeper. It was a feature that went with the job but sleeping alone was making him wake up early. So he resumed his morning run. He needed it both physically and mentally. He had seen too many athletes who had been superb specimens while they competed turn into blimps as soon as they stopped full-time training. He would be the first to admit that he wasn't the same man he had been at twenty-one. He had added a few pounds here and there, but his suit size had only increased by one size. He could attribute that to the work the doctors had done to get him back to full fitness after the IRA had tried to blow his arse off. The morning run had been part of an exercise regime that had been inflicted on him to bring him back to some level of fitness. Now it was something that he needed to do to ensure that his endorphins got him ready for the day ahead. There had been a heavy rain overnight. It was the kind of rain that the engineers hadn't taken into account when they had designed the drainage along the embankment of the River Lagan, which had become his preferred route. He didn't bother to avoid the large puddles that dotted the concrete pathway, but went straight through them drenching both his feet, and the ends of his training bottoms. The aftermath of the rain intensified the ozone smell of the sea rising from the river. He sucked in large volumes of air as he pushed himself to complete the sprint sections of the run. He hadn't been born beside the sea but after twenty years of living in Belfast, he felt that he would never be able to live away from the ocean. He eased the pace into his long-distance rhythm. This was when his mind was at its freshest. In general, he used this freshness to review cases but since his relationship with Kate had hit the skids, possible remedial actions occupied at least half of his thinking time. Today Wilson had to make an effort to push Kate into the rear of his conscience. He needed to use his mental capacity to consider the possible reason why three young men had been murdered. For some reason, his mind segued into the conversation he'd had with Kate's mother the previous evening. He didn't have a picture of her as a fanatical Ulsterwoman. She wouldn't exactly fit in with the women waving their Union Jacks on the Shankill on the twelfth of July. He wondered why his mind had strayed to Helen; there was no reason why it should go there. He needed to find the motive for the murders. He knew that he wouldn't get the answer from Baxter and Weir. If they proved to be the murderers of Malone and Grant, their motivation would be simple enough – money. The answer might not even come from Big George Carroll. Baxter, Weir and Carroll were the little men. They were expendable. He would have to go well beyond them to find the real motivation for the murders. He had almost reached the Belfast Waterfront and the round red-bricked building that was the Opera House. This was the point at which he turned for home. As he approached the Waterfront, he saw a figure standing under one of the lamps. The daylight had not yet hit Belfast and the yellow light from the lamp lit the figure up. Wilson tensed at once. More than one policeman had met his end in this kind of situation. He looked around and saw that he was alone. He kept up the pace of his run and as he approached, he realised there was something familiar about the man. He kept his gaze down while pounding the grey and blue concrete slabs that led to the Waterfront. The next time he looked up, he saw why the figure seemed familiar. Jock McDevitt was leaning back against the lamppost holding a cardboard tray on which two cups of coffee stood. Wilson continued at the same pace until he came level with McDevitt.

'Coffee?' McDevitt asked.

'No thanks.' Wilson stopped but continued to run on the spot. He didn't want to break his rhythm. He pointed at the coffee. 'I take that when I'm done, and I'm only halfway.'

McDevitt pulled the cap off one of the coffees and took a sip. 'I think they use special water to make this stuff. I've never been able to boil normal water to the temperature that McDonald's achieve with ease.'

'You didn't come here to offer me a coffee,' Wilson said, his voice bouncing up and down as he jogged on the spot.

'Maybe if you stopped hopping, we could have a civilised conversation.' McDevitt sipped at his coffee. 'I'm not usually up at this time of the morning so if I think it's important maybe you should too.'

Wilson stopped running on the spot and put his hand out for the coffee. His run was over. 'Okay, but you're going to have to walk back with me.'

McDevitt handed him the coffee and then fell into step beside him. 'A little bird tells me that my information from Glasgow panned out.'

'I hope that little bird wasn't DC Davidson.' Wilson pulled the lid off the coffee and sipped. The hot coffee burned his lips.

McDevitt smiled and shook his head. 'I have other sources. You have the names?'

'Aye, but they've scarpered. They could be in Timbuktu by now.' It was clear to Wilson that McDevitt also had the names.

He might be tempted to publish them but given the principle that people are innocent until proven guilty, the lawyers at the *Chronicle* would put a stop to that.

'You'll catch up with them eventually,' McDevitt said. 'But they were only the hired help. They're the monkeys. You need to find the organ grinder.'

A group of runners passed them, heading towards the Waterfront. Wilson envied them. He wished he'd been allowed to finish his run. 'We're aware of that. I suppose you're going to tell me that you know who the organ grinder is, and squeeze some quid pro quo out of me.'

'This morning's *Chronicle* has a story about Brian Malone being a murder victim,' McDevitt said.

Wilson thought about Malone's parents. As soon as that news broke, there would be the secondary shock that their son's death wasn't natural but had been contrived. 'I would have liked to have the opportunity to warn the parents.'

'Sorry 'bout that. My editor is rather anxious to keep up the pressure on this story. He's the one who'll decide how long the story will run.'

'Meaning?' Wilson's coffee had reached a temperature whereby it was drinkable.

'Meaning that there are forces in this Province who might be happier if the whole Malone and Grant issue would go away.'

'Not another bloody conspiracy theory, that's the difference between coppers and journalists. You people get to speculate up there in the air somewhere. We concentrate on evidence. Speculation doesn't put criminals behind bars, evidence does.' He looked out over the river and saw two double-sculls rowing their way against the tide. The young men at the oars looked fit and strong. He remembered himself like that.

McDevitt followed his gaze. 'Spring in the air,' he said and laughed at the double meaning. They were less than halfway back to the apartment and McDevitt was blowing hard. 'Can we stop for a minute? I need a rest.'

They stopped and leaned over the wall that separated them from the flowing river.

'What do you know about the Circle and in particular the Inner Circle?' McDevitt asked.

Wilson shook his head. 'Never heard of it.'

'Then I need to tell you a story,' McDevitt said and repeated almost word for word the tale he had told Carlisle.

Wilson listened while he watched the river. The scullers had turned around and were now rowing with the tide. Throughout his career, he'd heard a great variety of fanciful stories. He had been forced to conclude that everyone he had met had been deluded in some way. There was always a story that would explain why they did what they did. They were never really bad people. They were ordinary people who have done unimaginable things. By any standard, many of them had been monsters who had deluded themselves and now considered themselves saints.

McDevitt finished his story.

Wilson turned away from the river and sighed. 'And you're going to publish this?'

McDevitt laughed. 'That's one story that would be spiked at source.'

'But you want me to believe it.'

'It might help you with your case.'

'And Carlisle is involved?'

'He's not the organ grinder if that's what you're thinking.' McDevitt put up his hands. 'Don't ask me who is because I don't have a clue.'

'Now you're dragging me away from the realm of evidence and forcing me to speculate just like you.'

'Maybe you'll need to speculate to get to the answer.'

'I've got to get home,' Wilson said preparing to move.

'Remember me when you break the case,' McDevitt. 'Old Jock gets the scoop.'

'Aye, when we break the case.' Wilson tried to run but found that his body had lost its rhythm. He opted for a fast walk instead.

CHAPTER FIFTY-ONE

W ilson turned on the shower and increased the temperature of the water until it was almost scalding his skin. He hadn't worked up a sweat during his run/walk, but he was still wondering why McDevitt had interrupted him with his conspiracy theory. He was glad that he was a policeman and not a journalist. Ninety per cent of the so-called newspapers had already given up the pretence that they were about communicating 'news'. They pandered to what the customers wanted, and that was an article on the lives and loves of celebrities. The average citizen, who would be hard put to find Crimea on a map of the world, was totally enmeshed in the lives of the Kardashians and some crowd of idiots from Essex or Geordieland. That meant poor sods like McDevitt had to dream up conspiracies that might titillate both his editor and the general public. The financial crash of 2007 had exposed the excesses of the Masters of the World, as the bankers styled themselves. The man in the street was now aware of the astronomic bonuses and the extravagant lifestyles of those who ruled their financial futures. The existence of a tight-knit group at the top of Ulster's tree who wielded incredible financial power and, in effect, directed much of life in the Province would be sheer box office for McDevitt and the *Chronicle*. He appreciated that it was McDevitt's information that led to the identification of Baxter and Weir but the existence of an Inner Circle that might be behind the murders was a step too far into McDevitt's imagination. He jetted ahead to what his day was going to look like. He wasn't happy about the meeting with Gold. There was something in that silken voice that alerted him. If there was a flaw in the Prosecution case and he was to blame, there would be hell to pay. There was no question of Cummerford walking. They amassed a mountain of evidence linking her to the murders of three women. But Gold's time was money, and he hadn't invited Wilson to his office just to pass the time of day. He exited from the shower and towelled himself off before donning a bathrobe and making his way to the kitchen. The smell of freshly brewing coffee reached his nostrils before he got there. He was surprised to find both Kate and Helen fully dressed and facing him.

'Ian, I want to talk to you,' Kate said as soon as he entered the kitchen. 'Perhaps we should sit down.'

Wilson could see sadness in Kate's face and smugness on her mother's. He could already tell what was coming, and he felt an instant pain in the pit of his stomach. He pulled over a stool and sat down. 'We don't have to do this here and we don't have to do it now. We need to talk things out between ourselves.'

'We can't go on like this,' Kate said tears welling up in her eyes. 'The stress is making me a physical and mental mess. We shouldn't be living under the same roof at the moment. I found myself trying to stay on in the office last night to avoid coming home. That's not the way I want to feel.'

'We shouldn't be forced into decisions. There are people that we can talk to, experts in this area.'

'Maybe later.' A tear crept out of the corner of her eye.

Wilson started to rise but she held up her hand, and he sat back down. 'So there's to be no discussion.'

'It's only to give us a break,' Kate said, the initial tear was joined by others. 'I really don't want to do this, but we can't go on like this.'

Wilson looked at Helen and thought he could see satisfaction in her face. Maybe it hadn't been such a good idea to have her living with them when she was in Belfast. But it was always Kate's decision since it was Kate's apartment. 'So, I move out.' And leave the field to Helen, he thought.

'Temporarily,' Kate said. 'Until I get some time to think things out. Maybe then you and I can go see someone.'

Not if your mother has anything to do with it. The timing was rotten for them both. Kate needed to concentrate on the upcoming cases, and he needed to focus on finding the person behind the deaths of three men. Splitting from Kate, even temporarily, was not going to help. It would simply be a distraction. However, he could see that the die was cast. 'I'll pack my things,' he said simply.

'I'm sorry, Ian,' she said. 'I've agonised over this decision, and Helen has been a great sounding board.'

I'll bet, Wilson thought.

'I do love you.' There was a catch in Kate's voice. 'But losing our child.' Her voice trailed off.

Helen put her arms around her daughter and led her towards the rear of the apartment. She turned to Wilson. 'I'll get Kate off to work. The maid will pack a couple of suitcases for you. I've booked you a room at the Europa, and we'll have the luggage sent over.'

Wilson stared at the backs of the two women. Had he unwittingly let a serpent into his relationship with Kate? Helen McCann had researched him; perhaps he would return the favour. He looked around the kitchen, and he could not dispel the feeling that he was seeing it for the last time.

CHAPTER FIFTY-TWO

Peter Davidson was the star of the morning briefing. He had brought home the bacon from his trip to Glasgow. He led off the briefing with his report on locating Baxter and Weir. He told them how he had received an email from the Strathclyde police overnight. They had raided the addresses of the two men but had found nothing. The news wasn't unexpected, but it was disappointing. 'We'll find them, Boss,' Davidson said as a conclusion. 'The boys in Glasgow are among the best. As soon as Baxter and Weir resurface, they'll be nabbed.'

'Well done, Peter.' Wilson slapped Davidson on the shoulder. 'We now have one piece of the puzzle.' He turned to Eric Taylor. 'What about Big George?'

'It appears that he still lives with his mother,' Taylor said, 'although he pretty much sleeps wherever he finds himself when he's tired. The question is, how do you want him picked up, easy or hard?'

'I'd prefer easy,' Wilson said.

'So would I,' Taylor said. 'Hard might involve at least five uniforms. If George thinks he's going down, he might react and people could get hurt. He spends a lot of time with Rice, so we'll have to choose a time when they're not together.'

'I'd prefer to talk to him sooner rather than later,' Wilson said. 'This man appears to have been an accessory to two murders. I want him here in this station talking to us. I don't want him to run. So no all-points bulletin. Keep the uniforms out of it. It might mean sitting on his tail for a bit.' He continued looking at Taylor. 'What about the Infrastructure Agency stuff?'

'Christ, Boss,' Taylor said. 'I only have two hands, two legs, one nose, one mouth. In other words, I can't divide myself in two.'

'Thanks Eric,' Wilson said. 'I'm more than aware that everyone is overstretched. Peter, maybe you could be the point man on bringing Big George in. He's the next link in the chain, and he leads to Rice. That way, Eric can stay on looking at the Agency.'

Davidson nodded. 'Okay, Boss.'

'Moira, where are we with Traffic?'

'They've promised me something before the end of the morning,' Moira said.

'I want you to keep after them,' Wilson said. 'If we locate Big George, you and I will interrogate him.'

'Harry, anything new on O'Reilly?'

'I'm reassessing the results of the house-to-house,' Graham said. 'It's a busy intersection. Someone has to have seen something. I've collected all the CCTV from the area, and I'm reviewing that. Someone made their way into the apartment building, and I'm pretty sure they did it from the taxi station. That means they had a key. If I can't turn up anything from the interviews or the CCTV, we might have to bring Boyle in. He's more likely to crack than Dolan.'

'Okay,' Wilson said. 'You've all got lots to do. I'll be out for some of the morning. I've got to meet Laurence Gold. You should all keep it in mind that you might be next on his list. Cummerford is up in six or so weeks. My guess is that she's going to mount a defence, but I have no idea what it might be.' He saw a smile break across Moira's face. 'I'm serious.'

'Not even in pillow talk, Boss,' Moira said.

Wilson's face hardened. 'Now get on with your work.' He turned and strode towards his office.

Moira waited five minutes and followed him. She knocked on the glass door before entering and closed it behind her. 'Boss, I am really sorry if I said something inappropriate.'

'Don't worry about it,' Wilson said and returned to his papers.

'What's up, Boss?'

'Nothing you need to know about.' Wilson looked up into her eyes. 'Honestly, just some personal stuff.'

'Between you and Kate?'

He could see that she wasn't about to drop the questioning, and the fact that he would be staying at the Europa would soon be common knowledge. 'Kate and I have decided to take a break.'

'Oh no,' Moira said. 'Is there anything I can do?'

'No. We're both a bit overstretched these days. We always knew that our jobs would get in the way sooner or later.' It wasn't only the jobs though. There was the hand of Helen McCann in there somewhere.

'Where are you staying?'

'The Europa but that's between you and me for the moment. I know it'll soon become common knowledge, but right now I want it kept quiet. We don't discuss it again.'

'No problem, Boss. I thought you looked a bit down this morning.'

'It isn't over,' he said more in hope than certainty. 'We'll be back together again.'

'You're made for each other,' Moira said. 'Whatever the

problem is it'll pass.' She started for the door and thought about herself and Brendan. Would it pass too? And would she be in Boston when it did?

CHAPTER FIFTY-THREE

Big George Carroll watched the Blue BMW 520 drive slowly towards him on Ballygomartin Road. The previous evening, he had wanted to go back to his mother's house in Riga Street, but the Boss insisted that he stay the night with him. His mother wasn't best pleased when he'd phoned and told her that he wouldn't be home for his dinner. She had made him a steak and kidney pie and was looking forward to sharing it with him. His mother was the one constant in his life. Along with Sammy, she was the only person in the world who cared for him. Other people laughed at his size and the fact that he didn't always understand things. George's physical development and mental development were diametric opposites. While his bodily development went ahead at a pace, his mental capacity appeared to go in the opposite direction. As a young child, he had been diagnosed as being mentally retarded. His father wasn't up for dealing with a difficult child and decided to do a runner. George and his mother had never heard from him again after he left the house one evening to buy a packet of cigarettes. His mum stuck with him despite the tremendous difficulty in getting him through school. The psychologists and psychiatrists had a field day with him. They carried out test after test on him without coming to any conclusion on the particular genetic foul up that led to his disproportionate development. Sammy Rice had befriended him at school and made sure that the other kids who made a laugh of him only did it once. George reciprocated by helping Sammy to extort money from their classmates, and even from those in the older classes. He'd skipped school so many times that he had the reading age of a five-year-old. That didn't bother him because he only liked looking at the pictures. He was no good with numbers, but that was okay too since his mum and Sammy made sure that he didn't have to do any arithmetic. On the other hand, he could drive a car from the age of twelve, lift a truck with his bare hands and carry hundred-pound loads without blinking. He watched the Beemer until it pulled up beside him. The Boss had told him that he was going on a trip. He had no idea where he was going, but he hoped it would be somewhere beside the sea. Big George loved the ocean. It was nearly the first totally clear day since Christmas. The sky was blue and cloudless, although there was a nip in the air. He had already decided that if they were going to the seaside, he would have an ice cream, maybe even a 99. He liked the combination of the Cadbury's flake and the vanilla ice cream. And maybe they could have fish and chips afterwards.

Owen Boyle pulled in beside Big George and lowered the driver's window. 'Get in,' he said simply.

Big George walked around the car and opened the passenger-side door. He squeezed himself into the front seat.

Boyle could feel the weight of the Hi Point 9 millimetre automatic in his right-hand pocket. At 29 ounces, it wasn't the heaviest gun in the world, but he could feel it more because it wasn't his favourite weapon. He would have preferred a Ruger, a Sig Sauer or a Beretta. They were class guns. The Hi Point was a piece of American shit. Some people would call it cheap and cheerful, but if it's your intention to kill someone, you'd be better off beating them over the head with it than trying to shoot them. Sammy had told him what he wanted done with George. It was one of the only times that he heard emotion in Sammy's voice. That was highly unusual. He concluded that Sammy was either drunk or high, or maybe a combination of both. In any case, the result was the same. Big George had become a problem, and that problem had to disappear. Boyle felt oppressed by the body sitting next to him. The guy was a human ape. Boyle was astonished that Sammy had taken Big George on the O'Reilly business. He could just imagine the witnesses, 'it was a guy who was built like a brick shithouse officer'. Big George wasn't made for normal seats. They'd modified a black cab just for him, so an ordinary sedan was a bit of a challenge. At least, they weren't going too far and there would be more room on the return journey.

CHAPTER FIFTY-FOUR

The office of Laurence Gold QC was located in a modern office building in Arthur Street just around the corner from Chichester Street and the Royal Court of Justice. It was in the same area where Kate operated her office. Wilson stepped out of the elevator on the third floor and into the nineteen seventies. Whereas Kate's offices were decorated in Scandinavian chic, the heavy mahogany furniture and thick silk curtains that dominated Gold's office spoke of a long legal tradition and stability. This was no fly-by-night operation but a serious legal outfit that could be depended on to ensure that justice was well served, for a price. Wilson announced himself to the receptionist and was pointed to a leather button-back chair. The coffee table in front of him held magazines with titles like *Tatler* and *Field & Stream*. This was no place for the readers of *Football Monthly*. Wilson watched as juniors and paralegals raced around the offices trying to convince themselves, and each other, that they were enormously important. Those who did manage a look in his direction could see that he was either a client or a witness, both of whom ranked low on the scales of the budding lawyers.

The receptionist left her desk and approached Wilson.

'Laurence will see you now,' she said and headed off down the corridor.

Wilson followed, impressed at the level of democracy in the office whereby the lowly staff referred to their superior by his first name.

She knocked on a door and pushed it open. 'Detective Superintendent Wilson,' she announced moving away from the opening and ushering Wilson inside.

Wilson entered the large office that was almost the size of the murder squad room at the station. It was seven good long strides between the door and the desk from which Gold was rising to greet him. Laurence Gold was an imposing character. He was almost as tall as Wilson and although in his early sixties, he still stood at his full six feet two inches. His leonine head was set off with a mop of silver hair which was combed back from his forehead and terminated in what used to be known as a duck tail. He had two piercing blue eyes and a hooked nose, which would have done credit to a wooden Indian. His lips were full and most likely naturally so. He had put on some weight since Wilson had seen him last.

'Detective Superintendent,' he said rounding his large desk and striding purposefully towards Wilson. He held out his hand in advance. 'May I call you Ian?'

Wilson shook his hand. 'Absolutely.' Gold's voice was captivating. It had the kind of timbre that could have replaced the Pied Piper's flute in leading people astray.

'And you shall call me Laurence,' Gold said leading him towards the desk. 'After all you're almost a member of the legal fraternity by association.'

There was a knock on the door. The receptionist stuck her head in and announced 'Professor Guilfoyle'.

Wilson turned towards the door and frowned. He wondered what the hell Brendan Guilfoyle was doing here.

'Ian,' Gold said stopping at his desk. 'May I introduce—.'

'We're acquainted,' Wilson said quickly cutting Gold short.

Guilfoyle walked forward and offered Wilson his hand. 'Good to see you, Superintendent.'

'Better call me Ian,' Wilson said taking his hand. 'We all seem to be on first-name terms here.'

Gold smiled. 'No professional jealousy I hope.'

'The good professor is trying to lure my sergeant away to Boston,' Wilson said. 'And I'm afraid that he's succeeding.'

'I had no idea,' Gold pointed to two chairs in front of his desk. 'Because of his experience with serial killers, I asked Brendan along as a consultant.'

'Good,' Wilson said. 'I thought that this was going to turn into an episode of *Lie to Me*. I understand that Brendan is an expert at knowing when people are lying.'

'My last job in Belfast,' Guilfoyle said, a touch of sadness in his voice.

'We in the legal profession will certainly miss you, Brendan,' Gold said. 'Now I understand that Ian's time is limited. He's heavily involved in finding out who killed David Grant.'

'The investigation has expanded somewhat,' Wilson said glancing at Guilfoyle. He saw no sign that he was aware of the extension of the investigation to Malone and O'Reilly. The pillow talk was probably on more important topics, like their future life in Boston.

'Unfortunately,' Gold continued, 'there is one major point to be cleared up before we go to trial. We've examined all the documents, and we're wondering how Maggie Cummerford got to attend murder squad briefings.'

'There's a lot of research that shows that smart killers try to get themselves as close to the investigation as possible,' Guilfoyle said. 'They always seem to be around the investigating officers, drink where they drink, that kind of thing. In this case Cummerford wasn't just around. She was right in the centre of the investigation. She knew what leads you were following up, what your investigation strategy was. In fact, I was intending to use this case in my lectures.'

Wilson shifted uneasily in his seat. He saw that Gold recognised his disquiet.

'Ian?' Gold said.

'How important is this issue?' Wilson asked.

'A murderer who killed three women was at the very centre of a police enquiry into the killings,' Gold said. 'I have a feeling that the defence would be remiss in its duty if it didn't investigate for the jury how this situation arose. I should say that what is said within these four walls will stay here. But I need to know what happened so that I can prepare some kind of counter.'

Wilson tried to remember whether he had promised Jennings that he would bury the affair. Had he obtained something as a quid pro quo or had he simply used Jennings' written order to allow Cummerford access to the briefings in order to save his own skin? The look on Gold's face said that he was going nowhere until he explained. 'It all started when my old boss shot himself,' Wilson began, and the story of how Maggie Cummerford had blackmailed Deputy Chief Constable Jennings into letting her attend the briefings tumbled out of him.

'Holy Cow,' Guilfoyle said when Wilson had finished. 'I'm definitely including this in my lectures.'

'Now I understand your difficulties,' Gold said. 'And mine. There's a strong possibility that DCC Jennings will be dragged into the trial. You kept his written instruction, I assume.'

Wilson nodded.

'I must speak with the DCC.' Gold made a note on the pad in front of him. 'I'll try to keep your name out of the conversation.'

Wilson smiled. He could just imagine the fallout from that conversation. Jennings wouldn't need two guesses at who had spoken to Gold. That meant that he would find himself in the centre of the biggest shit storm in a career already noted for significant shit storms. 'Did I lie?' he asked Brendan.

'It's too bizarre to be a lie,' Brendan answered.

'Well I'd like to thank both of you for stopping by,' Gold said rising from his seat and extending his hand across the desk.

Wilson and Guilfoyle shook his hand then turned and left together.

'You really think I'm winning?' Brendan asked when they were at the elevator.

Wilson looked into his earnest face. 'I'm afraid so, and I'm about to lose a very talented policewoman.'

CHAPTER FIFTY-FIVE

Neither man spoke as the BMW left Belfast via Donegall Square and made its way towards the M1. Traffic was light, and they covered the two miles to the start of the motorway in ten minutes. Boyle looked occasionally at Big George, who just stared directly ahead. They took the M1 and travelled about eight miles before taking the exit towards Sprucefield. The weather continued to be kind. Ireland would be the most beautiful country in the world if it weren't situated directly in the path of the Atlantic weather systems. The rain and the wind always militated against the beauty of the countryside. Boyle was close to forgetting the purpose of the trip as he piloted the BMW onto the A1 and headed in the direction of Hillsborough.

'Are we going to the seaside?' Big George asked as they turned left onto Hillsborough Road.

Boyle was surprised by the question. Usually, George the strong silent type and his breaking of the silence was totally out of character. 'We'll run by the sea, but we won't be going through any decent-sized towns.'

'Can we get an ice cream?'

Where the hell was this coming from? Boyle asked

himself. Was it possible that Big George had a presentiment about what was going to happen? Boyle didn't answer but drove on through Dromara and headed towards Castlewellan.

'I'd like an ice cream,' Big George said with a deadpan expression.

What was with the fucking ice cream, Boyle thought. He turned and looked at Big George, who was examining the road signs. Either this guy was the simplest man on the planet or he was one of those savants who knew what was about to happen next.

'Can we go to Newcastle?' George asked. 'There's a really good ice cream shop there.'

'Maybe,' Boyle said. They were already on the Newcastle Road and while he had no intention of going into Newcastle itself, he couldn't think of any reason why a condemned man shouldn't get his final request. 'Okay,' he said. 'We'll do Newcastle, and you can have your ice cream.' He looked at Big George expecting to see a sign of pleasure on his face. He was disappointed.

Big George shifted in his seat. He was aware that he was crushing Boyle, but he never travelled in the rear and if Sammy wanted Boyle to drive that was his decision. He felt a certain level of satisfaction that they were going to the seaside on such a beautiful day. He loved the sea and more than that he loved ice cream.

Newcastle was a small town on the coast of the Irish Sea, set at the base of Slieve Donard mountain. The green and the purple of the mountain were perfectly set off against the light blue of the sky.

'I want to go to Maud's for a poor bear ice cream,' Big George said.

Boyle sighed. He knew Maud's was on Main Street and that parking was a nightmare, but a condemned man's wish and all that shit. He drove along the promenade and was lucky enough to find a parking place. They walked together to

Maud's drawing stares from people who saw this man mountain walking along with what appeared to be a midget. Boyle was five feet nine and weighed in at seventy-five kilos but walking beside someone standing six and a half feet and weighing a hundred and seventy kilos made him look like a ventriloquist's dummy.

Maud's was full of the elevenses crowd enjoying their coffees and cakes. George selected his poor bear ice cream and added two additional slices of cream cake. He stood waiting for Boyle to take care of the bill.

Boyle smiled and fished the money from his pocket. It felt like taking his son to the ice cream parlour. He took his change and motioned to George that they had to leave now. George was already stuck into his poor bear ice cream, white streaks hanging from the edges of his mouth. He carried his back-up cakes in his left hand as they left the café.

Boyle piloted the car back the three or so kilometres that they had strayed off their original path to satisfy Big George's wish. They passed through the minor village of Bryansford, and Boyle was on the lookout for the small side road that led into the Tullymore Forest. He saw it directly ahead and turned in. The BMW bumped over the rough path. Although Tullymore was a popular area for tourists, it was early in the season and with six hundred and thirty hectares, there were plenty of areas well away from prying eyes.

Boyle brought the Beemer to a halt two hundred yards into the forest and pulled it in near a copse of trees. 'We're here,' he said shutting off the engine.

Big George had finished his poor bear ice cream and was about to start in on his cakes.

'Put those away, for God's sake,' Boyle said. 'We've got work to do. You can have them on the way back.' He got out of the car and looked around the forest. The trees were bare and foreboding despite the warmth in the air. The only sound he could hear was the hammering of a woodpecker.

Big George eased himself out of the front seat and placed his cakes on the seat he had occupied. He was looking forward to the trip back to Belfast.

Boyle moved to the rear of the car and opened the boot. He removed a spade and shut the boot. He pressed the car key and locked the BMW. 'Come with me,' he said. They walked together off the path, and Boyle made a drama out of looking for a particular spot. In fact, he was just searching for a convenient place to plant Big George. He stopped in a clear area and motioned for his companion to join him. 'It's here,' he said pointing at the centre of the clearing and tossed the spade to Big George. He paced out a rectangle of approximately six feet by three. 'Dig it out to about two feet.'

Big George moved the spade along the rectangle that Boyle had laid out. He removed his pullover and tossed it onto a branch of a tree. The earth was soft, and the first spade of earth came out easily.

CHAPTER FIFTY-SIX

Wilson arrived back at the station and went immediately to the squad room. He had just entered when Moira rushed into his office.

'Traffic came through,' she said. 'Come out and have a look.'

Wilson went to her desk. Moira sat and began to run through the CCTV footage. 'They picked him up on the A57 on his way from the airport. You can get a good view of the passengers. It's definitely Baxter and Weir.' She moved the picture forward. 'Here he is on the M2 heading south into town.' She rushed the CCTV ahead. 'We have him in the street adjacent to Malone's apartment. There's no CCTV on Fitzroy Avenue, so he disappears for a while.' She moved the mouse. 'We pick him up next on his way to Ashley Avenue. He parks a bit away from Grant's house, and his passengers get out. They're carrying a case.' She moved the picture ahead. 'Here's one of them who comes back and collects Carroll.' Again the picture shot forward. 'Then the three of them return to the cab.'

'Stop it there,' Wilson said.

Moira pressed some keys, and the picture paused.

'Zoom in on the bag in Baxter's hand.'

Moira moved the mouse, and the picture zoomed in on Baxter's right hand.

'Grant's brother told me that he had bought his brother a very distinctive briefcase. Does that look like a distinctive briefcase to you?'

Moira looked up at him and smiled. 'If I'm not much mistaken, that looks like the kind of briefcase that is unique in the Province. We've got them.'

'Now we need Big George Carroll,' Wilson said. 'Where's Peter?'

'Out and about,' Moira said. 'Trying to get a fix on Carroll.'

'Get him on the phone and bring him up to date. We don't just want to talk to Carroll, we want him in an interrogation room, and we want him there now.'

'On it, Boss,' Moira said.

'I just ran into your boyfriend at Laurence Gold's office.'

Moira looked puzzled. 'What was he doing there?'

'Consulting for Gold,' Wilson said. 'Apparently.'

'Gold is on the side of the angels in this one, right.'

Wilson smiled. 'Laurence Gold is always on the side of the angels. I was just surprised to find Brendan there.'

'Brendan is a mercenary. If someone wants to pay for his expertise, he's constantly ready to oblige.'

'Always on the side of the angels?' Wilson asked.

'He likes to think so.'

'Get Peter, I want Carroll here.' He turned and went to his office. He could feel someone behind him. He turned sharply and found himself staring into Eric Taylor's flushed face.

'Boss,' Taylor held up a sheaf of papers, 'we need to talk.'

'Come in,' Wilson opened his office door. He walked to his desk and flopped into his chair. 'What have you got?'

'Something that's beyond my capacity, and certainly beyond my pay grade.' Taylor sat facing his boss. 'I've scanned all the building contracts awarded by the Infrastructure

Agency. One company has been particularly successful. You could even say that they've been spectacularly successful. It's called Robin Construction.'

'Who's Robin?'

'It's not a person. It's the national bird of the United Kingdom. Robin Construction has been successful in eighty per cent of the tenders that they've submitted. That's the kind of success ratio that companies dream about. I contacted Companies House to find out who Robin Construction is. On the surface, the company is owned and run by one Samuel Rice with an address in Ballygomartin Road, Belfast.'

'Sammy certainly has come up in the world. Who'd have guessed we had a construction giant in our midst.'

'I've been asking around about Robin Construction but nobody is talking. Anyway there's a lot of information from Companies House that I'm not in a position to evaluate. But there is one simple fact. Sammy Rice presents himself as the owner-operator of Robin, but he is, in fact, only a minority shareholder. A company called Carson Nominees holds ninety per cent of the shares. Unlike Mr Rice, Carson Nominees don't have an address in Northern Ireland. They're incorporated in the Cayman Islands, and their registered office is in George Town.'

Wilson leaned back in his chair. 'Any idea of the value of the contracts awarded to Robin?'

'I haven't worked that out yet but certainly in the high millions.'

Wilson was having one of his eureka moments. Malone worked at the Agency. Perhaps he stumbled onto the fact that Robin was winning a high number of tenders. If Malone discovered that there had been some skulduggery, what would he have done? He'd very possibly have gone to someone who was well known for attacking corruption head on. Malone was probably in no doubt that the documents relating to some kind of scam would be horrendously complicated. Grant was a lawyer, but he didn't have any financial expertise. That would be where O'Reilly would come into the picture. Wilson was connecting the dots and since all three men were dead, the conclusion he had reached was completely plausible. He waved at Moira.

'Boss,' Moira said when she entered Wilson's office.

Wilson asked Eric to repeat what he had found. 'I want you to take over this part of the investigation from Eric,' Wilson said to her when Taylor had finished.

Taylor let out a sigh. 'Thanks, Boss. The thought of going through all those legal papers was giving me nightmares.'

'Give Moira everything that you've got,' Wilson said to Taylor. 'Carroll is the key to this whole business. I want you to help Peter find him.'

Taylor handed the file to Moira and left the office.

Wilson expounded his theory as soon as Taylor left.

'Sounds plausible,' Moira said. 'But it's supposition until we have some concrete evidence. We have nothing to show that any of these three men met each other. It's one hell of a coincidence that they all owned computers but that none of them can be found. We've checked the agendas of the three and so far nothing. We're shooting in the dark.'

'I've made the link in a more or less logical fashion. Maybe Big George Carroll can lead us to the next step. In the meantime, I want you to dissect the information Eric has turned up. Get on to our fraud people and see if they can help. You met that finance guy at the Agency. You and I will go back there and shake his tree. And try to find out who owns this Carson Nominees.' He looked up at Moira expecting a 'Yes, Boss', and a view of her departing derrière. She was still holding the documents and hadn't moved. 'And?'

'I'm quitting the PSNI,' Moira said.

He saw a tear falling from her left eye. 'That's my girl,' he said. Inside he could already feel the pain of her loss. 'You're doing the right thing.'

'I'm not so sure.' Her voice was low and she brushed away the tear.

'Brendan is a fine man, and he loves you. I don't think you could have done better.'

'What about this?' She held out the file of documents.

'Go the distance on it but in the end, your life is more important. I'm sad to lose you, but it's for the best. Now I need you to work as fast as possible on that file.' Wilson was brought up as a man's man. His grandfather and father had been tough old bastards who never showed emotion. He was brought up to give no quarter on the rugby field, or indeed in life. Aside from Spence and his team, he hadn't made another friend in the PSNI. Since she joined his team, he'd developed a special relationship with Moira. If he and Kate hadn't got together, who's to say that that special relationship wouldn't have gone in another direction. That was the same level of speculation as he'd applied to the connection between Malone, Grant and O'Reilly. He thought about McDevitt's fairy tale and picked up the phone. He dialled the offices of the *Chronicle* and asked for McDevitt. There was a combination of banal music and clicking on the line then finally the croak of McDevitt's voice. 'Are you available to meet this evening?'

'Sure.' There was surprise in McDevitt's voice

'The Crown, seven o'clock.'

'I'll be there.'

CHAPTER FIFTY-SEVEN

I must have been fucking mad, Richie Simpson said to himself as he left the Republican Club in Andersonstown. He had attempted to enlist the assistance of the Fenians in taking care of Sammy Rice, but they'd laughed into their pints of Guinness and sent him on his way. His head was hurting. He had gone on a bender with some of Jackie's money and had already got rid of upwards of a grand. He was out of his mind taking a contract on Rice. He didn't do killing. That wasn't exactly true; he already had blood on his hands. So he could kill, but the chances were that if he tried to kill Rice, he was the one who would end up on a slab. The word on the street was that Rice had become his own best customer. However, a doped-up Sammy Rice was possibly a lot more dangerous than the sober version. He waved his hand at a black cab that pulled up beside him. He climbed in and said 'Donegall Place'. The driver looked at him in the mirror and drove away without saying a word. The phrase 'once in never out' was running around in his brain. He had no way to make up the grand he had squandered on drink, gambling and women. It was more fun than he'd had since Jackie's political party folded. So there was no question of giving the money back. Even if he could,

Jackie wouldn't accept it and he'd be the one with the contract on his head. The cab stopped, and the driver turned the clock around so that his passenger could see it. Simpson passed over a £5 note and didn't wait for the change. It was a perfect spring day, and he needed a coffee. Maybe a belt of caffeine would activate his brain cells. The coffee shops in Donegall Place had embraced the continental ethos and had already set tables and chairs outside their premises. Spring was in the air and summer wouldn't be far behind. He sat outside Clement's Café on one of the black metal chairs and ordered a double espresso. He watched the citizens of Belfast as they passed in front of him. Who the hell in this city would be willing to kill a lunatic for ten thousand pounds? His double espresso arrived, and he was in the process of stirring it when a man sat in the seat beside him. He looked up and recognised Davie Best, Gerry McGreary's top boy.

'Good to see you, Richie,' Best said motioning to the waitress. When she arrived, he pointed at the cup in front of Simpson.

'Davie, it's been a while.' Simpson continued stirring his coffee. Best was one of the most dangerous men in Belfast. He wanted to believe that this meeting was a coincidence, but he was in Belfast long enough to know that men like Best didn't meet you by accident.

They sat silently until the waitress delivered Best's coffee.

'I just got a call from one of my Fenian friends,' Best said stirring his coffee.

Shit, shit, shit, Simpson thought. This was exactly what he didn't need. Within days, every gobshite in Belfast would know that he was trying to organise Sammy Rice's demise. If one of those gobshite's worked for Sammy, it would be time to emigrate to Australia. That is if he was still alive.

'Seems you need a job done.' Best sipped his coffee.

Simpson looked at the people passing by. He was wondering if he ran, would any of them help him. But running would be pointless. Best or Rice would find him, and then he would be dead meat.

'It appears that Sammy is out of control,' Simpson spoke as lowly as he could and there was a nervous catch in his voice. 'Important people want Sammy put out of harm's way.'

'Important people?' Best asked.

'People who don't like a partner who is rapidly becoming a liability.' Simpson sipped his coffee. His mouth was dry, and he wished he'd asked for water.

'I think that you should meet with Mr McGreary.'

'I thought McGreary and Rice were friends.'

Best smiled. 'I wouldn't call them friends. More like business rivals.'

Simpson finished his coffee and called the waitress. 'Can I have a bottle of still water, please?' What in God's name had he got himself involved in? If McGreary wanted Rice dead, he could bloody well arrange it himself. He could see what was coming. He was going to have to do Rice himself, and McGreary wouldn't shop him as a quid pro quo.

Best finished his coffee. He removed a card from his pocket and laid it on the table. It had a mobile phone number on it. 'Call this number tonight and we'll arrange a meet. Do not fuck up on this Richie because if you do, they'll never find your body.' Best tossed a £5 note on the table. 'The coffees are on me.'

Simpson picked up the card and slipped it into his pocket. He felt totally calm. It was the calmness that came from the knowledge that he was a dead man.

CHAPTER FIFTY-EIGHT

ig George Carroll was very pissed off. He was working like a slave while Boyle got to walk around like he was the bloody foreman. The least he could have done was to spell him by doing a bit of physical work himself. George was thinking about the trip back to Belfast and the cake waiting in the car. He didn't bother to think about the hole he was digging. They were either digging something up or putting something down. George never got involved in the thinking part. He was always the doer. He was concentrating on making the hole as perfect as he could. He'd straightened off the edges, and he was almost down the two feet that Boyle had requested. He was lucky the earth was so soft. The rain of the previous few days had loosened the soil and made his work a lot less onerous. He hadn't hit a box or anything like that, and he was almost finished.

Boyle watched George as he was cleaning up the hole. You couldn't say a great deal about Big George, but he was a bloody good digger. It was just ironic that he had managed to dig his own grave without knowing it. Time to get the business at hand over with. 'I need a piss,' he said and moved deeper into the wood. As soon as he was out of sight, he removed the Hi

Point from his pocket and checked the magazine. There were eight slugs. They were good to go. He thumbed off the safety.

'Finished.' George climbed out of the hole and turned around. There was no sign of Boyle and he remembered he'd heard something about a piss. He was walking towards the Beemer when Boyle came out of the woods carrying a pistol in his hand. All of George's brain development had taken place in his amygdala, the oldest part of the brain that is dominated by the flight or fight responses. There was little or no development of the subcortex which governed basic thinking and passed messages to the cortex, the decision-making part of the brain, an area that was totally undeveloped in George's case.

'Sorry,' Boyle said and raised the gun. He fired.

Big George heard the click of the hammer and pulled his head to the side. He felt the wind from the bullet as it sped past the left side of his face. He felt an instant pain in his left ear and raised his hand. His ear felt squishy, and it was wet.

'Shit.' Boyle smiled. The man was as big as a fucking house, and he had managed to miss him. The fucking bullet had ripped George's left ear off, but he was standing there with a puzzled look on his face. He would have to spend a few quid on a session at a firing range. He'd assumed it was going to take a head shot to put Big George down but there was a lot more body to aim at. He lined up to fire a second shot and pulled the trigger. There was a click, but the gun didn't fire. It must have been a dud, he thought. He tried to eject the cartridge but wasn't able. The fucking gun had jammed.

George's amygdala was in overdrive. He was in a life-threatening situation, and if he didn't act fast, he would be dead. He let out a primal scream as he raced towards Boyle with the agility of a ballet dancer. It was a nimbleness that totally belied his bulk. As he moved, his right hand pulled back the spade. When he was within striking distance of Boyle, he swung the spade and aimed it at Boyle's neck. The edge of the spade struck the left side of Boyle's neck and cut through the external flesh, the trapezius muscle, the levator scapulae muscle, and the splenius cervicis muscle before cutting the blood vessels to the brain. It cut through the external ceratoid and the ceratoid sinus before slicing through the vertebral column. It continued on its way through the neck hacking muscles and ligaments until it exited on the right side of his neck. It was a stroke worthy of a medieval executioner. Boyle's head tottered on his shoulders before falling off and landing on the grass at his feet. His eyes looked up and the last image imprinted on his dying brain was the fountain of blood pouring from his headless body. The body slumped on the grass next to the head.

George dropped the spade and looked at the broken body on the ground in front of him. His brain struggled to make sense of what just happened. There was so much adrenalin surging through his body that he took no notice of the pain in his shattered ear. He walked forward and stood over Boyle's body. He bent and picked up the gun. Owen Boyle had tried to kill him. He took the car keys from Boyle's body and went to the Beemer. He opened the boot. It was empty. Where was the object that they had been sent to bury? It slowly dawned on him that perhaps he had been digging his own grave. That was impossible. Boyle must have gone crazy. He walked to the edge of the clearing and sat on a rock. The ground around Boyle was a sea of red blood. Boyle's eyes were wide open and there was a look of astonishment on his face. The adrenalin rush was beginning to subside and George could feel the onset of a searing pain in his left ear. He put his left hand to the side of his head and found that his ear had been turned into a piece of raw meat. He looked on the ground but there was no sign of the missing part of his ear. He walked across to Boyle's prone body and pulled out a large section of his shirt. He tore it off and wrapped it around his head. He wondered whether he should go to a doctor. If he did, they would ask him how he had been injured. That would lead to Owen Boyle and that would not be good for him. Maybe he could live with just one ear. He pulled Boyle's body to the hole he had dug and dropped it in. He kicked the head into the hole on top of the body. He picked up the spade and shovelled the earth over the dead man. If he went to the police, he would have to explain the dead body. He couldn't go back to Sammy. Boyle's torn shirt had staunched the blood somewhat, and he was becoming used to the pain. He took out his phone and called his mother. When she answered, he told her what had happened. After she assured herself that he was okay, she told him not to phone Sammy and not to accept any calls from him. He should return to Belfast and go to his uncle Ray's house. She and Ray would be waiting there for him. He didn't like it that he could hear her crying on the phone. He didn't like to make her unhappy. She told him that she loved him, and he was to take care on the trip back to Belfast. He closed his phone and walked to the BMW. His mother was the clever one. He would love to be able to think like her, but he had long ago accepted that there was something that didn't work right in his head. His mother had said that it wasn't his fault. It wasn't anyone's fault he was just made like that. If anyone was to blame, it was God. He opened the door of the BMW and smiled. The cream cake from Maud's was sitting on the passenger seat.

CHAPTER FIFTY-NINE

Moira couldn't believe that she had said it. She was going to quit the best job she could have imagined, something that she was more than good at, to take a leap into the unknown. Was she mad? It didn't matter. She had already done the hard part by telling Wilson. Now, it was just a case of writing the letter. The best phase of her short life was coming to an end. She wondered whether Brendan's love would be big enough to fill the hole. Now that the decision was made, she could stop agonising over what she was going to do and start concentrating on the case. Eric's information was easy enough to analyse. There was no doubt that Robin Construction was the preferred contractor of the Infrastructure Agency. The crux of the matter was whether undue influence had been brought to bear in order to achieve that performance. The fact that Sammy Rice was the frontman for Robin did not bode well. The question was whether Rice had the wherewithal to exert influence. She doubted it. Rice was a criminal and strong-arm man. He was the kind that would put a gun in your mouth to get your attention. That wasn't the kind of pressure that would make the bureaucrats toe the line. That type of pressure came from above. It needed political influence to create that level of compliance. Therefore, the focus on Carson Nominees. She got on her computer. Within a half an hour, she had a complete rundown on Robin Construction. The company was just one grade above a shell. It had employees, but they were not numerous. After Robin obtained a contract, most of the work was subcontracted. The declared profits of the company were totally out of line with the effort expended. Robin Construction was a cash cow providing its owners with substantial annual dividends. She next carried out a search on Carson Nominees and found that Robin Construction wasn't their only investment in the Province. She extended her search to look for information on Carson Nominees itself. That was where she hit the wall. There was nothing aside from the registered address in George Town on Grand Cayman. She needed help, very specialised help. She took out her mobile and called Brendan. She thought about telling him of her decision, but that could wait until this evening. She was on a roll and right now Carson Nominees was her top priority. She explained her problem, and Brendan said he would arrange something. She would receive a call within fifteen minutes. Seventeen minutes later, her mobile rang.

'Hi, can I speak to Moira?' The accent was an exact copy of Brendan's.

'This is Detective Sergeant Moira McElvaney,' she said.

'Hi Detective Sergeant Moira McElvaney. This is Professor Joel Feinstein of Harvard University Business School. I'm just gonna call you Moira, and I'm Joel.'

'Okay, Joel, sorry about the formality. It goes with the job.'

'What's the problem, Moira?'

She explained the situation with Carson Nominees, the Cayman connection and the link to a whole series of companies in Northern Ireland.

Feinstein said, 'While we were talking, I was looking into

some databases for information on Carson. I'm acquainted with their registered address in George Town. There are at least six hundred companies registered at that address, and I would guess that the only directors listed would be the guys who run that particular office. Brendan picked on me because I've written a book on the use of offshore banking to hide assets and ownership.'

'Is there any way we can find out who owns Carson Nominees?' Moira asked.

'If these people are serious, and I guess they are if they've gone to the trouble of registering in the Caymans, then they've already set up a series of shell companies in other jurisdictions that assist those who want to stay anonymous. It might take years of research by someone like me to sift through the ownerships to find out who owns Carson Nominees. And even then, the chances of success would be significantly reduced if they discovered someone was looking for them. I know this isn't what you wanted to hear, but these are the facts.'

'What can I do?' Moira asked.

'Not a lot, the guys who go this route are more slippery and sneaky than a snake. They couldn't set up this scheme, unless they had significant financial expertise, or at the very least access to significant financial expertise.'

'You're giving me a bad message, Joel.'

Feinstein laughed. 'Considering that there is more than $30 trillion out there in the so-called Treasure Islands, you can just imagine the kind of services that are provided by unscrupulous bankers for the real owners of companies like Carson. They have infinitely more resources than you and I could muster.'

'So they slide?'

'Unless they get careless, or you get lucky, and I wouldn't make a bet on either eventuality. Sorry. I got a class in ten minutes. I gotta go. It's been a pleasure speaking with you.'

'Thanks for your time, Joel.' Moira ended the call. Carson Nominees were probably at the centre of the case, and it was a dead end. Wilson wouldn't be happy. She stood up and went to his office.

CHAPTER SIXTY

Big George Carroll had disappeared off the planet. Well maybe not the planet but Peter Davidson and Eric Taylor were ready to conclude that he was no longer in Belfast. In fact, mention of his name was enough to strike most of the denizens of the Loyalist drinking holes of Belfast deaf and dumb. Now Big George, possibly because of his size, was usually not the most difficult man to run across, but nobody had seen hide or hair of George Carroll for days. Peter Davidson was at school with both Sammy Rice and Big George. A lot of the kids had treated George like the village idiot, and Davidson had watched as George had failed to advance in class with the other children. Sammy Rice had gone ahead with the other kids but at each play break he immediately made for George, and the two would get up to whatever mischief Sammy had thought of during class. Davidson had delayed heading for the one place that he knew for certain there was someone who knew where George was. Mrs Carroll had a pathological hatred of the police. Her family had been involved in criminal activity as long as Loyalists had lived in the Shankill. Her father and brothers had spent time in jail for a series of offences which ran the gamut of crimes that could draw a prison sentence. The family had often protested that they were being incarcerated for political offences, but the plain truth was that they were criminals, born and bred. Clare Carroll lived in a red-bricked maisonette in Riga Street. Davidson knocked on the door and stood back.

Mrs Carroll's large frame filled a crack in the door and looked at Davidson. 'You have some nerve coming around here, you traitor,' she said.

'Nice to see you too, Mrs Carroll.' Davidson creased his face in a fake smile. 'I'm looking for George. We want to have a talk with him.'

'And if he doesn't want to talk to the Peelers.' She held the door open just enough to look out.

'It isn't optional,' he said.

'He's not here,' she said and attempted to close the door.

Davidson blocked the door with his foot. 'It would be better if I found him. We don't want the uniforms looking for him. Someone might get hurt.'

'I'll tell him you were lookin' for him.' She pushed hard on the door.

Davidson's foot was throbbing. 'George might be in trouble, Mrs Carroll. He really should come and talk to us before it goes further.'

'When I see him, I'll pass on the message.' She pressed so firmly on the door that Davidson's resistance crumbled. He pulled his foot from the door and allowed it to close.

She knows where he is, Davidson thought. Ideally, he would like to watch her and see where she went but this was the Shankill and if he was seen standing around, it would stir up the local heavies. He'd have to hope that George would surface and that he would be in the vicinity when he did.

CHAPTER SIXTY-ONE

'So it's a dead end.' Wilson had listened to Moira's report on her conversation with Feinstein. 'Everything hinges on Carroll.' They were travelling in the car to the Infrastructure Agency offices in Central Belfast. 'This is like walking around in glue. The more we advance the more we seem to get stuck. I've asked for an international arrest warrant for Baxter and Weir. Sooner or later, we'll catch up with them. When we do, we can reappraise the forensics, and maybe we'll find something that links them to the crime scenes. Otherwise, the only person who can place them in both Malone's and Grant's residences is Big George Carroll.'

'What's the plan with Healy?' Moira asked.

'We shake his tree and see what falls out,' Wilson said. 'We don't have the expertise to follow up the corruption angle. Our speciality is murder, and I think we've already sorted out who killed Malone and Grant. We don't yet know why. The hypothesis that involves the Agency and the link with Robin Construction is only that, a hypothesis. We don't have a shred of evidence to confirm it. It might be different if we could find the missing computers. There wasn't a shred of evidence in any of their homes to indicate that they knew each other. We have to assume that Baxter and Weir cleaned up.'

'Baxter and Weir didn't do O'Reilly,' Moira said. They had arrived at their destination, and Moira pulled into a 'no parking' spot.

'Eric is going through the CCTV from Castle Street. The place is awash with cameras but there's a lot of it to go through. Eventually, we'll pick something up.' Wilson got out of the car and looked up at the impressive office building. 'At least we know where some of the money is going.'

They walked together to the reception and asked for Dr Healy after showing their warrant cards. They were shown to the lift and met at the sixth floor.

Healy stood as the two police officers entered his office. 'Sergeant McElvaney, back so soon.' He moved forward with his hand extended.

Moira smiled and shook his hand. 'Let me introduce Detective Superintendent Ian Wilson.'

'My pleasure.' Healy extended his hand to Wilson. 'I'm old enough to have seen you play at your best. You were a class act.'

'Thanks.' Wilson shook Healy's extended hand. 'It's nice to be remembered.'

'In your case it's easy.' Healy led them to his desk. When they were seated, he moved behind his desk and sat. 'Now how can I help you?'

'We haven't gone public yet, but we believe Brian Malone was murdered,' Wilson said. He noted the shocked look on Healy's face. 'I'm sure you've read about David Grant's murder.'

Healy nodded.

'We believe the two murders are connected, and that's why we've come to you,' Wilson said.

Healy looked confused. 'Brian, murdered. It's very hard to

take that on board. Who would want to harm someone like Brian?'

'We have a good idea about the "who",' Wilson said. 'What we're concentrating on is the "why". People don't get murdered for no reason, that's why motive is so important in our business.'

'I don't understand what that has to do with the Agency.'

'We have a hypothesis that I'd like to run past you,' Wilson said. 'Let's say that Brian Malone discovered something in the course of his work that smelled of corruption. We can further posit that he took whatever he discovered to David Grant who was known as being strong against corruption. We can now go further and theorise that this hypothetical information could possibly form the basis of the motive for the murder of Malone and Grant. You can probably see where I'm going. This hypothesis suggests that there's something rotten in the Infrastructure Agency.'

Healy was a whiter shade of pale. 'Have you considered that your premise may not be valid?'

'It is one of several lines of enquiry,' Wilson said. 'Perhaps you can help us either disprove or confirm the hypothesis I've just outlined.'

'How?' Healy asked.

'We've been looking into your operations,' Wilson said. 'Finance and operations are not our area of expertise, but we've noted some issues which need clarification.'

'If I can clarify them, I will,' Healy said.

'A company called Robin Construction appear to have been very successful in obtaining building contracts,' Wilson said. 'In fact they have been successful in eighty per cent of their tender applications.'

'Our tender procedures are set down by Government for all public tenders,' Healy began, comfortable now in lecture mode. 'In fact, PSNI is obliged to follow the same tender procedures. The tenders are submitted on a certain date, opened and a list of the tenderers drawn up. All tenderers can be present at the tender opening session. After the list of valid tenderers has been drawn up, the tenders are examined for compliance with the TOR.'

'TOR?' Moira asked.

'Sorry,' Healy said. 'Terms of reference, the compliant tenders are then examined for their technical ability to complete the project and the tenderers are marked on their technical capabilities. The final step is to open the financial proposal. Any unsuccessful tenderer can ask for a meeting to discuss the area in which their tender was lacking. The process is totally transparent. If Robin Construction has been very successful, it's because their tenders have been the best and the most complete.'

'Have you examined the ownership of Robin Construction?' Wilson asked.

'Our tenderers are required to provide us with the past three years' profit and loss account.' Healy said. 'And a list of contracts undertaken in that period. We only deal with bona fide companies who have a track record. Robin Construction would never have succeeded in a tender if they didn't fulfil these requirements. Overall ownership of the company is not an issue for us.'

'So it wouldn't be important', Wilson said, 'if it transpired that Robin Construction was owned by a Belfast criminal and a shadowy investor with a registered office in George Town in the Cayman Islands.'

'That would not be an issue,' Healy confirmed. 'I don't have the papers in front of me, but Robin Construction was obviously compliant in the tender procedure, presented valid technical proposals and their bid was the most economical.'

'And you'll stand by that?' Wilson asked.

'Absolutely,' Healy replied.

'And political influence plays no part in the allocation of contracts?' Moira asked.

Healy smiled as though he was dealing with someone who hadn't quite understood what he had said. 'The process is transparent. Any political interference would be instantly visible.'

Wilson stood. 'You've been very helpful, Dr Healy. And we've taken up far too much of your time.'

Healy stood. 'Would you mind if I asked you for an autograph, Superintendent?' He took a blank sheet of paper and a pen from his desk.

Wilson took the pen and paper and scribbled his signature. 'Thanks again,' he said handing back the paper.

They left Healy's office without speaking and climbed into the lift.

'So,' Moira said. 'We're no further ahead.'

'I wouldn't say that,' Wilson said. 'That guy was smooth. And clever, we were interrogating him but he found out a lot of what we were thinking. I think that you'll find the lights on in this building until very late tonight and that bags of shredded material will be on their way to the furnace by early tomorrow morning. Brian Malone might have found something but by tomorrow the chances of that happening again will be substantially reduced.'

'So we've had it,' Moira said opening the car door.

'We've had it since this thing started.' Wilson sat into the car. 'Whatever conspiracy is behind this has been around for a long time. The murders were a sign of panic. Someone screwed up. Malone got lucky and roped in Grant who roped in O'Reilly. Malone and Grant had no idea that they were signing the death warrant of the next man in the chain. We're into full cover-up at this point. Baxter and Weir are expendable because they have no idea what the whole affair is about. Big George is a danger because he can lead us to the next link in the chain, Sammy Rice. We get Rice, I have no idea where that might lead us.'

'So Big George is the priority,' Moira said.

Wilson leaned back in his seat. 'I haven't seen the letter,' he said finally.

'You're twenty years behind the times,' Moira said. 'It's all done by email these days. You'll find it in your inbox under the subject "Application for a leave of absence".'

'You know how many emails I get in a day.'

'I would have thought you considered it important.'

'I thought you were resigning.'

'Never burn your bridges.'

'What are you going to do in Boston?'

'Since I won't have a Green Card, I can't apply for the police. Brendan can arrange for me to follow some courses on criminal psychology. Since I already have a degree in psychology, it seems like the way to go.'

'What about work?'

'I've got some money saved so this is like a sabbatical. '

'I don't see you being on sabbatical for too long.'

CHAPTER SIXTY-TWO

Sammy Rice spent the day getting high and drinking. He wasn't happy about ordering Big George's death but it was a business decision and George was a liability that had to be removed. The Peelers were locked on to Baxter and Weir. They would have CCTV that would link them to George, and George would squeal like a stuck pig as soon as they had him in the interview room. It was the difficulty of using someone who was all brawn and no brains. He hadn't forgotten that Boyle was a link between Baxter, Weir and him but since no one had any idea where Baxter and Weir were, he had time to organise Boyle's demise. He had remained compos mentis enough to burn the laptops they had collected from Malone, Grant and O'Reilly. Those laptops and the information they contained were now a mass of charred plastic moulded together in some weird sculptural form. The whole business was a cluster fuck. The basic problem was that the people who ran Jackie had got greedy. They were the kind of people that wouldn't be happy making thousands if they could make millions, or millions if they could be making billions. Another hitch was that he had no idea who they were. He smiled. If he did have that knowledge, he might be tempted to take them out. He was the one who fronted up the construction company, but they were the ones who were pocketing most of the cash. He took out his mobile phone and called Boyle for what seemed like the fiftieth time. The phone rang out. He'd told Boyle to call him as soon as the job was done. Boyle was supposed to have a brain. It bothered him that his lieutenant hadn't obeyed his instructions. That fucker was living on borrowed time anyway. He took out his watch. It was four thirty. They'd left at 9 a.m., and Tullymore wasn't a million miles away. He cut two lines of coke with his Barclaycard. No point in worrying. Big George was history and one link in the chain had been erased.

BALLYMENA WAS a large town in County Antrim with a population of almost 30,000 souls. The casual visitor was left in no doubt as to exactly who controlled the town. The Loyalist paramilitary banners hanging from almost every lamppost were a dead giveaway. Most of the kerbstones in the town were painted red, white and blue, the colours of the Loyalist majority. Union Jacks fluttered from bedroom windows. Pictures of King Billy and masked Loyalist gunmen stared down from the gable walls of terraced houses.

Big George Carroll had long ago finished his Maud's cream cake, and his stomach was rumbling as he left the M2 motorway at Exit 26 and followed the sign for Antrim/Bally-mena/Coleraine. He was still unsure about what had happened in Tullymore but he was certain that he was a very lucky man to be still alive. He didn't like to think of Owen Boyle's head looking up at him from the ground. His mother and Uncle Ray would have the answers. They had the brains to put all the pieces of the jigsaw together. He would never be able to believe that Sammy was part of the plot to kill him. He and Sammy were friends since school. He had maimed and even killed people because Sammy had asked him to. He turned onto Lisnevenagh Road and drove the seven miles ahead to the Antrim Road. He turned onto Bridge Street. He was almost at his destination. Uncle Ray lived in a small townhouse in Waveney Avenue. Big George knew the area well and parked the BMW in the small cul de sac. He looked at his watch. It was four thirty in the afternoon. He had called his mother from the southern outskirts of Belfast, and she had told him that she would be waiting at Uncle Ray's when he arrived. He locked the car and knocked on his Uncle Ray's door. The door opened, and he was pulled inside.

'You weren't followed,' Ray Wright asked. He was a tall, red-haired man in his early sixties and one of the few men that George would allow to manhandle him. Wright looked at the shirt tied around George's head and suppressed a smile. 'Take that thing off and let me see the damage. You look even more of an edjit than usual.'

George started to remove the shirt from his head. The section directly over his destroyed ear was caked with blood and resisted being pulled away.

'Your mother's in the kitchen,' Wright said. 'We need to clean you up a bit before she sees you.' He led George to the bathroom and turned on the hot tap. He balled up a towel and soaked it in hot water then dabbed it against George's left ear.

George stood still. His threshold for pain was way beyond what Wright was doing to him. Gradually, the piece of shirt he had torn from Boyle's dead body came away and the extent of the damage to his ear was revealed. His left ear was reduced to a piece of red pulp. No amount of surgery was going to fix it.

'You're one lucky bugger,' Wright said examining the ear. If Boyle had been a better shot, he would have taken half his nephew's head off. 'Let's go talk to my sister.'

Clare Carroll sat at the kitchen table smoking. She'd stubbed out her cigarette when she heard the doorbell. She was waiting anxiously to examine the damage to her son. She was a child of the 'Troubles' and had seen torn and broken bodies before. But this was her only son, the boy she depended on to put food on the table. She knew that he was still in one piece, but she was hoping that his ability to take care of her had not been impaired. She looked up as her brother led her son into the kitchen.

George looked at his mother. He half-expected that she might cry when she saw that his left year was missing. However, she seemed unruffled. George moved his eyes to the two men sitting at the kitchen table beside her. He recognised Gerry McGreary and Davie Best.

'There he is Clare,' Wright said. 'He's as right as rain. Mind you, they'll have to change his nickname from "Big George" to "One ear George".' He smiled at his little joke. He turned to George. 'Mr McGreary and his associate are anxious to have a word with you. First, they want to know what happened in Tullymore. Sit down beside your mother, lad.'

Big George sat beside his mother She put her hand on his. 'Mr McGreary is here to help us, George. Tell him what he wants to know.'

Big George started to recount the events of his day. He went into detail and Ray Wright was about to stop him when he received a look from McGreary that said leave him alone. After a long discourse, George stopped. He looked at his mother. 'I didn't mean to kill Owen. He was my friend, but he shouldn't have tried to kill me. I only wanted to stop him from shooting at me.'

'Can you find the place where you buried him again?' McGreary asked. He ran protection, prostitution and drugs in Central Belfast. Like Rice he had been born and raised in the Shankill and had always wanted to control that area. At the end of the 'Troubles' the Loyalist paramilitaries had, like their Fenian counterparts, gravitated to what they knew best, crime. Rice and his family had grabbed West Belfast for themselves and that had pissed him off. He had been forced to settle but deep inside, he always wanted to get rid of Rice. The

Cummerford bitch had done him the favour of putting Lizzie Rice in a hole in the ground, and old Willie was too busy pickling his liver. Sammy was the de facto boss of the Rice empire. He was the one McGreary would have to get rid of if he was to become the number-one man in Belfast. Big George Carroll was the second present that had fallen into his lap that day. He had always considered Richie Simpson to be an arsehole and he'd proved it when he'd gone to the Fenians to recruit a killer for Sammy. McGreary had guessed, correctly, that Simpson hadn't the nous to come up with the idea of killing Sammy. That idea was way beyond Simpson's level. So the order had come from somewhere above and that probably meant Jackie Carlisle. And everybody who knew anything knew Carlisle was only a boy for the powers that be, the people who really ruled Ulster. If they wanted Rice dead, they might be grateful to the man who accomplished it for them. Simpson and Big George were a gift from God. And Gerry McGreary had learned never to spurn either a gift or God.

'Yes,' Big George said.

'Do you know why he tried to kill you?' McGreary asked.

Big George shook his head, making bits of loose flesh swing from his destroyed ear.

'The Peelers are scouring Belfast for you, son,' Clare Carroll said. 'You must have done something.' She was going to add 'think' but realised she shouldn't ask too much of her son. 'Boyle wouldn't have tried to kill you unless Sammy had told him to do it.'

Big George couldn't think of any reason why his best friend since school days would want to kill him. 'Maybe I shouldn't have thrown that man out of the window in Castle Street. But Sammy told me to do it.'

McGreary and Best looked at each other.

'And Sammy was with you when the man went out the window?' McGreary asked.

George nodded. 'He told me to throw him out and I did.'

McGreary nodded at Wright. 'Your nephew has had a busy day. He must be tired. Maybe you should let him rest in the front room.'

Wright stood up. 'Come on, George. I'm going to put on the telly in the front room and you can rest. I'll put your favourite cartoon channel on. I have to discuss things with Mr McGreary and your mother.'

Big George stood up and looked at his mother. She motioned him to follow his uncle.

McGreary turned to Best. 'Get on to the quack in Finaghy. We need to get that boy's ear fixed up. I have no idea what they're going to do to it but it's the least we can do. Alright, Mrs Carroll?'

'Thank you, Mr McGreary,' Alice Carroll said. 'You're a gent.'

Wright returned to the kitchen. 'He's watching the cartoon channel. He should be good for another hour. Between Rice and the Peelers, the poor boy is fucked. Rice can't leave him alive, and the Peeler'll have him for doin' that boy in Castle Street.'

'There may be a way out,' McGreary said. 'The Peelers're aware that George isn't the sharpest knife in the drawer. They'll live with a story where he was told by Sammy to toss the boy out the window. But if Sammy is there to contradict him, then it's one man's word against another. Sammy will buy the best legal brain in town that means he'll skate. And George will take all the heat.'

'But George would never do something without Sammy telling him,' Clare Carroll said.

'Tell that to Owen Boyle,' McGreary said. 'You know your boy, Mrs Carroll. Put him in an interview room and the Peelers will have his whole life history in an hour. Including the part where he decapitated and buried Owen Boyle in Tullymore Forest.' He looked directly into Clare Carroll's face. 'You'll never see him on the street again. You'll be in the cemetery before he gets out.'

Ray Wright was following the conversation. He had been a Loyalist paramilitary commander, and he was nobody's fool. He looked at his sister. 'Don't worry,' he said. 'I think Mr McGreary has a way that it won't happen.'

McGreary removed his wallet from his pocket. He peeled off two £50 notes and handed them to Clare Carroll. 'Why don't you go into town and buy yourself something. Your son might have to go to jail but he'll have the best brief that money can buy, and you'll be taken care of while he's away. When he gets out he'll come and work for me.'

She smiled as she took the money. 'What about Sammy?' she asked.

McGreary patted her hand. 'You leave Sammy to us.'

Clare Carroll put the money into her purse and left the room.

The men in the kitchen waited until they heard the noise of the front door closing.

Ray Wright looked at the other two men. 'Okay, Gerry, what do you have in mind?'

CHAPTER SIXTY-THREE

'Boss,' Eric Taylor almost jumped in the air as Wilson and Moira entered the squad room.

Wilson went immediately to Taylor's desk.

'You got to see this.' Taylor indicated the images on his computer. 'I've been going through the CCTV from every camera in the vicinity of Castle Street. Look what I've picked up.'

Wilson stared at the image on the screen. Two figures, dressed in black, were moving along Castle Street heading in the direction of Royal Avenue. They both wore woollen hats pulled down over half their faces. 'I can't see the faces. Can you give me a shot where I can identify them?'

'They don't want to be identified, Boss,' Taylor said following them down the street. 'The hats are pulled down and they keep their eyes on the ground. That's not the point. The one on the right is a man mountain. Who do we know that looks like that?'

'Big George Carroll,' Wilson said. 'If that's Big George, the other one must be Sammy Rice or one of his men. It all fits. O'Reilly weighed ninety kilos. Big George can probably bench press several hundred kilos. He could pick someone like O'Reilly up with ease.'

'And toss him through a window with equal ease,' Moira said from behind Wilson. 'It's all beginning to centre on Big George.'

'Where do they go from Castle Street?' Wilson asked.

'They disappear on Royal Avenue,' Taylor said. 'They cut into Berry Street where there are no cameras.' He turned and looked at Wilson. 'That's Big George. He was in Castle Street when O'Reilly went through the window. It's one hell of a coincidence.'

'It's no coincidence,' Wilson said. 'O'Reilly was murdered the same as Malone and Grant. Sammy Rice and Robin Construction are behind the whole affair.'

'Do we haul Rice in?' Moira asked.

'No,' Wilson said. 'We concentrate on Carroll. He hasn't disappeared off the face of the earth.'

THE SIX O'CLOCK briefing was upbeat. A large portrait photo of George Carroll dominated the whiteboard. Wilson gave a briefing on the visit to the Infrastructure Agency and the role of Robin Construction. He had drawn lines between the Agency, Robin Construction and Carson Nominees and then linked them to Sammy Rice and George Carroll.

'I think that we're almost there,' Wilson said. 'It not about the crime, it's about the cover-up. The crime was probably the corruption within the Agency that provided Robin Construction with a mechanism to win the majority of contracts. I'm willing to bet that all concerned made a whole lot of money. Exposing this level of corruption would be a career-maker for a minor politician like Grant. What none of them realised was that Sammy Rice was involved. Sammy isn't very good at thinking his way out of problems. His solution was to eliminate the trio and to do it in such a way as not to arouse suspicion. What they didn't count on was Professor Reid. O'Reilly looks like it was a rush of blood on the part of Rice. Like I said it all fits. There's only one thing missing, evidence. We'll get Baxter and Weir for Malone and Grant with George Carroll's evidence. We might even get Rice for O'Reilly but again it will require Carroll to rollover and put him in the apartment in Castle Street.'

'Boss,' Peter Davidson interjected. 'I've worn out a pair of shoes walking around Belfast today. Nobody has seen Big George in the past two days. He might have gone to ground, or he might even have left the country. I interviewed his mother. I got the impression that she knows where he is, but she isn't saying.'

'I know George,' Harry Graham said. 'He hasn't left the country. Removing him from both Sammy and his mother would be like putting him in an airless room. He would suffocate and die. He's still in the Province. The question is, where?'

'What about the international arrest warrants on Baxter and Weir?' Wilson asked.

'I've prepared the papers for the DPP,' Graham said. 'It'll be on the wire in the next few days. But it might take months before we get our hands on them.'

'It all comes back to George Carroll,' Wilson said. 'That's the focus of our investigation. Get me Carroll and we'll crack this thing wide open.'

CHAPTER SIXTY-FOUR

The snug is not a particular feature of Irish pubs. Special rooms for individual patrons is a feature of bars around the world. The snug in the Crown Bar had gunmetal plates for striking matches, and an antique bell system, very common in Victorian houses where servants were employed, which alerts bar staff to the liquid needs of the patrons. Drinking snugs, according to old records, were not originally built for comfort but to accommodate those people who preferred to drink quietly and unseen. Detective Superintendent Ian Wilson wasn't the first policeman, or clergyman, to favour drinking in one of the snugs in the Crown. As a patron for more than twenty years, his request for the reservation of a snug was always respected. He arrived slightly before seven o'clock and made his way to snug 'J' where a 'reserved' sign had been placed on the table. He ordered a pint of Guinness and waited.

Jock McDevitt was panting slightly when he pushed in the door of the snug. He sat down heavily, a film of sweat on his brow. 'Jesus, that was a bit of a rush,' he said and immediately pushed the bell. 'Pint of Guinness,' he said as soon as the barman's head appeared through the hatch between the snug and the bar. 'Just put my story for tomorrow's paper to bed.

Maybe I should have waited.' He looked expectantly at Wilson.

'It's payback time,' Wilson said. 'You've given me a lead that panned out so I'm going to tell you a story. It's hypothetical and I don't have the evidence to back it up, but I think the evidence is out there and someone like you might be able to ferret it out.'

McDevitt's pint arrived and he attacked it with gusto. 'I needed that,' he said simply when he was finished drinking. 'Go ahead.'

'It all started with the Infrastructure Agency,' Wilson began, and he connected the dots as he had done during the investigation. He explained the role of Robin Construction and the ownership of the company. 'We're nearly at the end of the road. Tomorrow we'll put out a statement that we're looking for two men in connection with the deaths of Brian Malone and David Grant. We won't publish the names, but we have firmly established that they're the killers. There's a conspiracy charge somewhere down the road, but we're not there yet.'

McDevitt finished writing in his notebook.

'We might never have cracked these cases if you hadn't tipped us off on the Glasgow connection.'

McDevitt picked up his glass and toasted. 'Glad to be of assistance, still think my little story about the Inner Circle is a fantasy?'

'I deal with reality. It's always easy to ascribe events we can't explain to shadowy organisations. Half the planet has read Dan Brown and believes that Opus Dei or the Masons have their hands in every pie.'

McDevitt laughed. 'And they don't? You know I have always respected your intelligence, but you can't possibly think that these organisations don't include people who only want to use them to make money. The Inner Circle is not Opus Dei, or the Masons. It doesn't promote religion or business contacts. It has only one God, money. It will turn its hand to anything that will make money. It's the Mafia, but it's our version of our Italian cousins. Opus Dei and the Masons would bend their knee to them. Who the hell do you think Carson Nominees are? Surely someone with your level of brainpower can connect those two dots.'

'Some professor from Harvard that my sergeant spoke to seems to think that we'll never find out who's behind Carson Nominees. Maybe that's where you come in.'

'Are you joking? I've been at this game twenty-five years, and I've dealt with as much scum as you. One thing that I've learned is that you don't step into the lion's cage. These people would chew me up if they had any inclination that I was interfering in their business. You remember that journalist who was looking into Maggie Thatcher's son's connection with the Pinochet regime. He was found dead in a Santiago Hotel. The conclusion of the coroner was that he wanked himself to death.'

'What a way to go.' Wilson couldn't contain a laugh.

'Yeah, it's funny but it happened.' McDevitt rang the bell and ordered two more pints. 'The Circle won't be broken easily, and if they wanted to, they'd swat me like a fly. They have connections that go way beyond this Province.'

'Then why tell me the story?'

'You know that saying that it only needs good men to look away for evil to win.' McDevitt stopped while the two pints of Guinness were delivered. 'I wanted to put them on your radar. This is an organisation that has existed for over one hundred years and virtually nobody has heard of them. If they were ultimately responsible for the deaths of Malone, Grant and O'Reilly, it's the first time in a hundred years that they've raised their heads above the parapet. Maybe the current crop of leadership is getting sloppy.'

'You didn't think that by putting them on my radar you might be putting me on theirs.'

'You're an honest copper, Ian. I think that maybe you are already on their radar.'

'We're off the record, right.' Wilson waited until McDevitt nodded. 'I think Sammy Rice was responsible for the murders of Malone and Grant and was probably in O'Reilly's apartment when he went through the window. I intend to prove that before this investigation is over. Are you trying to tell me that Sammy Rice is a member of this Inner Circle?'

McDevitt laughed. 'Not a chance, I have no doubt that he's their creature. They use people like Rice to do their dirty work. They've learned from the cell system developed by the Communists and terrorists. Rice probably hasn't any idea who is in the Inner Circle. He will have dealt with someone on the periphery who himself may never have met an Inner Circle member. It's the spider at the centre of an extensive web.'

They were both silent and took a drink together.

'If I were to believe you, I wouldn't even bother to go to work tomorrow,' Wilson said.

'It's the opposite. If you believe that the Inner Circle exists, it should be the primary reason for you to continue to solve crimes. Every time you put someone evil away or any time you put a block on one of their plans, you shake their web. Maybe they'll come after you and that might expose them.'

'So I should become the sacrificial goat?'

'No, you should just do your job to the best of your ability. The belief that the Inner Circle exists just adds an additional layer to your thinking. Maybe the next time you look at a dead body, you'll think that there might be an unseen hand behind that death.'

Wilson looked at his watch. 'It's time I was off.'

'Pity,' McDevitt said. 'I was looking forward to an evening of getting pissed and hearing a couple of saucy rugby stories from your past. I think in a parallel universe we could be friends.'

'I don't do friends.' Wilson stood up. 'But if I did, maybe

you'd be one of them. Tread easily on this Inner Circle shit. It might return to bite you.' He opened the snug door and walked into the bar. It was like passing through the Looking Glass in reverse. What happened in the snug was the fantasy. The bar filled with the noise of chatter and laughter was the reality. Most people just wanted to have a good time and enjoy themselves. He was not so naive to believe that there were not those who seduced and sucked the life out of others like a succubus. He made his way through the crowded bar and pushed into the street. He took a deep breath savouring the smell of the city of Belfast. The air was not sweet and without pollution. He loved this city with all its faults and failings. Belfast people were some of the best in the world. They were witty, friendly and intelligent. On the flip side, they could be religious bigots and murderers. But they were all human beings. The members of the Inner Circle, if it existed, were phantoms. Figures without substance, what could they have in common with the ordinary citizens of this great city.

CHAPTER SIXTY-FIVE

S omething was seriously wrong. Sammy Rice had been pacing back and forth for nearly an hour in the front room of his Ballygomartin home. He'd phoned one of his contacts in the PSNI but there were no reported accidents on the road to or from Tullymore. There was only one possible conclusion for the absence of contact. There was a screw-up. He was doped to the gills and that had increased his feeling of unease and paranoia. His mobile phone rang, and he snatched it from the coffee table. 'Yeah,' he said as soon as he'd made contact.

'Sammy?' The voice on the other end said.

Rice's first conclusion was that this wasn't Boyle. The accent wasn't straight Belfast. 'Who's this?'

'It's Ray Wright,'

'What's the problem Ray?' Rice had the words out before he remembered that Wright was Big George's uncle. He and Wright were tight during the 'Troubles'. Sometimes he'd had Wright's back, and often it was the reverse. They hadn't been in contact for several years.

'Big George is with me here in Ballymena.'

Rice said nothing. He was thinking as fast as his brain would allow. Fuck, it had surely gone pear shaped. Big George was alive and there was no contact from Boyle. It wasn't hard to draw the conclusion that Boyle was no longer in the land of the living, or at the very least hurt so badly that he couldn't communicate.

'Big George wants to meet,' Wright said. 'He's confused and so is his story. The bottom line is that something went wrong between him and Owen Boyle in Tullymore today.'

Rice badly needed a clear head but the cocaine was in the ascendance. If you wanted something done, you had to do it yourself. Boyle was given a fairly simple task and he'd fucked it up. Rice put on his calm voice. 'I sent those two muppets to Tullymore to bury something. What happened?'

'Not on the phone, like I said we need to sit down and go through this thing. Maybe you can make sense out of Big George's story.'

'I'll come to your place in Ballymena.'

'No. George wants to be with his mother. We're coming to Belfast.'

'I'll wait for you in Ballygomartin.'

'Not on, the Peelers have been scouring Belfast for Big George today. They even went to my sister's house. The Peelers want him and it seems they want him badly.'

Rice knew that Wright wasn't lying. 'What do you have in mind?'

'There's a warehouse in East Belfast that you use sometimes.'

'The one in Ballymacarrett Road?'

'That's the one. We'll meet you there in an hour. Come alone. Big George is a bit skittish. What with the Peelers looking for him and what happened in Tullymore.'

'Tell him we can work this out. We've been friends since we were able to walk. I'll sort out the thing with the Peelers no matter what it costs.'

'I'll tell him. He knows he can count on you. We'll see you in an hour.' Wright broke the connection.

Rice sat down and held his head in his hands. It was all going to shit. Boyle screwed up. Big George was alive and well and wanted an explanation for whatever happened in Tullymore. He had one hour to come up with something that would be believable. There was only one possible story that would wash. It was all Boyle's idea. He had wanted to get close to Rice and realised that Big George had the inside track. So he decided to off Big George. He himself knew nothing of Boyle's plan. Wright and Big George might buy that story, but that would still leave George alive and kicking with the Peelers on his tail. Forget the fucking story. He needed Big George dead and there was only man he really trusted to handle the job. Himself. He walked to the mahogany desk in the corner of the living room and opened one of the drawers. He took out a Beretta 92 automatic. It was his pride and joy. A beautiful weapon that only the Italians could have designed. He checked the magazine and smiled when he saw it was full, fifteen rounds of 9×19 mm Parabellum. That would be plenty enough to take out Big George and his uncle. In a few hours, his remaining problem would be floating in the Lagan.

CHAPTER SIXTY-SIX

W ilson sat in his room on the third floor of the Europa Hotel. In front of him were the two suitcases holding all his worldly goods. Before Kate and he had decided to live together, he had been the owner of a fine four-bed house in Malwood Park that was stuffed to the gills with knickknacks his wife had bought. When he sold the house, he had auctioned all their goods. Despite the current state of his relationship with Kate, he didn't regret selling either the house or its contents. He long recognised that he had remained in the house in an effort to cling on to the past, and he welcomed the move to Kate's stunning apartment as an opportunity to move on. Something he should have probably done as soon as his wife died. The result of the sale of the house and the de-cluttering was that he had a substantial cash amount in his bank account. He looked across to where the remnants of a club sandwich and a beer sat on the dressing table. This was not going to be his new life. He might, or he might not, be able to rekindle his relationship with Kate. In either case, it was time for him to decide on what his life was going to be moving forward. It had only taken him a few hours to conclude that his future life would not include being based in a hotel. So he put a limit of one week on his stay in the Europa. Tomorrow he would start looking at apartments. Initially, he would rent but as time passed, he would select something suitable to live in. He could kick himself in the behind that he had left the proceeds of the sale of the house and contents in a bank just gathering dust. Since Kate and he hadn't really gone the full distance on commitment to their relationship, he should have had a place that he could at least have called his own. Their relationship might be over, but life still goes on. As soon as the dust settled on his current case load, he would sit down and decide what his future life was about. His second decision was that the PSNI could no longer be the centre of his world. Everything had changed. He was watching the news bulletin when the phone in his room rang. He rushed to pick up the handset.

'You'll be pleased to learn that I'll be leaving Belfast tomorrow.' The voice of Helen McCann came over the line. 'My business in Belfast is almost concluded.'

'And what business was that?' he asked. 'The business of getting me out of Kate's life.'

'I assure you I had nothing to do with Kate's decision to have a temporary break.'

'I wondered what all the whispering and the secret conversations were about.'

'When you look into your heart, you'll see that you were responsible for Kate's feelings towards you. I suppose insensitivity goes with your job.'

'And you're the sensitive one?'

'I love my daughter and only want the best for her.'

'And I'm not the best?'

'I never said that. But you are consumed by your job. Look at the David Grant business. That pathologist woman declares it murder, and you're away like a hound after a stag. Kate has needs too.'

'You've had a bee in your bonnet about that case from the

start. Several people have tried to block that investigation. Has someone asked you to interfere?'

'Absolutely not.' The tone was indignant.

'Ever heard of Carson Nominees?' he asked.

There was silence on the line. 'Carson Nominees,' she said. 'No, I'm on the board of several financial companies, but I've never heard of Carson Nominees. Who are they?'

'They're just some shadowy financial outfit that seems to have its fingers in a lot of pies here in the Province. Strange that you haven't run across them in your business life.'

'Don't give up on Kate, Ian. She's worth fighting for. I'm sorry but I have a dinner engagement.' The phone went dead.

MOIRA AND BRENDAN GUILFOYLE were snuggled up on the couch in her flat. Before them on the coffee table was the detritus of an Indian takeaway. Moira had received an email confirmation that Wilson had approved her request for a leave of absence and had forwarded it to Personnel. Hierarchical approval was a given and she would be on her way out of the PSNI in a matter of weeks. Brendan was ecstatic, and she would have liked to have the same feeling. Despite having made the decision, she was still unsure that she was doing the right thing.

Brendan leaned across and kissed her for the twentieth time. 'You're going to have a ball,' he said. 'Boston in the summer is something else. We'll spend a lot of the time on the Cape with my parents. They can't wait to meet you.'

'It's all happening so fast,' she said.

'You'll love it and it will love you. I've heard back from the department, and you're on track to audit the criminal psychology course next year. It's a win all the way.'

Then why doesn't it feel like a win, Moira thought. She kept telling herself that it wasn't a permanent break. She was going for a minimum of one year. If things didn't work out with Brendan, she would be back and she would have Harvard on her curriculum vitae.

'Where are you on the death of those two guys?' Brendan asked.

Moira brought him up to date on the investigation.

'Stellar job.' Brendan smiled. 'You guys really are the bomb.'

'I'm afraid I didn't contribute much to the result. My mind has been a million miles away. Well at least three thousand miles anyway.'

'It's all about the team. At least you get to finish on a high.'

She broke down and cried. Brendan held her, stroking her large expanse of red hair.

CHAPTER SIXTY-SEVEN

S ammy Rice parked his Audi A4 on Ballymacarrett Road and walked in the direction of the unused warehouse. He dropped his hand into his pocket and felt the comfort of the Beretta. He was going to blow the shit out of Big George and his shit-arsed uncle. Two bodies dumped in the Lagan would show people what he was made off. He pulled at his nose. Snot was running freely and he leaned over the side of the road, pinched his nose between his first finger and his thumb, and expelled a thread of snot into the road. He felt strong. He was going to clear all his problems. After George and his uncle, he would take care of his bitch wife and then take aim at McGreary. Tomorrow, he would squeeze some names out of Jackie Carlisle. He would torture the old bastard to within an inch of his life, but he would have some names. He stopped outside the warehouse and removed the key for the lock from his pocket. He looked down and saw that he wouldn't need it. The lock had already been broken. He smiled. The muppets had already arrived. They had no idea what was waiting for them. He pulled the door aside and entered the large open space. He looked around. There was no sign of either George or his uncle. He moved into the warehouse. 'George,' he shouted. 'Ray, where the hell are you?' He heard a noise behind him and turned quickly. He found himself staring into a Browning Hi Power held by Davie Best.

'Move one fucking muscle, and I'll blow your head off,' Best said. 'I mean it, Sammy. Put your hands behind your head and kneel down.'

Rice opened his mouth to speak.

'Hands behind your head and kneel,' Best shouted. 'You can talk later.'

The gun in Rice's face was rock steady. He put his hands behind his head and knelt on the rough concrete floor of the warehouse. What the hell was Davie Best doing at the meeting? Synapses were rushing between his amygdala and his subcortex. He had already decided that an attempt to make a fight of it would be futile. This was one he was going to have to negotiate his way out of.

'Good boy,' Best said. 'Now lie forward with your hands spread out.'

Rice lay down and spread his hands wide like the crucified Christ.

He heard a shuffling behind Best and looked up from the floor to see the obese figure of Gerry McGreary.

'Gerry,' Rice said from his prone position. 'Tell your boy to get that gun off me.'

'No can do,' McGreary said.

Rice heard more shuffling, and two other figures appeared. He looked up from the floor and saw Richie Simpson and Ray Wright standing beside McGreary. His heart sank. He might have been able to handle Best. He might even have been able to handle Best and McGreary, but four to one were very bad odds for him.

'He's definitely carrying,' Best said. 'Search him, Ray, and don't stop until you find his gun.'

Wright came forward and stood over Rice. He started patting him down and found the shape of the Beretta in his pocket. He took out the gun and showed it to the other three men.

'Keep going,' Best said. 'We don't want any surprises.'

Wright slipped the Beretta into his pocket and continued the search but found nothing. He moved back to the other men.

'Stand up, Sammy,' McGreary said.

Rice stood up slowly. He knew that he was in mortal danger and that the only possibility he had of walking out of the warehouse alive was to make some concessions to McGreary. 'Gerry, we go back much too far for business like this.'

Wright brought a chair from the rear wall of the warehouse and put it beside Rice.

'Recognise the chair,' Best said keeping the gun on Rice. 'It's the one that you tied me to when your guys lifted me. You let them beat the living shit out of me.'

'But I didn't kill you,' Rice said.

Best smiled. 'Maybe that was a mistake.'

'Where's George?' Rice asked.

'He couldn't make it,' Wright said. 'Don't worry he's okay. Which is more than can be said about your pal Boyle. The asshole tried to shoot George but only clipped him in the ear. The gun jammed, and George hit him with a spade. Took his head off and then stuffed him in the hole he was supposed to go in.'

'Boyle was acting off his own bat,' Rice said. 'I had no idea he was going to off George.'

'George told us everything,' Wright said. 'He was the driver on the Malone and Grant kills, and he was the one who tossed that guy out of the window in Castle Street. That was why he had to go.'

Rice turned to McGreary. 'Okay, Gerry, what do I have to do to make things right?'

'You're out of control, Sammy,' McGreary said. 'We're

passed the point where we could have sorted this out. You've been in the position I find myself in now, and you know what's going to happen. You should try to take it like a man.' He turned and started for the door. 'I don't need to be here.' He kept walking until he was through the warehouse door.

Best turned to Simpson. 'Get that piece of shit out of your pocket.'

Simpson took the gun, which he had procured earlier, from his pocket.

'Do him,' Best said. 'Go behind him and put one in the back of his head.'

Simpson's legs wouldn't move. Sweat was running down his face and his back. He had killed but it was personal; he was obliged to murder the man who had abused him. Killing someone like Rice was a totally different matter. He wasn't a natural-born killer like some of the Loyalist paramilitaries he'd met.

'What's the problem?' Best asked. 'You're the one who got paid for doing it.'

'I'll do it, Davie,' Wright said removing the Beretta from his pocket. 'He can give me the money.'

Best smiled. 'No, Ray. He has to do it himself.' He turned to Simpson. 'You do it, or you'll join Rice tonight for a swim in the Lagan with concrete boots.'

Simpson knew it was no idle threat. He forced himself to move and walked towards Rice. For a moment, he passed between Best and Rice.

Sammy Rice realised this would be his only chance. He leapt from the chair and lunged at Simpson. He was on his way when the first shot hit him in the left shoulder. It spun him around and away from Simpson who looked dazed.

Best moved to where Rice was lying on the floor. Blood was pumping from his shoulder. Best had served with the Paras in both Iraq and Afghanistan. He'd seen all kinds of wounds, and he knew that unless Rice was in a hospital within the hour he was a dead man. The shot had hit one of his main arteries. He moved to Simpson and grabbed him by the throat. 'You almost fucked us,' he said his face inches from Simpson's. 'Now go over there and finish him, or you'll join him.'

'But he's dying,' Simpson protested.

Best raised his gun and pointed it at Simpson's forehead. 'Finish him. One to the head.'

Simpson moved and stood over Rice. He pointed the gun at Rice's head. Rice's eyes were dim. There was a pool of blood on the floor beside him, and the coppery smell was already in the air. Simpson tightened his finger on the trigger.

'Do it,' Best shouted from behind him.

Simpson pulled the trigger. He felt the recoil and looked away from Rice.

Best moved forward and took the gun from Simpson's hand. Then he looked at Rice. Sammy was stone dead. The bullet hit him square in the side of the head. The twenty-two had rambled around in his head destroying his brain and anything else it had encountered. 'You go home now, Richie. Ray and I will handle things here.' He looked down at Rice and then kicked him in the side. 'You shouldn't have beaten the shit out of me. I never forget and I never forgive.'

'Why did you let that fool finish Rice?' Wright asked when Simpson left the warehouse.

He showed Wright the gun Simpson had used and dropped it into a plastic bag. 'Now we own him.' He dropped the plastic bag into his pocket. 'Let's get this bollocks into the Lagan. I need a drink.'

'Snap,' Wright smiled.

CHAPTER SIXTY-EIGHT

It was one of those spring days when the early morning sun banished the last vestiges of winter. Wilson had slept well, at least a damn sight better than he had in Kate's apartment of late. He'd spent an hour in the gym at the Europa working up a sweat. As was usual during his workout, he ruminated over the problems that would face him during the day. He decided to put the break-up with Kate to the back of his mind. He had long ago recognised that in life you can only act on the things that you control. If it were up to him, he would have woken up beside Kate. But that issue was no longer within his control. So there was no point worrying about it. The solution to the relationship problem was in Kate's hands. His priority right now was the meeting with Jennings. He and Jennings had been in Police College together, and their careers had parted as soon as they passed out. Wilson went on to become a copper's copper, passing through the ranks reasonably quickly but not at breakneck speed. Jennings was spotted by the powers that be at the College and went the administrative route. He had sped past Wilson and ended up at the exalted rank of Deputy Chief Constable. At College, Wilson had been not only the star pupil, but also an Irish international rugby player with the acclaim that such a position accorded. Jennings joined the Orange and Masonic Lodges and garnered his influence there. He detested Wilson at College because of his sporting and intellectual prowess. His hatred of his former colleague had stood the test of time, and nothing would have suited him better than to be the man who cashiered Wilson out of the PSNI. Unfortunately, the boot was now on the other foot. Wilson had in his possession the written instruction from Jennings that could end the DCC's career. He was in no doubt that the summons to Jennings' office had something to do with the content of his conversation with Laurence Gold. The meeting was going to be difficult. He was back in his room before he turned his mind to the hunt for Big George Carroll. He was continually amazed at how quickly time passed when he became engrossed in his thoughts. He showered and slipped a crisp white cotton shirt over his head. He felt there was a big day ahead.

THE JOURNEY from Great Victoria Street to PSNI HQ took ten minutes so Wilson left at eight forty so as to be certain to arrive on time. On the way, he contacted Moira and told her he was running late. Wilson felt the atmosphere was distinctly frosty in Jennings' outer office but what was new. He was kept waiting beyond the appointed time. He smiled as ten past nine passed. If this was an attempt by Jennings to unnerve him, it was failing miserably. At twenty past nine, he was ushered towards the door of Jennings' office and shown inside.

Jennings didn't look up from his paperwork as Wilson entered his office.

Wilson had always considered Jennings to be a puny runt and often wondered why he had chosen the police as a career. An even greater mystery was how Jennings had passed the physical exam. The DCC seemed to have shrunk even more in the past few days. There was obviously a lot of stress in the air.

He stood in a relaxed posture in front of Jennings' desk. After all, this was the police not the army.

Jennings finally looked up into Wilson's face. His eyes were red-rimmed, and dark bags hung beneath them. 'Sit,' he said simply.

Wilson sat in the visitor's chair before Jennings' desk. If it had been someone else, he might have felt a measure of compassion at the appearance of the man.

'I suppose you know why you're here,' Jennings said.

'Not really.' Wilson was being purposely obtuse, and he didn't care. Jennings didn't deserve empathy.

'That Jewboy Gold is going to crucify me.' There were red angry streaks in Jennings' pale face.

Wilson suppressed a smile. Perhaps Jennings was having a Jesus complex.

'He's going to open up the whole issue of Cummerford being admitted to the murder squad briefings at the trial.'

Wilson remained silent.

'I'm going to need that instruction back that you wheedled out of me.'

'I don't think that's going to be possible.'

'It's an order from a superior officer.'

'It's an order I cannot comply with.'

'Then I'm going to launch a disciplinary procedure against you. Your previous connections with Professional Services will be like nothing. I will get them to go through every minute detail of your career. Everything will be leaked to the newspapers. I wonder how your barrister girlfriend will react to that.'

'Personally I don't think she gives a hoot. She's headed for the top of the judicial tree whether my career hits the skids or not. Cummerford's trial starts soon. Two weeks after it starts you may not be in the PSNI. I think you should forget about making empty threats and try to come up with something positive to explain why Cummerford was given access that other journalists weren't. Of course, you won't be able to tell the truth because that would expose your vendetta against me, and Fatboy Harrison's role in leaking the results of an internal Professional Services' investigation to a journalist, possibly on your orders. It's all come back to bite.'

Jennings brought his hands together as though in prayer. 'If Gold has his way, he'll finish my career.'

Wilson thought that Jennings was on the verge of tears. Jennings had nothing aside from his job. His friends in the Lodge would undoubtedly take care of him but the reason he woke up every morning and got out of bed would be gone. 'Gold, wants to win his case. Maybe he'll go easy on the Cummerford issue.'

Jennings pressed his joined hands to his lips. 'I met with him last evening, and he left me in no doubt. The competence of the PSNI was at stake. That woman conned me into letting her attend the briefings.'

'You opened the door.'

'I need your help.' The words came out one by one as though Jennings had to drag them through his throat.

Wilson almost tumbled from his chair. 'I can't give you the instruction because that would be the equivalent of throwing myself under a bus, and that's not going to happen. If you come up with something plausible, I'll hold the written instruction back. I'll only produce it if it looks like I'm going down.'

'My mind's gone blank. I can't see a way out.'

'You're a student of Machiavelli. Maybe you should think about throwing Fatboy under a bus. After all he was the cause of it all.' Jennings' face brightened, and Wilson could see that Chief Inspector Ronald 'Fatboy' Harrison was sitting directly under the sword of Damocles. Wilson's mobile phone started to ring. It was Moira and it could wait so he cut the connection. His phone started to ring immediately. 'I think it's important. Do you mind if I take it?'

Jennings nodded. He appeared lost in thought.

'Boss, you need to get back here pronto.' Moira's voice was hoarse with excitement. 'Big George Carroll just walked in here with his solicitor. They'll only talk to you.'

'Put them in an interview room and get set up. I'll be there in fifteen minutes latest.' He broke the connection. 'I need to leave,' he told Jennings already standing.

The DCC nodded. His mind was far away, and the wheels were spinning at maximum speed.

CHAPTER SIXTY-NINE

Wilson had never moved so fast. He crashed through the front doors of the station and made directly for the interview room. Moira was standing outside with a buff-coloured file in her hand.

She handed him the file. 'Photos of the cab, Baxter, Weir, Malone, Grant and O'Reilly.'

Wilson looked in the small window. Two men sat on one side of the table that dominated the room. A uniformed officer stood just inside the door. Big George Carroll took up most of the space on his side of the table. He wore a bandage around his head with a large patch over his left ear. The man sitting beside him was dressed in a dark suit, light blue shirt and tie. He looked the very picture of a solicitor, and although he was of average height and build, he looked like a dwarf seated beside his client. 'Let's get on with this,' Wilson said pushing the door open. He nodded at the uniform who left the room after Moira had entered.

Wilson sat down heavily into a chair on the opposite side of the table, and Moira sat beside him. 'Moira, the preliminaries please.'

Moira looked at the two men across the table. 'I'm going to

switch on the tape. We will be making a voice record and a videotape of this interview. A copy of the audio tape will be available to your solicitor at the end of the interview. Please state your full name when requested.' She pressed the start button on the tape recorder and gave the time and date. 'Present are Detective Superintendent Ian Wilson, Detective Sergeant Moira McElvaney.' She pointed at Big George.

'George Michael Carroll,' the big man said. The words were slow and deliberate.

'Alex Joseph Brady,' the solicitor said.

'First of all,' Wilson started, 'I'd like to thank you both for coming here this morning.'

'My client was made aware last night that you were searching for him,' Brady said, 'and is anxious to assist in any way he can.'

Wilson opened the file and removed the photo of the cab, which had been taken by the CCTV camera, and put it on the table. 'Is this you, Mr Carroll?'

'Yes,' Big George replied.

Wilson took out photos of Baxter and Weir and laid them side-by-side. 'And these men were your passengers?'

'Yes.'

'Where did you take them?'

George looked at Brady, who nodded. He gave the addresses of Malone and Grant.

Wilson placed photographs of Malone and Grant in front of George. 'Are you aware that both men were murdered?'

Big George nodded.

'Please respond for the tape,' Moira said.

'Yes,' Big George said.

'Did you take part in either of the murders?'

Big George looked at his solicitor, who again nodded.

'Yes, I helped move Grant. But I didn't kill him.'

'Were these men a random fare?' Wilson asked.

'No. I was told to pick them up at the airport, bring them to two addresses and drive them back to the airport.'

'By whom?' Wilson asked.

Big George remained silent.

'My client will be happy to tell you,' Brady said. 'But we will need to make some arrangements regarding the charges that my client will face.'

Wilson ignored the remark. He removed a picture of Mark O'Reilly from the file and placed it on the table. 'Do you recognise this man?' Wilson asked.

Big George was about to nod but then said, 'Yes.'

'Were you in his apartment when he went through the window?'

'Yes.'

'Were you alone?'

'No.'

'Did you throw Mark O'Reilly to his death?'

George looked at his solicitor who nodded. 'Yes.'

Wilson nodded at Moira.

She stood. 'Mr Carroll, would you and your solicitor please stand.' They stood. 'George Michael Carroll, I am arresting you for the murder of Mark O'Reilly and as an accessory in the murders of David Grant and Brian Malone, you do not have to say anything when questioned but anything you do say will be taken down and may be used in evidence against you.'

Big George and his solicitor retook their places.

'Now that the charges have been established,' Wilson said. 'Is your client prepared to answer the two questions I put to him earlier?'

Brady turned and spoke into Big George's ear. 'Yes,' he said.

'Who instructed you to pick up Baxter and Weir?' Wilson asked.

'Sammy Rice,' Big George said reluctantly.

'And who was with you in Mark O'Reilly's apartment?'

'Sammy Rice.' Big George seemed to be choking on the name.

'Do you know why these three men were murdered?'

'No,' Big George said.

Wilson looked at Moira.

'Interview suspended at ten thirty.' She switched off the tape.

'We'll be back.' Wilson stood, and he and Moira left the room. They went straight to the squad room.

'Peter,' Wilson called as soon as he entered. 'We've got Rice for Malone, Grant and O'Reilly. Get a warrant for him. Then collect some uniforms and find him, arrest him and bring him here immediately.'

Davidson was astonished. 'We have him how?'

'Big George just rolled over on him,' Wilson said. 'Get a move on. I want the airport and the ports alerted. Find the bugger before he runs.'

'No way,' Davidson said. 'Big George and Rice are joined at the hip. There's something very wrong here, Boss.'

'Someone must have separated them,' Moira said. 'Big George is going to put him away.'

Wilson started for his office. 'I want to inform the Chief Super. Then we're back in the interview room. This could be a long day.'

During the recess, Wilson had informed Spence of the development, but he also consulted the file they had established on George Carroll. Social Services had been involved with Carroll since his early days at school. At the age of fourteen, they had assessed a reading age of five and his IQ was only marginally above the level of someone considered to be mentally challenged. They might be able to put George away, but he certainly wouldn't prove a stellar witness against Rice.

Fifteen minutes later Wilson re-entered the interview room. Tea and biscuits had been provided for Big George and Brady.

Wilson and Moira sat. Moira switched on the tape and went through the preamble again.

'You had no role in the Malone murder other than driving the car?' Wilson asked.

'Yes.' Big George was getting tired of all the conversation. His uncle Ray had told him what to say, and he was concentrating hard to remember everything. He didn't like answering questions.

'And Grant?'

Big George cast his eyes down. 'He was heavy. They made me help hang him. I didn't like what they did to him, it wasn't nice.'

'What happened with O'Reilly?' he asked.

'Sammy told me to throw him out the window,' Big George said calmly. 'I was just doing what Sammy said. I always do what Sammy tells me.'

'Why did Rice want you to throw O'Reilly out of the window?'

'I don't know. Sammy got angry with him.'

'What happened to your head?'

Big George looked at his solicitor, who nodded. 'Owen Boyle shot me in the ear.'

'When?'

'Yesterday.'

Wilson looked at Moira then turned back to Big George. 'Why?'

'I don't know. I think he was trying to kill me.'

'Why was he trying to kill you?'

Big George shrugged his shoulders. 'I don't know.' He wished the questions would stop and he could go home to his mother.

'Where is Owen Boyle now?'

'In a hole in Tullymore Forest.'

Moira gasped.

'Did you kill him?' Wilson was beginning to feel sorry for

Big George. It was evident that Rice wanted him out of the way.

'It was an accident. I just didn't want him to shoot me again.'

'Moira.' There was resignation in Wilson's voice.

Moira stood and arrested Big George for the murder of Owen Boyle. 'Mr Carroll, would you and your solicitor please stand.'

'Can you show us where the body is?' Wilson asked when Big George and Brady had retaken their seats.

'Yes.'

Wilson nodded at Moira.

'Interview suspended at eleven fourteen,' she said.

Wilson stood up. 'Let's organise some transport and see if Reid's available. I'll advise the Chief.'

'I presume you don't need me along.' Brady closed the pad on which he had been taking notes and put it into his brief-case. 'I will, however, attend any future interview sessions.' He handed Moira a card. 'You can contact me on my mobile anytime.'

Moira took the card and left the room. She returned with a uniformed officer who placed handcuffs on George Carroll's big hands.

CHAPTER SEVENTY

Two men sat in a Saab 93 fifty yards down the road from Jackie Carlisle's house. They had been in position since early morning, and the floor of the car was littered with empty hamburger cartons and crushed cardboard coffee cups. The man in the passenger seat wore a white jacket buttoned to the neck. To a passer-by he might possibly be an off-duty chef. They had been in place for more than three hours when the gates of Carlisle's driveway opened, and a car rolled slowly out. They watched carefully as the car passed them ensuring that the driver was Carlisle's wife. They waited ten minutes and then the driver started the car. He stopped outside Carlisle's house. The passenger picked up a bag from the space beneath his feet and left the car. He walked up the drive and knocked on the door.

Several minutes elapsed before Jackie Carlisle opened the door.

'Mr Carlisle.' The man smiled. 'My name is Bradley Mills and I've been sent by the hospice in Ballynahinch.' He held up his bag. 'I'll be coming to give you regular injections to combat the pain. Towards the end I, or one of my colleagues, will be here every day.'

'Aye, come on in.' Carlisle opened the door wide and stood aside. He would have preferred a woman, but one couldn't be choosy. The male nurse followed Carlisle through the living room and on into the conservatory where the invalid slumped back in his favourite couch. He was glad the nurse had come. The pain was becoming so heavy that the painkillers the doctor had prescribed were no longer capable of combating it.

The male nurse opened his bag and removed a syringe and a small bottle of liquid. He carefully filled the syringe with the liquid before removing a rubber band. Carlisle held out his right arm.

'We'll start on the left if you don't mind,' the nurse said.

Carlisle sighed and held out his left hand. The nurse gripped it harder than Carlisle would have liked. Mills wrapped the rubber band around his bicep. Carlisle noticed that the nurse was wearing surgical gloves, and he didn't remember seeing him put them on. He felt the needle enter his arm and watched as the nurse pushed in the plunger. Those gloves had been on the nurse since he had arrived, he thought as the morphine hit his bloodstream. They say that a drowning man sees his whole life flash before him. Jackie Carlisle saw the equivalent through his morphine rush. Episodes from his own life played across his eyes as he seemed to float above them. His school friends playing football, the excitement and camaraderie of the 'Troubles', his political career, rubbing shoulders with the great and the good. His eyes were glazing over. He glanced at the nurse and saw that he was watching intently. He looked down and saw the syringe still sticking in his arm. Everything was growing dim, but he was feeling euphoric. He thought he could see his long dead parents in the distance.

'Everything alright, Mr Carlisle?' the nurse asked.

Carlisle smiled and finally understood. Now there would be no pain at the end. His suffering and that of his wife was at an end. 'Thank you,' he said and closed his eyes for the last time.

The nurse waited several minutes and then checked for a pulse. There was nothing. He placed Carlisle's fingers on the syringe and the plunger. He removed the hand and wrapped it around the bottle and put the fingers on the rubber band. That should be enough to convince anyone that Carlisle had botched a morphine injection. He took a mobile phone from his pocket and took a photo of the dead man.

The nurse left the house and carefully closed the front door. He went to the Saab and sat in the passenger seat. He nodded at the driver, and they pulled away from the kerb.

Helen McCann sat in the Business Lounge at Belfast International Airport. Through the window, she could see her Lear jet sitting on the tarmac. Some of her friends considered the purchase of the plane a caprice, but as soon as she had bought it, she had set up a small aircraft leasing company. The jet more than paid for itself, and she had the use of it whenever it wasn't leased. She glanced at her watch. They would be airborne in half an hour, and she would be in the south of France two hours later. She was exhausted from her visit to Belfast. She had never anticipated that anyone, especially not her daughter's partner, would become a threat to something that was part of her life's work and legacy. She smiled. He even stumbled across Carson Nominees.

The Cayman-based company had been her brainchild. She conceived it in order to store the flood of money pouring into Ulster from the US, the UK and Europe – money that was intended to keep the zealots on both sides of the religious divide from each other's throats. She saw the flood of money as a business opportunity and she managed to make the members of the Circle very wealthy. Along the way, she bought bureaucrats, Members of Parliament and judges. And lots and lots of police officers. What a pity Wilson wasn't open to being bought. Named in honour of Sir Edward Carson, the man who created Northern Ireland, she buried Carson Nominees and its ownership deep, but unfortunately not deep enough. That was something she was going to devote herself to in the coming days. Carson Nominees had served its purpose. It would disappear and positions it had established would be wound down. She would have to create a replacement, but that wouldn't be difficult. A mobile phone in her handbag buzzed. She picked out the cheap mobile she had purchased the day before and looked at the screen. She opened the message. The picture on the screen brought her no joy. She had known Jackie for almost forty years, and she consoled herself for her part in his death by the thought that what she had done was to relieve both him and his family of pain. There were now several degrees of separation between the three dead men in Belfast and the Inner Circle. She removed the chip from the phone as her pilot entered the lounge and made directly for her. He picked up her bag and led her out of the lounge. As she passed a waste bin, she dropped the phone in. The chip would end up on the runway. She looked at the rain clouds that were beginning to billow over the airport. Thank God she was leaving this terrible place.

CHAPTER SEVENTY-ONE

As so often happened in Ireland, the good start to the day was illusory. By late morning, dark rain clouds had swept in from the Atlantic Ocean and were in the process of drenching the Province and all who ventured outside. The three police Land Rovers made their way along the narrow laneway into Tullymore Forest. Wilson travelled in the passenger seat of the lead vehicle which also held George Carroll, seated and chained to a uniformed officer in the rear. They were at the point where Carroll was directing the driver to their destination. Reid hadn't been available but had cleared her agenda and was only fifteen minutes behind them. They retraced the route that had been taken by Boyle the previous day and pulled up finally into the clearing where Boyle's death had taken place.

Wilson descended from the Land Rover and entered the clearing. Despite the rain, he could see a large stain of blood on the short grass. He looked across to the other side where a mound of earth indicated a freshly dug grave.

Moira joined him. She nodded at the earth at the other side of the clearing.

'Tape the area off,' Wilson said. 'Get the uniforms on the

job. And have them put a canopy over the whole of the clearing before the rain ruins whatever evidence there is. What's the story with SOC?'

'They're on the way,' she said heading back to the second Land Rover.

The officer chained to Big George climbed out of the first Land Rover. They came to stand beside Wilson.

'Is that it, George?' Wilson indicated the heap of fresh earth.

Rain was streaming out of Big George's dark hair. He nodded sending particles of water flying up and down.

'Put him back in the car,' Wilson said. He started to walk around the edge of the clearing examining the trees. He saw the bullet by chance. He had no doubt SOC would have found it, but there it was and it would probably corroborate Big George's account of what happened.

Moira was already in her plastic suit, and she tossed one in his direction. 'Find something interesting?' she asked.

'A bullet embedded in a tree.' Wilson pulled on his blue plastic suit. 'That bullet might verify Big George's story.'

'He's like a big child,' Moira said. 'I'd hate to see him go down for life.'

'He's a brief's wet dream,' Wilson said. 'He already has you in his corner. How do you think a jury will respond when his whole life is put before them? Don't worry about Big George. He's going to spend several years feeding the ducks in some open prison.'

'The dynamic duo.' Reid came up behind them and put her arm around Wilson's shoulder. 'Absence really does make the heart grow fonder. Haven't seen you lately.' She ignored Moira.

Wilson could see the hard look on Moira's face, and he smiled. He wondered what would become of him when his protector was three thousand miles away. 'He's in that mound over there,' he said to Reid. 'Shall we go take a look?'

'I'd go anywhere with you,' Reid said.

Moira sighed. She wondered whether Reid knew that Wilson and Kate had split. 'I'm too old to witness these futile mating rituals,' she said.

'And how is that lovely young professor chap you can be seen fawning over?' Reid asked moving off in the direction of the mound. 'Scene of crime?'

'On the way,' Wilson said falling into step beside her. 'Maybe ten minutes.'

She looked around the clearing. 'I think the victim lost most of his blood. Any idea how he died?'

'He was decapitated.'

She stopped and looked at him. 'That would certainly explain the blood.'

Wilson looked over her shoulder and saw two police vehicles arriving. 'Looks like SOC are here.'

'Let's wait,' Reid said. 'They can help to disinter the body properly. How's life with the Ice Queen?'

'Looks like Moira had a point. I thought we'd moved beyond the sparring.'

'I can't wait around forever.' she smiled. 'Although there's no sign of Prince Charming on the horizon. So you're still my number one choice.'

The Chief of the SOC team joined them. 'What have we got?'

Wilson told him. 'Let's just get the body disinterred so that Professor Reid can have a look. Also I found a bullet lodged in that tree over there.' He pointed out the tree.

'No problem.'

Twenty minutes later a canopy was set up over the clearing, and the remains of Owen Boyle had been exposed. Reid bent over the body and examined it. 'Neat job, he must have had practice,' she said from the kneeling position. 'There's no question about what killed him.'

'A case of beginner's luck.' Wilson was standing behind

her and saw the Hi Point still held in Boyle's right hand. 'Bag the gun,' he said to one of the SOC team. 'I want to know yesterday whether the slug that's dug out of the tree was fired from that gun.'

'I'm done here,' Reid said. 'As they say in the cop shows, "bag him and tag him". I'll see him on the table as soon as I can fit him in.' She stared at the giant in the rear of the police Land Rover. 'I suppose this is one of those open-and-shut cases.'

'Yeah,' Wilson said. 'Thank God for that. Now we need to talk to the man behind all the mayhem we've been experiencing.'

'Who is it?' she asked.

'Sammy Rice.'

'Son of the already-dead Lizzie?' She started pulling off her blue suit and was pleased to see that Wilson was taking more than a passing interest in her body.

'The same,' he said, aware that Reid was putting on a bit of a show but unable to take his eyes off her.

'I think we deserve that drink, don't you?' She threw her protective suit over her arm and picked up her bag. 'My God, here comes the Rottweiler just on cue. Do you have her trained to interfere with my plans to seduce you?'

'We're wanted back at the station,' Moira said joining them.

'Spoilsport,' Reid said and started to move away towards her car.

'Have we got Rice?' Wilson asked.

'Peter's been over Belfast with a fine toothcomb. There's no sign of Rice. The radio is reporting the death of Jackie Carlisle. You know the line, "at his home after a long illness".'

'Call Peter, tell him to get on to our contacts in the Gardai. Rice might have gone South. Get them to watch their ports and airports. We have to nail that bastard. We have to find out why he had Malone, Grant and O'Reilly killed.'

'It's already done, Boss. Wind it down. We'll get Rice and we'll get Baxter and Weir. It'll just take time.

WILSON AND MOIRA stood in the squad room in front of the whiteboard. Wilson traced the evolution of the investigation with his finger. From the victims, to the identification of Baxter and Weir, and on to Big George and Sammy Rice. He picked up a black marker and drew an arrow from a picture of Big George Carroll to a picture of Sammy Rice. 'Where the hell have you got yourself to?' he asked circling the picture of Rice with the marker. He then drew a box and drew an arrow from Rice's photo to the box. Inside the box he wrote 'Carson Nominees' and directly under it 'The Circle'.

'What's the Circle, Boss?' Moira asked.

'A figment of McDevitt's imagination.' He added 'I hope' in his own mind.

'I wanted to end on a high,' Moira said.

'It is what it is. Someone has been pretty damn clever keeping themselves out of the picture. It's a step too far in the imagination to think that Sammy was capable of setting up a complicated financial scam. That wasn't his style. He was a criminal and a thug.' He took the marker and drew five thick circles around the box he had drawn. 'I'm going to put a photo in that box some day and people like Sammy Rice are going to help me do it. Meanwhile you have a plane to catch.'

HELEN MCCANN SAT on the veranda of her villa in Antibes and looked across the blue waters of the Mediterranean. She felt confident that she had protected the Circle and herself. Carlisle was gone. He was the only one that could identify her. But Wilson had got a sniff of the Circle. And like the good gun dog he was, he would continue to root away until he exposed them. She had already identified him as an existential threat to her organisation. She would have to work out a plan to neutralise him, a plan that would destroy him without killing him. She picked up a glass of chilled white wine from the marble table beside her chair and sipped it. She already had something in mind.

EPILOGUE

Wilson parked his car in the outdoor car park and walked briskly towards Departures at Belfast International Airport. He was aware that he was late but wasn't sure whether it was by accident or design. He entered the airport terminal and saw the small group he was looking for standing at the entrance to the departure gates. Moira's parents had travelled from Omagh and there was a group of university types congregated around Brendan Guilfoyle. Wilson slowed his walk. He wasn't the kind of person who went for these types of events. He didn't have any close friends, and it was hard for him to accept that Moira was no longer a colleague but a friend.

'Glad you could make it.' Guilfoyle left his group and moved to greet Wilson. 'I know you're busy.'

'Moira has to be sent off properly,' Wilson said shaking the young man's hand. The official farewell party had been held at the station. The Murder Squad and the uniforms had tucked into the drinks and sandwiches while forced to listen to platitudes from Spence and himself. Moira had prepared a witty response but broke down so many times during the delivery that the impact of the humour had been lost. Two days before

her departure she had asked to stay on until Rice, Baxter and
Weir were arrested. Wilson had refused with as much grace as
he could muster. The three men had gone to ground, and it
would be months, if not years, before they would be brought to
justice. He knew you had to accept some things in the pursuit
of justice even though you may not want to. The bush tele-
graph was alive with rumours that the Murder Squad was to
be incorporated into a wider Serious Crimes Unit and he was
not being mentioned as the potential head. Jennings was
fighting for his career, and rumour had it that Laurence Gold
was going to skewer him during the Cummerford trial, due to
start soon. Wilson wished Gold luck. Jennings' farewell party
was an event that he would be happy to attend.

Wilson walked towards Moira and her parents. He kissed
Moira on the cheek and took the opportunity to whisper in her
ear. 'Get that look off your face, someone will think that your
dog just died.'

She smiled and introduced Wilson to her parents, who
looked like country mice on a visit to the city. Her father was a
small stout man with freckles and wispy red hair interspersed
on his head. It was easy to see where Moira's flaming red hair
had come from. Her mother was the one with the good looks.
Although she was in her mid-sixties, she looked considerably
younger; the only giveaway was the grey hair tied back from
her forehead. She wore a blue two-piece suit, which looked
like it had been bought especially for the occasion. They were,
as he had expected, salt-of-the-earth people.

Moira's father held his hand a little longer in the hand-
shake and pulled him slightly aside. 'I want to thank you for all
you did for Moira.'

Wilson was embarrassed. 'I was just her boss,' Wilson said.

'It's a little more than that,' the older man said. 'Moira
wasn't in a good place after the business with her ex-husband.
Now she's got a fine young man, and she's off on a new adven-
ture. It didn't just happen by accident.'

'Sorry, folks,' Brendan said. 'If we don't move now we'll miss our flight.'

Moira kissed her parents then Brendan put his arm around her and led her through the barrier. Wilson watched them disappear and said his goodbyes to Moira's parents. He left the terminal and walked to the car park. He looked up as a plane took off directly over his head. He wished he were on that plane heading anywhere. He never felt so utterly alone. He was an expert at losing people, his parents, his wife, his partner and now Moira. He took out his keys and opened his car. As he sat into the driver's seat, he wondered where the hell Sammy Rice had got to.

AUTHOR'S NOTE

I HOPE that you enjoyed this book. As an indie author, I very much depend on your feedback to see where my writing is going. I would be very grateful if you would take the time to pen a review on Amazon. This will not only help me but will also indicate to others your feelings, positive or negative, on the work. Writing is a lonely profession and this is especially true for indie authors who don't have the backup of traditional publishers.

Please check out my other books on Amazon and if you have time visit my web site (derekfee.com) and sign up to receive additional materials, competitions for signed books and announcements of new book launches.

Derek Fee is a former oil company executive and EU Ambassador. He is the author of seven non-fiction books. Dark

Circles is his sixth novel and the fourth in a series featuring Ian Wilson.

Derek can be contacted at derekfee.com.

Now,
Voyager —
Betty DAVIS —

DARK Victory
Betty DAVIS —

JEZBEL

Made in the USA
Coppell, TX
11 September 2021